An Unlikely Duchess

by

Nadine Millard

An Unlikely Duchess
by Nadine Millard
Published by Blue Tulip Publishing
www.bluetulippublishing.com

This is a work of fiction. Names, places, characters, and events are fictitious in every regard. Any similarities to actual events and persons, living or dead, are purely coincidental. Any trademarks, service marks, product names, or named features are assumed to be the property of their respective owners, and are used only for reference. There is no implied endorsement if any of these terms are used. Except for review purposes, the reproduction of this book in whole or part, electronically or mechanically, constitutes a copyright violation.

AN UNLIKELY DUCHESS
Copyright © 2014 NADINE MILLARD
ISBN 13: 978-1499313147
ISBN: 1499313144
Cover Art Designed by P.S. Cover Design

To my wonderful husband who makes me feel like I'm living in my very own romance novel!

To my beautiful children who bring me more joy every day than I ever thought possible.

And to my family who support me in all that I do.

Prologue

"You know, old chap, 'tis not a bad sort of life." This sentiment was expressed rather drunkenly by the gentleman being propped up, unsuccessfully for the most part, by another young gentleman in much the same state.

The two were exiting one of the more reputable gaming halls lurking on the wrong side of London. The Black Den, known as much for its light skirts as the light pockets people suffered when exiting, had become a regular haunt for the two friends since the beginning of the Season.

These were no ordinary gentlemen. They were considered the catches of the Season and, as a result, had suffered greatly at the hands of ambitious mamas with steel in their eyes and marriage on their minds.

The more drunk of the two, and younger by two years at twenty-eight, was Lord Carrington, future Earl of Ranford, whose seat would be a magnificent estate in Ireland. Having spent much of his twenty-odd years in England attending the best schools and then sowing his oats under the pretence of wife catching, the young lord had no real desire to be shipped off back to Ireland to waste away with no society or activity to speak of.

However, his father was getting on in years, and it was time to return home and learn the ropes before the mantle and responsibility fell to him.

The older, and even more of a catch as far as the mamas were concerned, was none other than the future Duke of Hartridge. The title alone was enough to have debutants swooning. Added to that his colossal wealth and number of properties, and even Prinny himself would not have caused as much of a stir as when Charles Crawdon, Marquess of Enthorpe walked into a room.

The gentlemen had been suffering the machinations of debutantes and their mothers since the start of the Season. Only that evening, the Marquess had literally had a young girl thrown at him by her mama in the hopes that the scuffle would look like some sort of scandal, therefore forcing an engagement.

He would rather face the entirety of the French army than the mothers of the *ton* hell bent on having their girls wed.

And whilst Henry Carrington had suffered his share of near misses, nobody was terribly thrilled about a son-in-law who would leave the country. After all, what was the point in having a peer in the family if one could not parade him around in front of one's friends? But he was still an Earl, so he was in their sights.

And so it was that the young scoundrels, determined to paint themselves as disreputable rakes, though not quite brave enough to suffer the collective wrath of their fathers, frequented places like the Black Den, and associated with the demimonde and the women who had neither the means nor inclination to trap them into marriage.

Outside, the biting wind helped to revive the gentlemen somewhat, and as they awaited the arrival of the ducal carriage they were both contemplating the same thing.

"The end of the Season is fast approaching." Lord

Carrington was the first to break the contemplative silence.

"Yes, it is."

"Your father expects an engagement."

"So does yours," Enthorpe bit back.

"Indeed he does."

There was a slight pause, and then a desolate sigh.

"I think our days of rakishness are numbered."

"Had they even begun?" Enthorpe enquired dryly.

"Not as much as I had hoped. I suppose I just do not have it in me to seduce widows and ruin debutantes."

"No," answered Enthorpe rather regretfully, "nor do I."

Another pause.

"So, who will you marry then?" This time Enthorpe broke the silence.

"Perhaps Lady Mary. She is a good sort. I think we would rub along rather well together. She has indicated, quite forcefully, that a quiet life in the Irish countryside would be no hardship to her. It may as well be her as anyone. And you?"

"The Lady Catherine, I think," was the eventual answer after some minutes pondering the question. "I must consider the duties of a duchess when making my decision. Nobody knows the rules of society as much as she. She is pretty and pleasant. And it will please my father to align ourselves with that family. She is on his list of acceptable wives."

Neither of the men spoke in terms of asking these women. They knew, everyone knew, that a refusal would be completely out of the question for any of the ladies in Town.

There was an air of finality about the conversation between the two young men. They both knew they were on the cusp of respectability and their days of misadventure would soon be behind them.

Thus, it was with a fond nostalgia that the conversation continued once they were safely ensconced in the warmth of the ducal carriage and making their way back to Mayfair.

"It has been a good ride Thorpe," said Lord Carrington

fondly.

The marquess grinned. "It has been at that Carry."

"I wonder how many brats you will have," Carrington quipped.

"Less than you I warrant! An heir and spare is all I require, though I believe ladies have a fondness for daughters too."

"I shall want at least four to fill up that museum of a house in Offaly. As long as one of them is a boy I shan't mind about the others."

"Boys will be infinitely more manageable than girls, Carry."

"Nonsense. Girls are pliable and pleasing. They do as they are told quietly and without fuss." Carrington answered this firmly and with confidence, having had no experience of sisters or close female cousins.

The marquess, however, had grown up with sisters and smirked at Carrington's innocence and naivety.

"And what of the trouble of marrying them off?"

"Well, what of it? I shall give them their Seasons and they will marry."

"My dear Carry, do think of the Season *we've* just had. You will subject your daughters to the likes of us?"

"I had not thought of that," answered Carrington, his sudden look of consternation confirming that he'd forgotten that his daughters would not be exempt from the ups and downs of the marriage mart.

The marquess gave him a moment to digest this new piece of information and to re-evaluate his desire for girls.

"I've got it," he announced so suddenly that Enthorpe almost jumped out of his skin.

"Damnation, Carry! You almost scared me to death!"

"Apologies, old man. But I've got it."

"Got what?"

"The solution, of course."

"To what?" the marquess asked in exasperation.

"Why, the marrying off of my children," announced Carrington in a booming voice. "I shall just marry them to yours!"

Now, neither of these young men were hair brained or stupid. However, both were very firmly in their cups and, in such a state, the idea seemed ideal. Having enough sensibilities between them still to actually hash out some details, they decided that since the duke's heir probably should live where his actual dukedom was, it would be more appropriate to marry off a daughter of the earl's to a son of the duke's.

And, as young men of vast wealth and power are wont to do, they immediately called upon the duke's solicitor and forced that poor man out of his bed to draw up a legally binding contract that would secure the futures of their children. And all this before either man was engaged.

Thus, both men went on to marry their intended ladies and start on the children they were to produce, safe in the knowledge that at least two of them could look forward to a very agreeable match…

Chapter One

Offaly, Ireland, 1815

"Remind me again what we're doing here." The command, issued in a bored drawl came from Edward Crawdon, Duke of Hartridge.

The ducal carriage was bouncing along a rather bumpy, if beautiful, road in the Irish countryside, carrying its passengers to stay with *Very Dear Friends*. A term oft used by his mother and usually, as in this instance, meaning people Edward had either never met or could not remember.

His mother speared him with a steely glint and slightly raised eyebrow, designed to quell his stubbornness even from infancy.

"I told you dear. Several times. We are to visit our very dear friends, the Carringtons."

"You do know, Mother," pressed Edward, "that I have never actually met the Carringtons?"

"You've met Ranford, dear."

"Have I?"

"Why, yes," the dowager answered sweetly. Too sweetly.

"And, how old was I when I met him, Mother?" He

speared her with a steely look of his own.

"I cannot recall the exact age…"

"Take a guess."

"Oh, about three or four perhaps."

Edward smirked as his suspicions were confirmed. There was something going on.

"It is odd, is it not Mother, that we would be invited to stay with Ranford six years after Father died, and for no real reason?"

"Of course not," Lady Catherine answered brusquely. "He and your Father were terribly close, and I have always maintained a correspondence with Lady Ranford. I expressed a wish for a change of scenery and she was kind enough to invite me to stay for some weeks before the Season. Would you have me travel here alone at my age?"

Edward looked at his mother and raised another eyebrow. His mother was far from in her dotage. At 54, she was neither old nor incapable of travelling without her son. She was fit, healthy and had retained much of the beauty of her youth.

She had aged some six years ago when his father had passed away suddenly in a riding accident but, being good *ton*, had recovered remarkably well and was happy to become the dowager at a relatively young age. Now she could sit back, relax, and pressure her only son into marriage and the production of grandchildren. Besides which, she wasn't alone, never going anywhere without her lady's maid, Annie.

Edward knew his mother well enough to know that something was going on. And he'd be damned if he'd walk into the situation, whatever it may be, blind.

He turned to question the other occupant of the carriage, his cousin Tom. Tom and he had always been close, more brothers than cousins he supposed. The son of a second son, he was very comfortable being a gentleman of means but little in the way of occupation. He had half-heartedly studied the law before settling himself in a small estate outside of London. He lived comfortably and well. His wealth could not be compared to Hartridge's but there were few men who could boast of that. His father was, by all accounts, a cruel and bitter man whose jealousy of Edward's own father had caused a lifelong estrangement. Tom had been taken under wing by the dowager and her late husband, saving him from his father's cruelty and allowing him to develop into a happy and pleasant young man without being poisoned by his father's moods. He was also very likely to be privy to whatever it was Edward was missing in this scheme.

"Well, Tom," he questioned, "are you going to tell me what's going on?"

"Your grace?" asked Tom, politely.

"Come now Tom, do not play the innocent with me. I've known you far too long for that to wash. What am I doing in an Irish backwater?"

"I am sure I do not know what you mean, Edward. Your mother wanted to visit with her very dear friends. It is only fitting that her son should come too." He blinked a few times, which was always a sure sign that he was nervous, but his face remained a cool mask of innocence.

Biting back a growl of frustration, Edward changed tact.

"You know, it is terribly irresponsible of me to take myself out of the country when there is work to be done. Our investments and properties will not take care of themselves."

"No, they will not," his mother agreed, "which is why you employ the most efficient and capable stewards for when you cannot be there. You are one man, my dear. It would be quite impossible for you to shoulder all of that responsibility yourself."

Too late, Edward realised his mistake. There'd be no stopping Mother now.

"If only you had a wife to unburden yourself with," she began. Predictably. "Someone who could help ease your worries, talk through your problems and–"

"And what Mother?" he interrupted, sounding sharper than he intended but annoyed by the same lecture yet again. "And spend all of my money, gossip with her dim-witted friends, and parade me around Town like a circus act?" he asked, unable to hide the distaste in his voice.

"Edward," his mother admonished, a little shocked at the bitterness in her son's tone, "you cannot believe that I would want anything less than a suitable wife for you."

"Our ideas of suitable are vastly different, Mother," he commented dryly, "you would have me marry a cow if it was from good stock."

The bark of laughter from the other side of the carriage brought Edward's attention to Tom.

"You," he snapped, his tone accusing, "should know better than to go along with Mother's schemes, Tom."

"It is no scheme, Edward. It is just a visit."

Edward turned away from them both to stare moodily out the window once more. They'd closed ranks and neither would tell him anything.

Well, maybe it was genuinely just a visit. It would be terribly awkward, and unorthodox to say the least. But if he hadn't agreed, his Mother would have gone on about it until the Season, with all its distractions, started and he really did not want to have to deal with that.

The carriage started to turn and Edward noticed they were approaching a pair of heavy wrought iron gates. The entrance, presumably, to the Earl of Ranford's estate. His steel grey eyes took in his surroundings as the carriage began its slow progress up a meandering gravel path set in sweeping verdant grounds.

Ireland was really breathtakingly beautiful, he had to admit. Though there were similarities to his own country estates in Surrey, Lancashire, and Wales, there really was an air of mystery and magic amongst these hills and dales.

Edward was never one for fanciful thoughts. He had great responsibility, which he took seriously. Though his friends and family knew him to have a kind heart and wicked sense of humour, he rarely gave way to thoughts which were illogical or insensible. He shook his head slightly, laughing at himself.

The carriage rounded a central water fountain and stopped before a rambling red brick house that was the formal seat of the Earl of Ranford.

The house itself was built on land which had been occupied by an old and important Clan in Irish history and there were traces still of that ancient civilisation dotted around the grounds. There were ruins that could be explored, and his mother took great delight in telling him about the hills of the faery folk and 'little people' of Ireland.

He should really have her looked at.

Aside from the supernatural nonsense it was a beautiful old house, very well situated with a central rectangle design flanked by extended wings on either side.

The afternoon sun bounced off the windows giving the place an altogether welcoming feel.

No sooner had their carriage stopped than the front door opened and a flurry of activity ensued.

Footmen were brought immediately to their assistance by the butler, who introduced himself as Murphy — a very well turned out man, appearing to be in his sixties and with a pleasant Irish brogue.

"Good day to ye, your grace, your grace, sir," he said deferentially, bowing to each of them in turn. "If you will follow me please, his lordship is waiting to receive ye."

Edward offered his arm to the dowager and together they walked up the steps and into the hallway of the great house. His mother gasped in approval and Edward could tell she was noticing striking similarities between here and his estate, Banfield, in Surrey.

The floor was covered in a similar light coloured marble, a central staircase veered out to a surrounding balcony on the first floor and a truly magnificent chandelier took pride of place in the centre of the ceiling, drawing the guest's eye up.

Murphy coughed discreetly and indicated that they follow him to a room on the left.

He heard Murphy announce them and a booming voice telling him to show them in at once. He shared a look with his mother— hers, one of pleasure, his, ever suspicious.

Tom hung back and appeared disinterested in the proceedings. Edward knew he would already be wishing to acquaint himself with the staff and kitchen. Mostly concentrating on the kitchen.

They were shown into a beautifully situated receiving room. Decorated in tones of palest yellows and whites it was bright and airy and perfect for a hot summer afternoon. The windows looked out onto a beautiful vista of green leading down towards what looked like a sizeable pond centred by yet another fountain.

"My dear Kate, how wonderful it is to see you again." This rather informal – greeting was conducted by a statuesque woman who had risen to greet them. She stood a good head taller than his mother, was slim and willowy and carried herself like a true lady, her blonde hair, showing shades of grey, pulled into quite a severe knot at the back of her head. Her dress, though simple in deference to her age, was excellently made. In short, here stood the very epitome of a lady.

"Mary, it has been far too long," the dowager responded equally as warm, which was unusual for his usually reserved mother, and the two women embraced.

His mother turned to him to draw him forward.

"You must remember my son, Edward, the Duke of Hartridge."

"I do of course, though it has been many, many years.

How good to see you again, your grace."

Edward bowed politely then turned toward the man who was awaiting his turn for introductions.

This man had been his father's oldest friend and, by all accounts, the pair of them could have given the duke and his set a run for their money, in their hay day.

The earl was a tall and broad shouldered man whose face was remarkably unlined, though his hair was a pure white.

It was quite a bittersweet moment for Edward, to see his father's best friend stand healthy and happy before him, when his own poor father should have been here too.

The earl stepped forward to kiss the dowager on the cheek, and then turn to clasp Edward's shoulder.

"My dear boy" —obviously the Earl wasn't one for formality— "how good to see you now after all these years. And what a fine gentleman you've turned out to be. Why you are the very image of your father at this age. A finer man I never knew, and I miss him still."

"Thank you, my lord. I miss him too, every day," Edward responded.

"La, let's have none of that 'my lord' business. Why, I held you as a babe in arms." The earl smiled warmly, his brown eyes twinkling.

Edward could not help but respond to this friendly old man with a smile of his own. He immediately liked the earl and countess very much and was beginning to think that maybe this visit would not be such a bad thing.

"You must call me Henry," the earl continued jovially.

"And I am Edward, of course," responded Edward. He really had no choice. Propriety did not seem to be high up on the earl's list of priorities.

"Your grace."

Turning he found Lady Ranford bringing a pretty young woman forward for introduction. Edward did not know how he had missed her before, she was extremely like her mother, though in the first blush of youth.

She was as tall and willowy as her mother, and where Lady Ranford's hair was greying and her skin gently lined, this lady's hair was as bright as the sun, her face unlined and blushing prettily.

She was dressed in a pale lemon summer dress, which highlighted her slim figure. Edward cut a quick glance to his mother. Standing before him was the very picture of what the dowager would want for a daughter-in-law, he was sure. His thoughts were confirmed by the sheer joy on his mother's face.

Biting back a sigh of frustration, he smiled politely and bowed over the lady's hand. Yes, she was pretty, carried herself well and was no doubt a lady.

And was just like every other debutante that had been flung his way since he reached the grand old age of eighteen. His father had warned him about the debs and their mamas, but to see them in action was quite an experience. And, as he got older, they got more intense and, well frankly, frightening.

"May I present my daughter, Lady Caroline," Lady Ranford continued.

"Your grace," Lady Caroline demurred, curtseying very formally, and very properly, to the duke.

"How do you do, Lady Caroline?"

"Very well, I thank you. And you? I hope your journey was not too tiresome."

Did she think he was ancient, for goodness sake? Incapable of travel in a plush and luxurious coach?

"No, not at all Lady Caroline, I only wish I could have ridden part of the way. I found myself in need of fresh air."

"Why Edward," his mother pounced like a cat on a mouse, "what a wonderful idea. Why don't you let Lady Caroline show you around some of these beautiful gardens?'

As subtle as a blacksmith's hammer, his mother.

"I'd be delighted to, your grace."

Well, he could not bloody well say 'no' now, could he?

He looked around at the faces of the occupants in the room. Every one of them wore matching expressions of calculated delight and it suddenly dawned on Edward, sending an icy chill down his spine, why it was he was here.

So they'd decided he and Caroline should marry, had they?

Damnation. He would be having serious words with Mother as soon as he had the chance.

Now, however, was not the time.

"Care to join us, Mother?" Edward asked through gritted teeth.

His mother blinked innocently at him. Too innocently.

"Oh no thank you, dear. I am quite tired out by the journey. I should much rather take tea and catch up with my very– "

"Dear friends," finished Edward bitingly.

He wanted to say to hell with the lot of them and storm out to the nearest inn.

But he was raised impeccably and good manners won out.

"Lady Caroline, it looks like it is just us," he said smoothly. Though she blushed rather fetchingly at his words, her eyes remained ever so slightly calculating and Edward could not help but feel that everything she was saying and doing was nothing other than a performance. Bearing that in mind, Edward turned to Tom who was studiously ignoring him and instead looking at his hands rather intently. "Tom, I do apologise. Did you not say you felt the need to stretch your legs too?" Edward's tone and expression remained unfailingly polite but Tom knew him well enough to know that this was nothing other than a command. Albeit sugar coated.

He coughed a couple of times before smiling. "Yes, yes I did. I should be glad of a walk." Edward nodded ever so slightly in approval and pointedly ignored his mother's audible sigh from his left.

AN UNLIKELY DUCHESS

He waited in the parlour, listening to the chatter of old friends while Caroline fetched her bonnet. Within a couple of moments they were ready to go.

As soon as they left, the earl puffed out a relieved breath.

"Well, that went very well," he commented happily.

"Yes," agreed Lady Ranford, "and how beautiful they look together."

The dowager smiled her agreement, but she knew that her ear was in for a bashing when her fiercely independent son returned.

****

Outside, the sun beat pleasantly down on the trio as they made their way down the sweeping lawn toward the pond.

They were silent for a moment or two, each wondering what they should say. Somewhat to Edward's surprise, it was Lady Caroline who broke the silence first.

"We are so very pleased your mother and you could come to visit with us, your grace. My mother has been quite beside herself with excitement." She smiled favouring him with a charming, if formal smile.

"I am happy to do so, Lady Caroline," he replied pleasantly. "I know my mother was very much looking forward to it also."

More silence ensued. Edward usually had quite a repertoire of conversation he could pull out when chit chatting with members of Society. At the moment though, he did not feel like it.

The silence was suddenly broken by a ferocious shout coming from a clump of trees to their left as they made their way toward the pond.

"Damnation Martin!" shouted the very loud, very *female* voice. "I told you not to let it go."

Edward and Tom both stopped walking and stared in

amazement. For as much as the voice was loud and swearing like a sailor, it was also very much the cultured voice of a lady.

Another scream rent the air followed by the shout of a young boy and suddenly a kite, being carried by the stiff summer breeze floated out from the trees and right over the lake, getting tangled in the up-stretched arm of one of the statues flanking the pond.

So intent was Edward on the progress of the kite, and on seeing who on earth was making such a racket, that he paid little attention to whatever Lady Caroline was currently mumbling. However, he distinctly heard the words 'warned', 'begged' and, rather ominously, 'murder'.

Moments after the kite got itself good and tangled, the trees rustled alarmingly and a young lady burst through onto the path at a dead run.

Though she was moving far too quickly for anything identifiable to be established, she was trailed by a shock of chestnut hair flying out behind her. She came to a screeching halt at the foot of the statue and, shielding her eyes from the sun, peered up at it.

The trio was not close enough to see her expression but they were definitely close enough to hear another unladylike word spew from her mouth before she hitched her skirts and began to climb the statue!

Edward and Tom shared a look of pure shock. Lady Caroline had, at this point, buried her face in her hands.

None of them moved to help the young lady. And she did not even glance their way. She leaned precariously and stretched her hand upwards to try and untangle the string of the kite, the tail of which was still trailing along the ground.

Edward, in the midst of the commotion, could not help but notice that she had the body of a goddess. Shorter than the woman beside him, her heavenly curves were very well outlined by the material straining against her body as she reached. Suddenly he found his mouth had gone unaccountably dry.

Her hair was magnificent and he found himself struck with an intense desire to see her face. If it matched the rest of her, he could honestly believe he was in the presence of a goddess or perhaps one of the faery folk these lands were so famous for.

Another shout snapped Edward's attention back to the copse of trees as yet another figure bounded toward the pond. This time, it was that of a young boy, maybe ten years old and, by the brief glimpse of his clothing, the son of a staff member.

He skidded to a halt as he looked up towards the beautiful lady stretching with all her might, now leaning even further and seeming a lot more unsteady.

Edward felt a sudden slam of fear in his heart and started towards her, albeit at a slow pace. He did not want to scare her into losing her footing by racing towards her.

He chose not to examine the reason for this acute fear for a total stranger's safety. He was just being a good human being. That was all.

"My lady," the lad shouted in triumph, "here's the tail. We can pull it free."

It all happened so quickly that there was nothing Edward could do.

At the young boy's shout the young woman turned towards him. She had obviously managed to untie the string and was clutching it in her small hand.

As she yelled 'no,' the young boy picked up the string and gave it a sharp tug.

For a few heart-stopping seconds she balanced on top of the statue, her arms flailing about. The little boy, realising what he had done, promptly let go of the string, the only thing helping her even slightly to maintain her stance.

With another scream she lost balance and hit the water of the pond with a huge splash.

The splash seemed to galvanise the little group of

spectators and they ran towards the pond, Edward leading the way.

Now, Edward had had his fair share of experience with women. Especially gently bred women. And, although he could not imagine a single one of them ever being in the position this young lady found herself in—running through woods, chasing kites, climbing statues, he knew how the female psyche worked.

He was fully prepared for the crying, possibly wailing that was about to assail his ears. He suspected there may be a touch of hysterics and could almost guarantee there would be swooning.

This is what he expected. What he did not expect was to find the fair maiden sitting in the middle of the pond, covered in debris, soaked from head to toe... and laughing. Genuinely chuckling until the tears rolled down her flawless cheeks.

The little boy, Martin presumably, had joined in and the pair of them laughed and laughed and gave no indication that they realised they had company.

"Rebecca," Lady Caroline's sharp voice rang out bringing an abrupt end to the merriment. There was a world of disapproval, admonishment and anger in that tone. *Rather impressive to have packed so much into one name,* Edward thought distractedly.

The lady, Rebecca, turned incredibly big and sinfully dark eyes toward Lady Caroline. Edward found he had to gulp around his dry throat again.

"Caroline, how nice to see you," her voice was warm and soft, terribly mischievous and made Edward think very inappropriate thoughts.

"What in God's name are you doing?" Caroline hissed. "Get out of there at once. Can you not see that we have company?"

At Lady Caroline's word, the lady turned the full force of her incredible eyes on Edward and Tom. Edward bit back a gasp as the impact hit him in an area that had no business feeling anything in broad daylight. He heard Tom's audible gasp and imagined he suffered the same affliction. For some reason, this irritated Edward.

"So we do." The young lady was speaking again. And rather than sound upset, or scramble to her feet in mortification, she grinned unapologetically at the two gentlemen. "The Duke of Hartridge, I presume, and his cousin Mr. Crawdon?" She spoke politely, for all the world like they were being introduced in a drawing room or ballroom in London.

Tom, finally unable to contain his mirth, burst into laughter, which he desperately tried to cover up as a cough.

Lady Rebecca grinned even wider at Tom's obvious amusement at the situation. Who was this woman? Edward had never seen anything like it!

Lady Caroline stepped closer to the edge of the pond, her back ramrod straight. "Get. Up," she hissed menacingly through clenched teeth.

Lady Rebecca gave a defeated sigh and stood. As she did so, the water gushed off her person. Edward found he had to bite back a groan of pure, unadulterated lust. Her gown had originally been white, he would hazard, but had now been turned a slight shade of mud from the contents of the pond. The fact that it was wet meant it clung to her form like a second skin.

As she stood there, dripping wet and futilely wringing out her long tresses, Edward found he could only stare like an immature adolescent. Never had he seen a body like hers. Never had he seen the curves of a lady so well, who wasn't also standing naked in front of him and preparing to make love.

The thought set his heart hammering and his body stirring. It was terribly embarrassing but he could not bring himself to care. There was a lump the size of a rock wedged in his throat, and he could no more have looked away than he could have plucked the sun from the sky.

"Must you be such a bore Caroline?" Lady Rebecca asked, not a bit concerned with the other lady's disapproval that was practically rolling off her rigid frame.

"I told you we were to have guests today," muttered Caroline in a frantic whisper. The gentlemen could still hear her very well but neither one was much inclined to pay attention at that particular time.

Lady Rebecca finally seemed to be taking in the gravity of the situation. Her eyes travelled from Lady Caroline's furious face to those of the two gentlemen who both looked like they wanted to eat her alive.

She drew herself up to her full height and inhaled a deep breath before speaking again. "I apologise, Caro, really. I had quite forgotten the time." Her apology was met with stony silence.

"Gentlemen," she continued turning slightly towards them, "pray forgive my – er – less than proper appearance. I assure you, I do not usually greet guests of my father in such a fashion."

Her words snapped Edward out of his frankly inappropriate daydream.

"You are Ranford's daughter?" he asked, and was irritated to hear how husky his voice was.

"His youngest," the goddess confirmed. "Lady Rebecca Carrington." She dipped into a curtsey worthy of any daughter of a Peer, but since she was still standing in the middle of the pond, it rather seemed a little late for propriety.

"A pleasure," he answered a little dazedly.

"Ahem."

"Excuse me. My cousin, Mr. Crawdon." Edward gestured behind him.

Tom stepped forward and gave a deep bow. "An honour to meet you Lady Rebecca," he said, his eyes twinkling with mirth.

Her responding smile felt like a punch to Edward's abdomen and he suddenly wanted to pull her out of the pond and shield her from Tom's appreciative eyes.

"Rebecca," snapped Caroline, a blush of embarrassment rising in her cheeks, "please return to the house and clean yourself up."

Lady Rebecca rolled her eyes slightly but Edward caught it and could not bite back a slight grin. The chit was incorrigible.

"Gentlemen, if you will excuse me," she said with as much dignity as she could muster. Which wasn't a lot, given the circumstances.

She trudged to the edge of the pond, her progress slow due to the weight of the water on her dress. Edward did not think he'd ever seen such a beautiful dress!

As she reached the edge and made to climb over, he rushed to her assistance, almost knocking both Tom and Lady Caroline to the ground and out of his way.

"Allow me," he said, extending his hand to assist her.

Rebecca looked into his eyes and time seemed to come to a sudden halt. He heard the breath hitch in her throat and it was all he could do to prevent himself from pulling her flush against him. Good God! What was the matter with him?

The air between them felt like it had been struck by lightning. She placed her small hand in his and it felt perfect. He could not resist rubbing his thumb along the delicate palm. He watched as her lips parted and almost groaned aloud once again.

Get a handle on yourself man!

He shook his head slightly to try to clear the sensual haze surrounding them and stepped back so she could climb over.

Her bonnet, he noticed was still tied at the front, though it trailed down her back. For some reason he found it incredibly endearing. She must have noticed his glance for she reached back, which did nothing for his current state, and pulled it forward again.

"Well," she said jovially, presumably trying to salvage some propriety from the situation, "I shall be on my way. Good afternoon Caro, gentlemen." She curtsied once again and lifted her bonnet to replace it on her head.

And, of course, upon tipping it over to replace it, proceeded to dump its contents all over herself.

She gasped in shock as the icy cold water dripped down her head, and spluttered most becomingly as it hit her face.

Lady Caroline groaned and dropped her face into her hands once more. Tom, once again lost control of himself and gave a shout of laughter.

Edward found himself biting his tongue enough to taste blood to stop himself from laughing too.

Lady Rebecca swiped the excess water from her eyes and shot them a rueful grin. Then, turning on her heel, she trudged her way back up the garden and towards the house.

They heard the squelch of the water in her boots until she had disappeared over the slight hill.

The silence she left behind with her departure was deafening.

"Your grace," Lady Caroline stuttered the words in the general direction of his chest, too mortified to look him in the eye, "perhaps you would like to return to the house."

It seemed they were not going to discuss the surreal incident they had just witnessed. If he was honest though, he could not think of a damned thing to say anyway.

So, throwing a quick look of complete amazement towards Tom, who was looking thoroughly entertained, he offered his arm to Lady Caroline. "I would indeed, my lady," he answered, all politeness.

Edward had no idea what he had let himself in for by coming here. But suddenly, he could not wait to find out.

Chapter Two

Rebecca refused, just refused to look back during the mortifying trek back to the house. She could hear the squelch of the pond water in her boots, so she could only imagine that the witnesses to that spectacle could hear it too.

She could not believe that had happened. Her father would be furious. Her mother would probably cry. Again. And Caroline, well Caroline would likely never utter another word to Rebecca as long as they both lived.

She heaved a sigh, slipping through the conservatory at the back of the property, thus avoiding any chance of her parents seeing her before she managed to clean up.

She felt torn between utter mortification and total amusement at what had just happened. Mortification because she had just thrown herself into the pond, having climbed a statue and half drowned in front of a duke. Caroline's intended. Dear God it could not be a bigger disaster. Amusement because, well, it was rather funny!

What must he think of her? His cousin had seemed highly entertained by the incident, if his laughter and friendly smile were anything to judge by. Rebecca herself had found entire thing hilarious. But she'd learned from bitter experience and constant remonstrations from both Mother and Caro that what she thought was good fun was actually the behaviour of a complete hoyden and not a lady of good *ton*.

Frankly, she did not care about being *ton*, good or otherwise. But could never blaspheme thus in front of the paragons she lived with.

But the duke...

As her mind turned toward the duke and what he must think of her behaviour, she came to a complete stop, halfway up the servants' staircase to her room.

A myriad of emotions came over her and she found, to her surprise, that her cheeks began to heat profusely. As someone who had spent most of her life making rather a spectacle of herself in front of the entire village, thus becoming somewhat immune to blushes, this was quite a feat.

Her eyes closed and she inwardly groaned when she remembered the look of undisguised shock on his face. His face. Never had she seen such a face! Her heart had actually begun to slam against her chest when she'd finally looked at him, so loud that surely he must have heard it. The breath had been quite stolen from her lungs!

Why, he was beautiful! If a man could be described as such. Handsome just did not seem to do him justice. No it was beauty. Dark, brooding, sinful beauty. His hair, black as jet, was perfectly cut; his grey eyes, the colour of winter clouds, bore into hers. And although his face was hard, looked like he was carved from the purest of marble, his lips were perfectly formed and beautifully kissable...

Her cheeks began to heat again, for a very different reason this time. Her thoughts were wanton and shocking! She had never had a reaction to anyone like she had had to the duke; never felt the sensations that had run rampant through her body.

Rebecca felt a powerful yearning when he touched her.

But, being an innocent, she did not know what for.

All she knew was that the mighty Duke of Hartridge was finally, after months of preparation and excitement, here. And within thirty minutes of his arrival she had exposed her legs, fallen into a pond, shouted enough curse words to make a naval officer blush, and developed feelings that were as confusing as they were unwelcome.

Rebecca felt sick when she thought of the clown she'd made of herself. Sicker yet that the man whose touch had sparked feelings in her that she never even knew existed, was the same man who had been brought here to marry her sister.

Feeling defeated and guilty that she'd upset Caroline so much, she finished the trek to her room and rang for her long-suffering maid. Within minutes Maura, a girl whose sunny disposition was a great asset as the lady's maid of the notorious Rebecca Carrington, had entered the room, taken in the image of her mistress dripping wet and miserable, and immediately set about preparing a bath and some sweet, comforting tea.

"Should I ask what happened, my lady?" Her Irish brogue was quite prominent when she was both exasperated and amused. Which was very often.

"Must you?"

"Not at all. If you'd rather not say."

"I fell in the pond."

"That is not so bad. Would not be the first time."

"Caroline was there."

"Ah. Well, I am sure after a nice chat about avoiding the pond, she will be just grand."

"And the duke."

The silence lasted enough beats for Rebecca to know that even Maura understood this was no mere mishap.

"Oh."

"Indeed." answered Rebecca dryly.

Maura remained silent while she ushered the downstairs

maids, who had arrived with the hot water for the bath, from the room.

"May I ask how you landed yourself in the pond this time, my lady?"

"I climbed a statue to rescue Martin's kite and lost my balance."

"In front of his grace, my lady?" Maura looked stricken.

Rebecca squirmed. "Yes," she mumbled, eyes cast downward. It was more than a little embarrassing to know that your own maid was ashamed of your behaviour.

When Maura did not answer for several moments, Rebecca finally looked up. Maura stood before her, with her hands clasped around her mouth while she struggled to contain her obvious mirth.

"It is not funny, Maura." Rebecca scolded. "You know I am in a world of trouble when Papa hears what I have done."

"I am sorry, my lady," replied Maura, though her wide grin suggested otherwise.

Rebecca fought to keep a stern countenance but Maura's laughter had her remembering just how ridiculous she must have looked, flailing about at the top of the statue before scaring the wits out of the fish in the pond.

And, as much as she worried about her parent's reaction to her little adventure, dreaded the set down that was no doubt coming from her starchy older sister, and as much as her reaction to the great duke intrigued and frightened her, Rebecca could not contain her own laughter and was soon laughing once again and feeling much more like herself as Maura left her to bathe and went to organise her tea.

Her family had seen her do worse. And although she was quite sure the Duke of Hartridge would be utterly appalled by her, ultimately it was only her sister he was interested in. And if that thought caused a pang of sadness well, she would ignore it and carry on regardless.

****

Edward stood against the enormous fireplace, nursing a pre-dinner brandy while he waited for the rest of the party to assemble in the drawing room. He had spent the remainder of the afternoon becoming acquainted with the earl, the house and avoiding his mother to the very best of his abilities.

As soon as they had returned to the house, Lady Caroline had taken her leave and disappeared. By the stiffness in her spine, he could only imagine that Lady Rebecca was in for a lecture of some magnitude. He felt a twinge of pity for the girl. He may not be well acquainted with Lady Caroline but if her icy glare were anything to go by, he would not want to be on the receiving end of her cold anger.

Icy, cold. They seemed apt indeed when describing that lady. She was beautiful, but coolly so. Her manner was impeccable, but lacked warmth. She was perfectly polite and amiable, but altogether too rigid and controlled.

How she was the sister of the absolute hoyden they'd come across in the garden, he had no idea. As his mind turned to Lady Rebecca, he felt a stirring in his body that frustrated and, frankly, baffled him. He had never reacted so strongly, nor so quickly to a female before. Not even in his uncontrolled adolescence.

What was the matter with him anyway? The unbending Duke of Hartridge, he so famous for his self-control, mooning about like a lovesick schoolboy? It was ridiculous.

But he could not help it. She was exquisite. He had felt the impact from those eyes right down to his toes.

When he took her hand in his, it was all he could do to stop himself from pulling her flush against him and kissing the breath from her lungs, and damned if he cared who saw!

She was the complete opposite of her sister. Fire instead of ice. Fun and full of life. He could well imagine the types of scrapes she managed to get herself into. He would wager they were often too, considering Lady Caroline had seemed more resigned than surprised, by watching her sister climb statues and fall into ponds. As if the occurrence were regular. Very peculiar.

Yet her manners were definitely those of a lady of breeding. Her curtsey, her eloquent speech spoke of training and good society. It made the fact that she'd been knee deep in pond water and laughing with abandon all the more strange.

Yes, the total opposite of her proper older sister. *And of you.* The tiny voice spoke in the back of his mind and brought him up short.

He was a fun-loving, free-spirited man was he not? He certainly had been in his younger days. But the mantle of responsibility that came with the dukedom weighed heavily on his shoulders. If he were to be brutally honest with himself, he knew he had become rather stiff and implacable himself.

He gave a deep sigh. Yes, they were opposites. Not well matched at all. He supposed he should be thinking of ladies like Lady Caroline. Proper, polite, pretty. Filled with elegant poise and gentle mannerisms.

And boring, the voice piped up, irritating thing that it was.

Boring or not, a duchess needed to be of a certain ilk. And when did he start thinking of *any* lady as a potential duchess anyway? He wasn't here to marry either girl. The brandy was addling his brain.

He heard his mother enter the room and prepared himself to face her. She had a lot of explaining to do. He turned to address her and noticed that she was flanked by the countess and Lady Caroline. Biting back an irritated sigh, he bowed deeply to the three although he kept his eyes trained on his mother.

He knew she had brought reinforcements so he could not confront her about this blasted arrangement.

Well damned if he was going to make idle chit chat while they all made wedding plans behind his back!

Excusing himself after a couple of well-placed compliments and enquiries after the ladies' wellbeing, he went to stand with Tom and the earl and was about to address a question about the local agriculture when a movement at the door drew his attention and that of everyone else in the room.

The lady who had been occupying his thoughts almost exclusively since their unorthodox meeting this afternoon had arrived, and Edward felt once again like he'd been punched in the gut.

She was altogether too beautiful and intriguing for his peace of mind. And right now he knew he would never again see anyone as utterly breath-taking as she.

He heard Tom clear his throat nervously beside him and felt a ridiculous urge to block his view, shield her from his appreciative eyes. He could not, of course, but he was oh so tempted. He could hit him. But that might raise some questions.

He could not tear his eyes from her as she made her way towards her mother. She was a vision from her glorious chestnut hair, piled on top of her head with a few wisps framing her delicate face, to the tips of her satin clad toes. His eyes raked her greedily. That dress. Dear God, it could be used as a torture device! The greatest spies in the country would sell their secrets and their souls for a glimpse of what was hinted at with that blasted dress.

Its low cut displayed her pale and smooth skin to perfection, managing to be perfectly decent while invoking completely indecent thoughts in a man's mind. It outlined her curves to perfection. It hugged her tiny waist. The skirts, made of delicate palest pink satin swirled around her ankles and clung ever so slightly to her legs as she moved, outlining them for the briefest of seconds, ensuring that any red-blooded male would spend the rest of the evening imagining what having a real view would be like. He almost groaned aloud. How on earth was he to spend weeks here? This was fast turning into his own personal hell.

Rebecca studiously avoided looking in the duke's direction, though she could feel the weight of his stare. She desperately wanted to look at him, to see if he would be glowering in disapproval like she imagined a duke would. But having no idea if everyone knew or what had been said about the incident, she was afraid of giving anything away.

She could not avoid it all night of course. But first, she must gauge the reaction of her parents. Her mama and Lady Catherine were all warmth towards her, and although Caroline did her best to ignore Rebecca's presence in their circle, it appeared that she hadn't yet told them of the incident. Rebecca breathed a sigh of relief and found herself relaxing. If Caroline had said nothing then it was perfectly safe to look in the duke's direction, even speak to him.

Rebecca made a great pretence of looking around the room, finally letting her gaze rest on him. As if she hadn't wanted to seek him out the second she walked in the room. With a jolt, she realised that he'd been staring at her. And rather than glance away when she caught his eye, he continued to study her intently.

Rebecca felt herself blush for the second time that day. As her eyes locked with his, her breathing hitched and her stomach flipped dramatically. She had thought him attractive this afternoon. Tonight he was indescribable! The black of his evening coat made him seem even more smouldering, more sinful than the bottle green of his coat this afternoon. The snowy cravat enhanced his sallow skin and was tied simply but elegantly against his strong throat. She could not take her eyes from his throat and the cravat nestled against it. She found herself rather jealous of that cravat. The way it got to be so close to his skin. Jealous. Of a piece of cloth! She'd be off to Bedlam in the morning if they got wind of her innermost thoughts.

Her eyes widened in anticipation as he made his way

across the room directly towards her.

Oh heavens! Even the way he moved made her squirm. He walked with a panther-like grace, his long, strong legs perfectly outlined by the tight breeches that encased them.

"Rebecca," her mother's sharp tone interrupted her rather too intimate thoughts.

Unfortunately, her mind was still on his body and rather than the 'yes, Mama' Rebecca intended, she rather embarrassingly blurted out…

"Legs."

Oh dear.

"Excuse me?" her mother asked in confusion. She looked up, realising that while she was staring southwards of his eyes, the duke was gazing politely at her.

Rather, his face was a mask of politeness but his eyes glinted with amusement and something else she could not define but made her toes positively curl.

"I mean, I – uh – I apologise Mama. I was wool gathering, I am afraid." She smiled sweetly at Mama, Caroline who squinted menacingly, and Lady Catherine who smiled kindly if a little bemusedly.

"I was trying to introduce you to his grace, dearest," her mother explained through gritted teeth as if trying to keep the scolding she was clearly desperate to dole out, inside her mouth by sheer force of will.

Rebecca turned toward the duke but refused to look into his eyes again. Instead she concentrated on that lucky cravat.

"Your grace, may I introduce my youngest daughter, Lady Rebecca Carrington. Rebecca, His Grace, the Duke of Hartridge."

Rebecca curtsied and waited with trepidation for him to say they'd met already. A statement, which would lead to an explanation, which would lead to uproar no doubt.

To her surprise, the duke merely executed a deep bow, lifting her hand to his mouth. His touch, his words, sent a jolt through her and her eyes flew up to meet his. They twinkled mischievously as he smiled up at her. His thumb once again rubbed over the palm of her gloved hands and Rebecca's mouth dropped open in a little gasp. "A pleasure, my lady. And Lady Mary, I must congratulate you on the charms of both your daughters. They both look quite lovely this evening."

Both the mamas beamed at this, as did Caroline. Rebecca rolled her eyes. She'd grown up on the insincere compliments of the peerage. Seen with her own eyes when Sarah Woodchester had been called a radiant beauty. Sarah, bless her, resembled more closely a horse than any other living creature Rebecca had ever seen. Besides an actual horse, of course. She was a little disappointed that the Duke of Hartridge appeared to have as little imagination as the rest of them.

Looking back at him, she realised that he'd caught her eye roll and wasn't pleased about it. He lifted a haughty eyebrow in an expression he no doubt rolled out to put mere mortals back in their place. However, given that she never could resist a bit of mischief she raised one right back.

His mouth dropped open in surprise before his face adopted a cool mask of polite indifference. Ever the boring peer, Rebecca thought cynically, it would not do to show emotion.

****

He nearly ruined her right there, in front of her blasted family when that mouth dropped open, when the tip of her pink tongue darted out to lick her lips. Dear God, the woman was surely some sort of sorceress. How could such a simple action affect him so?

His hand tightened involuntarily before he let her go and straightened to his full height once again. He towered over her. He was taller than most men, and she was an entire head smaller than her sister. The difference in size gave him an overpowering feeling of protection towards her. He could imagine her, almost *feel* her nestled under his arm, leaning her head against his chest…

For God's sake! Get a hold of yourself man. Rebecca needed protection like he needed matchmaking!

She was an utter minx. Imagine. Having the audacity to roll her eyes at him. Did she not realise he was a duke for God's sake?

She suddenly grinned at him and gave a sly wink, no doubt trying to provoke a reaction and it was all he could do to keep his hands from grabbing her.

He turned his attention toward Lady Caroline who looked resplendent in Grecian style white silk.

"My lady, I hope you are well?"

Caroline beamed once again, obviously relieved too, that he chose to keep this afternoon's escapades to himself. Edward was surprised to see the change it brought about in her face. She looked younger, softer and altogether more beautiful.

Strange, though he could see that she was much more attractive than he first thought, he felt completely unmoved. Perhaps because he was so enraptured with the imp standing beside him.

"I am, your grace, I thank you."

"Am I to receive an introduction to this beautiful young lady then?"

Tom's voice floated from behind Edward's shoulder. He watched in consternation as Rebecca's eyes lit up with mirth. He was sure they hadn't lit like that for him. The thought did nothing for his mood.

This time, his mother, who'd been watching his face intently for the entirety of the exchange and had a sort of bemused expression, was the one to carry out introductions.

"Tom, my dear. Allow me to introduce you to Lady

Rebecca, Lady Caroline's younger sister." She had a shrewd glint in her eye and watched in satisfaction as Tom bent over Rebecca's hand.

It seemed to Edward that he held onto that hand longer than was necessary. He felt like ripping Tom's arm off and beating him with it.

"Lady Rebecca, an honour to finally meet you. A shame we did not meet sooner."

The twinkle in his eye drew a responding smile from Rebecca. This was much easier, much less complicated. Here was a nice man, making light of the situation. Handsome, pleasant, wealthy presumably. And she felt nothing. No tingle. No hammering heart. Nothing. What a pity.

"I apologise Mr. Crawdon. I was somewhat indisposed this afternoon."

His answering grin sparked one of her own and Rebecca felt herself relax even more. She could quite enjoy having this lively gentleman around, even if it meant having to put up with her feelings for his cousin.

Chapter Three

Shortly after, Murphy announced dinner and the assembled guests began to make their way in.

Rebecca found herself seated to Tom's right. Being the youngest and therefore lowest ranking female member of the party, she was seated at the end furthest from Hartridge. She could not help the twinge of disappointment.

What on earth was wrong with her? This is how people sit. Always. Besides, she could still see him. And his cravat.

"My lady," Mr. Crawdon's voice drew her attention.

Rebecca turned to meet his gaze and automatically leaned in closer to him when he began speaking in low tones, meant only for her ears.

"Never have I been so entertained in the first thirty minutes of a visit in my life," he began.

"Oh Mr. Crawdon, I beg of you, please do not bring it up again. What must you think of me?"

"I think you are delightful," he answered sincerely.

Rebecca smiled shyly, a little surprised at the rather forward compliment. She did not know Mr. Crawdon well enough to know if he had a wicked sense of humour or not so she thought it best not to comment.

Turning back toward her plate she glanced briefly up the table to where the duke sat and found, to her shock, that he was staring quite murderously at her. Her gaze caught in his and she found that she had no will or desire to look away. What on earth was he angry about? She could not possibly have offended him in the short time since they'd left the drawing room.

Rebecca could see that her father was talking to him and she tilted her head ever so slightly to indicate that he should listen. Her father could talk for Ireland and there was no doubt that the duke would be missing out on a rather large amount of conversation.

He blinked as if coming out of a trance and issued her a small smile before turning his attention to her father.

She could not help her mouth forming a smile of its own. Really, the man was far too handsome for his own good. Or hers. When he smiled, his entire face lit up and he looked younger, more carefree, and even more beautiful!

She caught Caroline's eye at that moment and her spirits plummeted. Caroline was glaring at her. And by the venomous look and the way her eyes darted between the duke and Rebecca, Caroline had seen their little exchange.

But it was perfectly innocent, thought Rebecca in consternation. Caroline was still shooting daggers and Rebecca knew better than to try to placate her now. She would not listen. A mule was less stubborn than Caroline when she thought the conventions of society were being threatened.

So Rebecca turned her attention to her plate and there it remained for the remainder of the meal.

After the last course had been served and done justice to, the ladies retired to the drawing room while the men enjoyed their port and cheroots.

Rebecca trailed rather miserably behind the other ladies and took a seat on one of the chairs furthest from Mama and

Lady Catherine.

Caroline immediately came to sit beside her and Rebecca prepared for the upcoming lecture on propriety, how a lady should act and each variance of these themes in between.

What she wasn't prepared for was Caroline's eyes welling up with tears. Rebecca gaped but could not help it. The last time Caroline had cried was when she still wore her hair in pigtails. If she remembered correctly, it had been because Rebecca had accidentally —no matter what Caroline tried to claim— dropped a basket of apples on her head.

"Caroline," she leaned forward in concern, "are you well?"

"Rebecca" —Caroline seemed to be trying to gather her composure— "I do not pretend to know what your reasons are, but please desist from trying to win the duke's affections. You know he is intended for me. That I am to be the duchess."

Rebecca was so shocked she could not form a coherent word. After spluttering for a while she managed to croak out a disbelieving "What?"

"You heard me perfectly," responded Caroline coldly, her composure well and truly back in place and her spine once again stiff enough to snap in two.

Rebecca could feel herself getting angry. What in the blazes was Caroline talking about anyway? She could not remember having a more ridiculous conversation than she was having right now, including the time she tried to explain to young Martin that his chances of catching a real leprechaun were extremely slim.

"And what part of my behaviour gave you the idea I was bent on seducing your precious duke, Caroline? Was it when I threw myself into the pond perhaps? Swore in front of him, because we all know that is sure to secure a gentleman's affection! Oh, I know, it was when he was trying to compliment us both earlier and caught me mocking him."

Rebecca was so angry that she was shaking. She hated

having to summarise her disgrace to prove she wasn't duke snatching.

"I cannot begin to imagine what it is that so attracts him, Rebecca," muttered Caroline icily, "but given that he has been staring at you like he wants to gobble you up since he watched your little circus in the gardens, I would say that whatever it is you are doing is working. So stop it."

Rebecca would much rather Caroline had continued to cry. At least she appeared human then. This frigid anger was horrible to endure. Their tempers were so vastly different. Rebecca went up like a torch when baited, her temper rising to fiery and gargantuan proportions.

Caroline, in contrast, became even more cool and calm, her tone biting as she delivered merciless set downs.

"That is preposterous," Rebecca cried, drawing the attention of Mama and Lady Catherine.

"Rebecca," her mother scolded, "do try to keep it down dearest."

Rebecca had enough. This entire situation was grossly unfair. She stood up and made to storm from the room. What insanity to say she had any ulterior motive toward the duke. Her conscience pricked guiltily but she shoved it aside. She did not purposefully find him attractive and had certainly given no indication of her feelings.

And as for Caroline claiming that he looked at her like – like –

Well it was ridiculous. Utterly ridiculous.

She decided to take some air on the balcony that ran around the side of the house and made for the doors leading from the drawing room and out into the summer night's air.

Still in a temper though, she could not let her true feelings about their guests go unsaid so she marched back towards Caroline, leaned down and whispered fiercely, "Even if I was in the market for a husband, which I am NOT, I think your way of going about getting one is insane. I understand the contract was made before you were even born but my God Caroline, you know nothing about him save his wealth and title. He could have been the most ill-mannered, self-absorbed rake who ever walked in the world and you'd *still* want to see this through."

"But he is not, is he?" Caroline's soft question brought her up short. No, he did not seem to be any of those things.

"Do you dislike him so very much then?" asked Caroline.

Rebecca hesitated before answering.

"I do not know him so how can I dislike him?"

"Rebecca, you've always allowed your head to be filled with ridiculous, fairy tale notions of love, romance and heroes. But that is not how the world works. I must marry and marry well. The contract is made. We are both aware of what our duty is. When Charles inherits Father's title and estates, do you really want to be a spinster sister? Living off the kindness of him and his wife?"

"Well of course not, who wants to live with her big brother forever? But I am hardly in my dotage. There is plenty of time for me to meet someone whom I love, and who loves me."

"And where will you meet this wonderful man, hmm? Certainly not here. And you are refusing to have a Season–"

"So are you," Rebecca responded hotly.

"I am not *refusing* I merely pointed out how unnecessary it is for me, when I am betrothed to a duke. After all, I cannot very well hope to do better can I?" she asked smugly.

Her constant references to her engagement, and to the Duke of Hartridge were feeding Rebecca's anger and bringing it to a fever pitch.

She chose not to examine the reason why too closely.

"What happened to you, Caroline? When did you become this Ice Queen?" she bit out.

As soon as Rebecca said the words, she wished she could take them back.

A look of pain flashed across Caroline's face before she schooled it into impassivity once again. It tugged at Rebecca's all too feeling heart.

"I am sorry Caroline. I should not have—"

"Your problem, dearest, is that you have yet to grow up," Caroline interrupted Rebecca as if she hadn't even been speaking. "You think that your beauty alone will be enough to excuse your ridiculous behaviour."

Rebecca flinched as if she'd been slapped. In truth it felt like she had been.

"Our whole lives you've been the funny one, the pretty one, the wild one and it was acceptable when we were young. It is even somewhat acceptable now that we're hidden away here on the estate. But you would bring utter disgrace down on our name if you were let loose in society. Why do you think our parents have not pursued the subject? And as for the idea of you being a duchess, well it is madness."

"I never said I *wanted* to be a duchess," Rebecca insisted hotly.

Why she chose this one detail of Caroline's softly spoken tirade to hotly deny was beyond her. She was livid, past the point of reason. But it felt terribly important that Caroline knew she had no feelings toward the duke.

At least then one of them might believe it.

Rebecca could not bear to listen to any more. She and Caroline had been at odds for years but the venom coming from her sister now seemed excessive. She did not realise Caroline held her in such contempt. And, whilst she had always suspected that her family was embarrassed by her antics, it hurt more than she was willing to show to have it spelled out to her in such a manner.

She'd never set out to hurt them.

Rebecca could feel tears beginning to sting her eyes but she would be damned if she'd let them fall in front of Caroline.

Without a word, she turned on her heel and fled to the

balcony.

****

Edward leaned back against the wall and closed his eyes, enjoying the peace and quiet. He meant to enjoy his solitude before having to join the ladies and deal with his raging hormones. He had enjoyed the reprieve with the earl and Tom but, when talk turned, not very subtly, to marriage he made his escape promptly.

Until he spoke to his mother all he had were suspicions, but he could almost guarantee that they were planning on him leaving here engaged to Lady Caroline.

They would be disappointed, however.

He had no intention of marrying.

And whilst he could admit that Lady Caroline was very much duchess material, it would be deuced uncomfortable taking her up the aisle when his entire being was preoccupied with taking up her sister's skirts!

He began to think about returning indoors when a noise to his left caught his attention.

He said noise, but it was really a curse. And a very audible one at that.

He had to bite back his laughter as he realised that the chit was once again swearing like a sailor and unaware that she was doing so in his presence.

"Devil take him anyway. He is not even that handsome."

His ears pricked up. To whom was she referring? It could not be him, he thought rather smugly, he was quite the catch.

She groaned next and he moved nearer to get a better look.

He found himself conveniently hidden behind a huge potted plant, yet still perfectly able to see her.

"Perhaps he is handsome. Well, there is no perhaps. He IS handsome, blast it."

Was it odd that he found her endearing whilst talking to herself?

"How dare she? I could care less about Society. And I certainly am not trying to seduce the duke."

He froze.

Her ranting suddenly became a lot more interesting to him. Though not nearly as interesting as the idea of her seducing him.

He nearly groaned aloud himself at the mere thought. He could not help feeling slightly proud that she found him handsome.

As he watched she kicked out at a defenceless plant then slumped against the balustrade looking very young and very defeated.

His heart clenched and he desperately wanted to reach out to her. Oddly enough, to comfort her and not even think about the idea of her seducing him... well, perhaps a little, he was still human–

"The sooner he marries her and takes her away the better."

He froze again, this time in anger as the little minx inadvertently confirmed his suspicions.

And he, he who never lost his temper, felt a burning anger slam into him.

Stepping out from behind the plant, he addressed her in the haughtiest voice he could manage.

"I assure you, my lady, I have no intention of marrying anyone."

Chapter Four

Rebecca screamed in fright as the cool voice sounded behind her. Whirling around, she lashed out and landed a resounding smack squarely on Edward's chin.

Unexpected as it was, he reared back and lost his balance. In trying to right himself, he automatically reached out for purchase on the closest thing he could grab. Her!

And, given that he was decidedly taller and heavier than she, all he managed was to fall on his backside and drag her down to land on top of him.

He landed with a *thud* and proceeded to have the air knocked out of him by her body landing sprawled across his.

Though as he registered the feel of her pressed against him, he could not remember a single reason why having breath in your lungs was all that important anyway.

The air seemed to crackle between them. By sheer strength of will, he managed not to maul her.

She fit, as he suspected she would, perfectly against him. Her body felt soft and warm and oh, so tempting pressed against his.

She gazed into his face with those blasted eyes and he felt

like he was drowning.

"I, I am so sorry, your grace," she stuttered and began to push away from him.

He made no move to help. No move to answer. No move at all really. He was frozen. Completely mesmerized by her, bewitched by her.

"Your grace," her voice was a mere whisper.

"Hmm?"

"Please, let me go. I fear we will be seen."

He realised that he was still gripping her arms. He also realised she was absolutely right.

Cursing under his breath he bodily removed her and jumped to his feet.

She had scrambled up and was righting her skirts, studiously avoiding his face when he clasped her by the elbow and pulled her behind the very serviceable potted plant, shielding them from anyone who might come looking.

Rebecca bit back a gasp of surprise when the duke moved her behind the plant.

She was in so much turmoil she did not know if she was coming or going.

Not only had he presumably caught her speaking to herself. About him, no less. But she'd hit him in the face and then lain across him like a wanton!

In less than twenty-four hours she had committed the most ridiculous of social *faux pas* and very nearly ruined herself. With the man who would wed her sister!

It could not get worse. She risked a glance up at him and noticed his thunderous expression. Oh. Maybe it could.

"Your grace, I apologise for knocking you over, I truly did not realise my own strength. I–"

"I beg your pardon, Lady Rebecca. You did not knock me over. I lost my balance."

He looked mightily affronted.

"Well, yes. Because I hit you."

He started to make a weird strangled sound and she wondered if he were choking.

"Are you quite well, your grace?"

"I assure you, madam, I did not fall because a tiny chit of a woman hit me."

For heaven's sake. This was one of the more humiliating experiences of his life. She barely reached his shoulder, dammit.

Not only had she knocked him clear over, but he'd actually grabbed her and pulled her over with him. The end result may have been pleasant but still. One does not admit to being knocked over on to one's – well, it simply wasn't done.

He looked down haughtily at her and noticed a fiery glint in her eye. Ah. Apparently he'd awakened her temper.

"A tiny chit of a woman?" Rebecca glared menacingly at him. He thought she looked like a feisty little kitten. All angry and adorable. Probably best not to mention that though.

"Yes, well, you are considerably smaller than me. And it is rather preposterous that you think you are the cause of my fall. I am a duke," he finished, as if that meant he could not possibly be hit by a mere mortal.

"Since you appear to be confused by what just occurred, I can only conclude that you hit your head during your fall. Perhaps you should go and lie down, your grace. After all, a ducal head must be ever so much more important than the heads of us ordinary people."

Her voice positively dripped with venom. My, my. What a little shrew she was.

"You do have quite the temper, do you not?" he quipped. "What an impact you will make on Society."

The sudden change in her face surprised him. She paled at his words and then seemed to physically draw herself inwards, once again looking utterly defeated.

Hang it all, what had he said? Of course she'd make an impact on Society. There was no one in London who would hold a candle to her beauty, her spirit. She would be the toast of the Season. The belle of every ball. Gentlemen would be lining up to pursue her.

This last thought gave him a stab of jealousy that he did not care to think too much on at this moment.

The point was she reacted as though he'd kicked her favourite puppy, when he'd meant to offer her a compliment. Of sorts. He still thought her a hoyden and a shrew. An utter minx who must drive her parents to distraction trying to keep a handle on her. Just an especially beautiful and charming one.

"I need to get back inside. They will be wondering where I am. Please excuse me."

She gave a brief curtsy and almost ran to the door in order to get away from him.

Why was she standing there arguing with him, unchaperoned?

He was an arrogant brute! One who would soon be a brother to her. The thought was repellent.

His comment about her impact on Society had cut her to the quick and she needed to leave lest she burst into tears right in front of him. He wasn't to know that it was a particularly sore subject at that time, given she'd had the same thing said to her by her very angry sister not thirty minutes prior.

It had been a dreadfully trying day and now she wanted nothing more than to make her excuses and escape to her room.

"Wait." His hand shot out and grasped her upper arm to stop her from leaving.

Rebecca felt the jolt of awareness that she now associated with even his slightest touch. She had nearly expired on the spot when lying across his body. He'd felt so strong, so muscular and warm. Her throat dried at the mere memory. She could not allow herself to think this way.

"Your grace?"

"What did you mean, when you said I was to wed her

and take her away? To whom were you referring?" He knew. But he wanted to hear her say it.

She sighed, resigned and looked up at him, pinning him with her doe eyes.

"You are well aware your grace."

"I am afraid I am completely at a loss as to what you are referring, my lady. Enlighten me, please."

Rebecca studied him for so long he feared she'd fallen into some sort of comatose state.

"You really do not know?" she finally offered.

He shook his head.

She muttered under her breath, shaking her head and huffing and puffing a little.

Finally she looked up again and asked, "Are you aware of the contract that existed between our fathers?"

His confused look was answer enough.

"Oh dear," Rebecca bit her lip worryingly. Deuced lucky lip. "I do not think I am the best person to speak to about this, your grace," she began.

"Please," he interrupted, his curiosity well and truly peaked at the moment, "I am having a rather difficult time getting an answer from my mother as to what is going on here. And I can hardly ask yours."

Rebecca studied him intently for a few moments longer then seemed to make a decision.

"Very well. Forgive me for being so blunt about this but, well, there is no terribly easy way to soften the blow as it were."

He wished she'd hurry along. She was too damned distracting and he felt he needed a stiff drink. Or seven.

"Your grace, our parents made a contract before any of us were born. Before either of them were even married, if my father is to be believed. A marriage contract. The eldest son of the Duke of Hartridge to marry the eldest daughter of the Earl of Ranford."

Her announcement was met with a deafening silence. Rebecca gulped as she looked into his face. She thought she'd seen him angry up until now but clearly that had been mere irritation. For the look of fury currently on his face would be enough to send demons scurrying back to hell itself.

He did not speak for several minutes. Rebecca was just thinking of sneaking away, she doubted he'd notice so locked in his anger he seemed.

His clipped question halted her plans of escape.

"You were all aware of this, this contract? You all believe I've come here to pay my addresses to your sister? To honour this marriage deal?"

She wasn't sure what the right thing to say would be. He seemed frightfully angry but she could not be sure at whom it was directed.

"Er – yes?" she ventured.

"I see. So, your sister— she believes we are to be soon engaged?"

He noticed the flash of pain cross her face and it made his heart stop. Did the idea of his marrying her sister cause her pain?

Interesting.

"Well, well yes, your grace. That is was everyone believes. You really did not know? About the contract?"

"No, I most certainly did not."

"How strange."

Not strange at all. His mother knew him better than anyone. If he'd known about it he'd have taken steps to break it immediately. He would never follow through on such a ludicrous scheme. Never!

Even if it was the younger sister? Where had this voice suddenly come from? Full of difficult questions.

He would not be forced into anything. By anyone.

And he certainly had no interest in Lady Rebecca's sister. Lady Rebecca however…

His eyes turned smouldering as they raked her from head to toe.

****

Rebecca shivered, wondering at the sudden change in his mood. In the atmosphere.

He took a step toward her and her skin prickled in anticipation.

"I cannot possibly honour this contract, Rebecca."

So enraptured by him, she barely noticed his casual use of her name, though she had not given him leave to use it.

"Why not?" she croaked.

"For one thing, I have no interest in having a marriage arranged for me." He stopped mere inches from her. Rebecca inhaled deeply and almost swooned. He smelled delicious, of smoke, of sandalwood, of *man*.

"For another, I do not intend to marry at all for quite some time." His hand reached up and smoothed a stray hair from her cheek and tucked it behind her ear, lingering there until her breath was coming in short, and sharp gasps.

"And even if I were to marry soon, my choice certainly could not be your sister."

All at once Rebecca looked offended and he could not help the smile that stretched across his mouth.

"Why ever not?" she demanded.

"How could I marry her?" he continued and this time his arms reached out and pulled her slowly against his body. And she, like the wanton she obviously was, went willingly with no objection.

"How could I marry her, when all I can think about is this? And you?"

And with that his mouth came down to crush hers in a fierce kiss.

And Rebecca was lost.

Chapter Five

Edward had lost all sense of reasoning by the time his lips met Lady Rebecca's. In the back of his mind he knew he was courting absolute scandal. He knew he was on the way to ruining the lady. He knew that she was all wrong for him. And he did not give a damn.

Heat exploded through his veins as he wrapped his arms around her slim frame and crushed her closer, ever closer to his unyielding body.

Dear God, had ever a more sensual, tempting vixen walked the earth? How could a man be expected to control himself? She was the very embodiment of desire and he could not bring himself to pull away.

The kiss went on and on. He kissed her like his next breath depended on it.

The stars could have fallen from the heavens and he would not have stopped.

He had no idea what was happening to him. The feelings coursing through his body were beyond mere lust. He heard her soft moan and felt her arms cling to his neck and his heart clenched almost painfully in his chest.

He was afraid that this was more than attraction. He could almost believe that he was developing real feelings for the minx.

And that thought was like a jug of iced water being poured on his head.

With a jolt he pulled his lips from hers and set her bodily away from him, holding on to her arms as she staggered slightly.

Rebecca opened her big, dark eyes and he noticed, somewhat smugly, that they were glazed over. Her lips were bruised and swollen from his attentions and her breathing seemed as rapid as his own.

They stared at each other in silence, neither one sure what they would or should say.

There was a sudden noise from behind them, the sound of raucous laughter coming from the drawing room. It seemed to jolt Rebecca into action.

She lifted a hand to her lips and blinked rapidly.

"Oh dear," she sounded so distressed, so horrified that he wanted nothing more than to comfort her. He reached out to do so and she jumped back like a skittish colt.

"Your grace, I – that is you. Oh, I cannot do this!" And with this last distressed cry she brushed by him and ran right down the darkened balcony, presumably toward the door to another room where she could enter the house undetected.

Edward did not know how long he stood staring after her. His mind in turmoil, his body screaming for release.

He heaved a sigh and ran a hand through his hair. He needed to do his social duty then retire to his room to try and figure out what the hell had just happened.

****

Rebecca threw up a silent prayer of thanks when she found the door to Father's study open and slipped inside. The room was in complete darkness but thankfully she knew it like the back of her hand and was able to get to the door without mishap.

She hadn't made her excuses so could not just run away, much as she'd like to.

She could feel panic well up inside her and knew she'd have to get herself under control before entering the drawing room again.

Oh to have some of Caroline's stiff upper lip right now.

As her thoughts turned to her sister, the tears she'd been battling burst forth and she slumped back against the wall and buried her face in her hands.

Oh, God. What had she done? What had she done?

She looked around as if an answer to her problem was lurking in the hallway.

I need to calm down and think this through.

He had said he had no idea about the contract and, though she only knew him a day, she instinctively knew he was trustworthy. He wasn't lying. He really had no idea.

That meant that he *hadn't* come here to ask for Caroline's hand in marriage. The thought gave her more relief than she had a right to feel.

And what about what he'd said? That he could not stop thinking about *her*. Not Caroline. Not a perfectly proper, gently bred paragon of femininity but little old her.

Rebecca could not help a small smile at this. He'd seen her at her worst today — she'd assaulted him, accidentally of course, but still. And he still felt — well, *feelings* for her.

Her heart slammed against her chest.

He'd kissed her.

Her first kiss. And how glorious it was.

Rebecca had suspected when he'd stepped toward her that his intentions were to kiss her. She'd been rooted to the spot by excitement, a delicious, almost frightening anticipation. Having never been kissed she had no idea what to expect. She'd read the romance novels that her mother disapproved of so, but she'd also heard enough from the local married women to know that what was written was very different from what actually happened, which sounded rather disappointing to be frank.

Never had she imagined though that the reality would be so much *more* than anything she'd ever read. The women who complained were obviously kissing the wrong men.

As soon as his mouth had touched hers she had lost herself completely. Her heart had exploded and she'd seen actual stars behind her closed lids. Sensations that she'd only ever read about and even then hadn't fully understood had raced through her body as his lips had met hers.

She'd found her body reacting quite of its own accord, pressing itself wantonly against his hard, muscular frame, her arms reached up to twine themselves around his neck, clinging to him like a brazen hussy and she hadn't cared!

She'd heard the sound of moaning and had been shocked to realise it was her. And still she did not care. And still the kiss went on.

His tongue had darted out to dance with hers and she'd almost perished on the spot. Only his strong arms wrapped around her had prevented her from swooning to the ground.

When she'd read of such kisses she'd felt a little ill, not knowing how something so disgusting could bring pleasure to anyone. Oh, how wrong she'd been.

She could have spent the rest of her life kissing him.

But when he'd suddenly pulled away and pushed her from his body, the hard reality of the situation slammed into her like a runaway carriage. She could do nought but stare at him while desperately struggling to get her breathing under control.

She could not speak, could not move, and could not tear her eyes from his. He'd looked as dazed and confused as she felt. What had just happened between them? She was an innocent but was sure that the power of their kiss was rare.

His silver eyes bored into hers, as if seeing into her very soul. And she was terrified of what he'd see there. Terrified of what she was beginning to feel for him.

The sound of laughter had splintered the air and Rebecca had felt panic like she'd never known. She could not be seen there with him like that. She would be ruined! The scandal, her parents... Caroline!

Rebecca had tried to say something, anything, to make sense of what had happened. In the end though, she had felt the very last shred of her control slip and knew she would have to leave before the tears came.

And now, here she was. Hiding in the hallway of her own home and wondering what the blazes she was to do now.

****

Edward entered the drawing room as inconspicuously as he could. Which was rather difficult considering the second he walked in three pairs of female eyes honed in on him with disconcerting intensity.

He was most definitely *not* in the mood to talk politely with the Carringtons. He was furious with his mother, baffled by the contract his father had supposedly made and driven to distraction by the brown-eyed daughter of the house that seemed to have disappeared.

"Edward," Tom's voice came to the rescue and bowing slightly to the ladies, he made his way toward Tom and Carrington who were taking tea by the large fireplace.

"Where did you disappear to then?" enquired Tom, a glint in his eye. What the devil was he up to?

"I was taking some air on the balcony. When I returned to the dining room you had already left so I came here directly. Why? Is anything amiss?"

"Not at all, Edward," the earl addressed him now. "Just

wondering where all the young people were disappearing to, eh? Say, you did not happen across my daughter did you? It seems Rebecca has disappeared also."

Edward kept his polite ducal expression in place and thanked his lucky stars that the earl did not seem to be suspicious of the two disappearances. A quick glance at his cousin's amused expression however, told him that Tom was decidedly suspicious.

"Afraid not. Perhaps she retired early—" he began.

"Ah here she is," the earl's voice interrupted him and Edward snapped his eyes toward the door.

Lady Rebecca had entered quietly and made straight for the ladies, studiously avoiding even glancing in the direction of where he stood.

He swallowed hard. She looked pale and shaken and, if he was not mistaken, seemed a little red around the eyes. The idea of her crying because of his actions made him feel an utter cad. He knew better than to take advantage of innocents in darkened corners.

He'd left his rakish ways far, far behind him when he became the Duke of Hartridge.

"Rebecca," called the earl. She stopped on her way across the room and he saw her physically draw back her shoulders before turning and making her way toward the earl.

She curtsied prettily as she reached them and kept her eyes fixed firmly on her father.

"Where have you been, darling? We've been wondering."

She blushed self-consciously and her eyes darted toward Edward for a split second. He suddenly knew that she had no idea what to say. Neither of them had given any thought to what they should say about being missing at the same time.

"I, um."

"I was just telling your father that I've been on the balcony and had not seen you, my lady."

The duke's soft tones interrupted her frantic thoughts as

she tried to figure out what to say. Relieved that he'd stopped her from making a *faux pas* she rushed to answer, "I was just in the library Papa. I had, er, thought to play something and seemed to remember I had left some music there."

"Capital idea my dear." Her father beamed at her. "Where is it?"

"Where's what?"

"The music you went in search of."

"Oh. Well, it wasn't what I wanted after all," she answered weakly. Really, she just wanted to get as far away from Hartridge as the room would allow.

What must he think of her? What sort of lady kisses a virtual stranger? Rebecca wanted to cry again.

"Well, never mind. You can play something from memory," said her father jovially.

"No. That is to say, I do not think — her grace must be tired from her travelling and—"

"My lady, I am sure we would all be honoured if you would consent to play for us."

She looked up to find Mr. Crawdon smiling kindly at her. She refused to look at the duke and so did not know what his expression held.

Contempt and disapproval probably.

"What's that, Rebecca?" her mother's voice called from across the room.

"We were just asking Rebecca to play for us," her father answered. "She sings like an angel," he boasted proudly to the gentlemen.

"Really?" her mother sounded a little angry and Rebecca, seeing Caroline's thunderous expression, began to realise why.

Rebecca should not be the one performing and drawing attention to herself. Rebecca wasn't the bait to catch the duke, she thought bitterly.

She should blend into the background and let Caroline do all the performing and talking. And kissing.

Caroline's angry words from earlier came back to haunt her.

Even if he felt no attachment to her sister. Even if he had no plans to marry Caroline. Rebecca was so far from duchess material it was laughable.

There could be no future for her with the duke. Even if he wanted one, which she very much doubted.

"No. Not really," she answered interrupting whatever her father was about to say. "What I mean is, I had thought about it but, really, if we are to entertain our guests then surely Caroline should be the one to perform. She is exceptionally talented and will do us proud, I think."

Caroline looked closely at her for a moment and then smiled softly and Rebecca felt a sort of reconciliation.

"Thank you, Rebecca." Only the sisters knew that she was thanking her for more than the compliment. For Caroline, this meant that she had Rebecca's support in endearing herself to the duke. Little did she know that he was not here to marry her and would very likely refuse to do so.

Caroline made her way to the pianoforte and Rebecca took the opportunity to take her seat immediately, avoiding all temptation to sit beside Hartridge.

From now on, she would stay as far away from him as possible. Though it felt very close to heart breaking, she would keep her distance and do all she could to help Caroline.

Caroline was duchess material. Caroline had been preparing for this since wearing long skirts. Rebecca had been left to scamper around the countryside at her leisure and, though she was well loved, she could not help but feel that there'd been little or no thought given to whom she should marry!

The idea had never crossed her mind before. There was no rush. But her feelings for Hartridge and Caroline's harsh words were enough to make her take stock of her situation.

Rebecca was old enough for a Season. She had avoided

one because, frankly, she did not want one. But she could not stay single forever. She must marry.

She had hoped to marry for love…

Caroline began to play and sing a famous Italian piece, much favoured by the sisters. . The song was a good choice for Caroline as it showed off her obvious talent for the language. Plus, there was an ever so slightly husky note to Caroline's voice when she sang which lent the song a dramatic flair, perfect for the flamboyant Italian emotions of love and betrayal which the song described. Rebecca risked a glance across the room to see if Hartridge was enraptured with the sound of Caroline's voice.

Her stomach jolted when she looked at his strong face and realised that he was staring at her. She blushed profusely and quickly looked away before anyone saw their heated exchange. Good Lord, if he continued to pay such particular attention, people would start to notice. And then what would she do?

She thought again of her future prospects. She had no desire to remain a spinster, relying on the kindness of her brother for a home.

Imagine being underfoot whilst he married and began to have children. The thought did not appeal in anyway.

And, if Caroline *did* marry the duke? What then? Would she be expected to spend time with them? Watch them go about their married life, always in the background, always pining for—

No! She stopped the thought in its tracks.

She would not live that life, would not be that girl.

If she could not marry for love, she would marry for all the usual reasons— security, safety, family connections.

And who was to say that she would not find love anyway? Rebecca could easily meet and fall desperately in love with the perfect gentleman. Of their own accord her eyes drifted once more to the duke.

She had not known him long enough to feel anything. The kiss, it had been sheer folly. A moment of complete madness. A sign of her immaturity!

Well, it was time for Rebecca to grow up. She would speak to her father and make arrangements to have her Season.

She would hunt for a husband and would finally and firmly put the Duke of Hartridge from her mind.

Chapter Six

Edward listened politely as Lady Caroline sang and played. The lady clearly had talent which made the performance very enjoyable and, he had to admit, her face was beautiful when she played. Obviously, the music helped her to relax some of her rigid control.

She seemed softer, more approachable. Any sane man would find her immensely attractive as a potential bride.

Unfortunately, he had been driven to insanity by her younger sister.

He looked at her again. It seemed he could not *stop* looking at her. Damn the woman! This was a complication he just did not need!

He intended to speak to his mother at the very first opportunity. Find out what the devil was going on here.

Then, he intended to make his excuses to the earl, apologise to Lady Caroline and get the hell out of there.

He did not intend to spend every agonising second lusting after Lady Rebecca, driven to distraction by her mere presence in the same room.

What an absolute mess.

Lady Caroline finished playing and the assembled groups showered her with well-deserved compliments. She curtsied charmingly and made her way toward her mother and sister.

Edward heaved a sigh of relief and was about to make his excuses when the earl's booming voice interrupted his thoughts.

"Thank you my dear, you did very well. And now, your sister's turn."

Rebecca looked at her father in horror and then glanced toward her sister. *Quite an overreaction to being asked to play,* thought Edward. She certainly did not seem the shy sort given that she climbed statutes in company and punched unsuspecting peers in the face!

Young ladies of the house were always rolled out to play for their guests, whether their guests wished it or not.

Much as he'd been looking forward to retiring, he found his curiosity piqued. Was she shy? Embarrassed? Perhaps she did not have the talent her sister possessed and it made her self-conscious.

The thought softened his mood. That must be it. The poor thing must be ashamed of inferior talent.

It was to be expected really. She had a sharp wit. He'd discovered as much when he had been eavesdropping on her conversation at dinner.

She was incredibly beautiful. Funny. As charming a young lady as ever he'd met, if a little scandalous.

It only stood to reason that she would lose out somewhere.

He suddenly felt rather protective of her, as irrational as that was. He would sit and support her. Enjoy her performance, outwardly at least.

The sound of her wailing may even help to cure some of the lust raging around his body. He sat back and got ready to pretend to enjoy the performance.

Rebecca had leaned forward to whisper frantically to her sister but had, after a moment, made her way to the instrument although, from the way her feet dragged it seemed she did so reluctantly. She looked altogether miserable, poor dear.

As she rustled some papers looking for some music to play, Edward prepared his ears for possible bleeding. There was no telling how bad she was going to be. But he'd been tortured by enough debutantes in the past to know they could truly make some inhumane sounds when performing.

Finally, she cleared her throat and took a breath. And then she began to sing…

Edward's jaw dropped open. He could feel it but could do nothing about it.

Her voice was, quite simply, exquisite. When her father had said that she sang like an angel, he hadn't been exaggerating.

She had picked an Irish air about unrequited love. Full of sorrow and sweet poignancy. Her clear soprano soared around the room and made him feel like gathering her in his arms and never letting go.

Blast it! The girl was supposed to be terrible! She had no right to sing as well as she looked.

The situation was untenable and Edward felt his control slipping. Desperate for distraction, he looked around the room.

His mother was entranced, the earl looked proud as punch. Even Lady Mary and Lady Caroline were smiling while they watched the performance.

None of them were helping! They were too enthralled by the temptress.

Finally, he turned to Tom hoping for some whispered conversation to take his mind off Rebecca and her selfish talent.

But Tom's expression had Edward wanting to leap out of

his chair and throw it at Tom. He was bewitched. Utterly bewitched. Edward knew from his face because he was sure he wore the same expression.

Tom had no business feeling that way. He, Edward, felt that way. She was hi-

He stopped himself short. *She was his?* No. She wasn't. They'd shared a mistaken kiss. And even if that one kiss had brought about a stronger reaction in him than any other contact he'd had with a woman, she was still not his. It meant nothing. It could not!

He was a duke. He had responsibilities. One of which was finding and marrying a suitable young lady.

Rebecca Carrington was far from suitable. For one thing, her behaviour could be termed scandalous. For another, he'd never get anything done with her around all day distracting him!

He had no right to feel possessive of her. But he'd be damned if he would sit there and watch Tom salivate over her.

So, although he'd never considered himself to be the immature kind, he pretended to yawn and stretched his arms above his head, then brought them down, making sure his right one hit Tom squarely on top of the head.

Tom leapt and almost shouted aloud but managed to contain the shout and not interrupt the performance.

He glared at Edward, who gazed innocently back.

"Terribly sorry, Tom. How clumsy of me."

Tom just grimaced and turned his head back toward where Lady Rebecca was finishing up her beautiful solo.

It hadn't served to distract him, but it made Edward feel childishly better.

Still, he could not spend the next two weeks attacking his cousin! And he sure as hell could not spend it under the same roof as Lady Rebecca and manage to keep his hands to himself.

Mostly, he could not stay and encourage whatever

fantasy Lady Caroline and her family seemed to be nurturing.

As Lady Rebecca finished her performance and stood to graciously accept the applause and praise, Edward made up his mind.

He would speak to the earl first thing tomorrow morning. And then he was heading back to London. Away from the Carringtons, away from the pressure of his mother and away from the torturous temptation of Lady Rebecca Carrington.

****

Rebecca finished the performance and immediately made her way to her mother. She meant to make her excuses and take her leave of the assembled party. When her father had asked her to play, her stomach had dropped.

She had always loved to sing and did it well. But this was Caroline's night to shine, not hers. She'd bent toward Caroline to ask how she could get out of performing without seeming rude but Caroline had cut her off.

"Rebecca, I should not have said the things I said earlier. I beg that you forgive me. I would not have you stay quiet as a mouse on my behalf. Not that you could anyway," Caroline said gently, a wry smile on her face, "You must perform. We cannot embarrass Father. Now go."

With a quick pat of encouragement on her arm, Caroline urged her to stand. And so she had. For what else could she do?

She avoided eye contact with everyone in the room and began to rifle through the music sheets though she knew several songs by heart.

Her eye was drawn to a particular piece. A sweet song that had been taught to her by Mrs. Maguire, the cook.

It spoke of love, of heartbreak, of desire and loss. It seemed natural to her that she would sing this piece.

Once she began to play she forgot everything and

everyone in the room. She lost herself in the music and felt herself relax for the first time since this morning.

The song held extra meaning for her tonight as she thought of everything that had happened today. The duke with his overwhelming presence, the kiss and the knowledge that he would never be hers.

The song expressed feelings that Rebecca could not.

When she finished, she thanked the assembly for their compliments without really hearing a single one. She had reached the end of her tether tonight and wanted nothing more than to leave the room and even to be coddled a little by Maura. After all, it had been a very trying day.

After making her excuses to her mother and Lady Catherine, she bade a general good evening to the room, avoiding eye contact with everyone, particularly the duke, and made her way wearily up the stairs and to her room.

As she opened her door, she was filled with gratitude as she noticed the fire lit, her nightrail laid out and a cup of tea waiting for her by the bed.

Maura began to fuss about her, removing her dress and leading her gently toward the dressing table to brush out her long chestnut locks.

"How was your evening, my lady?" Maura asked jovially.

Rebecca looked into the eyes of her maid and confidante. Before uttering a word, she promptly burst into a fresh barrage of tears.

Maura stared in shock for several seconds before dropping the brush and folding Rebecca in her arms.

She had seen her mistress in some hairy situations and had nursed her through some terrible accidents. But rarely had she seen her cry.

"There, there my lady. It is not as bad as all that surely," she crooned leading Rebecca gently to her bed.

"It is, Maura. Oh, it is," sniffled Rebecca.

Maura settled Rebecca against the pillows and handed her the teacup.

"You should drink that up and get a good night's sleep and you will be right as rain," she assured pulling at the coverlet and plumping the pillows behind Rebecca's head.

After a few moments and some reassuring platitudes from Maura, Rebecca began to feel calmer.

She assured Maura that she was feeling better and dismissed her without any more tears.

Then, settling herself down she determined to sleep, dream pleasant dreams and forget all about the man downstairs who had been playing havoc with her emotions from the second she'd set eyes on him.

Rebecca willed sleep to come quickly and began to make preparations in her head for her upcoming Season and search for a husband.

Would he be handsome? Charming? Kind?

Hopefully he would be all those things. She closed her eyes and tried to envision his face. But all she could see was the face of the Duke of Hartridge.

Well, what harm would it be to dream that he was to be her beau? Nobody needed to know about her dreams. Nobody but her.

Chapter Seven

The next day dawned bright and sunny. Rebecca was awakened by Maura bustling in to draw the curtains.

For a moment, she was tempted to pull the pillow over her head and sink back into the dreams which had comforted her through the night. But that simply would not do.

It seemed impossible that she had only met his grace yesterday morning and so much had happened since.

But, although Caroline had apologised for her harsh words last night, Rebecca knew there was truth in them. The duke had been brought here to marry her sister and it would do Rebecca no good to continue on in her childish ways and ignore her duty to the family.

She must grow up and marry.

That meant she must make plans to go to London.

Her sense of adventure reared its head and Rebecca found herself quite excited at the prospect of a Season in London. She was quite sure that there'd be *faux pas* after *faux pas* but she'd also get to experience all the glorious sights, sounds and experiences London had to offer.

She sat up and bid Maura a cheery good morning.

"Oh, my lady. You seem so much better this morning," exclaimed Maura happily in her thick Irish brogue. "I was sick with worry for you last night. I've never seen you so blue devilled!"

"Yes, well, one cannot mope around forever," retorted Rebecca, somewhat embarrassed at Maura's outpouring. She would never put the duke from her mind if she were reminded of her reaction to him.

"Today is a new day, Maura. What's done is done. And you and I have plans to make."

Maura began laying out a morning dress for Rebecca.

"We do?"

"Yes, we do. We are to go to London."

Maura paused in the act of straightening the pale blue muslin she was handling and turned to stare at Rebecca.

"L-London, my lady?"

"Yes, London," answered Rebecca brusquely.

"But, my lady – whatever for?"

"It is time I found a husband."

Silence. Rather deafening silence, actually. Rebecca wasn't sure whether to be concerned or offended. Really! Was the idea of her marrying so strange that it would render her maid mute?

"A husband?"

"Yes, you know one of those men with whom you share the rest of your life? Well. I am getting one."

Maura hurried over to help Rebecca out of her nightgown.

"It is just—"

"Yes, Maura?"

"Well, you've never expressed an interest in marrying before."

"I am well aware that this must seem sudden." It was sudden. "But I am not getting any younger and I know my duty. I must marry. I will never do that by spending all my time here. I intend to ask Father for a Season and I fully intend to be engaged by the end of it."

"Oh," was the weak answer. A step up from silence, Rebecca supposed.

"Oh, and a walking dress please Maura. I think I shall take my walk this morning. I need fresh air and some time to think."

I also need to avoid the duke, Rebecca thought, but kept that to herself.

Rebecca stepped out into the garden and inhaled the fresh air and scents of early summer that surrounded her. She did so love her home and would miss it dreadfully.

She knew every inch of this land — the gardens, forests and lakes. She knew the tenants and their families and could often be found in one of the cottages helping the local children learn to read or chatting with the wives of the farmers.

Making her way to the partly obscured gate, which led from the garden and into the forest beyond, Rebecca felt a pang of sadness. If, or rather when she married, she would be leaving all this behind.

It was the only home she'd ever known. She knew that the likelihood was that she would marry an English gentleman, would settle with him and would come here only as a guest. The idea was strange and not at all pleasant. She would have a new home. Be *mistress* of a new home. She who had once tried to assist her mother in hosting a ball and had ended up writing the wrong date on half the invitations!

Rebecca wondered if her husband would have a large estate to manage. She could not do too much damage on a small one. Her father's wasn't exactly small and she'd learned enough from Mama to be able to run a household of that size. Balls and parties aside of course.

She found herself wondering about the duke's estates, sure that they were vast and plentiful. *Oh, stop it Rebecca,* she scolded herself.

She needed to put that man from her head. A brisk, early morning walk before she broke her fast was just the thing for it.

She made her way determinedly through the gate and down one of the well-worn paths through her father's lands and towards the lake. She would soon pass a row of pleasantly situated cottages belonging to some of the tenants. Though partly obscured by a wall, the children were always scampering about and Rebecca looked forward to seeing their happy faces peek over the wall.

They never failed to cheer her up and this morning she could really do with some cheer!

The morning dew still clung to the leaves and made the forest floor beneath her feet damp and springy. The only sounds she could hear were the birds singing in the trees and the distant cries of farm hands.

It was bliss!

Rebecca could feel herself relaxing. These woods never failed to bring her comfort. She enjoyed the peace and the uninterrupted solitude.

The sudden sound of a snapping twig shattered the silence and Rebecca whipped around to see who or what was behind her. To her consternation there was nobody there. A prickling feeling of unease settled on her as she continued to scan the woods behind her.

Still she could see nothing. She laughed a little at herself. It was a forest. Any number of animals could have made the sound! Smiling at her folly she continued on her way, humming softly to herself and enjoying the freedom of not having to behave in front of an audience.

She had reached the point where the path sloped downwards. In her youth, she would run down it until she thought she would never stop. The overwhelming urge to do so again had her hitching her skirts in quite an unladylike manner and running as fast as her legs could carry her all the way to the bottom.

She shrieked as she gained speed and gave a shout of laughter at the exhilaration of feeling so free! Her laugh was cut short, however, when, on reaching the bottom she noticed a figure leaning against the large oak and staring intently at her.

At first Rebecca did not recognise him. The uneasy feeling of moments ago returned and she felt the urge to turn and flee. Then, as the figure shifted and came slowly toward her she suddenly recalled whom he was. The feeling of tension did not leave her however.

"Mr. Simons." She smiled politely. Mr. Simons had recently inherited his uncle's farm and had moved here not long ago. Though she was little acquainted with him, she knew that his uncle had been quite well off and was very well respected. Sadly, he had had no children before he passed and the nephew had come from the north of England to take over the running of the farm.

Her father had taken Rebecca with him one day to meet Mr. Simons. His manner had been brash and impolite. He had stunk of whiskey and leered at her for the entirety of their visit. So much so that Father had forbade her from ever visiting alone, something she often did with the tenants. Rebecca had not needed telling twice however. This was definitely not a man she wanted to be around longer than necessary.

After they had returned to the house, Rebecca thought perhaps she was being unduly harsh. After all, she did not know this man. And it seemed unfair to judge him so hastily.

Yet, here she found herself quite alone with him and could not ignore the sense of fear. He said nothing. Just continued to stare, his black eyes boring into hers. Rebecca was struck by the thought that this was the second time she'd been stared at by a man. But the feelings the stares evoked were complete opposites.

The thought gave her some relief. After all, what sort of lady would she be if she went around nearly fainting at every stare!

He still hadn't spoken even while Rebecca's mind did what it usually did and flittered off to somewhere else entirely.

I shall try again, she thought, *polite chit chat then leave.*

"Er, I trust you are settling in nicely to your new life as a farmer?"

"No," was the gruff reply.

Oh.

"Why ever not?" she asked rather indignantly. The man had been handed a successful farm with the money and stability that came with it, on a beautiful piece of land and he wasn't happy?

He stared for a bit longer. In fact, he was starting to irritate her now. This was good. Irritation made her braver.

He smirked slightly and answered her in his Northern England brogue.

"The farmer's life ain't for me. I'd much rather do what I'd been doing until I was hauled back here."

"And what was that?"

"Enjoying myself."

He did not elaborate and Rebecca did not ask him to. She knew little of his life before he had come to the farm but from what her father had been told, it had been anything but virtuous. Certainly the Mr. Simons before him had never spoken fondly of him.

He took another step towards her and Rebecca felt fear once again slam into her. Her instincts told her that this man was dangerous.

"Well, good day then," she said and made to move around him and continue on her way.

He did not bow, tip his hat or return her farewell. She stepped around him and was about to continue on her way when his arm shot out and clasped hers.

Rebecca felt a fear unlike any she'd ever known but forced herself to relax. It would do her no good to show anything other than strength and confidence. She was his superior and though she never liked to treat people as inferiors she would not allow herself to be manhandled by this stranger.

She turned her head and eyed his hand on her arm then turned her eyes to his trying her best to channel Caroline's icy glare.

"Remove your hand," she bit and was delighted to hear that none of her fear was evident in her steady voice.

"I've watched you," he whispered.

His words froze Rebecca's blood.

"What?" This time, it was barely above a whisper but Rebecca was too frightened to care.

"You are a fascinating woman, my lady." His look, his voice, everything about him made Rebecca's skin crawl. She needed to get away from him and fast.

"I cannot help but watch you."

"Try," Rebecca replied through gritted teeth. She pulled her arm from him and for one horrifying moment his grip tightened and he would not let her go. However, moments later Rebecca nearly expired from relief as he gave a short laugh and released her.

Bowing slightly he muttered good day but did nothing to move away.

Slowly, Rebecca turned her back to him and continued on her way. She would not run knowing instinctively that he would find her running from him immensely enjoyable.

Much as she wanted to, Rebecca would not turn to glance behind her. She continued on at a sedate pace until rounding a corner. Shock and fear made her tremble from head to toe. She considered turning back but had no desire to come upon him again.

Good heavens. How could such a thing have happened on her morning walk? She considered telling her father, but really, what was there to say? He hadn't forced his attentions on her and the encounter had lasted only minutes. Her father would think she was quite mad.

No, the best thing to do was put it from her head and take care not to walk alone again. She would be leaving for London soon, hopefully. Then she would not have to see him again for the entire Season, or ever if she actually married.

Determined to put it from her head she made her way toward the row of cottages which housed a cottage belonging to Mrs. O'Dwyer of whom Rebecca had always been fond. Her children were a constant source of amusement and would serve as a great distraction.

She reached the wall where Martin, her partner in the kite escapade of the previous afternoon, and his family lived.

"My lady," the whispered voices reached her from behind the low wall and Rebecca's face broke out in a grin.

"Hmm. I wonder who could be calling my name," she called loudly making her way slowly toward the wall.

It was a game they played often. Martin and his younger sister would hide behind the wall, quiet as mice and when she neared they would scare the wits out of her! No matter how many times they did it, they always managed to make her jump which caused much mirth amongst them all.

Today however, she did not think her nerves would stand the fright so she decided to beat them to the punch. Staying as silent as possible, she used the uneven surface of the stone wall to climb up. Then, poised near the top she leaned over with a shout.

The children screamed in fright and ran away toward the cottage. Rebecca doubled over with laughter. In her enthusiasm however, she had leaned too far forward.

She was stuck! Balanced on top of the blasted wall! Her top half was leaning over into the small garden but, having kicked loose the stone she had been resting on, her feet were dangling over the edge of the wall with nothing to gain purchase on.

How did she manage to get into these sorts of scrapes? It was really quite ridiculous.

She called out for Martin and his sister to help but none was forthcoming.

Bother! She could not very well hang there all day. It was starting to hurt in any case.

Rebecca mulled over the predicament. All she could hope for was that Martin or Mrs. O'Dwyer would come out to assist her. In the meantime, she would try to move further down the wall and hope that her feet would land on something to hold her weight so she could jump back down. At least it could not get any worse.

"Lady Rebecca."

Rebecca paused in the act of trying to wiggle herself backwards. This could not be happening.

The voice was unmistakable having haunted her dreams for much of last night. She had been caught, once again, by the Duke of Hartridge.

****

Edward had woken early that morning and had gone immediately to seek out his mother.

He found her, unsurprisingly, already dressed and breaking her fast downstairs. She had always risen with the birds.

"Mother," his greeting was formal and emotionless.

The dowager was immediately on her guard.

"Edward, before you begin I must tell you –"

"No, Mother. You must not tell me anything. You must listen. I do not know what exactly was agreed between Father and Ransford. I do not know how they convinced you it was a good idea to marry me off. I do not know why you concealed the truth from me and I had to find it out from Ransford's incorrigible youngest."

His mother took a breath to speak but Edward held up a hand to silence her. He must get this out before she could manipulate or guilt him into being married by the end of the day.

"I will not be made to marry anyone I do not wish to marry. I will not be used as some sort of trophy for the earl or his daughter. I will not be sold off as a husband to Father's friend because of some ridiculous contract made, no doubt, when he was thoroughly foxed! I am not a piece of horseflesh, Mother," he finished with injured dignity.

The dowager bit the inside of her cheek to stop from laughing at her son's indignant tone. "My dear, please consider, you have a duty to marry a suitable young lady. Lady Caroline is perfect duchess material. She will handle herself beautifully and her family could not be better. Your father thought only to help you!"

"Help me? By deciding my future before I was even born?" Edward could hear his voice rising with his anger and he made a concentrated effort to calm himself.

It would not do for anyone else to be privy to this conversation.

"I know it is difficult to understand but, Edward, your father knew you would be subjected to the worst sort of husband hunting— hounded for your title and your wealth. I understand how shocked you must feel but the idea holds merit. That is why I agreed to it, after many discussions and careful consideration."

"How could you think I would agree to such a scheme?"

"I knew perfectly well you would not," retorted his mother. "That is why I did not tell you. I wished for you to meet the lady first and form your own opinion on her. You must admit, she is very suitable indeed."

Edward said nothing but went to fill his plate, though his appetite was truly suppressed by his anger. In fact, he was probably developing an ulcer.

The dowager waited until he had returned and placed his plate on the table. Rather than sit however, he loomed over her.

"She may be suitable, Mother. That does not mean I intend to marry her."

"And why not?" Lady Catherine asked mildly.

Edward flung himself into his chair and crossed his arms.

"I do not want to," he mumbled grumpily, not unlike a toddler throwing a tantrum.

"She would make an excellent duchess."

"Yes, Mother. So you have said. Several times. But so would a great many women."

The dowager decided to change tactics.

"Have you not always done what is right and proper? What is expected of a duke?"

Edward nodded resentfully, still sulking.

"Have you not always said that dukes do not have the luxury of marrying for love? That they must marry for, how did you put it— less airy fairy reasons than 'love' and 'passion'?"

Edward was silent for a moment.

"That does not mean that they should not get a choice in the matter."

The dowager studied her son's face for a moment. He looked truly angry and upset. She knew he would not take it well, being as stubborn and independent as his father had been. She had not anticipated him being so very troubled by the idea, however.

It had been a gamble but, given his stance on marriage, Lady Catherine had thought that he would be indifferent to who the lady was as long as she wasn't objectionable. Much as it pained her to know his views on love, she could see that they held merit.

A duke did have certain obligations and marriage to the right lady was one of them. Her dearest wish had been that he would fall in love with Lady Caroline. It would appear that she had been mistaken. She had watched them both last night and had not noticed any attraction between them.

She had noticed, however, the way her son had looked at Lady Rebecca.

The thought gave her pause.

Certainly, she was from the same family. Had the same upbringing. Her beauty was quite breath-taking.

The dowager had not had the opportunity to speak much with the girl. And it would be decidedly awkward if Edward developed a *tendre* for the girl when he had been intended for her sister.

But her son's happiness was paramount and she knew the Carringtons well enough to know that if either Edward or Lady Caroline were unhappy with the agreement, they would not be held to it.

"Edward," she began in a conciliatory tone, "you know that I would not ask you to do anything you do not want to do. If you have set your mind against Lady Caroline, then we will explain to the Carringtons at the end of our visit and go our separate ways. I am certain they would not hold you to the contract."

"My visit is ending today, Mother."

"What?"

"I will not remain here any longer, knowing what is expected of me and knowing that I will be disappointing these excellent people at the end of it all. I have no wish to hurt anybody's feelings and it will do no good to stay and prolong the inevitable."

"Well, of course dear, if that is what you wish."

There was a somewhat awkward silence. Edward was brooding and the dowager was contemplating the best way to phrase her next questions.

"Lady Rebecca seems to be a lovely young lady."

Edward's head snapped up and the mention of that lady and the dowager felt a spurt of triumph. She knew her son better than he thought.

"Yes, she does," was the curt reply.

"And how beautiful she is."

A grunt this time.

"Her voice was so wonderful to listen to."

A cough.

"I did not get a chance to speak with her for long. Is she a pleasant gel? She certainly seems to be."

"How should I know?" Edward asked quickly. *Too quickly?*

"Why, you spent so long speaking to her, dearest. I thought you would have formed some sort of opinion."

Edward spluttered for a moment or two, most unlike him, before finally answering;

"What makes you think I spoke to her for long?"

Was that a *blush*?

"She told you of the contract did she not? I assumed you had conversed for a while beforehand, or did she accost you in the hallway and blurt it out?"

The dowager found herself rather enjoying this. It wasn't every day her unshakeable son was shaken!

"Well, yes we spoke for — that is to say, we didn't. There was some conversation. Brief. Well, not very brief. Long enough for it to have come up in the course of the conversation at least."

The dowager smiled knowingly as Edward's rambling came to a halt.

"I see," she offered mildly.

Edward jumped up from his seat.

"This is ridiculous," he blurted. "Can I not enjoy a pleasant meal without being interrogated in this fashion?"

"You haven't eaten dear," his mother answered mildly.

"I am not hungry," he answered sullenly. "I am going for an early morning ride. To clear my head. It isn't *un*clear, I just — want to."

With that, he bowed and turned on his heel, marching from the room as though highly insulted.

How very interesting, the dowager smiled. It was a great shame he had fixed on leaving. She would have liked to see how he interacted with the lovely Lady Rebecca.

****

Edward stomped from the house and toward the stables.

He knew he had acted childishly and had thus created problems for himself. His mother was bound to be curious about his unusual reaction to the mere mention of Lady Rebecca's name.

It did not help matters that he'd gotten no sleep last night thinking about the girl sleeping mere feet from him.

Even if his mind tried to forget her, his body had different ideas and he'd spent the night tossing and turning and in a fit of frustration that did little to alleviate his foul humour.

Calling for one of Ranford's stallions, Edward muttered a few choice curses to himself while he waited for the horse to be readied.

His consolation was that he would be leaving shortly and would be able to put this whole sorry mess behind him.

He was quite sure that Lady Caroline would be married off within the year. As soon as she was given a Season she was sure to be snapped up. She was beautiful, pleasant and possessed a huge dowry, smart enough, too, not to be taken in by fortune hunters and rakes he would warrant. Yes, she would do just fine.

As will Lady Rebecca, whispered that damnable voice that

would not shut up last night. Blast it! He did not want to think about her marrying. Belonging to another. Sharing another's bed. The thought made him feel murderous.

How would she fair during a Season? She would be the toast of the *ton*, no doubt about it. Her beauty alone would have men falling to their knees. She was sure to be a firm favourite with the other debutantes too, if only because they could not resist a whiff of scandal.

And she would be scandalous. Gloriously so. Town would be as obsessed with her as he was beginning to be.

He almost groaned aloud as he thought of the type of trouble she could get herself into.

Rebecca may be a little wild but she was still an innocent and he could well imagine her being taken in by the rakes who would see her as a challenge.

His blood boiled as he thought about her being compromised. Certainly those types of men would appeal to her reckless character. She would be ruined before her first ball!

He needed to calm down. There had been no mention of her even having a Season. And when she did, it would not be his problem.

He would just make sure he wasn't there to witness half the *ton* falling in love with her. It wasn't that he cared, he just... did not want to be there.

He had spent time enough last night with his mind occupied by that lady. He would dwell on these thoughts no longer.

As soon as he cleared the grounds he set his horse on a gallop towards the woods planning to explore some of the beautiful estate before he left it.

The animal was obviously glad of the exercise and Edward gave him his head as they raced towards the trees.

When they reached the edge, Edward slowed the horse down and began a steady walk through the canopy of trees.

Shortly he passed by a lone man making his way out of the cluster of trees. From his attire, Edward guessed that he was a farmer and he was surprised to find him walking here at this hour. Surely there was work to be done for the farmers at this time. That was certainly the case with Edward's own tenant farmers.

The man shot him a thunderous look, which surprised him. He had never cared much for propriety, at least not the sort that made others feel inferior to him but open hostility was not something he was used to.

Edward pulled the horse to a stop and bid the man good morning. His curiosity was piqued.

Rather than return the greeting however, the man merely growled, "The lady don't want to be disturbed. Leave her alone," then turned on his heel and continued on.

What an odd character. Which lady? Edward hadn't intended to follow the path the farmer had come from but now he was curious and wanted to know who the farmer had been referring to.

He must remember to enquire as to whom that was. Edward hadn't liked him. There was something altogether menacing about him.

He made his way down the path, which sloped downwards before bending to the left. He allowed his mind to wander once again to Lady Rebecca. He was exhausted from fighting it, to be frank, and nobody was privy to his thoughts so he might as well get it out of the way before he had to see her later today.

He was brought up short, by the most extraordinary sight in front of him. Half a woman's body. Dangling over a wall. What in the blazes?

His blood began to stir as he took in the scene. He would recognise that body anywhere since it had kept him from sleep and all sensible thought since yesterday afternoon.

Lady Rebecca!

Once again in a dangerous and totally scandalous situation. His gaze swept the scene in front of him and his body jumped to the type of attention that was decidedly uncomfortable when seated on a damned horse.

How did she manage these things? She was wiggling rather deliciously, presumably trying to get down from the wall. What she was doing up there in the first place, he had no idea.

He was fast learning the futility of guessing anything when it came to the hoyden.

He was torn once again between anxiety for her safety and amusement at the sight of a grown woman hanging off a wall.

His eyes took in the shapely ankles and calves scandalously exposed by her position. Dear God! Thank the heavens he was leaving. He could not stand to be around such temptation for very much longer.

Although, he'd certainly miss the views.

Deciding that he'd done enough leering, Edward cleared his throat to offer his assistance.

He needed to get her off that wall and away from him as fast as possible.

For both their sakes.

Chapter Eight

"Lady Rebecca," Edward called, jumping from the horse and moving slowly toward her.

Rebecca froze in the act of wriggling which disappointed him, since it had been so entertaining to watch. He could watch her all day.

There was a beat of silence before he heard an audible sigh of defeat.

"Good morning, your grace," her voice floated toward him.

His face broke out in a grin. He could not help it. Was she really going to adhere to social niceties when she was halfway over a wall?

"Good morning, my lady," he answered politely.

Another silence. He should not drag it out but he really was enjoying himself.

"Lovely day, is it not?" she asked conversationally.

Edward could not help it; he gave a shout of laughter as he stepped closer.

"I wonder if I may be of assistance Lady Rebecca."

"Oh no, that is quite alright, thank you."

"Do you plan to stay here then?"

"Er – well, no."

"And can you get yourself down?"

This time the sigh was followed by a very unladylike curse that had Edward laughing in silent amusement.

"No, your grace" she answered in a small voice.

"Then, I will assist you, yes?"

"Oh very well then. Yes."

"Now, that is not very gracious, my lady."

He could imagine the thunderous expression on her face, but since he could not see the top half of her body he could not confirm it.

"My apologies, your grace," she sounded as if her teeth were clenched, "I would be eternally grateful if you would be so kind as to assist me."

"I would be honoured," he answered, smiling. He'd seen flashes of that temper the night before. She was hot headed, no doubt about it. And he was hot blooded. The combination was as dangerous as it was intriguing.

He was still smiling at her predicament as he tethered the horse and moved back to where she balanced.

He sobered greatly however, when he neared her. The only possible way to do this would be to climb up and lift her into his arms. He wasn't sure he could handle holding her body again without completely losing his mind.

But it was either that or leave her hanging there.

He cleared his throat nervously.

"Lady Rebecca, I believe I shall have to climb up and lift you from the wall. Is that — would that be acceptable to you?"

"Your grace," she answered from over the wall, "I am hanging upside down over a garden wall. I hardly think now is the time to worry about my delicate sensibilities."

He snorted with laughter. "Perhaps not."

"It is not funny," she bit out angrily.

"Of course not, I apologise."

Rebecca remained silent for a moment before answering. "I suppose it is rather funny," she conceded.

"A little, yes."

Her sudden burst of laughter filled the air and made him smile in response.

She was the only woman he'd ever met who would laugh at herself. Of course, she was also the only woman he'd ever met who would climb statues and walls and get stuck on both!

"Let us begin."

Rebecca's face flamed as she felt the duke climb up behind her and suddenly all traces of amusement left her. The air between them seemed to crackle with tension once again.

How was it possible that she had humiliated herself so utterly and completely twice in as many days in front of this man?

She could only imagine what must have appeared in front of his eyes when he rounded the corner.

At least he did not seem disapproving, which was a relief. If anything, it sounded like he was thoroughly enjoying himself, damn the man. Of course, now he was also standing at the wall with his large body pressed shockingly against hers.

Her heart pounded. If anyone was to happen by she would be utterly ruined. So why did she not care?

"My lady," his voice was low, a mere whisper that tickled her neck. Rebecca shivered in reaction. Oh God, she needed to get away from him. She had promised herself last night that she would do her utmost to avoid him.

And yet, here she was completely at his mercy and filled with a longing so strong it made her want to weep.

"I need to wrap my arm around your waist and lift you down. Do you understand?" His voice was hoarse and gravelly and tearing her nerves to shreds. She nodded, not trusting herself to speak.

She felt him lean over and grasp her tightly around the

waist. Surely he did not expect to be able to lift her whole body weight with one arm?

She was just about to ask him what he intended to do when she felt herself lifted bodily from the wall. His strong arm held her in a vice-like grip. She was pulled back tightly against his chest as he began the short descent down the wall.

She felt solid ground beneath her feet but made no move to turn or even to leave the cocoon of his arm. Truthfully, she did not trust herself to move, to even breathe.

Something beyond her ability to understand was happening to her.

And though she believed him when he said he did not intend to wed her sister, it did not matter. Her sister would be bitterly disappointed. As would her parents. His mother too, probably.

Plus, he had given no indication that he felt anything for her. It had been a mere kiss. She was sure that he had kissed countless women before her. Even if the thought made her want to stomp on his foot, it was still true. It must be. He was the most eligible man in the peerage for goodness sake!

This entire thing was a complete mess and she needed to distance herself from it. And him. Hide away until she could escape to London, get herself married and forget these ridiculous notions.

Rebecca started when his hands reached up to grasp her shoulders. He turned her to face him.

"Are you well?" he asked, concern was stamped across his face as his eyes raked over her.

Not trusting herself to speak, she merely nodded, unable to tear her eyes from him.

"Rebecca," he groaned, sounding as though he were in pain. "Do not look at me like that. I only have so much control."

"Like what?"

"Like you are remembering our kiss. Like you wish for

me to kiss you again."

She gasped at his bluntness.

"I am not," she insisted albeit in a whisper.

"Oh but you are. Those eyes, eyes a man could drown in, they give you away."

Good lord the man was far too charming, far too irresistible.

"You are mistaken, your grace."

He hadn't released her and she'd made no attempt to move away. Funny how the grip of one man could strike abject fear into her heart but this man's touch felt like coming home.

"Let's see then, shall we?"

Rebecca froze, torn between a desire so strong she could weep and complete panic. Had she not promised herself that she would stay away from him? Had she not told herself over and over of that to harbour dreams about him was futile? Yet here she was, about to be kissed and unable to do anything about it.

She had almost convinced herself that last night had been a fluke. That her reaction had been down to the fact that it had been her first kiss. She knew now, that she was very much mistaken. If anything, she wanted him even more.

His lips descended slowly toward hers and Rebecca closed her eyes in anticipation.

"My lady!"

The shout broke through the haze of longing surrounding them and Rebecca stumbled back, away from his touch.

Once again they stared at each other, neither knowing quite what to say.

"Rebecca," Edward started to speak but she stopped him with a delicate hand raised.

"Please. Do not."

"We cannot just—"

"My lady," the voice was nearer now and within seconds

Martin's head had appeared over the wall.

"You scared the wits out of us, my lady," he scolded but his grin was firmly in place.

Rebecca smiled in response.

"Ah, but how many times have I had the wits scared out of me, young man? It is only fitting that I should get my own back one day."

"Mam says to come up to the house. She is back from the village." Martin blatantly ignored the duke's presence which gave Rebecca much amusement. She wondered if he'd ever been ignored before and decided that it was very doubtful.

"I shall come directly."

Martin whistled tunelessly as he made his way back up the garden path to the small cottage where Mrs. O'Dwyer awaited their arrival.

The silence was thick with everything that was unsaid between them.

Rebecca decided the best way to handle it was to ignore it and hope that it went away. This was a method that, admittedly, had never worked in the past. But the alternative was to spend more time in his presence and, honestly, she wasn't sure how long she could bear that.

"Right then. My thanks again, your grace, for your assistance. Good day to you."

She turned to leave but he sidestepped swiftly and rather neatly blocked her way.

"Allow me to escort you, my lady."

She eyed him sceptically.

"Up a garden path?"

"The idea may seem silly but you forget, I've seen, twice now, what you get up to when left to your own devices. My conscience will not allow me to leave you unattended. Even if it is only up a garden path."

She hadn't liked that, Edward thought with amusement, as her eyes narrowed menacingly. He was reminded again of the kitten trying to be fierce.

The truth was he knew full well she did not need an escort from one end of a garden to another. But for reasons unknown to him and best left unanalysed, he found himself reluctant to let her go.

He planned to leave at first light tomorrow. Originally he had wanted to be gone today but on reflection it did not seem fair to pay such a disservice to Ranford and his family, he was sure his refusal to marry Lady Caroline would be insult enough without him sneaking off into the night.

No, he would leave first thing tomorrow and as such he knew it unlikely that he would see this lady again, at least not for a while. When she did eventually turn up in Town for a Season he would have himself well under control and would be able to witness the parade of men vying for her affection with equanimity. He *would*.

"Your grace?"

Her soft voice interrupted his thoughts.

"Hmm?"

"Are you quite well?"

"Of course. Why do you ask?"

"You looked as though you might murder someone just now. And since I am the only person in the vicinity, I wondered if I should fear for my life."

She really was entirely too outspoken.

He decided to ignore her.

"Shall we?" He extended his arm.

"You haven't been invited."

"I will escort you to the door and then take my leave."

"You cannot."

"Why not?"

"Because. You will frighten the poor woman to death, that is why!"

Well, that was just rude. "I beg your pardon?"

"You will scare her, your grace. She is not used to having

people like you on her doorstep."

"People like me?"

"Yes. People like you. You are too rich, too titled, too — too big."

Too big? "This from the daughter of an earl?"

"That is different. I grew up here, I've known Mrs. O'Dwyer and all the tenants since childhood. They like me."

"Are you implying that they will not like me?" he demanded, feeling terribly affronted.

Rebecca raised an eyebrow at his tone. *What a brat!* She would appease him then get rid of him.

"I am sure they would think you all that is charming, your grace. However, since you are not escorting me, it is hardly relevant, is it?"

"I am escorting you."

"No. You are not."

They stood glaring at each other for several moments. Her with her hands placed firmly at her hips and shooting daggers, him with such a look of smug superiority she wanted to smack him.

"My lady."

Their standoff came to a halt with the appearance of Martin.

"Mam says you must bring the gentleman with you before you both grow roots."

"Ha! There you have it. I am invited."

Rebecca could only shake her head and wonder at his delight in being invited into a country cottage. He who had graced the halls of royal families and fellow peers all over Europe. His delight came, she was sure, from besting her and not for any real desire to spend time with the O'Dwyers.

She hoped that he would treat them as equals and with respect. She had a genuine friendship with this family and would allow nobody to be rude to them.

He extended his arm, grinning triumphantly. Rebecca felt

the breath catch in her throat. He was really almost unbearably handsome.

They began to walk further along the path to the gate leading into Mrs. O'Dwyer's garden.

What would it be like to be married to him? Have him belong to her and her alone? Spend every day with him. And every night, she thought wickedly.

"Are you well, Rebecca? You seem rather flushed." He sounded amused and she blushed even more fiercely. Damn the man! She could not be married to him! She'd murder him within twenty-four hours!

"I am quite well, your grace. Though apparently I am suffering an affliction of memory loss since I do not remember giving you permission to use my name."

He gave a shout of laughter at this.

"You really are quite the shrew aren't you? But you are right, you have not given me leave to use your name. I had thought, however, that we had come to know each other well enough to forgo the formalities. After all, a lady should at the very least be on a first name basis with the man who gave her her first kiss, should she not?"

Rebecca blushed to the roots of her hair and pulled her arm from him. He was an arrogant, odious brute. How could he speak of that in such a casual manner? And mock her about it to boot?

Well, she would put him firmly in his place once and for all. How could she have dreamt of marrying such a creature? Her husband would be the complete opposite of him — humble and kind and not so overwhelming that she could not think straight when he was near.

Rather than slap him or stomp off, which she was very tempted to do, Rebecca looked steadily into his eyes with what she hoped was a patronizing expression on her face.

"My first kiss, your grace? How sweet that you should think so. You are quite mistaken I am afraid. But do not worry yourself, you did very well." She patted his arm reassuringly and turned to continue up the path. Let him stew on that for a while! It *had* been her first kiss, but he did not need to know that and his pride could stand to be a little dented.

Edward stood encased in a burning fury as she stalked off up the garden path, her pretty little nose stuck in the air.

Rage coursed through him, making him think he was going quite mad. He'd been enjoying embarrassing her, knew that she must yearn for his kiss again as he yearned for hers. Had thought to curb some of that impertinence that seemed to come so naturally to her.

Now, however, he found himself bested by her. Eaten up with a jealous rage the likes of which he'd never felt before. Who the hell had she been kissing? How dare she go around kissing everyone!

And to imply that he had somehow failed to impress? Well, he thought huffily, that at least could not be true. He prided himself on his seduction techniques. Was really quite famous for them. He just hadn't been trying with her that is all.

He knew he was behaving like a slighted debutante and angrily clamped down on his roaming and ridiculous thoughts.

It was of no matter. It did not mean anything anyway. But he knew she was just as affected by their kiss, by his proximity as he was hers.

He slowly followed her and thought back to last night. He believed she was bluffing. Her kiss might have set him on fire but it had been the kiss of an innocent and if her initial hesitancy did not tell him that, the look of shock afterwards would have done.

No, she was most definitely bluffing. She had been kissed by none but him.

And he was an excellent kisser.

Feeling mollified, he increased his pace to catch up to her.

She was captivating. He found his eyes once more drawn to the sway of her hips, the exposed skin of her neck. He wondered if her skin there was as silky soft as the skin of her shoulders. He longed to find out. But knew that he could not.

How he had controlled himself when he was assisting her off that wall he would never know. He was stronger than he thought but his control was within an inch of snapping. Her back pressed against his front was an exquisite torture he would never forget.

She had smelled divine, her glorious hair had been hidden by her bonnet but the scent of lemon still tingled his nostrils. He made a mental note to have buckets of lemons all over his homes.

He'd been about to kiss her again when the lad had interrupted them. And she had been willing. This could not go on! The sooner he returned to England and away from temptation, the better.

He had intended to ride straight back and speak to the earl immediately. But the idea of spending more time in the company of the delectable Lady Rebecca was a temptation he could not refuse.

He caught up to her just before she entered the cottage. The smell of freshly baked biscuits floated on the summer breeze and Edward suddenly regretted the tantrum that had seen him leave his breakfast untouched.

He bowed slightly to allow her to pass him and enter the cottage but rather than move, Rebecca placed her hand gently on his arm. His eyes snapped to hers at the touch. She was gazing pleadingly at him with those blasted eyes once again and he felt his control slipping.

No wonder she was spoiled. How was anyone to refuse her anything when she looked at them like that? Likely the lady had the whole of Offaly firmly wrapped around her tiny finger.

"Your grace," Rebecca spoke quietly, obviously not

wanting to be overheard.

"What is it Rebecca?" He had purposely used her given name again but she was obviously too distracted to notice.

She began to worry her bottom lip just like last night and Edward could not stifle a groan of longing. Did she know what she did to him?

Probably not. Which made it all the more tempting.

"My lady, what is it that you want from me? You only need ask." He spoke hoarsely, his voice belying his desperation. If she did not speak or move soon she would find herself thoroughly compromised, right here on the doorstep of this workman's cottage.

"These people, the O'Dwyers, they're my friends. I have the utmost respect and affection for them." She paused and Edward wondered why he was telling him this. It was clear from her interaction with the boy that there was a longstanding friendship between the family and her.

"Although I am of noble birth, Mr. & Mrs. O'Dwyer have known me since I was a babe and therefore, feel entirely comfortable and able to be themselves around me. I am — that is, I would appreciate if you did not act terribly — er — dukey around them."

"Dukey?"

"Yes."

"Is that a word?"

She huffed out a sigh and glared at him.

"Just do not be yourself."

Lovely. "Then who should I be?" he asked mildly.

"Oh never mind," she spat then brushed by him.

He wondered idly how many moods she actually possessed, since he'd witnessed about seven since his arrival.

If Rebecca had but waited a moment, he would have reassured her to the absolute best of his ability. A duke he may be, but he knew and spent time with all of his tenants, particularly at his main seat, and had spent hundreds of happy hours with those excellent families in his youth.

Well, she would see for herself shortly, he thought as he entered the home. Maybe he'd surprise her.

Chapter Nine

The cottage was as warm and comforting as ever and Rebecca felt herself relax as she was embraced in a warm hug.

Mrs. O'Dwyer was like a beloved aunt to her and Rebecca made herself right at home, sitting herself at the much-used, well-scrubbed kitchen table. No standing on ceremony here! If the duke did not like it, well he could leave!

She eyed him sceptically, wondering when he'd sneer at his surroundings and take his leave and hoped he would not upset her friends.

Mrs. O'Dwyer turned to face the almighty duke and nearly fell over herself curtsying to him. Rebecca rolled her eyes. The older lady had never fawned over the earl that way!

Mrs. O'Dwyer, being a hardworking soul all her life, was getting on in years and her muscles and bones were not what they used to be. Edward waited while she struggled back out of her curtsy, panting as she went.

The children stood behind Lady Rebecca's stool eyeing him suspiciously while the lady herself looked disdainfully at him as if she expected him to start abusing the woman still half prostrate in front of him.

He glanced quickly around the large room while the old dear gripped a chair to straighten. He did not think she'd appreciate his assistance and would probably have a fit if he touched her.

The room put him in mind of the cottages he frequented as a child. Homey and warm, and thoroughly welcoming. It made him pang for his childhood when his father had been in charge and Edward had been free to do as he pleased.

It had been too long since he'd spent any real time with his tenants, something he would rectify soon.

"Your grace," Mrs. O'Dwyer finally wheezed, "we are truly honoured to have you here. Please, come through to the drawing room, Lady Rebecca should not have brought you in the back way." Her tone was ever so slightly accusatory and Rebecca snorted. Most unladylike.

"My dear Mrs. O'Dwyer," he began making every effort to put the good lady at ease and show the madam sitting at the table that he wasn't the snob she expected him to be, "I am sure you have an excellent drawing room but this kitchen puts me in mind of the cottages I spent a very happy childhood in on my father's estates. I would just as well stay here and enjoy the wonderful smells coming from the hob."

Mrs. O'Dwyer's face reddened with pleasure and Rebecca thought the poor woman would literally burst with pride. She was quietly impressed with the duke. He had been all ease and politeness with not a trace of arrogance or superiority. She was grateful to him.

He took a seat on the stool next to hers and his thigh brushed against her as he settled himself. She felt the impact all the way to her toes. Surely this did not happen to everyone? If it did, husbands and wives would stay locked away forever, never entering society.

Not liking where her thoughts were going she turned instead to ask Martin how his reading and writing practice was coming along while Mrs. O'Dwyer bustled about preparing tea things.

They spent a very merry couple of hours with the O'Dwyers until Rebecca decided that they must, albeit regretfully, take their leave.

The smile she turned on Edward was both warm and genuine and it warmed his heart to see her look at him so. He could not remember when he last had such an enjoyable morning. He had chatted with Lady Rebecca and Mrs. O'Dwyer, silently listened while they discussed the local gossip and partook of Mrs .O'Dwyer's truly excellent culinary offerings.

Watching the pair of them, it was obvious that Rebecca was truly adored by this family, and from listening to the many enquiries after her health that locals had made, it seemed she was equally adored by all of the tenants and local merchants. He wasn't surprised. She was adorable.

He had played tea with Annie, the daughter of the family, much to Rebecca's amusement, and had watched as Martin soldiered through his letters and numbers with Lady Rebecca encouraging and coaxing him along the way.

He had been struck suddenly by an image of her as a mother and knew she would be a wonderful one. Would she have girls, just like her? Incorrigible little pixies that would drive their father up the wall? The thought made him smile. He wasn't sure the world was ready for any more Rebeccas!

Truly it had been a wonderful morning. The only blip had been when he had mentioned the strange gentleman he'd come across in the woods. Lady Rebecca had paled at the mention of him and Edward had wondered if she'd been meeting him for an assignation. Perhaps she had been telling the truth about being an experienced kisser?

The thought cut through him like a knife. He was surprised and worried to find that alongside the jealousy, which to be fair he'd been experiencing so much of at this stage it was becoming second nature, there was an overwhelming feeling of despair. Not wanting to look too closely at such an emotion or the cause of it, he ignored it completely.

But her countenance had not been that of someone with a pleasant secret, she had looked afraid. Terrified even. Why would she be so frightened by the mere mention of that man?

Mrs. O'Dwyer's chat interrupted his thoughts.

"That one, your grace? Oh he is bad news. Very bad news. Not at all liked amongst the townsfolk and with good reason. Does nothing but drink and gamble and other activities I will not mention in front of her ladyship. His uncle will be turning in his grave, God rest his soul."

Edward wasn't altogether surprised to learn that Mr. Simons was an unsavoury character, he had thought as much on meeting him.

But Rebecca's reaction piqued his curiosity and his concern. He would be sure to question her later. But he had put it from his mind and continued to thoroughly enjoy the visit.

****

Rebecca said her goodbyes and took the duke's arm as they made their way back toward the woods. She had enjoyed her visit, as usual, but her mind was filled with the man beside her. How surprised she'd been by his manner! There had not been a trace of the arrogant man she'd seen earlier. He'd been completely at ease in the humble cottage and had chatted with Mrs. O'Dwyer and the children as if he'd known them his whole life.

He'd laughed a lot too, and she could not help but notice how devastatingly handsome he was when he laughed. He seemed younger somehow. He'd been kind, attentive, amusing and unfailingly respectful. It was terrible!

If he'd been rude or arrogant it would have been much

better for her heart. As it was, that traitorous organ was in great danger of slipping out of her possession and landing firmly in his. But this was impossible! She'd known him but two days. You could not go hurtling head over heels into love with someone after two days. Could you?

They'd reached the duke's horse in total silence, Rebecca's mind filled with the confusing thoughts that kept circling round in there.

She finally noticed that they'd come to a stop and looked up, blinking as if waking from a trance.

"Well," she said jovially, wanting to escape him for a while to try to sort through the muddle of emotions she was feeling, "that was very enjoyable. Thank you, your grace."

"Thank you?"

"Yes, for being so – well – normal."

He smiled indulgently.

"You really do not have a good opinion of me, do you?"

"Oh I do," she replied emphatically. "Now."

He chuckled softly. "Well I am glad to hear it. I thoroughly enjoyed myself."

"Truly?"

"Oh yes. I particularly enjoyed the tales of your escapades."

She had the grace to blush slightly.

"There was a lot of exaggeration, your grace."

"Was there indeed? So you did not set Mr. O'Dwyer's hens loose? Or steal a horse and cart? Or land yourself upside down in the trough in the town square?" he asked with a wide grin. He hadn't been the least bit surprised to hear of her adventures. He did not think anything would surprise him about the lady.

"I apologised about the hens. Profusely. I really think it is time people let it rest. And I did not *steal* the cart. I borrowed it for a while and returned it. Almost in one piece!"

"And the trough?"

She sighed resignedly. "Yes, I fell in the trough. But I did not remember it was there!"

They both laughed, she in remembrance and he because he could picture it perfectly.

"I shall take my leave of you, then," Rebecca eventually broke the companionable silence. She was far too comfortable with him. Enjoying his company too much.

"Nonsense. I shall walk back with you."

"But your horse, your grace," she protested though secretly she thrilled at the idea of being alone with him for a little longer.

"My horse will walk too, I do not plan on carrying him," he quipped.

"Very well," she smiled and they set off on their way.

They walked some distance before his curiosity got the better of him.

"Mr. Simons sounds like an interesting character."

Rebecca glanced at him briefly before answering in a carefully smooth tone. "'Interesting' is an interesting way of putting it."

"Are you well acquainted with the gentleman?"

"Not very. I met him when Papa came to meet him."

"And not since?"

She hesitated and seemed on the verge of saying something but then changed her mind and answered quietly, "No, not since."

Hmm. Something was definitely going on here.

Edward did not want to pry but he felt desperate to know just what her relationship with this man was.

He needed to be subtle, to gently coax the information from her, to make her feel secure so that she would trust him.

"I thought when I saw him in the woods that you and he had been having an assignation."

Or, he could blurt it out bluntly as if he had no control over himself. Which he clearly didn't.

Rebecca stopped so fast that he yanked her forward before he had realised. She pulled her arm from the crook of his and stood glaring up at him.

Oh dear.

"You thought what?" She was angry again. This was not going to end well. He cursed himself and his jealous stupidity. They'd enjoyed a wonderful morning in each other's company and he'd ruined it because he could not shake the damned image of her in another man's arms.

"Rebecca–" he started.

"*Lady* Rebecca" she ground out.

"My lady," he amended, thinking it safer not to use her name at all at this present moment, "I am deeply sorry, I do not know what came over me to suggest such a thing."

He should have known. He *did* know that it could not be true. He was usually so logical, thought things through so well. She had him tied in bloody knots! He hadn't been able to think straight since he'd first seen her sprinting through the trees.

"How dare you say such a thing to me? How could you think that of me?"

Oh God were those tears? Edward did not like crying women. They were frightening and unpredictable and he endeavoured to stay as far away from them as humanly possible.

Strange then that the sight of Lady Rebecca's tears, rather than repulsing him made him want to draw closer and offer any comfort that he could. He felt like an absolute cad.

"I am sorry. I do not think — that is to say — I may have thought for a mere moment — he mentioned you, you see so I—"

"What do you mean he mentioned me?"

Now she looked terrified as well as upset. What the hell was going on here? The tears still glistened in her huge eyes. If one, just one, fell it would be his undoing.

"He said that you did not wish to be interrupted," he answered miserably. This could not have gone worse. He should have stayed quiet.

"Your grace," she at least seemed less angry with him now.

"Edward," he interrupted.

"Pardon?"

"Call me Edward."

He watched fascinated as a fierce blush stained her cheeks.

"I could not possibly, your grace."

"'Your grace' is far too formal. You forget I now know the secrets of your youth. We are much better acquainted than 'your grace' and 'my lady' are we not?"

He realised as he spoke that the words could have more than one meaning. Rebecca obviously realised too since her blush went from pink to puce.

"It would not be proper."

Probably not the best time to remind her that as a rule, proper young ladies did not show off body parts whilst hanging from walls and statues.

Of course, proper gentlemen did not pounce on unsuspecting ladies on darkened balconies either.

"Then at least call me Hartridge. All my friends do."

She smiled at this and he was relieved to see that the tears seem to have receded for now.

"And are we friends, Hartridge?"

Never had his surname sounded so good.

"I hope that we are, Rebecca?" He said her name like a question, not willing to break the tenuous peace that had descended upon them once more.

She smiled again, wider this time and he felt that the storm had passed.

He was loath to continue their conversation when it was so obviously distressing to her. However, now he needed to know what exactly was going on.

"So the gentleman," he tried once more, "Mr. Simons. He had not seen you before he said you did not want to be interrupted?"

She heaved a sigh of resignation and started to walk again, leaving him to catch up.

"We spoke briefly" —odd that she would deny it originally— "he was – very forward. I did not like it."

Rebecca missed the murderous expression that came over his features at her admittance. She decided that she might as well tell him the whole truth. It would be nice to unburden herself in any event.

"He made me uncomfortable. And when I tried to leave, he took hold of my arm and would not let me go. I told him–"

Before she knew it, Hartridge had turned on his heel and began marching back the way they had come.

"What are you doing?" she asked in surprise.

"I am going to kill him," he answered conversationally, as if they were chatting about the weather.

"What? Do not be ridiculous. Come back here." Her commanding tone brought him to a halt, if only because never in his life had someone commanded anything of him.

He turned back to face her.

"Please, do not do or say anything about this. It really is of no matter. I shan't be seeing him again for quite some time."

He briefly wondered how she could be so sure but was too furious to think long on anything except getting his hands on the man.

"I cannot just stand here and do nothing when he has treated you so abominably. It is not to be borne, Rebecca. I will kill him with my bare hands."

Rebecca's heart was in her mouth. He looked absolutely terrifying. She could not imagine that any man, any *person* would ever want to cross him. He looked like an avenging angel— beautiful, dark and angrier than she had ever seen a person.

"Please," she tried again, placing a restraining hand on his arm. He was trembling with fury. Goodness, it really wasn't that bad!

"Please, you must calm down. Truly it is not as bad as all that. As you can see, I am unharmed. He let me go almost as soon as he grabbed me. It will be worse for me if you do anything, can you not see that?"

"No, I cannot! You did nothing wrong."

"Your grace, Hartridge. My mother really does not need to hear another story of my being mixed up in something — unsavoury. She will not care whether it was my fault or not! Please."

Rebecca sounded so distressed that Edward was torn. How could he justifiably let this incident go without action or comment? At the very least he must tell her father. But she looked so distressed and was begging him. And touching him.

So, against his better judgement and mostly because she was still touching him, he conceded.

"Very well. Though it gives me no pleasure, I will keep it secret. But" —he clasped her shoulders and stared down into her eyes— "you must promise me that you will not travel out alone and that you will tell someone immediately if he so much as looks at you. Do you understand me?"

He was serious. Rebecca could tell. And she was so grateful to him she would have agreed to just about anything. Besides, she'd already decided not to walk alone in the future. And she may yet tell Papa. But she did not want to think about that right now.

"I promise," she said quietly. "Thank you."

They gazed at each other and once again that unmistakeable crackle seemed to build. Both were aware of it and both were powerless to stop it.

If he kissed her now Rebecca would not object, though she should. She trembled in anticipation. The truth was, she had been longing to feel his kiss since last night.

Edward stared at her, that strange mix of lust and protectiveness swirling around him. He could kiss her now and knew he would be lost, knew that she would not stop him. His whole body screamed at him to take her into his arms. And yet…

She'd been through a frightening ordeal with that damned Mr. Simons. He would not take advantage of her, or scare her even more with the power of his desire for her. He knew that she was not scared of him, but to add to her uncertainty now, after all that had happened this morning? His conscience would not allow it, though the rest of him was doing the utmost to shut his conscience up.

He leaned forward and placed a tender kiss gently on her forehead. He should be sainted! Then, without another word, he gathered the reigns of the horse, offered her his arm and they set off toward the house.

Was that it? Rebecca frowned in consternation as she took his proffered arm and began walking back. A kiss on her head? Her head? She'd been certain that he'd been about to kiss her. Really kiss her, not a brotherly peck on her head. Did he not want to kiss her? Had he not enjoyed their last kiss? She felt sure that he'd been as affected as she, but perhaps not?

Or maybe it was this nasty business with Mr. Simons. Perhaps he thought that Rebecca was somehow to blame? That she had encouraged that man's advances? Or that she went around kissing men the way she had kissed him last night?

The thought was depressing. Well, if he was to judge her based on her behaviour with him he was a hypocrite! Of course, it did not help matters that she'd as good as told him that she went around kissing men.

But he was hardly an innocent. Even a peck on the forehead was enough to turn her to a quivering wreck. And she was quite sure that being a handsome young duke lent him a lot of sway with ladies. Why, he'd almost had an apoplexy when she implied he wasn't a very good kisser! That meant that he had experience, coming out his ears most likely.

How dare he stand in judgement of her when his behaviour was doubtless a thousand times worse?

On and on went her thoughts, while her temper rose higher and higher. And so it was that by the time they reached the house, he had put her into a towering rage without uttering a single word.

The house loomed into view and Edward turned toward the stables. Rebecca removed her arm from his, quite forcibly he thought, and began to stomp off in the opposite direction.

"Rebecca?" What the devil was going on now?

"What?" she shouted back over her shoulder.

"Where are you going?"

She spun round as if he had given her the most heinous insult and marched back over to him.

"Do not worry yourself, your grace."

They were back to 'your grace'?

"I am going to my room. I will not be doing anything that your virtuous self could find fault with."

What in God's name? She was angry that much was clear. And though he would never claim to have a handle on the female psyche, he had to admit that this sudden outburst seemed more irrational than usual. They literally had not spoken since their conversation about Mr. Simons. It was impossible for him to have done anything to warrant this! He suddenly felt his own anger rising to meet hers.

He'd bloody well been the perfect gentleman. Sacrificed his own wants to do what was best for the little shrew and this was his reward? To have her shout at him? It was the outside of enough.

"What the hell are you talking about?"

"Do not shout at me."

"I am not shouting," he shouted.

She raised a disdainful eyebrow and the last of his control

slipped. This bloody woman had been driving him slowly mad since he arrived here.

"I always suspected that females were quite mad. I am sure I've never yet met a one who could compare to you, however."

"Oh I am well aware of your low opinion of me, you being such a paragon of virtue."

What? His head was beginning to thump. They were very close to the house now and he was aware that at any moment someone might happen upon them arguing in public like a pair of children. But he did not care a jot.

"My low opinion of you? What the blazes are you talking about?"

"I am talking about *you*—"

Did she just poke him?

"Thinking you are so *perfect*—"

Ouch. That hurt!

"Thinking you can look down on us mere mortals who fall so short of your God-like expectations."

If she poked him again she would leave a mark for Christ's sake. He already had a lump from when she'd belted him the night before!

"Madam. Will you desist from poking me?" he bellowed.

His roar seemed to bring her up short and she stepped back from him, though her fists were still clenched and her breathing heavy.

She was beautiful when she was angry. But that was of no matter.

"Now. You will explain what it is you are talking about."

"Don't you dare presume to tell me what to do."

He'd never felt so exasperated in his life! He wanted to tear his hair out, or hit something, or kiss her senseless.

"What are you talking about?" That was louder than he intended and echoed around the open grounds surrounding them.

"You! You and your pious judgement of me. You obviously think I encouraged that horrible Mr. Simons or else why would you not want to kiss me?"

Rebecca threw her hands to her mouth as soon as the words left her mouth, as if she wished she could hold them in. It was too late of course. They'd already been spoken.

He looked at her incredulously. Could she really think that? And there he'd been, patting himself on the back for treating her so well. The mind truly did boggle. He could not bloody win.

"Want to kiss you?" he ground out angrily. "I've been slowly expiring trying to keep my damned hands off you."

"Why?" she asked mutinously.

"Because I am trying to be a gentleman!" he yelled once again.

Granted, it was not the most gentlemanly behaviour, to be roaring at her in the middle of her own garden. But the chit was really beyond exasperating.

"Nobody asked you to be a gentleman."

God she was a stubborn little miss.

"So you would prefer I ruin you, is that it? And what will you tell your sister then, hmm?"

Her face paled and he knew he'd gone too far, yet something kept him going, spurred him on to say more. Perhaps if he hurt her, pushed her away, she would do what he could not and break the bond that was forming between them.

"Or has this been your plan all along? Ensnare the duke meant for your sister? Do one better than she? Finally be something more than a disappointment to your family?"

He was cut short by the sting of her small hand connecting with his cheek.

Rebecca looked horrified by her behaviour and stumbled back.

Her eyes were huge and filled with hurt. Tears brimmed

then began to descend freely down her cheeks.

He knew he'd done it then. Pushed her away. But instead of feeling satisfied, he felt an acute pain that he'd never felt before and all at once he regretted what he'd said.

He stepped forward and made to reach for her, to apologise to ease her hurt.

But she pulled away from him with a little cry of despair. Shaking her head she turned on her heel and ran toward the house.

Edward made to follow her but stopped himself after a couple of steps. Follow her? What for? What was there to say or do?

He would be gone from here in less than twenty-four hours. And spending a pleasant morning with her, though it was one of the happiest he'd had in years, did not change the fact that they were completely unsuited. Why then, did it feel like he'd made a colossal mistake?

He did not know how long he stood for, staring after her, contemplating the futility of wanting her. Finally, when the horse became anxious, he turned and trudged toward the stables, feeling the weight of the world on his shoulders.

****

The dowager, who had watched the highly entertaining exchange from her vantage point at the dining room window, shook her head and lifted her coffee cup in a silent salute to the lady as she watched her slap her stubborn, rigid son.

No doubt he deserved it!

Of course, she had no idea what the fight was about, but to see Edward lose his control, for even a moment, was a miracle worth saluting.

Lady Catherine remembered with fondness how utterly exasperating she had found her late husband. And the passion with which they'd loved each other.

She needed to get to know the force of nature that was Lady Rebecca. See what it was that her son was clearly falling for. The stories she'd heard from her abigail made her a little nervous. The child was bordering on scandalous. Well, there'd never be a dull moment.

Her thoughts turned to the Carringtons and to Lady Caroline. She felt sure that young lady's heart was not involved but it was a situation that would require delicate handling. She frowned as she watched her son stomp off in the opposite direction, looking like thunder.

Perhaps now would be a good time to have a quiet talk with Lady Ranford before Edward announced to the earl that he'd had enough and ruined an almost lifelong friendship.

****

Rebecca did not stop running until she'd reached the house. She entered through the back to avoid running into anyone and stumbled through the kitchen, keeping her head bowed to hide her tears.

The kitchen staff called out greetings but she could not even bring herself to return them, just kept moving until she reached the sanctity of the empty stairwell.

Good God, how had things turned so bad so suddenly? She had never experienced such a range of emotions in such a short space of time before. It was going to drive her mad!

She had never been so angry, nor so sad in her entire life. How could he say those things? *Think* those things? It was unbearable. She could not stand to think of him thinking ill of her.

Reaching her room she cried, sobbed rather, for the second time in as many days. She needed to take herself firmly in hand. It did no good crying over a man. Especially a brute such as the duke. And Rebecca could not, *would* not be one of those simpering misses who allowed the whims of a man to dictate her happiness.

After giving herself a stern talking to, she felt no better but had at least calmed down enough to act like she felt better.

But she decided to take nuncheon in her room, just to be safe. If she saw him now there was every chance she would cry again. Or throw a platter at him. And whilst the latter seemed very appealing, nobody else would appreciate it.

It did not take long, however, for Rebecca to feel listless and bored having never enjoyed being cooped up, especially on such a beautiful afternoon. She heaved a sigh of frustration and looked out the window wistfully. Perhaps an afternoon ride would help clear her head and lift her from her melancholy.

She was about to turn and ring for Maura when movement to her right caught her eye. It was Caro. With Hartridge! She leaned forward and promptly whacked her head on the glass. A couple of moments rubbing the sore spot helped ease some of the dizziness and she pressed her nose against the glass to resume her spying.

Where had they disappeared to? Rebecca felt a sinking feeling like none she'd ever experienced. What was going on here? Was he proposing to Caroline? She felt sick and dizzy and it had nothing to do with the window.

He had said he wasn't going to marry her. Had no interest in marrying her! So what had they been discussing? In the glimpse she had managed, they seemed to be having quite a serious conversation. What if he'd decided to marry Caroline and save himself from crazy women like her? Rebecca knew Caroline had no feelings toward the duke. She'd barely glanced in his direction or even conversed with him since he'd arrived. Meanwhile Rebecca felt like she'd been burning holes in his person she'd spent so long gazing at him. But Caroline had been bred to be a duchess and do her familial duty.

If Hartridge decided, for whatever reason, to ask her to be his wife, Caroline would not hesitate in accepting.

Rebecca felt as if her heart had stopped beating.

So that was it? He was to be her brother-in-law? The fates had a sick sense of humour.

Chapter Ten

A ride seemed all the more appealing now and Rebecca had a desperate urge to get away.

She rang for Maura and with record speed had donned her riding habit and set out for the stables, thankful not to have bumped into anybody on the way.

If the stable hands noticed that Rebecca was not herself that day they tactfully refrained from commenting and readied her horse, Athena.

She set out at a leisurely pace, meaning to pick up speed once she'd cleared the grounds.

She thought guiltily of her promise not to be alone but quickly dismissed it from her thoughts. There was no real danger. Mr. Simons was a tenant of her father's. He would not be stupid enough to risk his entire livelihood by acting untoward. She could only presume that he'd gotten a little carried away and would stay out of her way from now on, for fear of retribution.

Besides, she could not, would not allow herself to think of Hartridge. She was barely holding it together as it was.

She rounded the stables, picked up her pace to a trot and

made her way toward the meadows; once there she would gallop until Athena tired and hopefully by the time she got back she would be able to hear the engagement announcement without embarrassing herself.

But luck, it seemed, was not on her side, for as she approached the boundary of the formal gardens she came upon Caro and Hartridge. He was bending over her hand and Caroline was smiling. Rebecca felt her heart drop all the way to her toes.

As he straightened, their eyes locked and it seemed as if the world melted away. How could he still have this effect on her? He was in the process of proposing for God's sake. To her sister!

Caroline noticed Edward's gaze was focused elsewhere and turned to see Rebecca's stricken expression. Her own expression turned to one of confusion but before she could speak Rebecca had turned Athena and galloped at full force toward the boundary hedge and the meadow beyond.

Caroline gasped in horror, Rebecca was going full pelt toward the hedge. Athena was a wonderful horse and Rebecca had one of the best seats Caroline had ever seen but she would never clear that hedge, would she?

Caroline made to start forward but was brought up short by the expletive shouted from beside her! She turned toward the duke to see he was staring in much the same horror, toward where Rebecca was still galloping.

"What the hell is she doing?" he growled.

Caroline was confused by his reaction. He seemed equally terrified. And she knew why *she* was reacting that way— because she loved Rebecca. So why was he?

However, Caroline did not have time to wonder about the duke when her little sister was likely about to break her neck.

She started to run toward Rebecca though there was no chance to catch up with her. She called out to her but the stiff breeze took her cry and carried it away.

She was soon overtaken by the duke who was sprinting as if the very hounds of hell were at his feet. He called out too and his voice was so much more commanding, more desperate sounding too, that Caroline was sure that Rebecca would hear and stop.

But Rebecca did not stop, even if she heard his pleading cry. She reached the hedge and Caroline froze in horror. She would surely fall.

Edward screeched to a halt as Rebecca's horse leapt. He had never felt such fear in his life. He would wring her neck if she survived that jump. How could she be so bloody thoughtless?

The horse's hind legs skimmed the top of the hedge and cleared it! Edward let out the breath he'd been painfully holding. If he expected Rebecca to stop or turn back, he was disappointed. She kept running, not even breaking her stride.

"Ahem." At Lady Caroline's subtle cough Edward dragged his eyes away from the retreating form of Rebecca. He seemed to do a lot of staring after the lady.

"Your sister is quite the adventuress," Edward stated calmly, doing his best to bring his emotions back under control.

Lady Caroline eyed him sceptically. He did not like that look. It reminded him of her sister and he really did not need any more reminders since Rebecca occupied pretty much all of his thoughts already.

When the lady did not speak, he tried again.

"Well, I hope she will be more careful when riding in the future. I am sure you would all prefer her to be safe and not trying to kill herself on her horse."

Lady Caroline continued to look curiously at him without speaking. *For God's sake! Has she suddenly turned mute?*

"Well, I will um — shall I escort you back, my lady?"

Lady Caroline's ice blue gaze had turned from curious to

calculating.

"No, thank you, your grace. I believe I shall take the air for a while. And make sure Rebecca gets back in one piece. We none of us want to see any harm come to her. Do we?"

He felt suddenly nervous under her intense scrutiny. Resisting the urge to pull at his suddenly too tight cravat, he bowed and turned back toward the house. He just wanted to take his leave. He had made an appointment to speak with the earl and, since he'd just broken the arrangement with Lady Caroline, he did not want to add insult to what was sure to be injury by not turning up at his allotted time.

Lady Caroline had taken the news surprisingly well. Insultingly well, if he were honest. She did not seem to care. And he was a duke!

He had asked her to walk out with him, not wanting to do it in the house in case she swooned or, heaven forbid, cried.

He had hemmed and hawed about how best to break the news, gently and with compassion, he decided. After all, it would be a difficult blow to come back from and she did not deserve to be hurt. He already felt like an absolute cad.

And so it was that they had taken a stroll around the gardens and he had finally worked up the courage to approach the subject.

"My lady" —they were just beyond the stables, secluded enough to protect the poor dear's dignity.

"I cannot pretend to be unaware of the arrangement made between our fathers, though I only learned of it when my mother and I arrived here."

All right. Here it went.

"I would have you know that I hold you in great esteem. You are charming and beautiful and would make a perfect duchess."

Caroline smiled serenely, giving no indication that she knew what was coming. Edward took a big breath and blurted. "I am so very sorry, but I cannot pay my addresses to you. I really do feel that—"

"I know." She cut him off.

Oh.

"You... know?"

"Yes, your grace. I know."

She knew what?

"You know what?"

"That you and I are wholly unsuited. That we would not make each other happy. That our fathers were either insane or more foxed than I imagined when that contract was made."

Right. No swooning then.

"I had thought that you — I mean, that you were aware, had wanted—"

"Your grace, from the schoolroom I have been trained in the fine art of being a duchess. My entire life, I suppose, has been geared towards it. I had no problem with it. I was not romantic. I know the value of a good marriage, based on family alliance and place in Society. Rebecca is our romantic."

Why was he not surprised?

"I hadn't given much thought to how I would actually feel when we met."

She blushed and he was struck again by how attractive the girl actually was once he saw past the standoffishness of her demeanour.

"The truth is, whilst I have the greatest of respect for you, I cannot help but feel that perhaps there should be a little more feeling on both sides when entering a marriage. Respect — well, it is not very exciting is it?"

Edward felt a surge of affection for the lady. She had a sensible head on her shoulders and he was glad that she wanted more from marriage. She deserved somebody who would make her smile, laugh and evoke feelings more than respect.

He smiled fondly.

"I am very pleased that we agree on this, Lady Caroline. I

only hope your father does not break out the shotgun!"

Caroline laughed. "I believe he will take the news better than you think. He will, perhaps, be disappointed. He is terribly fond of you and your family, you know. I think the thoughts of an alliance were more important to him than it being you and I specifically."

Edward coughed nervously and looked away. Lady Caroline did not suspect that he had developed a — what? What had he developed for Rebecca? Apart from raging lust and the ability to age about 10 years from sheer frustration.

When he glanced back, Lady Caroline seemed uncomfortable. Did she suspect? Or was she thinking of something else? Hmm. How mysterious. Who could she mean?

There was an awkward little silence, as if they were both thinking things the other should not be privy to. Edward smiled to break the tension.

"I am very pleased to have had things work out so well, my lady. I truly wish you every happiness."

"And you, your grace." Caroline smiled.

Edward bowed over her hand and was about to take his leave when he had sensed, more than heard, Lady Rebecca's presence. His body had reacted to her before he was even aware that she was in the vicinity.

As Edward entered the house and made his way to the earl's study, he thought back to the look on Lady Rebecca's face. Her expression had been so stricken that he had felt his heart clench painfully. What was the matter with her? Surely, she did not think that he and her sister –

Before he could even finish the thought, she had taken off full pelt toward the boundary of the garden. And then he'd been left to do damage control with her sister who had appeared far too bright and far too curious for his peace of mind.

He would make sure Lady Rebecca, the scourge of his

blood pressure, got a proper talking to later. And if the earl would not curb his youngest's penchant for dangerous misadventure, then he damn well would.

However, all thoughts of punishment, especially the more exciting ones, needed to be firmly pushed aside. It was time for his meeting with the earl.

****

Rebecca felt infinitely better after her ride. Since the evenings were brighter as they approached summer, she had stayed out for longer than she had intended but it had done her good. Her mind felt clearer, and she felt better equipped to deal with the announcement that was surely to come at dinner.

There was just enough time to slip to her room and change, but first she needed to speak to her father.

Rebecca found him in his study, gazing out at the glorious grounds that could be viewed from this room. Decorated in a typically male fashion, all dark woods and blood red brocades, it was nevertheless one of Rebecca's favourites in the house.

In the past she had sat for hours reading in here while her father went about his business. The smell, the worn comfortable furniture had always put her at ease. Rebecca did not feel at ease right now, however. Though she was sure her father would have no objection to her having a Season, she did not want him inquiring as to her sudden interest in the marriage mart when she had shown a distinct *lack* of interest up until now.

Still, it had to be done. And she would just avoid difficult questions as much as possible. She hadn't left very much time for discussion anyway and hoped that would aid her in skipping over any difficult bits.

"Papa?"

The earl turned toward her with a smile.

"Ah Rebecca. I take it you have heard the news?"

Oh God. So much for avoiding difficult topics. Well, perhaps it was best to get it over with now. If she cried in front of Papa he would send her off to her Mother and at least this way she would not have to try and save face in front of the entire party later.

"About the engagement, Papa?"

"Well, yes. Or rather lack of engagement, eh?" he asked jovially.

"Pardon me?"

"Even your mother does not seem that put out. I am disappointed, I must say. But then, I suppose it was the wish of two foolish young men who really took very little into consideration."

Rebecca was growing more confused by the second. Was he saying that there *wasn't* an engagement between Hartridge and her sister? Then, what had she witnessed in the garden?

"Father, are you saying—"

"Of course," he continued, "it would have been quite a feather in your sister's cap. And then, there is the desire to have our families finally aligned. Old Thorpe always did feel more like a brother than a friend. Still. No matter. I would not have either of them unhappy. And your sister has suddenly gotten romantic notions in her head, or so it would appear."

"Father!" Rebecca rather shrieked.

The sound brought the earl up short.

"Forgive me. But, has there not been an engagement between his grace and Caro?"

"No, dear. That is what I've been saying. Edward came to me a short while ago to cry off. Though, I suppose he hasn't cried off as such, since there was never really an engagement in place."

Rebecca listened in shock as her father rambled on. Her heart soared and she felt quite lightheaded with relief. Though she had no right to. *They were not engaged!*

He was still an absolute swine for the things he'd said. But he remained an unattached one.

"Anyway, I am not a complete tyrant so I broke the contract willingly. I was worried about your sister but, as I said, she seems to have developed notions of love." He said the last with an air of amazement.

Rebecca could not blame him. Caroline was not exactly known for her softer side, though she had a heart of gold.

"Well, good for her I say! As long as she takes care to attach herself to one who is worthy of her, I shall be well pleased."

Rebecca smiled weakly in response, too overwhelmed by shock and a torrent of nameless emotions to form any coherent answer.

"So, what can I do for you, dearest?"

Her father's question gave her pause. What could he do? She'd been all set to ask for a Season, to tell him that she had every intention to wed. But now that Hartridge was not to marry Caroline it changed things, did it not?

Or did it?

What difference did that make, really? He was still an arrogant snob who thought the most terrible things about her.

And, even if he were not, she was still most definitely not duchess material!

Her resolve once again strengthened, she squared her shoulders and said "Papa, I want to find a husband."

Chapter Eleven

Rebecca made an extra effort with her appearance for dinner that night. At first she'd decided to dress as plainly as possible, to wear no adornment in her hair or on her body and to blend into the background as much as possible. She sent Maura away saying she could ready herself.

After all, Rebecca did not want Hartridge to think that she was trying to 'win him' from her sister.

Then, she decided that he could easily assume that *had* been her plan, and now that he'd discovered it she was reverting to type. She rang for Maura immediately and instructed her to lay out her silver silk evening gown, one of her favourites and most eye catching. Then she sat down in preparation for Maura to dress her hair.

She did not want him to think that she was dressing plainly because of him.

But, if she did make too much of an effort, would he think she *was* trying to attract him? After all, hadn't she screeched at him like a fishwife for not wanting to kiss her? She told Maura to leave again.

Maura refused on the grounds that Rebecca would call

for her again in a matter of moments.

So she stayed.

"There, my lady." Maura leaned back having braided a silver ribbon through the intricate style piled on top of Rebecca's head. It left her neck exposed apart from a few tendrils, which curled at the nape. "As pretty as a picture."

Rebecca smiled gratefully at Maura, pleased now that she had decided, or been forced by Maura really, to dress well. *Stuff the arrogant Duke!*

She would be in London this Season proving to him that she had no interest in him.

Ignoring the clenching in her heart at the thought, she gave herself one last looking over and, happy enough with the results of Maura's ministrations, she swept downstairs.

****

Edward had been worried about the reception he would get from both his mother and Lady Ranford but he found to his relief that the ladies treated him as warmly as ever. He had spoken to his mother earlier of course, and explained that he had met with both Lady Caroline and Ranford, and neither had seemed overly disappointed in his breaking the contract.

The dowager had barely batted an eyelid. How strange. He'd been dragged all this way to marry the chit and now nobody seemed to give a damn!

Now, he stood engaging in a lively discussion about the recent goings on in Parliament with Tom, the earl and the vicar, Mr. Davids, who had been invited along with his wife to dine this evening. The vicar was an intelligent man and Edward was quite enjoying the verbal sparring. As the conversation grew livelier, he noticed that Tom seemed suddenly distracted and that his eyes had glazed over slightly. *Rebecca must be here.*

Preparing himself for the impact, he turned in the

direction of Tom's stare.

She wasn't here! Edward felt a moment of confusion before he realised that Lady Caroline had entered, looking resplendent in ice blue silk. He looked quickly back at Tom who still seemed quite starry eyed.

Well, well, well. It seemed Edward would not have to shoot his cousin after all.

He was about to turn away when a flash of silver caught his eye and now it was his turn to stare. For there she was, the woman who had made him feel more emotions in the last two days than he'd felt since being a hormonal lad.

God, she was so beautiful it almost hurt to look at her. Her gown was a soft silk and, in the candlelight the silver colour made her look ethereal. Her dark hair was shot through with silver ribbon. Edward swallowed past the lump, which seemed to have taken up residence in his throat, as his eyes travelled the length of the gown.

The neckline was low, though not obscenely so, showing just enough flesh to drive him mad for the entire evening. It skimmed her body, falling in soft folds but rather than completely hide what was underneath it hinted at it enough to keep a man guessing until he was driven to the brink of insanity.

He needed a drink.

Slowly he came round to the oddest, rasping sound. His brows drew together until he realised that the earl was coughing to gain his attention.

He schooled his features into a mask of indifference but the earl did not seem fooled in the slightest. The vicar was smiling in great amusement. Edward noticed that Tom too looked decidedly uncomfortable. It seemed they'd both been caught.

Fortunately they were saved from further embarrassment by the butler's announcement that dinner was served. Glancing sheepishly at each other, they made their way to the ladies to escort them to dinner.

Rebecca sat and prepared to make more conversation with Mr. & Mrs. Davids than she ever had in her life. Anything to stop herself from being drawn into conversation with Hartridge. She still wanted to throw a platter at him and was currently eyeing up the silverware to pick her best weapon. Not too heavy, or it would not reach him.

"My lady," Mr. Crawdon's voice brought her out of her less than innocent musings. She turned to him with a smile.

"I wondered if you liked to play whist."

"I do indeed, when I am allowed to," Rebecca answered mischievously.

"What can you mean?"

"Only that I have such a talent for the game, my father rarely allows me to play." She leaned in to whisper, "he does not like being beaten by girls, you see."

Tom laughed loudly drawing the attention of the rest of the table.

Rebecca looked up to see Caroline shooting daggers at her. What was that look for? What in God's name had she done now? She hadn't even spoken to the blasted duke.

Her thoughts seemed to propel her gaze toward him, though she had told herself to ignore him completely. It seemed she could not help it.

His expression made her throat catch. He was looking murderously at his cousin but when his eyes snapped to hers his expression changed. Rebecca did not know what to call it, but she felt the impact of it right down to her toes and a shocking heat pooled in her belly. She felt her face flush and looked away.

"What can be so amusing, cousin?" Edward asked, all politeness. His tone was friendly enough but there was an underlying hardness to it. Rebecca wondered if anyone else noticed it.

"Lady Rebecca and I were just discussing her prowess as

a whist player. It is quite something to behold I hear," Tom answered calmly, seemingly unfazed by the iron in the duke's tone.

"It seems the lady has many talents," Edward replied.

Rebecca's eyes flew back to his. She did not like his tone.

"Why earlier I found myself quite amazed with her horsemanship."

Oh no.

"I was very impressed at her ability to jump the boundary hedge from your stables to the meadows, my lord," this to her father.

She hated him!

The earl looked momentarily confused then, as realisation dawned he looked in horror at Rebecca. She wanted the ground to swallow her.

"Rebecca," his voice was low and controlled since they had guests, but she knew that had they been alone, he would have railed at her until he grew hoarse. "How could you take such a risk?"

Rebecca looked again at the duke, feeling a stab of betrayal. Why would he say such a thing, knowing she would be in trouble? She only prayed that he was finished trying to humiliate her and that he would not mention Mr. Simons. Or anything else, for that matter.

"It was fine, Father. I am quite capable of jumping the hedge. I did not even—"

"And I have told you before," the earl interrupted her, fury stamped on his expression, "that I will not have my daughter taking such ridiculous risks and acting like anything less than a lady."

Rebecca's cheeks burned with humiliation. She dared not look at anyone else at the table, lest she see scorn, disappointment, or worse, pity on their faces.

There was an uncomfortable silence at the table broken at last by the dowager duchess.

"Well, I for one admire your energy Lady Rebecca, though I do urge you to take care. Beauty such as yours is so rare. I find myself quite excited about the impact you will make when you make your come out."

Rebecca smiled gratefully at the dowager. Not only had she broken the tension but had raised the subject of the upcoming Season, thus giving the ladies at the table a subject to discuss and allowing them to quite forget Rebecca's set down.

Mr. Crawford engaged her once again in a conversation about her card playing abilities and Rebecca forced herself to relax. It seemed her humiliation was done for now. But she felt utterly heart sore.

It was obvious to her that the duke still held her in as much contempt as he had displayed this afternoon.

Edward allowed the conversation around the table to wash over him while he inwardly called himself every bad name he could think of. And since he spoke three languages, he had quite the repertoire. Had he really just gone out of his way to shame and humiliate the girl? Had he really sunk so low? And why? Because he was jealous that she was laughing with Tom?

If ever there was proof that he needed to leave here at first light, this was it. Rebecca would hate him now, if she did not before. The damage done this afternoon had just been reinforced by his own jealous stupidity.

"Is that not so, my dear?" His mother leaned across the table to gain his attention.

"I am sorry Mother, I did not quite catch that."

"I was telling Mrs. Davids how sorry you are to have to leave tomorrow."

"Indeed. Very sorry. But urgent business calls me to Town I am afraid."

Rebecca, who had been chatting with Mr. Crawford heard the dowager announce Hartridge's leaving. Her head snapped up. Leaving? She listened carefully to his answer. Tomorrow? He was leaving tomorrow? She felt a stab of disappointment, which was ridiculous. She hated him!.

And, wasn't Rebecca herself planning on leaving for London just as soon as her father could make arrangements? Though she did not want to clap eyes on him while she was there.

London was filled with enough people that they could happily avoid each other, though they would attend much of the same functions.

So it should not make a difference to her when he left. It *did not* make a difference.

"Is your whole party to leave, your grace?" Caroline asked the dowager in a small voice. Rebecca felt Mr. Crawford tense beside her at Caroline's question.

The dowager answered, "No, my dear. I have so wished to visit you all for so long. Tom has been kind enough to offer to stay behind for the duration of my visit."

"How wonderful," Caroline answered weakly. Rebecca frowned. Between Caroline's reaction and Mr. Crawdon's statue-like posture beside her when Caroline had spoken, she felt something very strange was going on here.

"We shall be joining you in London this Season too, my lady," the earl announced, his tone still not as jovial as before but sounding a little less angry.

"Indeed?"

"Yes, Rebecca has decided to hunt for a husband!"

For Heaven's sake! Her father was the least subtle man in the realm.

The earl was cut short by the sound of choking to his right. It seemed the duke had swallowed something that did not agree with him.

"Good heavens man! Are you alright?"

Hartridge took a long drink of wine before apologising.

"Pray forgive me sir, I must have bitten off more than I

could chew."

This earned an unladylike snort from Rebecca, which in turned earned another angry glare from Caroline. And her father. Best she stayed quiet. She risked a quick glance at Hartridge and found his eyes boring into her. His face was rigid and his jaw clenched as if he was struggling to stay in control. He was probably disappointed that an ocean would not be separating them for long after all.

"Do continue, Charles," the dowager urged excitedly, "are you really to come to London for the Season?"

"So it would seem," the earl continued, "Rebecca has gotten it into her head to settle down, and now that Caroline and Edward have decided against each other, we may as well launch the both of them." Her father had never exactly been renowned for his tact.

"But this is wonderful," the dowager exclaimed. "My dears, you will be the toast of the Town!"

Caroline stared at Rebecca from across the table. Rebecca hadn't had a chance to confide her wishes to her older sister. And judging from their father's announcement Caroline was now to seek a husband, whether she wanted to or not.

Rebecca leaned forward and spoke as low as possible, "I am sorry I did not get a chance to speak to you Caroline, I hadn't thought that father would expect you to come too, unless you wanted to."

Caroline looked down at her lap and kept her head bowed for a moment and Rebecca wondered if she was truly terribly upset by the idea but then Caro's head raised and she fixed a determined smile on her face.

"I think it is a wonderful idea. We must both marry, mustn't we? Why not go and see what London has to offer?"

Rebecca could not help but feel that something else was going on in Caro's head but now was not the time to question her. The dowager, her mother and Mrs. Davids were chattering excitedly about balls, soirees and London wardrobes; her father was discussing his plans to open up the Townhouse with the vicar and none of them seemed to be paying attention to the tension emanating from Rebecca, Hartridge, Caroline and, strangely, Mr. Crawford.

The atmosphere was as untenable as it was confusing and Rebecca just wanted the night to be over.

****

Edward listened to the buzz of conversation around the table but he could not drag his eyes from Rebecca's face. She was coming to London, would be attending functions with him all Season. Well, perhaps not *with* him but in the same room as him!

And she was on the hunt for a husband?

He wanted to punch something.

This was all his fault. He had antagonised her. Insulted her. And now he would have to watch her marry some dandy, no doubt.

His jaw clenched even harder until he thought his teeth would disintegrate. Who amongst the *ton* would be good enough for Rebecca? Those with the right lineage would bore her to tears. And the ones who were not boring were downright dangerous.

It was ridiculous! Rebecca no more wanted a husband than he did! What the hell was she going to do? Stifle all that personality by becoming a proper society wife? Or have her heart broken and fortune stolen by a rake?

She would not even look at him.

In total exasperation he looked across the table to Lady Caroline. Judging by the earl's announcement, that lady had not even been consulted. Perhaps she would be able to disabuse her younger sister of the notion to marry. But Caroline looked as miserable as he felt, and decidedly caught up in her own thoughts.

And hadn't he heard her tell Rebecca that she *liked* the idea? Well, she would be no help!

Help in what? Edward almost cursed aloud as that damned voice popped into his head yet again. It always appeared at the worst times and it never said anything he wanted to hear.

Help in stopping Lady Rebecca from marrying? Why would he stop her from marrying someone else? Was he going to marry her himself?

He hesitated as his mind threw up images of what it would be like having Lady Rebecca as a wife. But his mind wasn't much use since the only images it was throwing up were not images he should be conjuring in front of her parents.

He had no intentions of marrying her. She was unsuitable. She climbed statues for God's sake. And he did not love her. He could not. No, Rebecca did not suit.

So then, what was it that he wanted? Lady Rebecca to remain unattached because he did not want to see her married to someone else? Yet, having no intentions towards her, did he want her to be a spinster? Forever alone? No, he did not want that either. It was unfair. She deserved a life filled with love. And passion.

Do not think about passion, he warned himself! *Not in a room full of people.*

Dear God this Season would be excruciating. Standing idly by, watching men throw themselves at her until she picked one and walked out of his life forever? Perhaps they'd meet at social occasions, her on the arm of her husband and he forever lusting after someone unattainable?

"No."

Oh wonderful. He'd just bellowed 'no' aloud. He'd finally taken leave of his senses.

His outburst brought a shocked ending to the buzz of conversation. Edward needed to think of something fast.

"No doubt," he recovered addressing the earl, though

how he would finish the sentence he'd started was beyond him. Plus, since he'd started off shouting he felt the need to continue in an excruciatingly loud voice. "No doubt you — er — will be wanting someone to keep an eye on the ladies at the functions you are unable to attend, Ranford."

What in damnation was he saying?

A quick glance down the table confirmed that everyone was mightily confused by this rather random statement.

"Well," began the earl hesitantly, "their mother will be there to sponsor them, naturally."

"Yes, of course."

There was a pause while Edward continued to rack his brain.

"But, between you and me sir," he leaned forward conspiratorially. The rest of the party leaned forward too.

"You are a man of the world, as am I. I think we both know that there will be a certain type of gentleman most desirous of company with your daughters."

What was he saying?

"What's he saying?" hissed Rebecca to Mr. Crawford only to be shushed by his flapping hand.

"I am listening," he whispered.

The earl looked gravely at the young duke.

"Yes, yes I suppose you are right."

Edward inwardly breathed a sigh of relief. At least the older man thought he had genuinely meant to shout 'No' at him and hadn't had some sort of episode at the dinner table.

"I have no doubt your excellent wife is more than capable of bringing the girls out. However, I believe it would be prudent to have a gentleman escort the girls to functions and keep an eye on them, so to speak. When you are not attending functions yourself, that is."

Had he really just volunteered to be a nanny to the ladies Carrington?

"A capitol idea, dear fellow," the earl beamed. "I will feel much more comfortable knowing that you will be looking after the girls' interests. Need to keep those who would take advantage of them in dark corners away, eh?"

Edward decided not to dwell overly long on the fact that, to his knowledge, the only man who had accosted either of the earl's daughters in a dark corner was him!

Instead he smiled weakly and was left to contemplate exactly how stupid or insane a man had to be to offer to watch over the very lady he wanted more than anything in this world while she set about picking someone else to spend her life with.

Chapter Twelve

Rebecca could not sleep. No matter how hard she tried, she tossed and turned but she did not sleep. Despite her best efforts, she could not get her mind to stop whirring, throwing up thoughts about London, the marriage mart and, mostly, Edward.

She whispered his name. It sounded right on her lips. And he'd told her to use it, though she would not dare to outside the sanctuary of her room.

Her heart stung a little at his offer to escort her to functions. He knew that she was intending to find a husband and was obviously so unaffected by it that he was going to *help* her find a decent one!

Well, what did she expect? There was nothing between them save a stolen kiss and his low opinion of her. To be fair, he'd seen her at her worst. Twice. His opinion had been formed.

And what did Rebecca care for his opinion anyway? He meant nothing to her.

Sighing in frustration she stepped out of bed and slipped on a robe to cover her flimsy nightrail. Perhaps a book from the library would help to soothe her mind.

She slipped quietly from the room, instinctively avoiding the floorboards that creaked loudest and hurried down the stairs.

Tiptoeing into the library, Rebecca noticed with some surprise that a lantern was already burning low in the room. Usually the servants were more diligent. Still, she was grateful for the extra light. She turned it up to better illuminate the room, then took her candle to scour the shelves.

Her mind however, wasn't on her task and she skimmed the titles without really seeing them.

"Looking for something in particular?"

Rebecca whipped round at the sound of the low voice behind her and let out a terrified scream.

Without thought to her actions she flung the candle she was holding at the person who'd spoken and scared the wits out of her.

The flame thankfully flickered out mid-flight and there was a rather sickening *thump* as the candleholder met its mark.

The ensuing string of expletives, some of which sounded as though they were in a different language, confirmed what Rebecca fearfully suspected. She had, once again, attacked and injured the Duke of Hartridge.

"Bloody hell woman. Are you insane?" His voice was no more than a loud whisper but she could hear the anger embedded in it and it made her temper flare in response.

"Am *I* insane? What are you doing creeping up behind people in the middle of the night?" Rebecca bit back equally quietly but ferociously nonetheless.

The whispering, however, seemed futile. Since she'd screamed blue murder not two minutes ago and nobody had come to her aid!

"I am not creeping up behind you, my lady," he sniffed haughtily. "Besides, I was here first," he finished rather childishly, rubbing his shoulder — presumably where her weapon had hit.

"Why are you still up?" she demanded.

"Why are *you* still up?" he countered.

She sighed and relented. After all, they were not getting very far standing here bickering, yet again, like children.

"I could not sleep," she answered stiffly. She could be civil but did not have to be happy about it.

"Excited about the prospect of your new husband are you?" he sneered.

And just like that her temper peaked yet again.

"Your grace," she bit, managing to make the address sound like an insult, "you have made your opinion of me painfully clear. You have strived to humiliate me in front of both my family and yours and you have insulted me in every way imaginable. You do not like me. I understand. You have made it abundantly clear. So why do you persist in speaking to me? Why do you care about whether or not I wish to have a husband? What does it matter to you?"

Her chest heaved by the end of her speech, so caught up in her anger was she. She was glorious in her anger.

Edward stood stock still, shock and something she could not define stamped on his arrogant face.

"You think I do not *like* you?" he eventually choked out. He laughed but there was no humour in it.

"Trust me, my lady," his voice was low and slid over her jangled nerves causing her to shiver, "*not* liking you is not the problem."

"Then what is?" she could not help but ask.

He stared at her for so long Rebecca thought he would not answer. He took a step closer so that there were mere inches between them.

Suddenly, it seemed as though the temperature in the room shot up and Rebecca felt the now familiar stirrings he had awakened in her.

Slowly, so slowly, he lifted a hand and grazed his

knuckles softly down her cheek. His eyes, a darker grey now, like the sky before a storm breaks, bored into hers and held her captive. She could not have moved away had her life depended on it.

"The problem is," he eventually spoke, "that I like you too damn much."

And as his lips plundered her own Rebecca thought desperately that they appeared to be suffering from the same problem.

Edward kissed her as though his very life depended on it. At that moment, he felt like it did.

He pulled her closer and felt, with some satisfaction, her arms reach up and wind around his neck. He felt like he could kiss her forever. His tongue slipped out to taste her lips and he took full advantage of her gasp by slipping inside to taste her properly.

He could not help the groan of pure lust that escaped him as he plundered her mouth. Dear God, had anyone ever been so consumed by just one kiss?

He hadn't meant for this to happen. He'd intended to keep his distance. Had tried to. Had sat in this very room for hours trying to numb his emotions, emotions he wasn't ready to examine.

But he hadn't been able to stop his mind from wandering. And always to Rebecca. To her smile, her eyes, her body. Her wit, her laugh. The woman was haunting him.

And when he wasn't thinking all of these pleasant things about her, he was driving himself insane with thoughts of her in London flirting and dancing with other men. Other men holding her like this, kissing her like this.

And then, worst of all, her marrying someone. Someone whom he was sure would not be good enough to be her husband. Someone whose hands held her supple body, moulded her shape to his own, just as Edward was doing now.

The jealousy that coursed through his veins caused him

to pull her closer yet, to lift her into his body, to let her feel what she did to *him*. His hands roamed the contours of her body, made so much more accessible by the flimsy cotton that covered her shape now.

He remembered how she'd looked with her dress plastered to her like a second skin. And now he felt it and it seared his soul. He would never have enough of her. Never.

But he must. The lady wasn't his.

The thought was like being doused in cold water and pulled him abruptly back from the point of no return. His control was hanging by the merest thread and he was closer to the breaking point than he had ever been.

He broke the embrace and held himself away from her, gripping her shoulders when it looked like she might stumble.

The sight of her standing in front of him, wide eyed and looking thoroughly kissed nearly brought him to his knees. Her robe had come undone during their embrace and the flimsy nightrail she wore did little to disguise her curves. And her hair, that glorious hair he'd had fantasies about since he'd arrived, flowed down her back like a river of mahogany satin, framing her face and making him wish he could see it spread out on the crisp white sheets on his bed. He could have wept. The temptation to pull her back to him was all encompassing.

With herculean effort, he spun away from her and paced to the other side of the room. Distance was needed. Distance and brandy.

He walked to the end table where he'd been drowning his sorrows and poured himself another healthy measure. He turned and silently offered her the same by holding up the bottle. To his surprise she nodded her assent. Neither had yet spoken a word.

Making his way back across the room to her, he handed her the glass of amber liquid before downing his own, doing all he could to stop his eyes from raking her body and his hands from touching her.

The silence stretched on. Rebecca, unsure of what to say and still feeling shaken to her core by the power of his kiss, gulped back the contents of the glass. The amber liquid burned a trail down her throat and caused her to cough and splutter in a most alarming manner.

"My God." Edward was by her side in an instant, clapping her back in what he assumed was a helpful manner but what was really rather *un*helpful. And sore.

He led her to the chaise he'd been sprawled on when she'd entered the library and sat her down.

Eventually, Rebecca got the coughing under control, though tears continued to stream down her face, which was now flushed though from the brandy or the near choking, he could not tell.

"Are you alright?" he asked gently, grasping her hands and hunkering in front of her.

"Yes, quite thank you," she rasped, her voice made hoarse from the exertion.

"When was the last time you drank brandy, Rebecca?"

"Never."

"*Never?*" he repeated amazed. "And for your first taste you decide to gulp it like a drunkard?"

She smiled ruefully and shrugged her delicate shoulders. "I rather thought I needed it."

He returned her smile with a rueful one of his own and let go of her hands to sit beside her. Rebecca tried not to feel disappointed at the loss of contact.

Edward heaved a sigh before turning to face her.

"I am sorry for my behaviour," he muttered, trying his damndest not to be distracted by the glimpse of skin at the neckline of her attire or the way the light from the lantern shot her hair through with a blazing red.

"Which part?" she quipped.

He smiled wryly. "I deserve that. I've been a cad. For all of it, really. I haven't exactly been a gentleman."

"And why is that, your grace? You who is the epitome of a gentleman if everything I've heard of you is to be believed."

"The epitome of a gentleman?"

"Indeed. Or so I was told before your arrival here."

He frowned. For some reason, that description did not sit well with him. It made him sound — well — boring. But then, hadn't that been exactly what he was since his father's demise? Never putting a foot wrong. Never doing anything without thinking it through methodically, logically. Never stepping outside the role of duke for one second… until her.

"What can I say? I've never felt the need to act like anything less than a gentleman. Until I met you."

Her eyes widened before she lowered them to her lap demurely.

Rebecca's breath hitched. He really should not say those things. It was most improper. As was the thrill that shot through her when he did.

She risked a quick glance at him and found him staring at her again with that expression on his face, one she could not quite decipher but which made her feel hot and tingly and scared, all at once.

"I should return to my bed," Rebecca said softly and was annoyed to hear the tremble in her voice.

"As should I. I have an early start."

At the mention of his leaving, Rebecca's stomach lurched. She did not want to want him to stay. She wanted to be as furious with him as she had been earlier today. But he'd apologised. More than that, he'd kissed her. And now she could not help wanting things that were, frankly, dangerous and impossible.

She needed to remove herself from this room and from him. An apology, though very nice, did not really change anything.

"Ah yes. Your urgent business in Town. I do hope it is nothing too serious. After all, you have kindly volunteered to take Caroline and me under your wing, remember?"

He muttered a couple more choice words before answering.

"That was an accident."

"An accident, your grace?"

"Your grace?"

She blushed slightly and he had to grip the seat to stop himself from reaching for her.

"Hartridge," she amended.

He waited, one eyebrow raised haughtily.

"Fine. Edward," she huffed.

He smiled in triumph. "As much as being around you gives me more pleasure than it should, I cannot say I am looking forward to the task."

"Why ever not?" she asked curiously, "It was your idea, was it not?"

"Yes it was. Curse my mouth."

Her eyebrows rose slightly and, though he knew he should keep things distant and aloof, he felt that he owed her an explanation. Especially in light of his terrible behaviour.

"You are young and innocent Rebecca. You do not yet realise the impact you have on any normal, red-blooded male. I will have my work cut out for me fighting them off in London. With you *and* your sister."

"Oh." Her voice was barely more than a whisper. "Well, we do not wish to give you more work."

He chuckled softly.

And then, because he could not help it, he touched her face, placing a finger under her chin and raising it until she looked at him.

"It is not the work I am worried about, sweetheart. It is stopping myself tearing from limb to limb any man who even looks at you."

Rebecca did not know what to say. Nor did she move, trapped by him, by his words, his scent, his presence, everything.

He leaned forward and kissed her tenderly. Not like the passionate embraces they'd had thus far, but a soft brush of his lips against hers.

"Goodnight, my lady" he whispered against her lips. And then he was gone.

Rebecca made her way slowly up the stairs and to her room. She'd forgotten to take a book but it was of no matter now. Nothing now would be able to take her mind off Edward.

She walked as if in a trance. Her mind and heart focused on one thing and one alone— he'd called her sweetheart.

Chapter Thirteen

The next couple of weeks passed in a blur of planning, packing and, much to the earl's despair— shopping.

A trip to London for a Season was not a matter to be taken lightly. Particularly when you had not one, but two daughters hoping to make an impact.

The dowager and countess were in fits of happiness choosing gowns and events with military precision. Caroline grew more excited as the days went on. And Rebecca did too, though she had not been able to shake the strange *ennui* that had come on since Edward's departure.

Try as she might she could not put from her mind that last night in her father's library. It felt like something had shifted between them. Like they'd crossed an invisible line and had made things all the more complicated.

Rebecca found herself wishing she'd never asked to go to London. She could not imagine Edward escorting her to balls and soirees knowing that she was there to search for a husband. The things he'd said, the way he kissed her; it made her feel like perhaps she was coming to mean something to him. And yet, what could it mean, really?

He did not profess to love her and she certainly did not love him. Of course not. Besides which, all the old problems still existed. Rebecca Carrington was far from fit to be a duchess!

Nothing had changed. Not really.

She resolved to put Edward from her mind once and for all and concentrate on what was needed for the great move to London.

The day after Edward had left, the ladies had made a trip to Dublin and sought out their favourite mantua maker and now, just days before they were due to set off, their purchases had arrived. Rebecca knew the poor woman must have worked day and night to have readied so many gowns in so little time. But the Carringtons were one of the leading families in the country and when the countess wanted something, she got it!

There was much excitement at the breakfast table that morning.

The earl had listened ruefully to the excited chatter before turning to Mr. Crawdon.

"A day for a hunt I think, Mr. Crawdon?"

"An excellent idea, my lord," answered Tom with considerable enthusiasm.

The gentlemen bid them good day and made a swift escape and the ladies retired to their rooms to re-examine the gowns they'd purchased and make last minute arrangements.

The morning was a flurry of excitement — gowns, ribbons, bonnets, gloves and on and on until Rebecca's head spun with it.

The excitement was infectious and even the servants were caught up in it. Rebecca barely thought of Edward or the prospect of a husband. She looked forward to the sights they would see, the parties they would attend and, admittedly, the fabulous gowns they would wear.

The ladies shared a light nuncheon before returning to

their packing and Rebecca and Maura had settled down to some last minute sewing when a commotion sounded in the entrance hall.

Rebecca glanced at Maura in confusion before they both ran to see what was going on.

There was pandemonium down below. Footmen scarpered here and there and Mr. Crawdon stood in the centre barking directions. What on earth was going on?

Rebecca rushed to the top of the stairs at the same time as Caroline and her maid, Betsy, arrived.

Her mother and the dowager shortly appeared from the morning room on the left.

"Mr. Crawdon, what are you about?" Rebecca shouted down.

Her cry drew his attention. She could see that he was deathly pale.

"My ladies," he answered turning his attention to Caroline and then to the dowager and countess, "I am afraid I have some bad news. Lord Ranford, he has taken sick."

"What?"

"We were hunting and he complained of a malady with his chest." The ladies stared in horror as he continued with his tale. "We started to ride back at once but—"

He was interrupted by the arrival of several footmen carrying what appeared to be a heavy sack. Rebecca felt the room spin alarmingly when she realised the sack was her father. And he wasn't moving.

The countess screamed and promptly had a fit of the vapours. Caroline burst into tears and Mr. Crawdon was shouting above the din that someone should go for a doctor.

Rebecca felt sick at the sights and sounds surrounding her.

"My lady" —Maura had clasped her hand— "are you well?"

Rebecca took a steadying breath and took in the scene

once more. She would be no good to anyone, least of all her father, if she were to swoon now. In the absence of their brother Charles, who was still at Oxford and would likely spend the Season in London, being something of a man about town, and given that her mother and Caroline were currently indisposed, it fell to Rebecca to take control of the situation.

"I am well, Maura." Her voice shook alarmingly but she forced herself to stay calm and gradually felt less dizzy.

Rebecca marched over to Caroline and pulled her into a quick hug.

"Come, Caro. We must help Mama." Guiding her older sister by the shoulders, she rushed down the stairs.

"Murphy," she called to the usually unflappable butler who was looking decidedly uneasy at this moment. "Have them put my father in his study. The chaise there should be big enough for him. And loosen his cravat."

"You there," she pointed to a footman who was hovering by the door, "fetch the doctor immediately."

"Your grace," she lowered her tone in deference to the older lady who was kneeling by her mother's prostate form. Mama had not yet succumbed to a dead faint but did not seem far off. "Please accompany my mother to her room. I shall come directly."

"Of course, my dear," the dowager moved immediately, coaxing the countess from the floor and instructing the lady's maid to go on ahead of them.

"Maura, please fetch the smelling salts and bring them to my mother's room along with some strong, sweet tea. She will want to see my father soon but must calm herself first."

Maura bobbed a quick curtsey and went on her way.

Rebecca took a fortifying breath. She had not even looked properly at her father yet, but felt a little better having taken some control of the situation.

She turned to address Caroline and was, for a moment, struck dumb by the sight before her. Caroline was still weeping, though silently now and Mr. Crawdon was holding her in a tight embrace, his lips close to her ear murmuring something that Rebecca could not hear.

What shocked Rebecca was the intimacy of the pose. Mr. Crawdon looked *pained* by Caroline's distress and Rebecca could not help but feel that she was witnessing a private moment. But it was far from private; they were in the entrance hall for goodness sake.

"Caroline," she called gently and her voice seemed to pull both Caroline and Mr. Crawdon back to their senses. They jumped apart and Caroline looked even more distressed.

"Caro," Rebecca repeated, "I am going to sit with Papa until the doctor arrives. Perhaps you can check on Mama?"

Caroline nodded her assent mutely and, studiously avoiding making eye contact with either of them, she swept off to assist the countess.

Rebecca did not have the time or inclination to question Mr. Crawdon about his rather familiar behaviour. Her mind was wholly occupied with her father.

She set off toward the study with Mr. Crawdon falling into step beside her.

"Allow me to say, Lady Rebecca, you would be a great asset as a military general! I've rarely seen a person bark orders with so much authority, certainly not a person who does not come past my shoulder," he quipped.

Rebecca allowed herself a small smile.

"I am my father's daughter in many ways, Mr. Crawdon," she answered lightly, then immediately sobered. "Please, tell me exactly what happened."

"Truly, my lady, I do not know. He complained of pain as I said and, on the ride back he — he just slumped over. He almost came off his horse but thankfully we were close to the house and the footmen who accompanied us were able to support him while I rode ahead to raise the alarm."

They had reached the study and both slipped inside

quietly. Murphy had done as he was instructed and her father lay tucked under an array of blankets on the large and comfortable chaise under the window.

Rebecca felt ill again looking at his deathly still form. His breathing was terribly shallow and she'd never seen anyone look so pale.

She felt tears spring to her eyes as she made her way slowly to his side and dropped to her knees, grasping his hand. It was freezing.

Behind her, Rebecca heard Caroline and her mother enter the room. The countess came immediately to her side and Rebecca moved away to allow her mother to take her place.

She turned back and noticed that, although he wasn't now touching her, Mr. Crawdon had moved to her sister's side and was standing protectively over her.

It made Rebecca yearn for someone to watch over her, protect her. Her mind threw up an image of Edward and she nearly sobbed aloud. She knew that if he'd been there he would have made everything better. Just having his commanding presence in the house would have made her feel safer and less scared.

None of them knew what to do or how to help. So they stood in silence, keeping vigil until the doctor's arrival.

That man thankfully came soon after. The countess rushed to the door and out into the hall before he'd even removed his hat.

"Dr. Austin, please follow me."

The doctor came immediately to the study and having glanced briefly at his patient, turned and shooed everyone from the room save the countess who would not be budged, and Murphy who would offer assistance.

Rebecca stood outside with Caroline, their hands firmly clasped.

"My ladies," Mr. Crawdon spoke quietly, "please allow me to escort you to the drawing room and have something brought to you. Some sweet tea, or a glass of wine perhaps? To help with the shock."

They consented for there was little point in standing in the hallway. Making sure a footman knew to come directly when the doctor had left, they made their way to the drawing room where they found the dowager had already called for tea things.

She fussed over the sisters and Mr. Crawdon did all he could for their comfort.

But silence soon ensued broken every now and then by a reassurance from the duchess or Mr. Crawdon. Rebecca noticed that his gaze focused most of the time on Caroline.

He had the same brooding expression as his cousin, Rebecca noticed distractedly. Their looks were vastly different, though both exuded a maleness and strength that was hard to find in other men. But where Mr. Crawdon's demeanour was always sunny and rarely as serious as it was now, the duke's was more brooding, and much more serious.

Rebecca's eyes took in Mr. Crawdon's crystal blue gaze trained on Caroline and his ever so slightly too long, sandy hair streaked with blond. She smiled in spite of the grave situation. Edward's hair would never dare to be over long! It had probably stopped growing altogether for fear of his displeasure.

At that moment Caroline's gaze found Mr. Crawdon's and he smiled tenderly, offering comfort in his expression.

Rebecca looked away to glance out at the lake she'd fallen into on that most memorable of days. Mr. Crawdon appeared to be enamoured of her sister. It was a shame. Caroline would never marry a gentleman who was not titled. She probably would not be allowed to. Their parents were wonderful people but very much believed in traditional Society rules.

Just as Rebecca could never be a duchess, Caroline could never be less than one, or at the very least less than a countess.

Rebecca looked back and could not help the envy she felt

knowing that Caroline had a pillar of strength waiting for her to want him.

She yearned for Edward with an intensity that shocked her once again.

The door opened and Rebecca and Caroline jumped to their feet. But it was not a footman who entered. Their mother came in looking pale and older than her years.

Rebecca's heart clenched in abject fear at the tears streaking her mother's face.

But the countess smiled and held out her arms to her two daughters.

"He is going to be just fine my dears. All is well."

Chapter Fourteen

As soon as the countess was settled with a snifter of brandy, Mr. Crawdon had insisted they all needed something stronger than tea, she told them what had occurred with Doctor Austin.

"Murphy is arranging to have your father removed to his rooms. Doctor Austin said complete bed rest is absolutely vital for the coming weeks."

"But what happened Mama?" Rebecca gripped her mother's hand tightly.

"He had a heart attack, dearest," the countess replied gently. "We must ensure now that he is given total relaxation, a stricter diet and an altogether healthier lifestyle."

Rebecca and Caroline nodded in agreement, all the while trying to process the information that their father, a giant in their eyes, had been taken so very ill in so short a time.

"But, he will make a full recovery?" the dowager enquired softly.

"Doctor Austin sees no reason why he should not, so long as we follow his instructions to the letter."

The party lapsed into silence borne mostly from

emotional exhaustion the past hour had inflicted on them.

"May we see him, Mama?" Caroline asked anxiously.

"Of course, my dear. Just give Murphy a chance to speak to Stevens, his valet," she explained to Mr. Crawdon and her grace, "and get him settled into his room. A half hour should suffice. Though I warn you he has had laudanum so will likely be in a deep sleep for the rest of the evening."

"I suppose that we should use the time then to speak to the servants and have our trunks unpacked," stated Rebecca making her way to ring the bell and call for a maid.

"Goodness me, I had quite forgotten we were to leave. Of course we will need to cancel our arrangements immediately."

"Do not distress yourself, Mama. I will speak to the staff at once and Cook must be informed that the family will be here after all, lest we all starve." Rebecca tried to lighten the mood. In truth, she felt such relief that her father was going to be fine it made her almost giddy.

Not travelling to London was not the end of the world. There would always be next year when Papa was stronger. Rebecca tried not to think about the duke and the fact that she would not be seeing him again as she had thought.

The door opened and Rebecca asked the young girl who entered to send Murphy to them directly when he had finished with Stevens and her father's needs.

"Mary," the dowager spoke up, "if I might speak with you for a moment in private?"

The younger occupants of the room, somewhat surprised at the dowager's uncharacteristic impoliteness, immediately made to leave.

The countess looked equally surprised and bid Rebecca to stay in her room so that she may summon her when Murphy collected the staff to deal with the announcement. Rebecca was much like her father in that she was a born leader. Charles would be the same. Caroline had taken after Lady Ranford in that she was quiet and, although efficient, wasn't given to taking a leadership role in anything.

Rebecca nodded her agreement and swept from the room with Caroline and Mr. Crawdon. Crawdon took his leave directly, explaining his intention to write to the duke and inform him of the change of plan. He felt, and was probably correct, that the dowager would extend her stay to offer assistance or even merely a shoulder to cry on for her old friends.

Rebecca and Caroline, not wanting to be alone and craving the sibling bond, had both repaired to Rebecca's room. Though they were disappointed about the cancellation of their plans, both were ready to do so without a second thought.

As soon as the young people had left the room, Lady Hartridge leaned over and grasped her old friend's hand in hers.

"My dearest Mary, I cannot tell you how pleased I am that Charles will pull through. What a fright he gave us all."

Lady Ranford shuddered at the memory of her husband's still form being carried in.

"Indeed, I have never been so frightened. Rebecca handled things beautifully, did she not?"

"Unsurprisingly," replied the dowager, "that girl could rule the world."

The countess smiled proudly. No doubt Rebecca had caused more headaches in this household than every other occupant combined, but she was a treasure.

"What was it that you needed to speak with me about, Catherine?"

"Ah, you mean when I was rude enough to demand your own daughters leave them room?" the dowager quipped.

The countess merely smiled and awaited the answer.

"Of course Charles will not be travelling now, and nor will you I warrant. And nobody could or would expect you too. However, I would like to still take the girls to Town for the Season."

The countess gaped at her old friend. "Catherine, that is excessively kind. However I do not think—"

"Hear me out, please. Before you decide. I realise that your mind is wholly occupied with Charles at present. And, of course, the girls probably would not even want to have a Season now. But, Charles is in no serious danger if Doctor Austin is correct and there is no reason to suppose he is not. All of the preparations have been made. And, if you will permit me to speak candidly, your daughters are a true joy though perhaps they are not as — er — *relaxing* to be around as some."

The dowager awaited her friend's reaction. She meant no slight on the young ladies of whom she'd become excessively fond. But there was no denying that the youngest in particular was quite a handful at times.

Her description of the girls seemed to set the countess thinking.

"The house would certainly be quieter," Lady Mary started hesitantly.

The dowager nodded but stayed quiet.

"And, though I would miss them, I have no real *need* for them to stay. We are more than capable of seeing to Charles' needs."

"You would not be too lonely?"

"Oh no, think nothing of that. I have plenty of friends who will not remove for the summer."

A silence fell while the countess thought on the proposal.

"Charles would dearly love to see them married," she finally said. "And I am sure my son could be prevailed upon to stay in our house in Mayfair with the girls. He usually takes rooms for himself if he prefers not to return home."

Again, the dowager nodded but did not comment, wanting to allow her friend to make her own decision.

"I am not sure that he would be a suitable chaperone for the girls, however. He certainly is not as responsible as I'd like him to be, though his youth plays a large part in that."

"Of course," answered the dowager, "but I confess, I had thought that perhaps the girls could stay with me for the duration."

"Oh Catherine, you are too generous! I could not expect you to take on full responsibility for two ladies' coming outs. Especially when one of them is Rebecca," she added drily.

The dowager laughed aloud at this.

"What nonsense! They would liven the place up. And there could be no impropriety as Edward occupies his own townhouse. I would appreciate the company. And Rebecca, for all her *energy* is vastly entertaining. I think we would rub along quite well together."

The countess began to see the merits in the plan.

It would no doubt ease Charles' mind to see at least one of his children married off. And she did so hate to disappoint her girls quite literally at the last moment. After all, they had been due to leave at first light.

She trusted her friend implicitly and had already had the duke's assurances that he would help to keep them safe.

Plus, Charles would be there. Though she presumed he would return home first when he received word of his father's sickness, he was sure to return to London for at least some of the Season.

All in all it seemed a good idea.

Her mind made up, she smiled at her friend and said "Thank you, dearest Catherine. I should love the girls to go with you."

****

Dinner that night was a solemn affair, though Mr. Crawdon did his utmost to keep the tone jovial.

The earl had not woken yet from his deep sleep, but Doctor Austin had convinced the ladies that this was perfectly normal and, indeed, a good thing. He had returned home for a few hours' respite but was returning to spend the night and would be a constant presence at the Hall, should the earl need him.

However, aside from the worry about the earl's health, there was the standoff that Rebecca and her mother were currently engaged in.

Rebecca and Caroline had not long repaired to Rebecca's room to await their Mama when the countess swept it and announced that they were still to travel to London the next day, and were to remain in London for the Season with the dowager duchess.

They protested immediately and loudly, neither one willing to leave their father while he was so ill, or leave their mother to deal with his sickness alone.

"My darling girls," the countess had done her best to appease them, "I have already written to your brother and had the note dispatched this very afternoon. I am quite confident that he will return home with haste when he reads our news. Not only that but it will give your father and I great pleasure to know that you are enjoying your Seasons, and putting yourselves into the path of marriageable young men."

"Do you not see?" the dowager, who had accompanied their mother piped in, "your father's greatest wish for you both is for you to make a good match. Think how pleased he would be, how *relaxed* he would be to know that you were out there, pursuing a marriage, putting his mind at ease..." she finished coaxingly, her impassioned plea seeming more than a little contrived to Rebecca, who suspected it had been rehearsed.

Caroline immediately looked shame faced and went to the countess to grasp her hands.

"Oh Mama, I feel this is all my fault. If the duke and I had agreed to the contract, perhaps Papa would have been less stressed. I shall go to London with her grace and endeavour to make you and Papa proud."

Rebecca, however, eyed the dowager with a sceptical expression.

"If I may be so bold, your grace, you would have made an admirable career on the stage," she quipped.

The countess and Caroline gasped at her affront but the dowager laughed aloud.

"We shall get on famously, you and me," was her answer.

Rebecca could not help but smile at the cunning matriarch.

She heaved a sigh. "Caro, do not blame yourself. You are not to blame. I think we can all agree that if any one of us was going to drive poor Papa to a heart attack, it would be me."

Caroline smiled wanly at her, but Rebecca noticed, she did not actually argue with her.

"It seems my sister has fallen victim to your blackmail scheme, your grace," she turned once again to the dowager and was suddenly struck by a likeness between her and her son. Everyone said that he was the very image of his late father but there was definitely a striking familiarity there now. Perhaps it was the look of self-satisfaction, Rebecca thought ruefully.

"And you?" the dowager asked.

Rebecca looked to her mother. The countess smiled and said, "It is my wish that you do this Rebecca."

Oh marvellous.

She looked to Caroline who whispered, "Please Becca."

"I do not wish to leave Father while he is so ill, Mama."

"I promise to keep you fully informed. If anything changes I shall write direct. Besides, with plenty of rest he may be able to make the journey for the end of the Season."

Rebecca had to admit that she had been looking forward to seeing London in all its glory and to seeing Edward again. She felt such pangs of guilt though, at the thought of her father bedridden and her mother alone.

The countess, as if sensing her conflict, grasped her by the shoulders. "Her grace is right, Rebecca, though I am sure she meant it only to lighten the atmosphere. It will give your father great comfort to know that both you and your sister are endeavouring to make good matches. I know it will be hard to leave him, to leave us. But it is our dearest wish."

Eventually Rebecca had relented though somewhat grudgingly.

****

Since Mr. Crawford was the only male at dinner that night, he chose to retire to the earl's study for his port and cheroot.

The ladies retired to the music room where Rebecca and Caroline played until the tea things came.

They made idle chit chat but nobody's mind was really on the conversation, a mixture of excitement for tomorrow, worry for the earl and guilt for leaving in the first place swirling through the ladies.

Rebecca made her excuses as soon as was polite and was unsurprised to hear Caroline follow in her wake.

She readied herself for bed dismissing Maura and instructing her to get some sleep for the early start tomorrow.

Soon she would be in London. Soon she would be with the duke again. She wondered what the Season would hold for them all.

Chapter Fifteen

The day dawned bright and clear and Rebecca rose with the larks. She was filled with nervous tension. The reigning feeling was one of excitement. What would the Season hold for her? How would things develop between her and Edward? She was feeling much better about leaving having spent some time with her father last night.

The earl had woken for a brief few moments and the girls had rushed to see him. Though he was weak and frail, he was able to reassure his daughters that he wasn't quite ready to shuffle off this mortal coil just yet, and tell them that he was excessively pleased about them continuing with their plans to travel to London.

It would be some hours before the rest of the household rose. They were due to set off directly after breakfast.

Rebecca pulled the drapes and looked across her father's lands, still crowned with dew drops and glistening in the weak morning sun. Spring was her favourite time of the year. Not cold enough to be confined to indoors and not yet stifling warm.

Thinking of the long hours before breakfast, Rebecca

decided a ride through the grounds would be just the thing to settle her jangling nerves. After donning her old, chocolate brown riding habit and hat in record time, she quickly made her way to the stables. Her new, deep red velvet habit was already packed away and she could not wait to wear it, but wasn't going to risk ruining it on the muddy ground before getting the chance to show it off.

She would be leaving her beloved horse at home for the duration of their stay in London. The dowager had assured both her and Caroline that the duke's stables had plenty of horses, which would be available to them.

Rebecca would miss her mount terribly and spent several minutes brushing her beautiful mane, spoiling her with oats and crooning promises of her swift return before saddling her.

She mounted the animal and set off at a leisurely trot, making sure to steer clear of the woods, her encounter with Mr. Simons still fresh in her mind. Unfortunately, however, it appeared the man did not only lurk around trees for as she rounded the stables he stepped out in front of her, stopping her progress.

Deciding that he deserved no politeness and refusing to be cowed by him, Rebecca lifted her brow haughtily and demanded, "What do you want?"

Rather than be intimidated, he merely smirked not removing his eyes from her face.

"I heard about your father."

"So did everybody, I imagine. Though it is no concern of yours." She knew she was being unspeakably rude but the man terrified her and Rebecca just wanted him to leave her alone.

"He is my landlord is he not?" Again that awful smirk, that deeply uncomfortable stare.

"Please move out of my way," was her only reply.

There was a long pause as she awaited his response but he neither moved nor answered.

Blowing out a sigh of frustration, Rebecca made to move around him but her anger getting the better of her, she turned back slightly and addressed him.

"Your manner and speech are as insubordinate as they are insulting, Mr. Simons," she stated coldly, "In future, do not address me unless I speak to you first. And there is little likelihood of that. Consider yourself lucky that I leave for London soon so will not take matters further. When I return, I expect to see and hear as little of you as possible."

Hoping to give him a set down, she was disappointed to hear his chuckle.

"You will be seeing a lot more of me than you think, my lady."

Rebecca did not give him the satisfaction of responding or even breaking her stride.

But what, she wondered, *did he mean by that?*

Mr. Simons watched her go and finally gave way to the furious feelings that he'd kept in check. So, the lady thought him a nobody did she?

It did not surprise him. The upper classes had always treated the likes of him like something unpleasant they'd stepped on.

He'd had it often enough while he lived in London before his doddery old uncle met his demise and left him his farm.

He'd only planned to come here for long enough to make whatever money he could from the place and then jump the first boat back to London and the gaming hells and low-brow establishments that awaited him.

And then he'd seen her. She'd come to call with her father. Never had he seen a tastier morsel. She was obviously as uppity as the rest of her class but then he'd always liked the idea of taking one of them down a peg or two.

From that day on he'd watched her, far more than the lady was aware. She was definitely more free spirited than her icy sister, though that lady was just as beautiful. And just as much a snob.

His lip curled menacingly when he thought of what he'd do when he finally got his hands on her.

What started off as lust had turned into a raging obsession. He felt a murderous rage thinking of her with that bastard who'd come to marry the older one, but had clearly got his eyes on the younger.

Well, George Simons wasn't afraid of him or anyone else who tried to get in his way.

The lady would be his whether she wanted it or not. In fact, the less she wanted it, the more exciting it would be…

****

Edward arose early on the morning that his mother and her guests were due to arrive in London. He'd received her missive a few days ago telling him of the earl's state of health and was now waiting to find out what news they would bring with them.

His mother had explained her plans to bring the girls along with her and he hadn't been able to stop the smile that broke on his face as he read of Rebecca's rather vocal objections.

He would expect nothing less.

A frown broke quickly replacing the smile however as he thought of the earl's health. He remembered with sorrowful clarity how his own father had died. The circumstances were much the same except the late duke had been in his study enjoying a late night brandy and had, by their reckoning and the doctor's, taken suddenly ill.

Thankfully Tom had been with Ranford at the time and was therefore able to call for help. It was presumed that the heir, Charles, would return home when he received the news. In point of fact, he could even be there by now, or very close. Edward was glad to know there would be someone there to run things.

Probably not as efficiently as Rebecca, however.

He smiled again, a ridiculous grin that he could not seem to wipe from his face. He chose not to examine why he felt so elated at the thought of seeing her again and instead called for his valet.

They would not reach Town until later today and were sure to be exhausted from the long journey, first on the boat and then the long journey from the port at Holyhead to London. He could not imagine that several days of travelling would have any of them arriving in an overly joyous mood but he meant to be there, regardless.

It would be remiss of him as a son, after all, not to welcome his own mother back home.

"Ah, good morning, Bailey," Edward greeted his valet as he entered the room in his usual quiet way.

"Good morning, your grace. You seem rather happy today."

"I am, Bailey. I am."

"Might I enquire as to why? Tis rather unnerving."

Edward raised a brow at the valet's sarcastic tone. Bailey had been with the family since before Edward's birth and was more like family than servant. Of course, this gave him leave to say what he wanted, when he wanted to. And he was never afraid to voice whatever thought was on his mind.

"Can't a man wake up happy, ready to face whatever the day holds in store?"

"A man, yes. You?" he trailed off without finishing the sentiment, though his meaning was clear.

"You are fired."

"Very well, your grace. Shall you wear the blue coat today or the green?"

Edward relented. He'd never best Bailey, not if he lived to be 100, which he suspected was Bailey's age.

"The blue, I think. I shall be gone for most of the day but

please have my best dinner jacket prepared for this evening."

"You will be out dining, your grace?"

Edward wasn't surprised that Bailey was confused. The Season had only just begun and, even were it in full swing, Edward avoided more events than he attended as a rule. He was not blind to the fact that he was a prize the ladies of the *ton* thought worth catching.

And if they played fair, he would not mind. But they didn't! They were ruthless and terrifying, lurking behind corners and pretending to faint in front of him so he'd have to catch them. It was exhausting.

"Perhaps. My mother returns to Town today."

Bailey looked none the wiser.

"She will have guests with her. Ranford's daughters. I want to be prepared in the event that I am expected to dine with them."

Bailey made little effort to hide his smile. Having been made privy to the entire marriage contract farce on Edward's return, he suspected that the arrival of a certain young lady was the cause of such sudden happiness.

"Lord Ranford's daughters? So that would be the Lady Caroline then… and of course, Lady Rebecca?"

Edward cleared his throat. "Yes, that is correct."

"Hmm."

"What is that supposed to mean?"

"What, your grace?"

"That face. That 'hmm'?"

"I am not following, your grace."

Edward stared at him suspiciously for a moment but Bailey being ever the professional remained as blank-faced and expressionless as ever.

Edward huffed and turned away to begin dressing. He would just ignore Bailey's knowing look. The man was exasperating.

He meant to send a footman to watch his mother's house

this afternoon. It would be hours before the party arrived but Edward wanted to know the moment they were back. He wondered what the ladies would make of their first trip to London.

****

Rebecca strained against the window as she tried to take in all of her surroundings at once. The excitement building in her was barely containable. She was here. Finally! After a gruelling journey that seemed to take weeks rather than days, they had arrived in London.

It was a cacophony of sounds, sights and smells. Completely overwhelming and completely wonderful.

Caroline had long since given up asking Rebecca to choose a side to sit on and stay on in the dowager's luxurious carriage and had resigned herself to having Rebecca jump from side to side, half on top of her, every time something new caught her eye.

"Caroline, is it not just wonderful?" Rebecca's eyes shone and her face was flushed with excitement. She looked enchanting.

Caroline smiled indulgently.

"Yes, dear. It is very exciting," she answered composedly.

Rebecca frowned at her older sister. Caroline looked as pristine as if they'd just set off not one hour past. Her carriage dress was wrinkle free, her gloves immaculate and her hair still perfectly in place. In short, Caroline was the very picture of ladylike beauty.

Rebecca had not yet seen her reflection but could only assume she looked like she'd been dragged through a hedge. Her gloves were stained and a little torn from when she'd fallen out of the carriage. For the second time.

Her hair, barely containable on most days, had succumbed to the long hours, the bumps, the sea air, and was now a bundle of unruly curls being valiantly secured by dozens of pins.

Something was going to lose the battle and Rebecca's money was on the pins.

But none of that was of any consequence now. They were finally here and she was elated.

They passed through streets of vendors packing up their wares for the evening. They passed so many people, shops and beautiful buildings that her head fairly spun.

Rebecca could not wait to explore it all.

The rough and tumble of the city began to give way to a much more dignified setting, which in turn gave way to pure opulence and Rebecca knew they must be nearing their destination.

She was proved right when the dowager, who had slept for some of the journey, awoke and gave an exclamation of relief.

"Finally. Here we are girls. Not long until we reach Mayfair."

After a few moments of silence, Caroline exclaimed, "Look Rebecca. That is our Townhouse."

Rebecca gazed out at the imposing structure they were passing. The house was white, like those surrounding it, with huge black wrought iron gates and black doors. It was as opulent and beautiful as she expected it to be. Her father's family had exquisite taste.

She wondered if they'd get to see inside it before they left. If Papa would truly be able to come.

Her thoughts were soon diverted however by the carriage rolling to a stop in front of an imposing townhouse, even more grandiose than the Ranford one. It looked to be larger and more intimidating, though perhaps it only seemed that way to Rebecca since her nerves were once again well and truly rattling.

She was about to be launched into the absolute cream of

London Society. In fact, she *was* the cream of London Society! Rebecca Carrington, who sometimes forgot to pin her hair up and had to be bodily removed upstairs by Maura to rectify her *faux pas*. Who rode astride when she could get away with it, for Heaven's sake. Who climbed trees and fished and generally did the opposite of what she should.

She swallowed convulsively as they made their way up the steps to the front door, which had already been opened for them. Footmen scrambled about removing their luggage and a rather imposing butler stood waiting to receive them at the door.

"Welcome home, your grace."

"Ah Jeffries, good to be back. Please allow me to introduce you to Lady Caroline Carrington and Lady Rebecca Carrington, the young ladies who will be breathing life into our house for the Season," the dowager answered with a smile.

The dowager seemed truly excited about having them there. Rebecca dearly wished that she would not let the older woman down and decided then and there to do her utmost to conduct herself like an absolute lady at all times.

She would act with poise, calm and aloof grace. Basically, she would mimic everything Caroline did. She just hoped it would be enough.

"Now girls, I shall get Mrs. Humphries here to show you to your rooms," the dowager continued indicating an older woman who had made her way over to them with a broad and welcoming smile. "Please, freshen up from our journey and then join me in the drawing room for tea. I am sure we are all far too tired to even think of going out tonight but I intend to show you both off in style tomorrow."

Caroline and Rebecca smiled excitedly as they thanked the dowager and made for their rooms.

Thankfully, the carriage carrying Maura and Caroline's maid along with the luggage would follow not too far behind.

Rebecca was sure she would be able to change from her carriage dress to the simple afternoon muslin she'd brought in her valise without assistance.

Before she'd even removed it from her small bag however, a knock sounded at the door and a young maid entered bobbing a curtsy.

"Beg pardon, my lady," she spoke in a soft voice, "her grace has sent me to assist you if I can."

Rebecca smiled kindly at the shy young girl.

"Thank you, I was just going to change into my dress but I am sure I shall manage."

"Oh, my lady, it is all creased from the bag. Let me press it for you. I will not be a minute."

Usually Rebecca would have insisted that it would be fine just the way it was. But given that she was to try her hardest to be the best sort of lady, she nodded and thanked the maid.

The young girl scurried off and Rebecca set about washing the dust from the journey from her face and hands. She hadn't long removed the dusty carriage dress when her dress was returned, pressed and looking much better for it.

To add to her pleasure, Maura came soon after and set about redoing Rebecca's hair so that by the time she joined the dowager downstairs she felt a hundred times better and ready to deal with anything London could throw at her.

When Rebecca entered the drawing room, however, she was alone. Presumably a real lady took longer than half an hour to freshen up. She felt a little uneasy being alone but decided the best thing to do would be to stay put in case she got lost in the sprawling house.

She had just settled herself when she heard the click of footsteps outside. She turned with a smile toward the door thinking that Caroline or perhaps the dowager was about to join her.

Her smile froze and her heart beat shot up when the door

opened and Edward, Duke of Hartridge walked in.

Chapter Sixteen

Rebecca felt sure that Edward would be able to hear her heart beat, so loud did it sound to her. She had known she would see him, of course. And somewhere deep down she had desperately wanted to see him. But now? On her arrival? Her heart just wasn't prepared for the impact.

She had thought that three weeks of separation would cool her longing for him. Or that perhaps she had imagined him as more handsome than he had been, making subtle changes in her mind. But no, here he stood just as breathtakingly handsome as ever and her longing, rather than cooling, raged up inside her like a river about to burst its dam.

"Edward," Rebecca breathed his name before even realising she'd spoken and immediately flushed with embarrassment. She hadn't seen him since the last night he'd spent at the Hall and memories of that night came flooding back.

Surprise registered on his face when he spotted her quickly followed by something she could not define. His eyes glittered like molten silver as he gazed at her.

"Rebecca." His voice sounded hoarse but he did not

speak again.

She stood up to face him, feeling the need to break the tension suddenly permeating the air around them.

"We are not long arrived, your grace. We are going to have tea now and plan our day tomorrow, since we're far too tired to venture out this evening. Your mother will be here directly. And Caroline."

Rebecca knew she was rambling, but she was a bundle of nerves in his presence and felt an overwhelming and entirely inappropriate need to throw herself into his arms. Instead, she wrung her hands as she waited for him to reply.

To her surprise, after a moment's pause, he smiled a little wickedly and prowled towards her, closing the door quite scandalously behind him. Her breath hitched and she felt her cheeks flame.

"Your grace?" he questioned, his voice low and smooth as velvet.

His hand lifted and he stroked an errant curl back from her face and tucked it behind her ear.

"The last time we met, you conceded and called me Edward," he murmured. His voice was lower still and Rebecca felt a delicious shiver run through her.

Her breathing quickened and her heart still slammed loudly against her chest.

"I am afraid I do not remember, your grace," she muttered piously.

Hadn't she said she would act like the perfect lady? Discussing late night brandy swigging and earth-shattering kisses with this rogue was hardly ladylike behaviour.

He smiled a wolf-like smile at her answer.

"What a shame you seem to forget. But do not worry, sweetheart. I remember it well enough for the both of us. I've dreamt of nothing else. Perhaps I should try to jog your memory."

Rebecca's eyes widened as she registered his words. He

was truly wicked and oh so tempting. She knew he meant to kiss her and nothing would have made her prevent it. He reached out a hand and cupped her chin, raising her face to his.

Rebecca felt molten desire pool in her lower abdomen. She needed his kiss more than she needed her next breath. How she'd missed him!

Edward leaned forward, his lips inches from hers.

The door suddenly banged open and Edward and Rebecca sprang apart guiltily. The dowager glided into the room, her expression one of calculated regard.

"Edward, my darling. How good of you to come and see your old Mama," Lady Catherine said dryly as she took in Edward's frustrated countenance and Rebecca's flaming cheeks.

Edward, ever the duke, drew himself up and bowed to his mother before leaning over to kiss her cheek.

"But of course, Mother."

"Your timing is impeccable. We are only just arrived."

At this he looked ever so slightly sheepish.

"Yes, well I — uh — I had a footman notify me of your return."

The dowager grinned widely, making Edward remember that it was extremely difficult if not impossible to get anything by his formidable mother.

"How solicitous of you, dearest. And I must thank you for keeping my young guest company in my absence."

Edward glanced sharply at her to see if there was a hidden meaning but her face was bland and non-committal. Which meant she was up to something.

The dowager rang the bell for tea then pulled Rebecca gently to the sofa to sit with her. Edward could not seem to drag his eyes from Rebecca's face. Her cheeks were still flushed and she avoided his eyes. But it mattered not. Seeing her again was like a feast after having been starved for weeks.

When he'd walked in and seen her smile up at him, her sinfully dark eyes warm and inviting, all thoughts of propriety and even decency flew from his mind.

He felt like a blind man who'd been given sight. His heart had sped up and a savage lust had pierced his body. He would surely go mad from wanting before this Season was through, so utterly bewitched by her was he.

He could think of little other than tasting her lips one more time. Seeing if her kisses were as irresistible as those his mind had conjured up every single night since he'd left her in Ireland. And she was going to let him, too. It seemed she was as eager for his kiss as he was hers.

His mother had the worst damned timing in the world.

Well, perhaps it was just as well. If they'd been spied kissing he surely would have had to offer for her. And he was starting to think maybe that would not be such a bad thing, after all. Which was utter madness, of course.

"How is your father, Lady Rebecca?" he asked, trying to gain some equilibrium.

Rebecca looked up but did not quite meet his eye.

"He seemed well settled when we left, your grace, but we are awaiting word from home as to his progress."

"I am sure there will be a letter awaiting us, my dear. The post does travel much quicker. I shall have Jeffries bring it directly."

Rebecca smiled her thanks to the dowager.

Edward came over and sat across from them to study her face again. When he'd first heard the news his instinct had been to go straight to her, which was of course ridiculous since he knew from the same letter that she was coming here. But every part of him had wanted to be with her, to comfort her. He could just imagine what his mother had described, and Tom too, Rebecca taking charge, giving orders, not giving way to tears and hysterics.

But he also knew how much she loved her father. She

would have been scared to death but refused to show it. And while Rebecca was busy being strong for everyone else, nobody had been strong for her. His heart ached at the thought and he found himself wanting to take her in his arms again, this time though to offer comfort. To protect her and cherish her.

What the blazes was wrong with him?

The tea things arrived just minutes before Lady Caroline.

"I apologise for keeping you waiting, your graces," she said after Edward had bowed to her and enquired after her general health, "I had misplaced my valise when we arrived."

"Not to worry, my dear. Ah, Jeffries, tell me, has there been a letter from Lady Ranford?"

"Yes, your grace. It arrived just yesterday. I shall bring it directly."

Rebecca and Caroline glanced at each other worriedly. They could do nothing but hope that it was good news.

The butler returned with a letter addressed to Caro on a silver platter. She took it and placed it on her lap with a smile of thanks.

Rebecca stared at her.

"Aren't you going to open it?" she demanded.

"Rebecca," Caroline gently chided, "it would not be polite to open it in company. I shall excuse myself later."

"Hang politeness, I want to know if he is well," Rebecca said sharply.

"Rebecca," Caroline admonished in her familiar icy tones.

"Lady Caroline, my dear, I am sure we are all anxious to know how the earl fares. Please feel free to read your letter."

Rebecca looked over to see both the dowager and Edward looking rather amused at her tantrum. What a great start.

On reflection, the plan she had made not one hour ago to be nothing but a genteel lady had already started to go swiftly downhill with her almost being caught in a scandalous clinch with the duke and then shouting at her sister in front of the duke and dowager. She wondered idly if good intentions counted for anything.

Caroline smiled demurely and immediately opened the letter. She was obviously the consummate actress, Rebecca thought, for while she had given the appearance of complete calm, her hands shook as they unfolded the pages. Rebecca leaned over her shoulder and scanned the pages.

Her chest lightened considerably and she almost felt weak with relief.

"Oh thank goodness," Rebecca exclaimed and, to her mortification and consternation, she felt hot tears prickle behind her lids.

"All is well?" the dowager asked.

"Yes, yes it is," Rebecca beamed. She looked at the duke who smiled encouragingly but something wicked smouldered in his stormy eyes as he took in her smile.

She immediately felt hot and flustered all over again and began to worry her bottom lip with her teeth lest she do something silly like throw herself across the room and into his lap.

Edward's eyes darkened even more as they took in the small action and Rebecca was sure he groaned quietly. He jumped suddenly from the chair.

"Won't you tell us the news, Lady Caroline?" he bellowed, causing them all to jump. He cleared his throat and tried again in much more dulcet tones, "We are anxious to hear how he is getting on."

"Of course," answered Caroline swiftly though she looked a little nonplussed at the duke's erratic behaviour. "Mama says that his health is improving daily. Doctor Austin is elated with his progress. He has been sitting up already for some of the day and Doctor Austin believes that by the end of next week he will be well enough to be up and about a little."

Caroline's face was a picture of relief and happiness and she leaned over to squeeze Rebecca's hand reassuringly, her earlier remonstrations forgotten in the midst of such good news. Rebecca returned the squeeze with one of her own feeling as if a massive weight had been lifted from her and that she could now enjoy her time her with her sister, knowing her father did well.

Caroline turned back to continue scanning the missive.

"Oh, Charles is to return home," she exclaimed. "Mama says she received a letter to say he was making the journey. He may even have arrived already."

"I am sure your mother will be very pleased to have him back," said the dowager kindly, "Your father too I warrant. Well. This is excellent news and I believe we all feel much the better for it. Usually I would suggest going out to the theatre or opera to celebrate but I believe we are all fatigued from our journey. I think perhaps a quiet evening at home tonight, and tomorrow we can begin our socialising."

The sisters nodded in compliance, neither really wanting to do more than write to Mama, eat and then catch up on some much needed sleep.

"Edward, you will dine with us tonight won't you?" asked the dowager.

He glanced at Rebecca before answering.

"Of course, Mother. I should be delighted."

"Excellent. You may fetch Tom from his home too and bring him along. I am sure he would be glad of it and is anxious to hear news of the earl too. He was most attentive to the ladies during the crisis, was he not girls?"

"Oh yes, he was wonderful," Rebecca enthused. Caroline merely smiled but stayed silent.

"Well, I shall leave you ladies to letter writing and unpacking and so forth. I shall return later. Good day Lady Caroline, Mother. Good day Lady Rebecca." He bowed over each of their hands in turn and Rebecca's blood heated when he lingered over hers only a little longer than necessary.

His thumb circled her hand and she felt his lips sear her skin wickedly before he released her and took his leave.

The man was going to cause her to perish on the spot one of these days.

"Well, I shall look forward to having you all with me tonight," the dowager said, her eyes twinkling, "What an interesting few months we shall have. If you will excuse me ladies, I shall speak to Cook directly about our dinner plans. Please feel free to explore the house and grounds and of course, write to your Mother. I want you to treat this house as your home." She smiled kindly and swept from the room.

"I do hope she is right, Rebecca. I do so hope we have a wonderful time."

Rebecca smiled at Caroline and linked her arm as they strolled from the room.

"Oh, I am sure we shall."

****

Edward tracked Tom down at White's having first called to his house.

"Drowning your sorrows, Tom?" he quipped as he took a seat next to him and signalled for an extra glass.

"Something like that," answered Tom, not his usual jovial self.

"Ah, travelling with only ladies for company has taken its toll, has it?" Edward asked slapping him on the back. "Well, prepare for more of their company. We've been summoned to dine with Mother tonight."

Tom heaved a sigh before answering in the same light vein Edward used, "I do so like to eat other people's food. And besides, it is not as if the view will not be ravishing across the dining table," he answered with a wink.

"No, it will not be much of a hardship, will it?" answered

Edward frowning slightly, wishing to make sure Tom was speaking only of Lady Caroline but unable to say anything for fear of being sent to Bedlam. He knew that any man with eyes in his head and blood in his veins would know what a beauty Rebecca was, but that did not mean he had to like it. When she had bitten that blasted lip… but no, he could not think of that now or things would become very embarrassing very quickly.

"Lady Caroline received a letter to say that the earl is making excellent progress so the mood too should be jolly enough."

Tom's face lit up. "Wonderful news. They must be ecstatic."

"They certainly seemed to be. Their brother is to return home to the family seat apparently."

"I know that is what they'd hoped for."

"I do not think I've met the young viscount," continued Edward conversationally. "Do you know ought about him?"

Tom thought for a moment. "Not much," he answered, "He is finishing up this year in Oxford before learning the ropes of the estates as far as I know. Something of a rake, but not debauched. Not unlike you really."

"Or you."

"Ah yes, but he is titled, wealthy and suitable. There will be nothing standing in his way."

This sounded rather bitter for Tom, and Edward was taken aback. Tom usually did not have a bitter bone in his body. He was always cheerful, always the charming joker. He was renowned for it. That and his prowess with women.

"You cannot tell me anything's ever gotten in your way, Tom," answered Edward, "Besides, nobody could accuse you of being poor."

"But my money has the whiff of trade behind it, don't you know," Tom answered sarcastically.

Edward frowned as he looked at Tom's downcast expression. This really was most unusual.

"Tom," he began cautiously, "is there something troubling you?"

The question seemed to rouse Tom from whatever morose state he'd been in. He stared intently at Edward for a few moments, so much so that Edward began to grow a little paranoid.

"Let me ask you something," he suddenly spoke, slurring slightly. He was more in his cups than Edward had first thought.

"Yes?"

"Have you ever wanted something so badly you would do anything, *anything* to have just a taste of it? Even just for a brief, wonderful moment? You'd swim an ocean, cross a desert, walk to the ends of the earth!" Tom was starting to get louder and more dramatic as his speech went on, drawing some laughs and raised glasses from the surrounding men.

Then he quieted down again and looked so bleak that Edward became rather alarmed.

"But," he spoke so softly now that Edward had to lean in to hear, "no matter how much you want it, how much you would do for it... it can never be yours?"

The words made Edward's heart stop. Yes he had wanted something that badly. Still wanted it that badly. Rebecca.

He was suddenly overwhelmed with the same sort of melancholy that seemed to afflict his cousin.

"Yes," he answered sadly, rather dramatically himself, "yes, I have. And it is hell on earth."

Both men were so wrapped up in their own problems, they each failed to ask the other what exactly was bothering him.

It was only later, as they shared a carriage to the Dowager Townhouse, somewhat more sober, Tom turned to Edward and asked, "So, who is she?"

Edward started. He'd been thinking, not necessarily purely, about Lady Rebecca and Tom's sudden question unnerved him.

"Who?" he asked defensively.

Tom smirked.

"The lady who has created this hell on earth."

Edward regarded him cautiously. "What makes you think it is a woman?"

Tom barked out a harsh laugh. "Isn't it always?"

Edward chuckled. "Yes, I suppose it is."

"So, are you going to tell the gory details?"

"Are you?" Edward shot back.

Tom smiled. "Touché cousin."

They made the rest of the journey in contemplative silence.

Chapter Seventeen

The next day dawned bright and clear and Rebecca leapt from bed, a sense of excitement bubbling in her stomach.

Last night, they'd enjoyed a quiet but excellent dinner with Hartridge and Mr. Crawdon. Though Rebecca had been a bundle of nervous anticipation, she'd actually thoroughly enjoyed the night. The food had been delicious, the wine delightful. And though she had been sure she would feel uncomfortable in the duke's presence, he had been a witty and entertaining visitor. Between them both, Edward and Mr. Crawdon had managed to keep them entertained with funny anecdotes about each other's past escapades.

The strong relationship between them was evident in their banter and Rebecca had been relaxed for the whole evening. The only time she'd had a wobble was when the duke had been taking his leave and had once again kissed the back of her hand. The now familiar longing had shot through her and she'd felt the urge to stroke his raven hair between her fingers as he'd bent over her hand.

Still, she hadn't, thank goodness, and now she knew she could spend some time in his presence with equanimity.

Maura bustled into the room with Rebecca's morning chocolate and started pulling garments from the drawers and wardrobe.

"What would you like to wear today, my lady?" Maura was in fine spirits, filled with excitement at being in the city at last.

"I do not know what the dowager has planned, I believe she mentioned something about shopping so perhaps one of my new afternoon dresses."

"How about the pale lemon muslin, my lady?" Maura asked, pulling the beautiful dress from the wardrobe.

The colour showed off Rebecca's dark colouring to perfection and it was ideal for a clear spring day. Rebecca nodded her approval and looked forward to wearing the new gown.

It wasn't long before Maura once again worked wonders with Rebecca's hair, gathering most of it at the back of her head and leaving a few curling tendrils to frame her face. The style was simple but extremely flattering and Rebecca felt more than ready to take on her first day of the Season.

As they broke their fast, the dowager confirmed her plans to take the girls shopping and so it was agreed that they would leave at two o'clock and go directly to her grace's favourite mantua maker. The girls had bought no more than one or two evening gowns in Dublin after the duchess' insistence that they wait to meet Madame Elodie Barousse.

Madame Barousse was famous throughout England for her talent in dressing ladies of the *ton*. She was difficult to secure an appointment with and even more difficult to convince to actually make gowns for the ladies who came to see her. But Madame had long since been patronised by the Duchess of Hartridge so the dowager was confident that the girls would be well attended to.

"She will, I am sure, be delighted to dress two such beautiful girls," the dowager told them excitedly as they approached Madame's shop later that day. "Dressmakers always want to show off their clothes on a beautiful face and form."

Rebecca and Caroline waited with some trepidation for the footman to lower the steps so they could alight from the carriage. Maura had told them the servants' gossip about the famous Madame. Apparently only last week the daughter of the Duke of Bandon had been seen running out in tears as the volatile dressmaker had hurled insults at her.

Caroline had then spent a goodly part of the morning begging Rebecca to be quiet, calm, not rise to any bait and conduct herself with quietness and decorum. "In short," finished Caroline after a lengthy sermon, "just do not be yourself." Lovely.

Rebecca was the first to exit the carriage and stood taking in the sights and sounds of the busy shopping street while she waited for the other ladies.

So much busier than Dublin, which she had thought to be bustling, London seemed fast paced and relentless. *So many carriages and people,* she thought. Her eyes scanned the crowd taking in the elegant ladies and handsome gentlemen. She froze suddenly as she spotted a man watching her from across the street. An icy dread filled her. No. It could not be he!

"Rebecca."

Rebecca yelped as a hand touched her arm.

"Goodness, what is the matter? You look as if you'd seen a ghost." Caroline, who had touched her to draw her attention, was frowning in concern.

Rebecca spared her a quick glance but then turned back. He was gone. She scanned the street both ways as far as possible but there was no trace. Perhaps she'd imagined it?

"Rebecca. Truly, what is wrong?"

"It is nothing, Caro. I thought I saw someone I knew that is all."

Caroline seemed appeased and turned to enter the shop.

Rebecca, however, was uneasy and felt a little ill. She could not speak to Caroline about what had frightened her so, since Caroline had no idea that the man had caused Rebecca any problems.

No, there was only one person, Edward, who knew and even then he was not aware of her last nasty meeting with that man.

For standing across the street watching her had been Mr. Simons.

But how and why was he here? Rebecca resolved to speak to Edward as soon as she could. He was the only person who could advise her on what was best to do. Besides, he made her feel safe and right now she felt anything but.

It could, of course, be an unhappy coincidence. But an Irish country farmer had no business in London during the Season. And he had been watching her so closely…

The sooner Rebecca could speak to Edward about this and figure it out, the better.

Entering the shop proved a welcome distraction. Indeed, Rebecca thought one could not help be distracted on entering this shop.

As soon as they were inside a young girl approached to welcome them. She recognized the dowager at once and immediately led them to comfortable seats then scurried off to fetch Madame.

The booming voice was heard before the person was seen. Barking orders like a military general it was deep and loud and definitely caused the girls to be nervous. They shared a look of alarm before the curtain parted and Madame Barousse stepped into the room.

Madame Elodie Barousse was certainly a sight to behold. As big as her voice had indicated, in both stature and height, she towered above the ladies who rose to greet her.

"My dear duchess. How wonderful to see you again," Madame boomed in her thick accent. "Who have you brought to me today? Let me have a look."

She reached out and grabbed each of the sisters in a vice-like grip, dragging them to stand in front of her while she squinted and inspected them closely.

After a few moments silence, and a couple of circles around their bodies, Madame clapped her hands together causing them to jump.

"Magnifiqué," she declared, "They will do my creations justice. I will dress them."

Madame began watching them with the squinty expression again. Rebecca wondered if they were supposed to be doing something.

"Bien," she shouted, causing them to jump yet again, "I will start with the blonde. I have just the thing."

Some hours later, the ladies left Madame Barousse's with their smiles bigger and their allowances lighter. They had commissioned Madame to make several evening and ball gowns each, along with the accompanying slippers and wraps. Each girl had purchased an utterly exquisite gown for the end of Season ball, which was put on by the dowager every year. It was the social event of the Season. Everyone would be there and so it was imperative that the girls had something special.

They could not wait to see what Madame created, having seen samples of fabrics that she intended to use. The dresses themselves, she informed them, would be surprises. But having seen some of her gowns they knew they were in the hands of a genius.

They stopped off for ices to regain their strength and then headed straight back into the fray, coming away from each shop with new fans, bonnets, ribbons and decorations for their hair, gloves, slippers and plenty of other things they did not need. The dowager was a very persuasive shopping companion and had, in fact, purchased several items for the girls as gifts.

When they objected she clasped them both by the hand

and said, "Please, girls. Allow me to do this. I never had a daughter that I could share these things with."

The girls had thanked her and offered no more objections.

Finally, after hours of exhausting but thoroughly enjoyable shopping, the ladies were ready to return home. There ensued a complex few moments of arranging the various purchases in the carriage, with some of them having to be stored on the seats inside. The footmen managed it however and the ladies were just getting ready to embark when a shout sounded behind them.

"Ah, mother. I see you've been buying up Bond Street yet again." Edward smiled indulgently and Rebecca felt her heart warm at the sight of him.

He peered into the carriage at the excess boxes.

"Good heavens! It seems your cohorts share your talent for shopping."

"They do indeed," answered the duchess enthusiastically. "We have enjoyed a very successful afternoon."

"I hope there is something in there for the March's dance this evening. It is your first event, is it not? You must make sure to draw attention."

Rebecca watched Edward as he chatted and smiled, his demeanour friendly and easy-going. She rather liked this side of him, usually being only privy to the arrogant 'duke' side.

"Oh do not worry on that score my son," the dowager answered, "The girls will have marriage-minded young men beating down the door by as early as tomorrow, I warrant."

Her words fell like rocks into the jovial mood of the group. Rebecca had quite forgotten her assertion that she was here to find a husband, though her sponsor had clearly not.

Edward's face went from smiling to thunderous in a second and he shot a dark look at Rebecca before pulling his features yet again, into his haughty 'duke face'.

"But of course, eyes on the prize, eh ladies?" he asked

sarcastically.

Rebecca felt her hackles rise but she bit back a retort and instead smiled sweetly at Edward.

"Did you not promise to escort us, your grace, so that you may help us to pick suitable husbands?"

Edward's jaw clenched so tightly, she thought rigor mortis had set in. But he soon recovered his composure enough to bow slightly and answer, "Of course, my lady. I should be delighted."

"If that is delighted, I dread to think what your unhappy face looks like," she quipped.

The dowager burst out laughing. Caroline stepped on Rebecca's toe.

"You've seen it, my lady, when we've been interrupted," Edward answered scandalously, wanting to get one up in this verbal sparring, his smouldering eyes reminding her of the incidences he was talking about.

Her own eyes widened at his audacity. What on earth was he doing, saying such things to her in front of his mother and her sister? Had he run mad?

There was a pause in the conversation as Caroline and the dowager thought about what he'd said. Rebecca did not want to give them a chance to start speculating so she began shooing, *shooing*, the Dowager Duchess of Hartridge into her own carriage.

"Come now, your grace, we should be returning to ready ourselves for the dance tonight."

The dowager looked a little shocked at being manhandled but allowed herself to be escorted into the carriage. Caroline shot daggers, again, at Rebecca before following the dowager.

Rebecca spun to face Edward, her eyes glinting with anger.

"How could you? Do you not realise they will start supposing things with your cryptic remarks?"

Edward merely grinned unrepentantly.

"What is there to suppose but that I have been happy in your presence Rebecca? And I have been happy. Very, very happy."

To Edward's great amusement, Rebecca swore quietly but profusely.

"Come now, do not upset yourself. I promise to behave like the perfect gentleman from now on."

Rebecca should not have felt a pang of disappointment at his promise. But she did. And it obviously showed since Edward's face broke into a wicked grin.

"In company of course."

She should not smile, should not encourage him but he was incorrigible and she was more drawn to him by the day.

"Then I shall just have to make sure we are not alone together."

"And I shall have to make sure we are."

The air crackled between them.

"Are we to stand around all day then?" came the dowager's voice from the carriage, "Lady Rebecca seemed in rather a rush to go."

Rebecca's face flamed as she apologised to the dowager and made to enter the carriage. Edward grabbed her hand and kissed it wantonly; Rebecca gasped as she felt sure his tongue had just darted out. But his face was expressionless as he rose up again and handed her into the carriage.

"Good day, ladies," he said as he closed the door, "Until tonight."

Though he spoke to the group, his eyes remained on Rebecca.

Chapter Eighteen

The door sounded downstairs and Rebecca knew it must be Edward come to escort them. She had completely forgotten to ask to speak to him earlier so that she might share her concerns, fears rather, about Mr. Simons. But perhaps there would be an opportunity tonight.

Maura had just put the finishing touches to her hair and was retrieving Rebecca's wrap from the wardrobe.

"Now, my lady, let's have a final look at you before you go down."

She turned Rebecca toward the looking glass and sighed happily. "You really are a picture."

Rebecca looked over herself with a critical eye, needing to make sure that she looked her best tonight. She did not want to let her father down now.

She had chosen a cream silk evening gown for tonight's festivities. The square cut neckline was a trifle low, though not as low as some she'd seen. A row of tiny pearls had been sewn along the neckline. The cap sleeves were lined with the same pearls. Yet another row was sewn onto the empire line of satin ribbon before the dress fell in folds to her feet.

Cream satin slippers and white evening gloves completed the picture. At her neck and throat she wore the diamonds that her parents had gifted her for her sixteenth birthday and Maura had cleverly dotted diamonds throughout the curls piled on her head. An elegant cream fan and satin wrap were the finishing touches, handed to her now by Maura.

"You will cause an absolute sensation, Lady Rebecca," exclaimed Maura happily.

"I just want to be sure to live up to my family name, Maura," answered Rebecca a little nervously.

"Sure and why would not you? You will be the belle of the ball."

"I hope so," answered Rebecca quietly, looking once more at her reflection. Her cheeks were flushed from excitement and nerves and her eyes glistened with anticipation. It was now or never. Rebecca gave Maura a quick hug and swept from the room.

Edward stood in the hallway and awaited the arrival of the ladies of the house. His mother was not exactly renowned for her punctuality. Lady Caroline, however, seemed far too well mannered to keep a gentleman waiting and indeed within moments of his arrival, the lady began to descend the stairs.

She really is very beautiful, Edward thought. Strange how her beauty failed to move him.

"Lady Caroline," Edward bowed to her as she reached the foot of the stairs, "may I say how beautiful you look tonight?"

Lady Caroline smiled graciously and thanked him. She wore a gown tonight the colour of the sky in spring and it suited her very well. It made her eyes seem bluer and her hair brighter. Her jewels were sapphires and she looked so well put together Edward knew that she'd be fighting them off in droves.

He wondered if he should enlist Tom's help in keeping the wolves at bay.

His mother arrived on the heels of Lady Caroline looking resplendent in deep purple velvet. She was still a woman of beauty and Edward was pleased to see how happy she looked. It did her good having the Carrington girls stay with her. He felt a little guilty that he did not visit more often.

He'd purchased his own townhouse a few years ago after it became apparent that his mother was trying to marry him off. He'd grown tired of bevvies of debutantes laying siege on his house and had judged it best and safer, really, to remove himself to another equally beautiful but mercifully debutante free household.

His mother was far from lonely, being one of the leading ladies of the *ton*. But to see her excitement now made him resolve to spend more time with her. And he really should think about providing her with those grandchildren she so desperately yearned for.

It seemed an odd sort of coincidence that Lady Rebecca should choose the moment he thought of grandchildren to make her entrance. His heart stopped. Simply stopped dead in his chest. This woman would be the death of him.

He watched her descent with eyes wide and jaw open. She looked like Aphrodite, Goddess of Love and destroyer of the souls of men everywhere.

The cream silk of her dress caressed her body lovingly before falling in folds to the floor, hiding what he knew to be utterly gorgeous legs. He swallowed convulsively as she came to stand in front of him and bent into a curtsy.

Still he remained unmoved.

"Edward," his mother's voice sounded more than a little amused, "bow to the lady. And close your mouth."

Edward snapped to attention at his mother's voice.

"Lady Rebecca," he said though it sounded embarrassingly like a squeak, "you look –"

There was a pause as he tried to form a coherent sentence.

"I believe what my son is trying to say is that he approves, my dear," the dowager seemed to be thoroughly enjoying herself.

Rebecca smiled, secretly delighted to have caused such a reaction in him. She was honest enough to admit that was precisely what she had wanted.

"Shall we, your grace?" she asked with a confidence borne of knowing she had caused such a reaction.

Edward, still unable to speak, merely nodded before standing back and allowing the ladies to precede him to the ducal carriage. It was going to be a long night.

****

The ballroom of the March's townhouse was bedecked with sweeping folds of white material, hundreds of candles and vase upon vase of white flowers. It was also filled to bursting and Rebecca found it enchanting.

As they waited in the receiving line to meet their hosts, Rebecca was aware of looks of curiosity from the ladies and frank appreciation from the men present. Edward's hand on her lower back guided her through the crowd and Rebecca felt that she was being branded by it.

What would it be like, she wondered, *to be his wife? To have him look after her like this all the time?* She quickly quashed the thought before it could fully form. She'd been through this hundreds of times. It was not going to happen.

Several people approached them for introductions and soon Rebecca's head spun with names, titles and connections. The ladies, for the most part, seemed pleasant enough though there were some discernible scowls from those who noticed Edward's protectiveness over his charges. The gentlemen were polite but rather forward and Rebecca found she had to bite her tongue on more than one occasion when a remark or impudent look set her teeth on edge.

Rebecca obviously wasn't the only one to notice. It seemed that for every lascivious glance, Edward took a step closer, usually accompanied by a none-too-subtle swear word.

And so it was that by the time they reached their hosts, Edward was pressed so closely to Rebecca's back that a fan would not have fit between them.

The dowager introduced them to their hosts, Lord and Lady Marsh, who were simply delighted to have the daughters of the Earl of Ranford at their event.

The dowager was very well pleased with the stir the girls were creating. "What a buzz surrounding you, girls. I am elated. Edward you must make sure to dance with both of the girls, secure their standing at once, not that they need any help in that department."

With a wave of her fan, she made her way to the other matrons of the *ton*, sitting in a corner of the room, reigning over all who passed them.

The evening took off at a whirlwind pace. There were introductions, polite chats and so much dancing Rebecca's feet ached!

Mr. Crawdon had arrived not long after their party and had immediately asked Rebecca to dance. She took great pleasure in the cotillion they danced together. Mr. Crawdon was an easy partner to dance with. He evoked none of the strange feelings in her that his cousin did and he was terribly amusing.

After he returned her to Edward, Rebecca fully expected the duke to ask her to dance but before they even got a chance to talk, another gentleman approached, then another, then another. Soon Rebecca's card was completely filled… and Edward had not asked her to dance once.

Rebecca did her best not to look disappointed but she could not help but wonder why he did not ask her to dance. He had danced with Caroline while Rebecca had danced with Mr. Crawdon. She knew because Mr. Crawdon had kept his eyes trained on the couple for almost the entirety of the dance. Rebecca had refused to look.

She had not stopped dancing all night and was taking a much-needed moment to catch her breath from her partner, a young baron with far too much enthusiasm for talking, dancing and treading on toes. Her feet ached from the amount of times they'd been trod on.

She glanced around the ballroom, vastly impressed by the glittering array of brightly coloured gowns and jewels. The ladies here most definitely dressed to impress. She had spent some time with the dowager who had introduced her to the other matrons of the *ton*. Each of them had looked her over thoroughly and each of them had declared her to be a success. Rebecca presumed this was a good thing.

As Rebecca continued her perusal of the ballroom, she spied Edward. Her stomach dropped. There was a lady attached to him as if they'd been sewn together and Rebecca felt a stab of jealousy such as she'd never experienced. Her eyes narrowed as she studied the scene. Edward was smiling down at the beautiful woman who was clinging to his arm like a leech and gazing up at him adoringly. Rebecca did not like the way the lady kept rubbing his arm, nor the way she looked proprietorial about him.

The scene did nothing to help her already sad mood concerning the duke, and Rebecca had seen enough.

She spotted the doors to the balcony opened on the other side of the room and began to make her way toward them, meaning to make her escape before the return of her young dance partner.

She made it outside without incident and exhaled in relief. She had been enjoying herself immensely but the ballroom was stifling and the duke's snub had taken the shine off the evening somewhat. *Not to mention the fact that he seemed to have grown an entire person out of the side of his body*, she thought bitterly. Rebecca knew that people must have noticed his ignoring her. Caroline had definitely noticed since she'd asked Rebecca if they had gotten into an argument.

Rebecca felt like crying. Why was he doing this now? She thought of the look on his face when he'd first seen her this evening. She thought of how he'd stayed glued to her side before they'd entered the ballroom. Why then, had he disappeared and paid her no attention at all since?

She huffed out her frustration and made her way to the balustrade to lean her arms on it and contemplate the duke's behaviour and her upset at it.

That was where Edward found her moments later. He had seen the second she'd left the ballroom. He'd watched her all night.

"Surely you know by now not to wander outside alone?" he asked gently.

There were other couples walking up and down the terrace, taking the air and he did not want to draw their attention. What he wanted was to drag her off somewhere private, though he knew he could not.

Rebecca turned at the sound of his voice but, besides a small, polite smile, gave him no greeting. He got the distinct impression that he was in trouble. He must tread carefully.

"Are you cold?" he took a step closer.

Rebecca shook her head in response.

He stepped closer still.

"How are you enjoying your first venture into Society?"

"Oh, it is wonderful," she replied brightly. But it sounded false.

"You did not look as if you were enjoying it just now," he answered.

"And how would you know?" she bit out, "You seemed wholly occupied by your 'companion'." She spat the word as if it were an insult.

Edward frowned as he thought about whom Rebecca meant.

"My companion?"

"Yes. The lady who could not seem to stand up by herself and required the assistance of your arm. In fact, you should probably return to the ballroom in case she has collapsed in a heap since you are not there to hold her up."

Edward bit back a grin though he had to admit to feeling smug at her obvious jealousy. As baffling as it was, she seemed to feel threatened by Lady Sarah. It was almost laughable.

"Are you speaking of Lady Sarah?"

"I do not know, your grace. I am speaking of the elderly lady in the red dress," she sniffed.

Edward had to bite back another grin.

"Elderly lady?"

"Well, I do not know her age of course. But she looked frightfully old."

"She is not yet thirty."

"How tragic, then, that she looks so much older."

Edward could not hold back the chuckle this time.

"Oh, sweetheart. You really are one of a kind."

Rebecca spun to face him and her eyes glinted with an angry fire.

"Lady Sarah, you will learn, has a tendency to cling to any and every man in the room at an event. She is the goddaughter of Lady March so is tolerated by that lady's friends. She drinks too much and is quite scandalous but is harmless enough."

"She is also," he continued drawing closer to her, "married."

Rebecca began to feel foolish for letting her jealousy loose. But nothing of what he said explained away the fact that he'd ignored her all evening.

"I must admit, I am rather pleased that you are jealous."

"Jealous!" she scoffed. "I am not jealous, your grace."

"Really? You seemed to be. And I am rather an expert on

jealousy."

"Oh, really? And how's that?"

"Because I've been eaten up with it watching you steal hearts all evening."

He really had an unnatural talent for making statements that took her breath away.

But she refused to be charmed by his honeyed words, knowing them to be untrue.

"Really, your grace, there is no call for exaggerating. I am aware that whatever interest you had in me has — has waned."

As difficult as the words were to utter, they had to be said. Rebecca had been foolish to spend her time dreaming of Edward, of spending the summer together. While they'd been alone he had been flirtatious and attentive. But now, on the first public outing of the Season, he had ignored her entirely. And, though it was hard to accept, those were the cold, hard facts.

It was better to get things out into the open now so that they could both move on.

"Believe me, it has far from waned. Much as I've tried, Rebecca, I cannot fight the effect you have on me. And more and more, I am finding I do not want to."

"But you've ignored me all evening," Rebecca blurted out, sounding like a spoiled child but not caring.

"Ignored you! I haven't stopped watching you from the second you came down the stairs in my mother's house," he retorted almost angrily. "I could not ignore you even if I wanted to."

"Yet you have not asked me dance," she muttered.

"And when was I supposed to do that, hmm? Was I to fight my way through your sea of admirers? To do battle for a cotillion? I did not get a chance to ask you to dance. But believe me, I have not been ignoring you."

Rebecca felt warmed by his words and relief flowed

through her. He had not lost interest in her. If anything, he seemed rather put out that she had been attended to so much by other men. Did he not realise that none of them even held a candle to him?

She suddenly felt younger and more carefree. Happier than she had since they'd arrived. All of her resolutions to stay away from him, all of her assertions that distance between them was for the best flew out the window.

Rebecca suddenly beamed at him and Edward felt as if the sun had come out.

"So, you will dance the dinner waltz with me?"

"I cannot, your grace. I have promised it to—"

"I do not care. You are dancing it with me."

"I beg your pardon?"

Edward smiled ruefully.

"Pardon me, my lady," he said with a bow, "What I mean is, would you do me the honour of dancing it with me?"

Rebecca giggled and hit him lightly with her fan.

"Oh do get up," she admonished since he still hadn't straightened.

"Not until you say yes."

She laughed again. "I cannot. I have promised it."

Edward straightened and sighed dramatically.

"Alright. To whom is this most scandalous of dances promised then?"

Rebecca checked her card.

"To Viscount Hadley. Though, I confess, I cannot remember who he is."

"Let me escort you back in and we will find him."

Rebecca took his arm and steeled herself against the familiar shiver of need that coursed through her. She would never get used to that feeling.

They re-entered the ballroom and Rebecca immediately spotted the Viscount. He was talking to the dowager and seemed to be searching for Rebecca given the way his eyes travelled the ballroom. He spotted her and a smile broke out on his handsome face. The smile, however, did not quite reach his eyes and Rebecca felt less than comfortable at the idea of spending even moments in his arms. Especially in such a dance as the waltz.

He straightened his cravat and bustled toward them. Rebecca bit back a sigh and planted a polite smile on her face. He reached them and bowed so low Rebecca thought he would tip over.

"My lady," he spoke smoothly, "I believe the next is mine?"

Rebecca really did not want to dance a waltz with him and had, in fact, been somewhat shocked that the dowager had permitted it. Although it was more often done in London than in the small assemblies back home, it was rather unheard of to dance it with a man one had only met. But the dowager had been most insistent that the Viscount should ask Rebecca and he had been more than happy to do so.

"Good evening Hadley," the duke's pleasant tone sounded before Rebecca could answer, "I am sure you will not mind giving up your claim on the dance to me?"

The young viscount looked surprised at Edward's addressing him.

"Your grace, I did not see you there."

Edward merely smiled and waited for the young man to answer his request.

Rebecca bit back a smile. Really, it wasn't fair for Edward to use his ducal arrogance on young bucks of the *ton*. They were ill equipped to deal with it.

"Y-your grace," Hadley stammered, "I am — that is to say — the lady said – well…" he stammered on some more while Edward's expression remained coolly aloof and completely unchanged.

After an excruciating moment of silence, the younger man relented.

"Of course, your grace," he mumbled unhappily before bowing to them both and taking his leave.

Edward led Rebecca onto the floor.

"That was badly done, your grace," Rebecca chided, though she was thrilled to be in his arms at last.

"Must we continue with this 'your grace' business, Rebecca?" was his only reply.

"Edward," she conceded, "you intimidated the wits out of him."

"Any man willing to give up your hand so easily is not worthy of it, sweetheart."

The first strains of the waltz started and Edward gathered Rebecca closer. His hand seared her waist and she felt her breathing quicken.

They started to move to the music and Rebecca felt as if the world drifted away, until it was just Edward and she. The only two people in the world. He was a wonderful dancer.

The atmosphere seemed to intensify between them as a magic spell started to weave its way around them. Neither spoke for words were unnecessary. And both were afraid to break it.

They moved around the floor of the ballroom, completely oblivious to the attention they were attracting. They made a stunning couple, for one. Their intense regard for each other, too, was extremely obvious in the way they gazed into each other's eyes, the way the young Duke of Hartridge held her as if he were holding a prized and rare jewel, the way Lady Rebecca gazed adoringly into the young man's handsome face.

The dowager heard the whispers and agreed with them all. In the normal course of events she would be concerned that Edward was subjected to such speculation. Since he'd become Duke of Hartridge he'd developed a seriousness about his character that, while completely necessary given the sheer volume of responsibility, was also sad since he seemed to have been robbed of his youth and former vivacity for life. Seeing him now, smiling and genuinely happy made her heart swell. She could very well see what was developing between these two young people, even if they could not. And it seemed it was becoming just as obvious to everyone else.

Chapter Nineteen

The dance had finished but Edward was reluctant to let go of Rebecca. She was perfect, at least to him. Her hand felt tiny within his, her body, he knew, was a perfect fit too. He gradually became aware of a strange sort of stillness and when he looked up he was surprised to see so many faces standing stock-still and staring at them.

"Rebecca," he whispered.

"Hmm?" she was still gazing at him and he felt like picking her up and running from the eyes of the *ton*, from the speculation, from everything until it was just the two of them.

"We seem to have drawn a crowd."

Rebecca blinked slowly then looked around. Immediately her cheeks flushed and she stepped away from him.

The bell rang for dinner and the crowd began to disperse.

He wondered if she was upset but when he looked at her again, he saw that she was grinning ruefully.

"What's the smile for?" he asked, adding, "Though I am not complaining. I love your smile."

She looked a little startled at his declaration but made no comment.

"I was just thinking of how determined I was to cause no scandal this Season. To make my parents proud. And since yesterday I've almost been caught — well," Here her cheeks blushed profusely. Edward thought it was adorable, "Well you know. With you."

He smirked but she ignored it.

"Then I shouted at Caroline in front of you and your mother and now it appears I've committed some terrible crime by dancing with you. In short, I find it tragically amusing that even when I do not mean to do so, I stir up trouble wherever I go."

She laughed and shook her head.

He watched her a moment before he replied.

"Come. Let us take some air," he said. He knew she was laughing about it but it must hurt for her to think herself a failure.

"But the bell has gone for dinner."

"I will not let you starve, I promise."

Rebecca did not put up any more of a fight because she really did not want to fight it. Taking her arm once again, Edward led her outside. She suddenly remembered that she had not yet spoke to him about Mr. Simons.

As soon as they were outside, she turned to him.

"I am glad you've asked me to walk alone with you, Edward."

Before she could continue his eyes gleamed a silver fire and he grabbed her by the shoulders and pulled her towards him.

"Me too, sweetheart," he said hoarsely before crushing her lips beneath his.

All thought left Rebecca as soon as Edward's lips touched hers. *Hang Mr. Simons,* she thought a little frantically.

Edward kissed her with more passion than ever before and it scared and thrilled her all at once. Her last coherent thought was that he'd obviously been holding back those other times. This time Rebecca felt as if there was a fire raging between the two of them. She shook with the sheer force of it.

"Ahem. I've been sent as a search party to find the two of you. Not very well hidden are you?" Mr. Crawdon's voice came from behind Rebecca. She made to jump back from Edward but he grasped her shoulders and kept her pressed against him.

"Go away, Tom," he growled, his head leaning against Rebecca's, his breathing as laboured.

"But your mother—"

"Now." His eyes never left Rebecca's. And she continued to shake with longing, not really caring that they'd been discovered.

"Fine, fine," laughed Tom, "I surrender. But I hope you are prepared to make an announcement should anyone else happen upon you."

Edward appeared not to have heard for the second Tom was gone, he captured her lips once again.

But Rebecca had heard.

She pulled away again.

"Edward," she heard the breathlessness in her voice, "Edward. Stop."

He stared at her with pure desire in his eyes and it was all she could do not to throw herself back into his arms and hang the consequences. But it would not be fair to either of them.

The last thing Rebecca wanted was for him to be trapped into a marriage with one so unsuitable as she. She loved him far too much to see him suffer forever for a moment of madness.

Oh my God.

As the full force of her thoughts hit her, Rebecca reeled in shock.

She loved him? She loved him!

Dear God, this was an utter disaster. How could she have

been so stupid?

Edward watched the emotions flit across Rebecca's face and was more than a little alarmed when her face paled and a look of horror passed over her features.

She stumbled a little and paled so much he thought she would faint.

"Rebecca," he said in alarm, wondering at the sudden change in her countenance. "Sweetheart, what is it? What's wrong?"

"Nothing," she mumbled miserably, refusing to look at him. What the devil?

"Look at me." Nothing.

He grasped her shoulders. "Rebecca, *look* at me."

She glanced up reluctantly and to his dismay, her eyes glistened with unshed tears.

"Oh, my darling, please do not cry. I am sorry. I have frightened you with my attentions." He pulled her into his strong arms and rubbed her back comfortingly, interspersing his speech with kisses to the top of her head. "I am sorry, I know that you are young and innocent. It seems I cannot remember my famous self-control when I am around you. I would never hurt you. I would never want you to be frightened of me."

He sounded as if the thought pained him.

"No. Truly, you have not frightened me."

"It is just, when you said you were glad I asked you to be alone, I thought you'd been as anxious for privacy as I."

Rebecca smiled a little at the uncertainty in his voice. If only he knew how anxious she was for privacy, for *him*. How much her heart longed for far more than he was willing or able to give.

But, there would be plenty of time to deal with that little problem later. Right now, she had to concentrate on getting through the rest of the evening without blurting out her feelings for him.

"Mr. Crawdon," she started nervously, "He will not say that we — that you…"

"Tom? He will remain the soul of discretion. I promise."

"How can you be so sure?"

"Well, because I will shoot him if he does not," he answered as if this were perfectly obvious.

Rebecca had to smile at that. Everything was so logical to him. He never seemed shaken or worried by anything; which led her to why she'd actually wanted to be alone with him before his kisses forced her to acknowledge the loss of her heart.

"I did want to speak to you about something rather, rather strange I suppose," she started self-consciously. What if he laughed at her? Or thought her mad? Still, there was nobody else that she could turn to.

"It is about Mr. Simons. I — I do not know if you remember him."

Edward's jaw tightened. "You mean the bastard who manhandled you."

Right. He remembered then.

"Er, indeed. Well, anyway the morning that we left for London I was riding. Just in the grounds," she added quickly, remembering her promise not to be alone. "He was at the stables and he approached me again."

Edward's expression went from mildly irritated to murderously angry.

"Did he touch you?" he spoke through clenched teeth.

Rebecca swallowed convulsively.

"No! No, I was on my horse. He did not try to, well he did not touch me," she finished weakly.

Rebecca wished she'd never spoken. He looked furious and she did not know why.

"Go on," he instructed gently.

"He, he said something which I thought unusual at the time. He said that I would be seeing him sooner than I thought. I had delivered a rather severe set down you see and had told him how damned lucky he was that I was leaving," she spoke hotly and remembered how indignant she'd felt at his insolence.

Edward smiled a little as her temper clearly got the better of her. He waited for her to calm down before she continued.

"Well anyway, he had said this unusual thing about me seeing him. I did not give him the satisfaction of asking what he meant and I thought no more of it. But then, yesterday outside Madame Barousse's I saw him. I am sure it was him. Standing across the street and staring at me. It scared me, I admit."

She turned and began to pace in remembered agitation. Had she stayed put she would have seen his expression change yet again. If Rebecca had thought him angry looking before she would have been truly terrified by the expression on his face now.

"He disappeared not two minutes later and though I looked, I could not see where he had gone. I suppose I could have imagined it, or that it was a coincidence. It is just that, coupled with what he said it seemed… strange."

Rebecca turned back to face him and he was careful to school his features to appear unconcerned and calm. Inside he was burning with the need to find the man and pummel him for causing her any discomfort. He had no doubt that she had seen him and it set him on edge to know that he had come all this way. To follow her?

"I cannot speak to anyone else about it. Nobody else knows of my encounters with him. I realise I was foolish not to tell Papa but, well I would not worry him with it now anyway. And I thought I was free of him and, well, it just did not seem all that serious but now—"

Edward could see that she was getting worried again so he took her gently by the shoulders and lowered his head so that he could look into her beautiful eyes.

"Rebecca, love, pray do not worry yourself. We shall get to the bottom of it."

"But how?" she whispered miserably.

"I will deal with it," he answered firmly. "You do trust me, don't you?"

He was suddenly aware of how important her answer was. How much he wanted her trust.

She gazed up at him for a moment, as if considering his question.

Finally, she nodded and he felt a surge of pride that this brave, beautiful woman was willing to put her trust in him. He vowed not to let her down.

"Good. Now, let's re-join the party and I shall call on you tomorrow to take you driving in Hyde Park. We shall discuss our plans."

Rebecca felt as if a massive weight had been lifted from her shoulders and she beamed happily up at him.

"If you look at me like that again we will not move past this isolated balcony," he warned her.

Rebecca felt a little thrill at his words and, feeling happier than she had in weeks, she gave him an outrageously flirtatious look before answering, "Then let us be gone before another search party comes along." And she swept inside with a sly little wink.

The minx. She was going to cause him no end of trouble.

Chapter Twenty

The next day Rebecca stifled a yawn as she listened to Viscount Hadley drone on and on about Tattersall's, horseflesh, his new mount and various other things equally horse related and equally boring.

Dear Lord, did the man speak of nothing else?

The dowager had been correct in her prediction and all morning the girls had received gentlemen callers. The calls were interspersed, thank goodness, with calls from young ladies and friends of the dowager so the morning wasn't a complete loss.

How, Rebecca thought a little desperately, did people *do* this every day without being driven completely mad?

Even Caroline, all that was proper and well mannered, was starting to fade a little and Rebecca caught her slight eye roll every now and again.

The room was filled with people as well as flowers brought by the gentlemen. Rebecca had noticed that when a lady called at the same time as an eligible gentleman, the lady was reluctant to leave and so it was that by one o'clock the drawing room was filled with boring young bucks and simpering young misses. Rebecca felt like screaming.

"Lady Rebecca," Hadley was mercifully interrupted by Miss Cavendish, the pretty young daughter of a baron to whom she'd been introduced last night. The girl had wide violet eyes and golden ringlets and looked, Rebecca thought, perhaps a little meanly, like an overgrown doll. She'd lost count of the flounces on Miss Cavendish's pink-trimmed dress. And she'd been trying her hardest to count them all, since the alternative was listening to Viscount Hadley.

Rebecca turned to her with a smile.

"You really must tell us your tricks! We are all quite anxious to hear of your methods."

Rebecca frowned in confusion.

"My methods?" she queried politely.

"Why yes," the lady exclaimed, "Lady Marsh's party was abuzz with talk of you and the duke. He has never shown a preference for a young lady before. Never!"

Rebecca felt her temper rise at the impertinence of the young girl. She noticed that the quiet buzz of conversation had ceased at the question and everyone awaited her answer.

Along with Miss Cavendish were that lady's mother, of course, Lord Hemming and his sisters, and a plethora of other young gentlemen all vying for the attention of the Ladies Carrington. Rebecca did not particularly like any of them.

She did her best to remain calm and polite.

"I am sure you are mistaken, Miss Cavendish. His grace danced only one dance with me, after all."

"Well that is one more than he has ever danced with any of us," answered Miss Cavendish, not giving up, "Why he seemed positively enamoured of you."

Rebecca's cheeks flamed and she glanced at the dowager to check the lady's reaction. The dowager looked intrigued rather than affronted. And she did not look as angry as Rebecca thought she would, given that this little madam was gossiping about her own son. In her own drawing room no less!

"Miss Cavendish," Rebecca tried to maintain a cordial yet distant tone of voice. "I assure you that the duke is no more interested in me than I am him."

Rebecca stumbled over the lie. Had she not spent almost the entirety of last night tossing and turning, unable to sleep or to escape the knowledge of her love for him?

She had thought of nothing else since they'd re-entered the party last night and she had thought of nothing else during the carriage ride home. Being close enough to Edward to smell him, to have his leg accidentally brush against hers.

The things that she had believed about love — the fairy tales, the knights in shining armour, they seemed ridiculous to her now. Love wasn't a fairy story. It was a painful, burning emotion that did not abate and brought no peace.

If only he loved her back.

But she might as well wish for the stars.

The thought was painful enough already, trying to convince her heart not to hope for him and here she stood, having to convince perfect strangers of his lack of regard for her, too. It was the outside of enough.

"The duke has shown no particular interest in me, of that I am certain."

She could have kicked him, literally kicked him or perhaps stomped on his foot when he chose that very moment to burst into the room and declare, "My lady, our carriage awaits," before bowing low and presenting her with a beautiful posy of hothouse flowers.

Rebecca almost groaned aloud at the look of smug disbelief on the faces of Miss Cavendish and the others present. The dowager chuckled merrily and Caroline lowered her head to hide the grin plastered on her face.

But Rebecca had seen it and did not see what was so amusing. People were getting ideas about her and the duke. Ideas that she wished with all her heart were true but were the figment of overactive imagination and nothing more.

"Your grace," she answered weakly, dropping into a curtsy before thanking him graciously yet formally for the flowers.

Edward frowned at her greeting but did not question her. Instead he turned to greet his mother, Caroline and the other occupants of the room. He was more than a little displeased to see that the majority were unattached men.

"Miss Cavendish was just commenting on how little you seem to dance, your grace," Rebecca told him, hoping that he would read between the lines and see that their dance had drawn attention.

"Was she indeed?" he asked, his eyebrow rising and his face taking on its 'duke mask.'

The young lady had the grace to blush at least.

"We were just talking of how lovely you and Lady Rebecca looked dancing together, your grace," she demurred, her eyes downcast.

Rebecca rolled her eyes at the performance. The girl was clearly trying to insinuate something but did not have the courage to come outright and say something truly improper to the duke's face.

Edward regarded her silently for a moment and the young lady flushed a bright crimson under his scrutiny. Rebecca started to feel almost sorry for her.

Finally, Edward spoke and his voice was as detached and emotionless as ever Rebecca had heard it.

"Of course, Lady Rebecca would look lovely no matter the partner," came his smooth reply.

He turned to Rebecca then and said, "If you are ready then, my lady?"

She grinned at him, happy to be escaping the monotonous conversation of young dandies who had nothing of consequence to say, and the deadly dull debutantes hanging on their every word.

"I shall just fetch my pelisse and bonnet, your grace."

As Rebecca made to leave the room, she noticed Caroline's look of desperation. Caroline was just as bored as Rebecca, though far too well-mannered to show it as Rebecca was wont to do.

And though she would treasure any time spent alone with the duke, Rebecca could not sacrifice her own sister.

Making a swift decision she turned to Caroline and said, "Caro, make haste. We do not want to keep his grace waiting. You have not forgotten our promise to take the air with him this afternoon, have you?"

Caroline beamed at Rebecca as if she'd rescued her from the gallows.

"Of course not," she jumped up hastily, "I shall be ready directly." And with that the two ladies bid goodbye to their guests and swept from the room.

They were positively giddy a few moments later as Edward handed them into his landau. He could not be disappointed at the added guest. Not when he saw how miserable the girls were amongst their sea of admirers, interspersed with gossips such as Miss Cavendish.

He was a little shaken to hear that he'd been the subject of Society gossip. He was never gossiped about. He had never given cause to be gossiped about. He did not particularly relish the idea.

But even had he known, would he have passed up the opportunity to dance with Rebecca? No, he did not think he would.

"So, holding court over the young swains of England was not to your liking?"

"Good God no. If I am told how beautiful my eyes are one more time, I shall gouge them out," grumbled Rebecca dramatically.

"At least your hair hasn't reminded at least a dozen gentlemen of the sunrise in springtime," complained Caroline bitterly. And Caroline never complained.

"We are indebted to you, your grace, for rescuing us from such utter nonsense." Rebecca smiled at him and Edward felt it like a punch to his gut.

"I would rescue you a thousand times over to have you smile at me like that, my love," he whispered for her ears only and was smugly satisfied to see her pupils dilate and her breathing quicken.

Conversation between them then ceased for a while as Edward needed all his concentration to navigate the busy route to Hyde Park. He listened to the sisters' idle chatter and was pleased to hear how happy they sounded and well they seemed to be going along.

They had not long entered the park with they happened upon Tom, taking a leisurely ride on his stallion, Brutus. He greeted them all jovially enough but Edward noticed a definite set to his jaw when speaking to Lady Caroline. His curiosity was piqued and he made a mental note to question Tom about what was going on between him and Lady Caroline.

His thoughts were soon cut short however by the arrival of Lady Sarah herself. He felt Rebecca stiffen beside him and an imp inside him awakened. He rather looked forward to introducing the two formidable ladies and sitting back for the fireworks.

"Eddie, my darling." Lady Sarah had never been given to following the rules of propriety. She was a well-known flirt and her flirtations were known to extend beyond the innocent whenever the mood struck. Her aging husband rarely made the trip to Town, giving his much younger wife free reign over his household and his purse.

Sarah was harmless, once one made it abundantly clear that her advances were not welcomed. Nothing ever seemed to entirely put her off, however.

Today, she was dressed in true scandalous style, her scarlet dress more suited to evenings and even then evenings in certain places only. She was beautiful and voluptuous and made no apology for it.

Her deep red hair was more down than up and she did not wear so much as a spencer to cover her scantily clad form.

Lady Sarah instructed her driver to bring her barouche to a stop beside Edward's vehicle.

"And Tom. How are my two favourite boys?"

"How do you do, my lady?" Edward answered politely, while Tom tipped his hat and grinned at the lady.

"May I introduce my lovely companions for today — Lady Caroline Carrington and Lady Rebecca Carrington, the daughters of the Earl of Ranford?"

Lady Sarah looked them over rather disdainfully before shrugging as if wholly unimpressed. The look made Rebecca itch to slap her.

"Pretty little things," was all the answer she gave.

Rebecca felt her blood boil but Caroline, because she knew her sister as well as she knew herself, grasped Rebecca's hand and answered politely. "A pleasure, Lady Sarah."

"A shame you girls have only just arrived, you missed a wonderful party last night at my dear god mamma's, did they not my darlings?" she reached out and rubbed Tom's arm rather obviously and Rebecca nearly yelped as Caroline's hold on her hand became a death grip.

Edward replied smoothly, "The ladies were present, Lady Sarah."

"Indeed. I confess I did not notice."

This was sure to be a lie since the party was awash with speculation on the two ladies. Both unattached, both extremely wealthy and both, it was rumoured, looking for a match.

Rebecca had had enough of the rude woman and her blatant lasciviousness when looking at Edward.

"Perhaps your eyesight is failing, my lady. That can happen with age."

There was a moment of shocked silence before Tom

barked out a laugh and even Edward chuckled, though more softly than his cousin.

Rebecca heard Caroline whisper "oh no" but she was far too het up to pay any heed.

Lady Sarah's eyes narrowed dangerously and her demeanour lost its insincere friendliness.

"My, my. Quite a fiery one, aren't you? One would not think so to look at your – er – rather demure clothing." She smiled nastily.

Rebecca wanted to throw something at her.

Lady Sarah had basically said Rebecca looked dowdy. Rebecca had been rather pleased with how she looked. She wore an afternoon dress that had come from Madame's the other day. It was a white muslin skirt with a light lavender bodice and white ribbon trim. Madame had insisted Rebecca take it as the original buyer had not returned and she'd been "as ugly as a horse's backside" regardless, according to Madame.

Rebecca had been too scared to refuse.

For their outing she'd teamed it with a white pelisse and white bonnet with lavender trim. Rebecca knew she looked becoming in it and Lady Sarah was just being a spiteful old hag.

Rebecca smiled sweetly and replied, "I shall be sure to pass on your opinions to Madame Barousse, whose creation it is. With such a discerning pallet, she will be most curious to hear others disagree. Though I am sure you are not familiar with that mantua maker. I cannot imagine her creating something of yours."

Lady Sarah looked both mortified at having insulted a creation of the House of Barousse and furious at being delivered such a set down.

Rebecca, having said all she was willing to say to the lady bid her a polite good day and stepped down from the vehicle intending to walk off her temper a little.

She had not gone far when Edward caught up to her.

"Alright. Put the claws away little cat, she is gone."

"I am sure I do not know what you mean," answered Rebecca innocently.

Edward just grinned but made no more comment on the subject. In truth he had expected nothing less when introducing those two. He knew Rebecca could hold her own in any war of words. She'd made light work of Lady Sarah.

His only worry now was that Sarah would try to find her revenge in some way. The lady did not like to be bested.

"Be careful with Lady Sarah, won't you?" he warned, "She does not like to be embarrassed and she does not like to be outdone."

"If she does not like to be embarrassed perhaps it would benefit her to invest in a looking glass so she can see herself before leaving her house." Really, Rebecca had never been so unkind about anyone. That lady quite simply grated on her nerves.

"My, my. Such viciousness from such an angelic looking person. Remind me not to cross you."

"You already have. Several times."

"Ouch," he winced, "True perhaps. But have I not also caused you some joy?"

They had come to a stop under a sprawling oak and Rebecca noticed for the first time that they seemed to be alone.

"Where is Caroline?"

"Further back, talking to Tom. Or rather arguing with, judging by her countenance when I left them."

"We should return."

"Yes," he agreed, "we should."

Neither of them made any move to turn back however. It seemed they were equally reluctant to leave. The thought should have caused her pleasure but all it did was cause confusion. Rebecca knew that she was reluctant to leave him because she loved him and was happier in his company than anywhere else. What then, was his reason?

She turned away lest her feelings show in her expression when her heart stopped dead as she spotted a figure watching them from across the small pond.

"Edward." Rebecca gripped his sleeve.

"What's the matter?" He frowned.

"There, by the pond. Is that not Mr. Simons?"

Edward spun around in time to see the figure's swiftly retreating back.

"Was it him?" he asked urgently.

She nodded shakily. "I am almost certain. No, I *am* certain. It was he."

"Right." Edward grimaced and he seemed to be forming a decision in his head for he nodded decisively then gripped her elbow and led her back to the landau. "Let us get you home. I will have a man make some enquiries. I do not want you making yourself ill worrying about this, Rebecca. I will deal with it."

Rebecca nodded again and admitted to herself that she felt far less frightened having Edward by her side than she had done the first time she'd spotted Mr. Simons.

They returned to Caroline and Tom. Rebecca watched them closely for any sign of argument but both were their usual selves, if a little quiet.

Edward returned them to his mother's house but took his leave directly. He drew Rebecca to a corner of the drawing room before departing.

"I shall keep you informed of every development. In the meantime do *not* go anywhere alone. And try, at least, to stay out of trouble."

She gave him every promise to try. At least. And with a swift kiss to her hand he was gone.

****

Lady Sarah Whitting fumed as she made her way through the park and toward the small but serviceable house she kept in Chelsea. She was in the mood for one of her assignations and could certainly do with the distraction.

How dare that little upstart speak to her in such a fashion?

And the way Edward hung on the brat's every word! It was not to be borne.

She scowled as she thought of the dance the previous evening and how everyone had watched the girl and her Ice Queen sister. For God's sake. Earl's daughters were two a penny; there was no call for the fuss they were creating.

And then she'd seen Edward dance with the chit.

Edward had always tolerated Sarah's outlandish ways. He had never guessed at the very real desire she felt for him. Sarah had never minded since he had shown no preference for any lady of the *ton*. Until now.

And would it not just wipe the smug little grin from Lady Rebecca's pretty face to know that, however platonic their friendship was now, it had not always been so between Edward and Sarah.

A white lie here, an embellishment there and she could have the girl thinking quite interesting things about Edward and her.

Her thoughts were abruptly interrupted by the unwelcome arrival of a rather dishevelled young man, who jumped in front of her horses causing the driver to swear loudly and pull up.

"What the devil do you think you are doing?" he shouted at the young man.

The man ignored him completely and sauntered over to Lady Sarah's side of the vehicle.

She looked down her nose at him. He was handsome. Very brooding. But he was clearly one of the lower class and therefore unworthy of her notice.

"My lady," he addressed Sarah with a bow, which seemed rather mocking. "I believe you and I may have something in common."

Sarah regarded him disdainfully. What in heaven's name would she have in common with a creature such as this?

"Perhaps you are mistaken, boy," Sarah spoke venomously, "I am sure I could have nothing in common with the likes of you."

George Simons' temper flared as yet another toff treated him as though he were something she'd stepped on. But he needed her on his side if she was to help him with his cause and he needed help. From the looks of things, that damned duke wasn't going to leave Rebecca's side.

So, making sure to hide his dislike, he doffed his hat and said, "I apologise for interrupting your afternoon, my lady. But I noticed your little chat with Lady Rebecca and the duke just now and, well, you did not seem right pleased at seeing them together."

Lady Sarah's brows rose, not only at the man's obvious acquaintance with the horrible Lady Rebecca but his impertinence at addressing her about so delicate a subject.

"I did not get your name, boy."

He grinned and she noticed a couple of missing teeth, though they were not right in the front and not too off putting.

"That is because I did not give it."

Really. He was shockingly insubordinate.

"What exactly do you have to do with the lady?" she asked leaning forward, her curiosity definitely piqued now.

"Not as much as I'd like to," came the bitter reply. Sarah was confused by his response. There was something odd about the man to be sure. She'd had enough.

"I've had enough of this. Drive on," she ordered. But before the driver could move, the man had taken hold of Sarah's lower arm.

"How dare you," she screeched. "Unhand me

immediately."

Her driver had jumped down from his seat and was rushing round to remove the odious creature from Sarah's notice.

But the man easily pushed him off and turned back to Sarah.

"Seems to me that the lady has slighted you and you do not strike me as a woman who likes to be crossed." This certainly got her attention, the anger at Rebecca's treatment of her still very much present.

"No, I am not" she agreed.

"Now," he continued while Sarah gestured for the driver to return to his seat, "I do not want those two together any more than you do."

"What the devil would you know about what I want?"

"I have eyes, my lady," was his only response.

Sarah looked him over again. What the devil was going on here? He was far from gently bred and she could not imagine the snooty Lady Rebecca having anything to do with him. But, clearly there was *something* going on here and Sarah was intrigued.

"I cannot be seen talking to you here," she finally uttered, "God knows what people would think."

Sarah missed the curling of his lip at this statement.

She continued on, oblivious.

"Follow me to my house in Chelsea. My man will give you the address."

Without another word, she turned away and waited for her driver to finish with him so they could move. She'd hear what the fellow had to say before deciding what to do with him.

Chapter Twenty-One

Some nights later the sisters made their first visit to Almack's. The dowager was not only in constant possession of vouchers, but was bosom friends with several of the patronesses. The girls were extremely excited about it, not in the least because Madame had arrived in person to deliver the girls' gowns for the evening.

Rebecca's was a masterpiece of cream silk which hugged her form. It was daring but far from vulgar and Rebecca loved it.

Madame had, in fact, delivered all but one of the gowns the girls had ordered, stating that their final ball gowns were not yet finished.

Her work was exquisite. There was no other word for it.

Caroline's dress was a confection of palest pink chiffon, which made her look softer and more feminine than usual. Her maid had even arranged her hair in a softer style, in keeping with the silhouette of the dress, and the overall effect was stunning.

"Caroline," breathed Rebecca when they met in the drawing room, "you look like a fairy princess."

Caroline giggled, *giggled* and flushed happily.

"Thank you, dearest. I must admit when I first saw it I thought it was a trifle girlish but it really is beautiful."

"*You* are beautiful," corrected Rebecca fondly.

Rebecca's looks had always drawn notice quicker than Caroline's because she was darker than most young ladies of the *ton* but growing up she had always envied Caroline's hair like spun gold and her icy blue eyes.

"Especially," she continued mischievously, "your hair, which puts me in mind of the sun in springtime."

The sisters were still laughing when the dowager entered the room, declared them both to be equally beautiful and swept them out to the carriage.

Rebecca tried not to look for Edward the moment they arrived. She had seen little of him since the day in the park and her emotions swung between worry, disappointment and anger at herself for being worried and disappointed.

Really, this business of being in love felt like nothing more than a constant headache!

Immediately after they were announced, the dowager took them to meet the patronesses themselves. Rebecca was slightly worried since Caroline had spent the morning explaining the intricacies of the rules of the *haute monde*.

Apparently, Rebecca should not have waltzed at the Marsh's ball the other night. Waltzing should only be considered after it had been deemed acceptable by one of the patronesses of Almack's.

"But," Caroline reassured her, "I am sure there is nothing to worry about since the dowager is sponsoring you and gave you permission. And really, who is going to argue with the Dowager Duchess of Hartridge?" she asked laughingly.

"Er – nobody?" Rebecca guessed.

"Well, of course nobody! The dowager is above reproach. Hartridge wives have always been perfection personified.

They do not break the rules. I am sure there will be no adverse consequences."

Rebecca thought miserably that Caroline could have said nothing more to convince her that Rebecca was definitely NOT Duchess of Hartridge material, though she did not really need convincing on that score. Still, the whole fuss seemed ridiculous to her.

"Caroline, it was just a dance! What possible consequences could there be?"

"Becca, do you remember Lady Louise Trent, the Earl of Donbury's daughter?"

Rebecca racked her brain.

"No."

"Exactly!" Caroline exclaimed. "That is because she waltzed for an entire Season without having even *attended* Almack's, let alone gained permission to dance."

"Oh my God," Rebecca was horrified, "you mean they *killed* her?"

"What? Do not be ridiculous! She lives at her father's country estate. Engaged to a local vicar so I am told."

"Oh," Rebecca was vastly relieved. "So then, what is the problem exactly?"

"Did you not hear me? She is an earl's daughter."

"Yes?"

"She is marrying a *vicar*."

"So?"

Caroline huffed a sigh of frustration and refused to continue with the conversation.

Although Rebecca did not think of marrying a perfectly respectable vicar as a punishment, the moral of the story was clear. One simply did not offend the patronesses of Almack's!

The dowager greeted the ladies warmly then drew the girls forward.

"May I present Lady Caroline Carrington and Lady Rebecca Carrington, daughters of my dear friends the Earl and

Countess of Ranford?"

Caroline curtsied beautifully and Rebecca followed suit, hoping to impress the formidable group before her lest she be shunted into obscurity for the rest of her days.

Rebecca watched helplessly as several pairs of eyes looked her over thoroughly. She was beginning to think that obscurity sounded like a holiday.

Finally, one of the ladies, and in her panic Rebecca forgot which, addressed her.

"I believe you danced a rather sensational waltz with our dear duke, Lady Rebecca."

Rebecca froze. What should she say? It was hardly sensational; it was just a damned dance!

"I did, Lady—" she froze once again. Oh God! She could not remember the name! Her mind was a total blank. Just as she was beginning to hyperventilate, a voice sounded from behind him.

"How goes my favourite coven tonight?" sounded Edward's deep baritone. Rebecca could have kissed him.

She breathed a sigh of relief as the ladies chuckled at his wicked question.

"Edward, my dear boy. How nice to see you."

It appeared that the duke was a favourite of the gathered ladies.

There were several moments of chit chat during which Rebecca was wonderfully ignored, then Edward turned to her, "My lady, may I request the pleasure of the first dance?"

Rebecca glanced at the ladies watching them closely, unsure if she was allowed to just accept or if she should wait for them to grant permission.

"Um," she started a little hesitantly, giving somebody the chance to speak up, "I would be delighted, your grace. Thank you."

She took his arm and turned to leave when they were stopped by a subtle "Ahem."

They both turned back to face the little group. There was an awkward pause. Well, a pause which felt awkward to Rebecca, who was starting to turn scarlet under the collective scrutiny of the leading ladies of the *ton*.

Finally, the one whose name Rebecca could not remember spoke again.

"Be sure to dance the waltz together. My interest has been piqued."

Edward smiled and bowed then, without another word, turned Rebecca gently and led her to the floor.

He chuckled softly as Rebecca heaved a huge sigh of relief.

"Come now, sweetheart. They're not the worst in the world."

"Easy for you to say, they clearly adore you."

"Well, I am adorable," he quipped.

"Hmm. Modest too."

He grinned unrepentantly. The steps of the cotillion took them away from each other and when they returned Edward's wide smile took her breath away.

Why did he have to be handsome?

"So, what news on Mr. Simons'?" Rebecca asked, more to take her mind off the overwhelming attraction she felt towards him than anything else.

"None, I am afraid. Though that is not necessarily a bad thing, I think."

"Do you think then that I am worrying unnecessarily?"

"No, I would much rather you were vigilant. I have a man still making enquiries and another watching my mother's house."

He had someone watching the house? Rebecca frowned, she had not even noticed.

"Does that not seem a little excessive?"

Edward's eyes darkened. "No, it does not," he snapped. "I will not have anything happen to you."

Rebecca told herself that his concern was nothing more than that of a family friend. That it did not mean anything other than he took his role as protector seriously.

If only she could get her foolish heart to listen.

The night went by without incident, save Rebecca's pouring a glass of champagne over Sir Roger Dalton's head. Caroline had been furious, naturally. But it wasn't as if she'd done it on purpose. She'd been standing near the gentleman's chair being accosted, yet again, by Lord Hadley. There was a moment of panic when the viscount, swaying slightly, had reached for her hand. Rebecca had jerked it back a little more forcefully than intended and her drink had ended up on Sir Roger's head.

It hadn't been the worst thing she'd ever done.

The audible curse afterwards was slightly less excusable.

Caroline had marched her to the dowager and begged that they be taken home. Rebecca had not even had a chance to say goodbye to Edward, so unceremoniously was she removed from the room. They had not had a chance to waltz.

To her relief, and Caroline's consternation, the dowager had found the whole thing vastly amusing.

Their carriage pulled to a stop outside the dowager's townhouse and the ladies alighted into the cool night air. Rebecca glanced around to see if she could spot Edward's man but saw nobody. She'd never make a spy that was certain. Smiling a little to herself, she entered the house behind the dowager and her sister.

Standing in the shadows, George Simons watched her move into the house. Her jewels glittered in the moonlight and the light colour of her cape stood out in stark contrast to the darkness around her.

The longer it took to have her, the worse the pain was getting. That is what it was like. A constant, burning pain. The only thing that would relieve it would be to finally have her, to slake his thirst for her. He would not wait much longer. He could not.

His focus was interrupted by the arrival of another carriage. He saw the crest on the side and scowled. That damned duke was getting in his way far too often. It was time to put his plan into action. All he needed now was an opportunity.

****

The ladies had just settled in the drawing room to take a final cup of tea before bed when the door burst open and Edward marched into the room.

"What the hell are you playing at?" he shouted at Rebecca.

Predictably, without wondering *why* he was in a towering rage, Rebecca's own temper immediately awakened.

"Me?" she screeched.

"Why did you disappear without even telling me? Do you have any idea what I was thinking when I searched and could not find you?"

He'd been worried about her. Rebecca began to soften toward him. Until—

"Besides, it is extremely ill mannered," he continued piously.

And just like that, the flame of her temper caught again.

"Ill-mannered? You are joking. You forget, it seems, that I have borne witness to less than gentlemanly behaviour from *you* in the past."

Since neither Rebecca nor Edward paid even the tiniest bit of attention to the other occupants of the room, neither was inclined to be careful about what they said lest they reveal more than they wanted people to know.

"Perhaps so," Edward conceded grudgingly, "but do you not think that I should have been informed? Did you not think that I would assume the worst?"

Rebecca thought, albeit reluctantly, of what it would seem like to him to have her disappear without a trace especially in light of their conversations about Mr. Simons.

She softened again.

"'I am sorry, Edward" Rebecca spoke softly now, not noticing that Caroline and the dowager almost fell over in shock. Caroline, because Rebecca had actually apologised for something and the dowager because her son, the stickler for rules and regulations looked delighted that Rebecca spoke his Christian name.

Rebecca continued on, oblivious to the sensation they were causing.

"We had to leave quite hurriedly and unexpectedly and there was no time to say goodbye to anyone. I should have known that you would worry. I am sorry," she repeated.

Edward's anger deflated. He was sure it took a lot for her to apologise since he guessed she'd rather stick pins in her eyes.

"Why the sudden departure?" he asked curiously.

His eyes narrowed as her face took on a pink hue, which told him she had either gotten into trouble or done something silly.

"I cannot remember," she murmured and turned away to retake her seat.

"You cannot remember?" he questioned disbelievingly.

She shook her head in answer and raised her teacup to her lips.

"I can," the dowager interrupted gaily and both Rebecca and Edward realised that they'd put on quite the display. The dowager however, seemed unfazed and actually rather happy about the whole thing.

Caroline was smiling knowingly at Rebecca. Rebecca chose to ignore the lot of them.

"We left because Rebecca poured a glass of champagne over Sir Roger's head."

There was a stunned silence from Edward as he took in this new information.

Then he turned to Rebecca, his expression serious.

"Do you make a habit of drowning old barons in champagne, my dear?" he asked politely.

"Oh shut up," she snapped not caring, in her state of embarrassment, whether people thought she was acting appropriately or not. "It was one glass, hardly enough to drown in. And it was an accident."

"It always is dearest," Caroline, the traitor, piped up.

They all laughed and Rebecca felt like a silly little child. She bowed her head miserably.

Edward refused his mother's offer of tea, taking his leave instead.

"It appears I shall have to keep an even closer eye on you, Lady Rebecca, lest you find yourself in any more scrapes that seem so unique to you," he said by way of goodbye.

Rebecca stuck her tongue out at him. Which wasn't terribly mature but made her feel better.

Yet even though she was annoyed with him, with herself, with the world in general at that particular time, when he kissed her hand her heart still cried out for him. There really was nothing else for it. She was hopelessly in love with the arrogant swine.

Chapter Twenty-Two

Edward called the next day to take Rebecca driving again. This time, he was accompanied by Tom who requested Caroline's company for a drive.

Rebecca was shocked to see a flush creep over Caroline's cheeks at the request. She really had meant to ask Caroline if something had happened between her and Mr. Crawdon but lately Rebecca's head had been so filled with thoughts of Edward she barely managed to dress herself in the morning.

Thankfully Maura did not require much help in that department.

And so it went, for the next week or so. Edward called every day. Sometimes with Tom, sometimes not. Sometimes he just visited; sometimes he took them out to museums, parks, for ices and he even braved a shop. Though it was a bookshop. And he waited outside. But it was a valiant effort at chivalry nonetheless.

Her favourite thing about these outings and visits was not the token gifts that Edward was always giving to her in secret; a book she mentioned, her favourite flowers, even a little figure of an imp he'd seen once and bought because it reminded him of her, it was that they talked. Really talked. About their fathers, Edward's having gained the title of duke so unexpectedly and the pressures that entailed, Rebecca's fears that some of her more outlandish behaviours would bring shame to her family's honour and general conversations that had no real purpose but allowed them to understand each other and get to know each other more and more every day.

Rebecca had never been happier or more concerned about her own heart. The Season was plodding on; she was receiving gentlemen callers every day. Her dance card was filled every night. But the only thing that gave her any pleasure was being in Edward's company.

He danced with her every night. The first dance and the supper dance, ensuring that they were seated together at dances and balls.

It could not be said that he showed much of a preference, however, since he always made sure to dance two with Caroline also. But rational thought really had no place in her fantasies and the longer she spent with Edward the more lost to any other man she became.

****

Some weeks after their arrival in Town, the dowager took the girls to the Opera. They were thrilled at the prospect for although they'd seen performances in Dublin, the dowager assured them that a trip to the Opera during London Season was quite a sight to behold.

She was not wrong. As their carriage pulled up in front of the theatre, directly in front of the carriage holding Edward and Mr. Crawdon, Rebecca could see that the ladies truly did not hold back when dressing for the opera.

She and Caroline had once again dressed in Madame's creations and were infinitely pleased to have done so. They would have looked positively dreary in anything less than

Madame's designs here amongst the most glittering of the *beau monde's* ladies.

Caroline had reverted to her favourite— blue. A light azure whose colour was a little daring for a debutante but Madame had refused to dress Caroline in white and Caroline had, wisely, stayed quiet.

Rebecca was in an unusual choice for her, a pale mint green. She was surprised to find that colour suited her very well.

As they stepped from the carriage, Edward came to assist Rebecca and his mother up the stairs to the grand entrance, which was lit with the most beautiful chandeliers.

Mr. Crawdon was escorting Caroline and there appeared to be none of the animosity between them that sometimes radiated from them. Rebecca was pleased. Something felt rather special about tonight and she did not want any of them to be unhappy.

"Your beauty never fails to steal my breath, sweetheart." Rebecca was surprised and pleased to hear Edward's whispered words in her ear. His breath tickled her neck and she shivered at the tingling sensation that shot through her.

Rebecca looked up at him and took in the immaculate black evening coat, needing no padding for his shoulders were the broadest she'd ever seen, his arms muscled and taut. She swallowed over the sudden lump in her throat. Rarely did Rebecca allow herself to study him anymore, unless she knew for certain that he was not watching her.

His valet had done an impeccable job with his cravat; it was blindingly white and tied with none of the flamboyance of the dandies of the *ton*. It was sensible and well suited to the sensible man. Rebecca smiled.

"What's that for?" Edward asked.

"Oh, I was just thinking of your cravat," Rebecca blurted out, before even thinking about what she was saying.

"Oh. Right." He seemed confused. Rebecca did not blame

him.

"It is just I noticed yours is tied without all the pomp and fussiness of some of the other gentlemen of my acquaintance. It is sensible and practical. Like you, really."

His smile was quickly replaced by a frown.

"Sensible and practical? That is how you see me?"

Rebecca paused, surprised at how unhappy he seemed. He was not *only* those things. He was so much more. But he was, first and foremost a duke and therefore had a huge amount of responsibility. It only stood to reason that the head of such a vast empire would at least have a sensible head on his shoulders.

"Well. Yes" she exclaimed. "But that is not all you are," she hurried on to explain.

"What else am I?"

"Oh no. You shall not fish for compliments with me, your grace. I believe your ego is quite inflated enough."

"Minx."

Rebecca merely smiled and walked ahead toward their box.

Edward shook his head slightly, as if to clear his brain of her spell once again. *Sensible and practical?* He may be those things now, having been forced to do a lot of growing up when his father had died.

But prior to that his life had been one of a decided rake. Though he had never shirked his responsibility, he was honest enough to admit that he had enjoyed his life of few problems, plenty of wealth and the good looks that reduced women to pools of trembling wrecks.

He remembered the times fondly.

Since he'd taken over as Duke of Hartridge, however, he'd had to leave all that behind. He would not disgrace his father or his name by damaging the estates or the name of Hartridge.

He'd settled down. Stopped gambling. Stopped drinking

excessively and although he hadn't become celibate, he was a man with needs after all, he was certainly much more discreet about it. Though only one woman had held any interest for him since his trip to Ireland.

The one who thought him sensible and practical. Wonderful!

He felt a primitive urge to show her just how insensible he could be, right here in the theatre. But of course, he would not. She deserved better. She meant far too much to him to be treated as anything less than a duchess.

He frowned to himself as the thought formed in his head. That was it, the problem that kept him awake. When he was not lusting after Rebecca, he was wondering if he wanted her as a wife. No, that was not strictly true. He wanted her, quite desperately, as his wife.

He, Edward, just the man that he was, wanted her so desperately it was driving him insane. And he'd come to the monumental and, frankly, terrifying conclusion that he did not just lust after her. He could very well be in love with her. He *was* in love with her.

Love. He'd actually fallen in love with the girl who climbed things, fell into things, poured drinks over the heads of peers and swore like a sailor.

But however much Edward the man might love her, could Edward the duke really chose her as his duchess?

"Edward," Tom's voice interrupted his tortured reverie, "I've been sent once again to search you out. Though this time it seems as if you are not having as much fun as the last," he added wickedly.

"Shut up, Tom."

"Now, now. Be nice. You are not going to try any of that on me are you?" Tom continued unrepentant, "Because I must tell you, you are a little too hairy and big for me. Plus, I confess, I have a preference for blondes."

"Do you have a death wish, Tom?"

"Only in the mornings," came the laughing reply.

Both men turned to enter the box and Edward decided to try to put his musings from his mind and enjoy sitting in a darkened room with Rebecca by his side.

"I say blondes," Tom started again, "but Lady Rebecca would change anyone's mind on that score, she—"

"Tom," Edward had stopped and put his arm out to stop Tom preceding him into the box. "I vow on all that is dear to me, if you mention Rebecca's name in the same sentence as your 'preferences' again I will put a bullet in you. Understand?"

Tom merely laughed and clapped Edward on the back.

"Oh my poor cousin. You really are a lost cause." He slipped inside before Edward could retort. Or hit him. The latter seemed the most appealing.

****

Edward's evening went from bad to worse when he entered the box and discovered Rebecca had been wedged between her sister and his mother, leaving him no option but to take the back seat beside Tom. He sat directly behind her and knew immediately that he would spend the entire performance distracted by her. If he leaned forward slightly, he would be able to smell her hair. That wonderful citrus scent that almost brought him to his knees.

If he reached out he'd be able to graze his fingers along the smooth curve of her neck, exposed now because her glorious hair was piled on top of her head. He could not see the pins that held it in place, but he knew that they were there and that loosening just a few would release her hair, leaving it to tumble down her back like a river of chocolate.

He'd better stop. It was getting deuced uncomfortable sitting in this position and the performance had only just started.

He clenched his fists to make sure he did not lean forward and maul the lady where she sat and glanced over at Tom to make sure that he hadn't seen Edward panting at the top of Rebecca's head like a stray dog who'd followed her in here. But Tom's head was turned toward the stage where the performance had started. His fists, however, were clenched just like Edward's. *How interesting.*

****

Rebecca felt her shoulders droop with relief when the curtain closed for intermission and sincerely hoped nobody asked her about the performance for she knew not a whit what it had been about.

She had felt it the second Edward came in and sat behind her. If she leaned back slightly, she would be able to smell the glorious scent of sandalwood that one could only smell when standing closer than was acceptable. It was her favourite smell in the world.

What would it be like to be his wife so that he had leave to touch her in public, and she him? Would he caress her neck? Play with her hair?

Rebecca wondered if anyone would notice should she start to fan herself. She'd better stop her thoughts in their tracks. They were becoming far too heated.

The gentlemen left the box to procure some refreshments. Rebecca knew that now they would be inundated with visitors to their box.

People often used the interval as an opportunity to call on acquaintances and since they were in the ducal box it stood to reason that there would be a steady stream of well wishers heading their way.

Standing up, Rebecca begged the dowager and Caroline to excuse her while she stretched her legs. She did not really feel like making polite chit chat with boring old peers or young gentlemen who were desperate to court her dowry.

Slipping out before they were invaded, Rebecca made her way down the corridor, nodding politely to familiar faces but not stopping to speak to anyone. She headed in the opposite direction of the foyer in order to avoid the crowds and, to her relief, noted that the amount of people began to dwindle. Glancing up the corridor she wondered if she should return because, really, a single lady should not be alone for long and Caroline was sure to deliver a sermon on the subject if Rebecca did not get back, when she spotted Viscount Hadley's face. It looked as if he'd just exited the duke's box and was scanning the crowd.

In a panic, Rebecca whipped round and ducked behind a heavy velvet curtain hanging to her left. To her surprise, she had a straight view to the stage. How odd. Perhaps there was a purpose to the nook, perhaps something to do with the performances. She idly watched the crowed below for a few moments, enjoying the peace and quiet and for a moment, was tempted to stay here for the rest of the performance. But that would not do.

Reluctantly, she judged that it was time to return and turned to leave when she heard a distinctive tearing sound. What on earth? She stepped forward again and noticed that she was stuck. And there was the tear again.

Oh no. She was stuck on something. And her gown was ripped! Frantically she pulled at the material but it would not budge. It was too dark to make out what was catching the dress so she leaned forward, wincing at another audible tear, and moved the curtain slightly to allow some light into the tiny room.

It seemed her dress had gotten itself caught in the bottom of a disused chair and was hooked on a leg that had broken and come away slightly from the rest. The tearing, to her horror, was worse than she thought and her petticoat was almost completely exposed on her right side! The material had bunched on the bottom and every step or movement was tearing it more.

There came the distinctive sound of people beginning to return to their seats for the second half of the performance. Oh dear Lord. Caroline would *kill* her. Rebecca needed to think. She could not stand here with the curtain halfway parted and her dress hanging off a broken chair!

The only way to free her gown would be to let the curtain drop and try to free herself from the chair blindly. She let go of the heavy material and was immediately pitched back into darkness.

Where would they think she had gone? Would someone come to look for her? She prayed with all her might that if someone did come, it would be Caroline.

Rebecca had talked herself out of a lot of scrapes in the past but Mr. Crawdon or Edward seeing her undergarments? Even she could not think of a way out of the scandal of that one!

She began to feel her way down the dress, wincing as she fingered the massive tear. Madame would be distraught! If she found out, she'd probably force Rebecca to return all her creations and have her horsewhipped.

The material had bunched really, very tightly at the bottom of the tear. She tried to manipulate it in order to lift it off the leg but it was really wedged in. *What to do?*

Rebecca thought for a moment before deciding that there was nothing else for it. She had to get free. Nobody knew where she was! She would have to pull with all her might and hope that the dress gave way. As for returning to the public eye with half her dress torn and her petticoat on display? Well, she'd worry about that when the time came.

****

The dowager and Caroline did their best to look unfazed

while they held a whispered, frantic conversation with Edward and Mr. Crawdon about the whereabouts of the little hoyden. Only Rebecca could get herself lost in a building with two exits.

Edward dampened the panic that reared up when he realised she wasn't returning. It was highly unlikely that George Simons would have gotten to her here. For one thing, his mode of dress would have stood out immediately. For another, Rebecca was unlikely to calmly go anywhere with him or even speak to him when there were so many people around from whom she could get assistance.

Caroline made to rise from her seat. "I should go and find her."

Edward, however, placed a hand gently on her shoulder and said, "You remain here with Mother, Lady Caroline. Tom, please look after the ladies. I will find Rebecca.

Caroline looked uncertain but the dowager patted her hand and reassured her that Edward would find her and return her to them.

"Quickly," she finished with a glint in her eye.

Edward rolled his eyes and exited the box. Really, what did his mother think he was going to do? Seduce Rebecca in the middle of the corridor? The thought had appeal, he'd admit. But if he were to marry her he would treat her — wait! *Marry her?* He still hadn't decided, had he?

She was still unsuitable. That had not changed. Or had it?

To be fair, Rebecca had hardly been scandalous at all since their arrival in London. Granted she was now missing, alone, in the middle of an opera performance. And she had poured a drink over Sir Roger's head. Oh, and there had been the little set to with Lady Sarah in the park, though Rebecca had behaved like the perfect lady. Even if she'd looked like she wanted to gouge the other lady's eyes out!

But those things were not so bad.

Of course, he could not forget their ride in Hyde Park the

other day when he'd beaten her in a race and she'd issued a string of expletives, oblivious to the fact that her hair had come lose, her hat had flown off and they had an audience. He hadn't been oblivious. Though he had been ridiculously distracted by her since he'd gone to pick her up that morning.

Her habit had been red for God's sake. Red. The colour of sin. And the cut of it did nothing to diminish her curves. If anything the masculine, military style just highlighted them all the more. And it was red! Edward had wanted to weep.

But he had noted these things. He'd also noted the 'incident' where she'd dived in front of a carriage on Regents Street because a kitten had been standing in the road.

She had saved the kitten and completely charmed the driver of the carriage and the gentleman inside, unsurprisingly, but Edward had nearly lost his life. When he'd yelled at her, he could admit *now* that he'd yelled though he'd refused to at the time, she'd hotly defended herself by claiming that anyone would have done the same.

Edward had asked what she planned to do with the scrawny stray now that she'd almost caused a collision to save it. Suffice to say, his mother was now the proud owner of a cat.

All these things aside though, there was no denying Rebecca was a well brought up lady. She was kind, caring, funny and spirited. And more beautiful than was good for his common sense. And, quite simply, he loved her to distraction.

Perhaps she wasn't duchess material but did it matter? She was all he could ever want in a partner. And he was starting to suspect that she was exactly what he needed to save him from a life that was 'sensible and practical'.

He thought of presenting her to the stiff and staid members of his family and the peerage and could not supress a grin. He would pay money to see it!

His mind raced with thoughts while his heart fought desperately to get him to admit what he had subconsciously known for quite some time now; Rebecca was his destiny. He loved her. Loved her more than he ever thought possible. He loved her wholly and completely. And he would never be satisfied unless he had her by his side, every day, for the rest of his life. He resolved there and then to make her his own. To hell with propriety and what was expected of him. Rebecca was made for him and Edward would make her his wife.

Besides, she may not be exactly conventional but really, she had never done anything too sensational and—

His thoughts were interrupted by the sudden appearance of Lady Rebecca. Falling. Backwards. Through a curtain. Straight onto her backside. And yelling curses as she went.

—And maybe he'd spoken too soon.

It seemed that the lady had decided to stay on the floor, lying flat, gazing up at the ceiling and breathing heavily. *Was that her petticoat?*

"Good evening, my lady." He approached slowly, wondering what on earth had happened.

Rebecca started at his voice and turned her head to watch him approach.

"Oh no," she groaned and threw her arm over her eyes. "Go away."

He hunkered down beside her and pried her arm gently from her face.

"I am afraid I cannot do that, darling."

"Oh you can. It is really very simple. You just turn around and walk back the way you came."

"Are you going to get up off the floor?"

She contemplated his question for a moment before heaving a sigh of resignation.

"I suppose I must."

Edward smiled gently at her.

"Shall I assist you?"

"No that is quite alright. Although…" Here her face flushed and Edward was intrigued.

"My dress, it appears to have a, uh, a slight tear."

Edward's eyes raked her body. Her dress was torn completely open on one side, thankfully though, not past the bodice. He did not think he'd survive that. It was hard enough keeping his head together seeing her petticoat and the outline of her legs underneath it.

"Sweetheart, I can see your petticoat."

"Yes, I would imagine that you can."

"I think perhaps lying on the floor is not the best idea, given that it highlights the — what was it? — slight tear in your gown."

She huffed again then sat up. Edward reached out a hand and Rebecca clasped it as he hauled her to her feet.

"Are you hurt?" he asked gently.

"Not at all. Apart from my pride," she smiled ruefully and he could not have loved her more than he did in that moment. Had it been any other female she'd have been crying her eyes out now and scaring the wits out of him.

"So what are we to do about this 'little tear'?"

"I must leave immediately," she said, "before anyone sees it! I will be quite ruined and then murdered, I am sure, by Caroline."

"I can imagine," Edward agreed gravely. There was a moment's pause before he spoke again.

"You stay here. I will make our excuses and then escort you home. Tom will stay, I am sure, to escort the other ladies."

He made to leave and Rebecca reached out and grabbed his arm.

"No! Edward, no. You cannot, *we* cannot travel alone together. What will people think?"

Edward's eyes swept down her gaping dress, her dishevelled hair. "Are you quite sure you want anyone else to see you like this?"

Rebecca looked down at herself and grimaced.

"Caroline will come with me."

"Fine. I will tell your sister too. But I am not leaving two ladies to travel alone any more than I will leave one lady to travel alone so I shall escort you nonetheless."

Rebecca smiled. Always the gentleman.

"Very well. Thank you."

"Of course," he continued with a sigh, "my mother will not stay with just Tom for company and she'd been so looking forward to the performance. One of her favourites, you understand. But she will not mind having to leave because you are afraid to be alone with me."

"I am *not* afraid" Rebecca argued, "and I see what you are trying to do. Your mother will have plenty more opportunities to come to the Opera."

"Of course she will. I will just go and tell her she must leave then. I shall return directly."

He turned to go and could not supress his smile at yet another huff behind him before—

"Wait. Do not make her leave. I am certainly *not* afraid to travel alone with you. Do please give my apologies and tell the dowager and my sister I shall see them at home."

Edward turned back and bowed then swept off to do as instructed. Damn the man. He knew exactly what he was doing. Blackmailing her! And forcing her to lie. She had said that she was not afraid to be alone with him. Nothing could be further from the truth; for she was terrified he would see how much she loved him. And even more terrified that she would not be able to resist him in the close confines of a darkened carriage.

Chapter Twenty-Three

Edward tried not to feel smug about how he'd gotten his way and was now sitting across from Rebecca in his carriage on the way back to Mayfair.

Of course, he'd used underhanded tactics. But that was allowed when you were in love. However, now that he was alone with her, he felt stupidly nervous and did not know quite what to say.

It did not help matters that her petticoat was still on display. And as hard as she tried to cover it up, his eyes could not un-see what they'd seen and his body certainly could not forget it.

"Now are you going to tell me what happened?" He broke the tension with the question he'd been dying to ask. Never had he known someone who managed to get herself into such ridiculous situations at such regular intervals.

There hadn't been time to question her in the theatre. He'd bent down and whispered to his mother and Caroline that Rebecca was fine but had had a little incident and needed to be returned home. The fact that neither questioned him further was testament to how unsurprising this news was.

After asking Tom to ensure the ladies got home safely, he plucked up Rebecca's cloak and was out of the box within minutes.

His heart had clenched when he came back down the corridor and spotted her, alone and forlorn. With her hair a mess and her dress torn, she looked miserable and utterly endearing.

Without a word, he threw her cloak over her and fastened it at the neck. Then, because he could not help it, he raised her chin and planted a swift, tender kiss on her lips. Her eyes widened fractionally but she smiled brilliantly at him and Edward thought if he hadn't already tumbled into love with her he certainly would have in that moment.

Still silent, he turned her and led her down the stairs and onto the street where his carriage awaited. And now, here they were and he was more than a little curious as to how they ended up this way.

"I think it probably looked worse than it was, you know," Rebecca started. Edward said nothing and waited for her to continue.

"I knew that people would be visiting during the interval and I did not feel like making polite chit chat so I left to stretch my legs. Only that blasted Viscount Hadley was sniffing me out so I ducked behind that curtain and got stuck in a chair."

"I am sorry. Did you say 'stuck in a chair'?"

"Yes, well my dress caught in it and when I went to leave it tore even worse. I had to keep pulling at it, it was quite stuck you understand, and eventually, it gave."

"This would be the point where you came tumbling through the curtain, swearing like a sea captain, yes?"

"I did not swear like a sea captain," she sniffed, "I am a lady."

He burst into laughter and she looked mightily offended. But before she could speak a word or give way to that temper of hers, he leaned over and swept her onto his lap.

Rebecca gasped in shock.

"Edward! What are you doing? You cannot –"

"I can and I am," was all he answered before his lips claimed hers.

He told himself to hold back. That they had not even spoken of a future together. That he had not told her how she owned his heart completely and utterly.

But as soon as their lips met the fire he'd been trying too hard to keep in check burst into the brightest of flames. Rebecca groaned and wrapped her arms around his neck, pulling him closer.

Her tongue reached out to dance with his and he thought he would explode right there and then.

Rebecca could not stop the moan that escaped her as Edward's mouth crushed hers in a passionate kiss that left her mind blank and her body screaming. She was shocked by the visceral need that rose up inside her. She wanted him. In the most intimate way possible.

The fact that she loved him so only added fuel to the fire of her yearning. He kept her anchored to him with one strong hand while the other slipped beneath her cloak and began a slow, torturous exploration of her body.

He broke away from her mouth to rain kisses along her jaw, down her neck and to nibble wickedly on her ear. Rebecca felt like she would expire. Instinctively, she pressed closer to him and was rewarded by a desperate groan. She felt hot and flustered and more than a little excited by the evidence of his desire for her.

When did I become such a wanton, she wondered desperately. She felt a swift moment of disappointment when Edward's hand left her body, only to be shocked all over again when he moved her to lie on the plush velvet cushion of the carriage seat and then stretch out above her.

He held himself away from her on his elbows before once again lowering his head to claim her mouth. Her thoughts scrambled wildly as she reached up and pulled at the lapels of his jacket. She wanted to feel his weight on he, wanted to run her hands over his broad shoulders, his muscled back and lower still. She wanted to explore every wonderful inch of him.

By this time, Edward's hands had found the tear in her dress. While he once again administered kisses along her neck, his hand was stroking her thigh over the flimsy petticoat and the heat of his skin scorched her. When had he removed his gloves? He was driving her slowly mad and Rebecca felt a desperate need for more.

"Edward," she whispered frantically, "please."

Her whispered plea cut through the haze of longing that surrounded him and Edward dragged his body back under control.

What the hell was he doing? He could not take her here, in a damned carriage. Much as he wanted to she deserved so much more.

Reluctantly, he dragged himself away from her and sat up then reached down to pull her back into a seated position. But he was still human so he settled her onto his lap once again. They were both panting and Edward leaned his forehead against hers while he caught his breath.

"I am sorry, sweetheart," he murmured, "I do not know what I was thinking. I *wasn't* thinking. You'd make a saint lose his mind. And I am no saint."

"Well, I am sorry too," she whispered, "sorry you stopped."

His eyes snapped up at her bold statement and he was momentarily distracted from his raging lust by the annoyed look on her face.

He felt amusement as well as a pure masculine pride well up inside him.

"Believe me, it took more strength than I knew I possessed to stop. But I had to. You do not know what would have happened."

"I am perfectly aware of what would have happened, thank you." She paused then and conceded, "Well, I have a general idea."

He chuckled softly and kissed her forehead, not daring to touch her lips again.

"Rebecca, my love, you deserve more, much, much more than having your innocence taken in the back of a filthy carriage."

"It is a very nice carriage," she argued mutinously.

"Yes, it is," he agreed, "but it is still a carriage and your first time making love will not be in one."

Rebecca stared at him a moment then moved to sit on the other side of the vehicle. He saw hurt and embarrassment flash across her face.

Oh no, he thought, bracing himself for a storm, what was she thinking now?

Rebecca's head had finally cleared and she realised just what they'd been doing and what he must think of her. Dear God, she had thrown herself at him and then practically begged him to — to — oh, she could not even think it. And in a carriage? If anyone knew what a wanton she was, she would be disowned by the lot of them.

He would despise her now; think her even more unworthy. She went from the most exquisite happiness to torturous misery in seconds. And here came the damned headache again.

I should say something; apologise or explain or, or something. Clearing her throat she steeled herself to look into his eyes. Oh they were so beautiful in the moonlight, all silver and shining and—

No Rebecca! She scolded herself. Do not get distracted.

"Your grace," she began only to be interrupted by his snort of incredulity.

"Your grace?" he questioned disbelievingly.

"Your grace," she repeated firmly, "I must apologise for my behaviour just now. I do not know what came over me. I, I am not usually so w-wanton and..." she trailed off miserably, finishing with a whispered, "What must you think of me?"

Edward gazed at her in amazement. If he lived to be one hundred he would never understand the female mind.

"What must I think of you? I will tell you, shall I?" he grasped her arms again and this time deposited her on the seat beside him so he could grip her hands. "I think you are the most infuriating, stubborn, scandalous little minx I've ever come across." Her eyes narrowed and she opened her mouth, no doubt to issue a tirade but he continued quickly, before she had the chance to speak.

"I also think you are the kindest, warmest, wittiest and brightest person I've ever met. And you are far, far too beautiful for my peace of mind. It seems that I have no thoughts left anymore, but thoughts of you. You are the first thing I think of when I wake in the morning and the only thing I dream of at night. I am completely under your spell."

Rebecca's mouth hung open by the end of his announcement.

"That is quite a speech," she said a little breathlessly.

"Not even rehearsed," he stated proudly.

At this she laughed. He really was terribly arrogant and she loved him so much it hurt.

"So do not worry about anything I think of you," he continued, "and your wantonness, as long as it is reserved for me, is certainly nothing to apologise for," he finished with a wicked wink and a grin.

"It is," she confessed, "only for you. I've never even experienced this, this *want* before, until you."

Rebecca wanted with all her heart to tell him that she loved him. But he had not said that he loved her and though his words warmed her heart, they were not words of love.

His eyes gleamed at her words and he kissed her again.

But before either of them could get swept away again, the carriage rolled to a stop outside the dowager's house.

Edward pulled away reluctantly. He would have the rest of their lives to kiss her once they were married. He should probably mention that to her, actually.

"Let me see you inside," he said as he stepped out of the carriage and handed her down. He kept his hand on her lower back as she walked up the steps and into the house before him.

Once they entered the hallway, Edward dismissed Jeffries and led Rebecca to the drawing room. There was a fire burning merrily in the hearth and candles bathing the room in a soft, warm glow.

"My mother will return soon so I will take my leave lest she berate me for my impropriety," Edward spoke quietly.

Rebecca merely nodded. If only his mother knew of her son's impropriety!

"It would not do for her to see us alone together. Again."

Rebecca nodded again but felt her heart sink. If the dowager saw them alone and acting in any way inappropriately, she would demand a marriage. This was obviously not something Edward wanted. And Rebecca did not want it either.

Oh, she would love nothing more than to be married to the man she loved. But to be married to Edward when he did not love her, when he'd been forced into it, and when he thought her wholly unsuitable? He may lust after her now. He may even care for her. But lust would fade and he would grow to resent her.

And then, what if one day he fell in love? He would stay married to Rebecca because he was an honourable man. But he would not love her. His heart would belong to another. Would he take a mistress? The thought was unbearable.

Rebecca steeled her shoulders and smiled.

"No it would not do. She would have you wed to me without a moment's pause. It would be a disaster."

She was trying her best to be brave, but could feel tears burn the back of her throat and she wanted him to leave so she could cry and wail in peace.

Edward's heart froze when Rebecca spoke of a marriage between them being a disaster. But he was coming to know his little tigress quite well and he could see in her eyes that there was something else going on in that infuriating head of hers.

"A disaster, sweetheart?"

He walked toward her so he stood mere inches from her. Clasping her shoulders, he smiled softly and said, "It would be a lot of interesting things, but far from a disaster."

Rebecca's breath caught in her throat. What was he saying? Was he saying he *wanted* to marry her? Or at the least that it would not be horrifying for him?

He could practically hear the wheels turning in her head. He was so very tempted to open his heart to her but he did not want to overwhelm her. She was young and innocent. And thought him 'sensible and practical'. How could someone like him appeal to someone like her?

They both had quite enough to think about tonight. There would be time tomorrow to discuss the confusing emotions radiating from both of them.

"Goodnight Rebecca" he whispered, still clutching her shoulders.

"Goodnight Edward," she responded shakily.

He pulled her forward and placed a tender kiss on her head, just like that afternoon on her father's estate when she'd yelled at him for not kissing her properly.

The thought made him smile. It seemed a lifetime ago.

He turned to leave, thoughts of how to convince her that he was not the boring and sedate man she seemed to think him swirling around his head.

He glanced back before he left and ground to a halt. She was so heart-achingly beautiful. He would not rest, could not rest, until he made her his.

Swiftly crossing the room again, he gathered her in his arms and gave her an earth-shattering kiss.

"Tomorrow," he whispered against her lips, "we will discuss our future tomorrow. Dream of me, my love."

Rebecca raised her fingers to her lips, still tingling from his kiss. *We will discuss our future tomorrow.* What did that mean?

That night, for probably the first time in her life, Rebecca did as she was told. She dreamed of Edward.

****

Outside, it took all of George Simons' willpower not to murder the duke as he left the Townhouse. He knew he would not get very far with the duke's man watching the house. George had had to settle for watching from a further distance than he wanted.

He took another slug of whiskey, the burn in his throat unnoticeable above the burn of anger in the pit of his stomach.

She was *his*. The sooner that duke got that into his head, the better.

George wasn't stupid. He knew his life would be forfeit if he put his hands on a peer. But things were progressing between the duke and Rebecca. Even a blind man would be able to see.

It was time to act.

Tomorrow. She would be his. Even if it killed him.

Chapter Twenty-Four

Rebecca slept surprisingly well and awoke the next day filled with an excited anticipation.

She had thought about her conversation with Edward last night. She had thought a great deal *more* about everything else that had happened with Edward last night, but had given some consideration to what they'd said and realized that she had left a lot unsaid and thought that perhaps Edward had too.

And he'd spoken of their future.

Rebecca had decided in the night, while tossing and turning trying to make out Edward's meaning, that she would be honest with him. After all, what did she have to lose? Only her pride. And pride was no substitute for having Edward by her side.

She was going to tell him that she loved him. She knew, of course, that she was still wholly unsuitable to being a duchess but she would try her hardest to change. She meant to ask Caroline, the dowager, her mother, anyone to help her become the type of lady deserving of the title.

Of course he could have meant that they *had* no future

but Rebecca could not believe that. Not after his kisses. Not after the wonderful things he'd said to her. No, he must feel something for her and even if it was not love it could perhaps develop into love over time.

Rebecca joined the dowager and Caroline for breakfast and, try as she might, she could not keep the smile from her face.

"Why, Rebecca you are positively glowing this morning," remarked the dowager.

Rebecca blushed and thanked the older lady.

"Is there a reason for such a happy countenance?" she asked.

"No, your grace," answered Rebecca staidly. "None that I can think of."

The door to the dining room opened and Edward swept in with Tom following behind. They could see Jeffries shaking his head in despair behind the two gentlemen.

"Do calm down, Jeffries," Edward called behind him, "there is really no cause to announce me in my own mother's house."

He walked round the table to kiss the dowager on the cheek and take a seat to her right, beside Rebecca.

"Technically, it is your house darling," said the dowager with a smile.

"Nonsense, I have a house. This is yours to leave to whomever you choose."

The dowager looked surprised but extremely pleased.

"Why, Edward. I had no idea. That is very kind, my son. Though who would I leave it to, but my son? Or perhaps my adopted one who has yet to greet me?" she answered mischievously drawing the attention of Mr. Crawdon who was busy filling his plate.

Tom smiled widely and after dropping his plate on the table beside Caroline, he hurried around the table to plant a loud kiss on the dowager's cheek.

"That is better." She grinned.

"So what brings you two here this morning?" the dowager asked.

Edward had moved to the sideboard to fill his plate and Rebecca tried to keep her eyes away from him but she was struggling not to watch his every move. He had not spoken save to give a general greeting to her and Caroline but as he was passing her chair she'd felt the brush of his hand on her shoulders.

"No idea," answered Tom who had resumed his seat and started to demolish his breakfast. "I was woken with the birds and told to come!"

Edward resumed his seat and looked a little flustered.

"Was there a reason you needed to come so early, dear?" asked the dowager innocently, though there was a mischievous twinkle in her eye.

Edward glanced quickly at Rebecca before answering.

"Do I need a reason to want to break my fast with my own mother? Really, mother one would think you did not want us here."

"My dear, you know you are always sure of the warmest of welcomes from me. It is just a little unusual, that is all."

Before Edward could answer, Jeffries entered with a silver tray bearing a small card.

"For you, my lady," he bowed, presenting the card to Rebecca.

Rebecca was a little taken aback. Though they had received plenty of invitations since their arrival, they usually came to the dowager or even Caroline, being the eldest. And their morning calls would not begin for a couple of hours yet.

"There is a footman awaiting your reply," Jeffries explained.

Rebecca took the envelope and studied the direction. The penmanship was unfamiliar to her though it certainly belonged to a lady. Intrigued, she opened the missive and her jaw dropped in surprise.

"What is it?" asked Caroline curiously.

"An invitation to the Vauxhall Gardens" —Rebecca's confused look remained on her face— "for tonight, for you and I, Caroline."

"How nice," answered Caroline, "though it is a little rude to issue an invitation at such short notice. Who is it from?"

Rebecca gave Edward a loaded look before answering, "Lady Sarah."

Now everyone looked confused.

"Lady Sarah?" asked the dowager, "Are you acquainted with that lady?"

"As much as I want to be," answered Rebecca bluntly.

Caroline laughed a little nervously.

"Rebecca and Lady Sarah seemed to have a little, um — clash of personalities, your grace," she explained.

"She is vile," said Rebecca, which was another way of putting it, Caroline supposed.

"Good heavens," said the dowager, clearly amused, "I cannot say I feel anything more than the merest tolerance for the lady but I do not think I've ever heard her described as 'vile'."

"Oh that is not all Lady Rebecca had to say on the subject of Lady Sarah, Aunt," Mr. Crawdon piped up with a wide grin. "She also called her old and ugly."

"I did not," said Rebecca hotly, "I said her dress was ugly. And she started it."

The dowager burst into gales of laughter.

"Oh, my dear you never fail to amuse me."

"Yes, well as amusing as this all may be," began Edward, who had been silently studying the invitation, "it makes it abundantly clear that Rebecca and Lady Sarah are hardly friends. Why then, the sudden invitation?"

"You suspect something?" asked Rebecca.

"I am not sure. Lady Sarah is mostly harmless, though

she does not like to be bested. And you, my dear, put her very firmly in her place."

"Well, it does not signify anyway, since we will not be going," said Caroline.

"What? Why not?" asked Rebecca.

Caroline stared at her.

"You cannot *want* to go?"

"Well, if I were to choose a companion it certainly would not be that haggard old b—"

"Ahem," the dowager's well-timed cough cut into Rebecca's tirade.

"But," Rebecca continued more demurely, "I have always desperately wanted to go the gardens. The dancing, the performers, the fireworks! It sounds so magical."

"It is also highly improper for a group of ladies to attend unaccompanied. The place itself is barely proper as it is. Besides, she has left it far too late to ask us. I am sure the dowager has plans for us."

Rebecca frowned. Much as she disliked Lady Sarah, she was intrigued by what the woman was up to. And she did so want to visit the gardens.

But Caroline was right, it would be unspeakably rude to accept the invitation at such short notice when the dowager was bound to have plans for them already.

"Oh do not worry on that score, my dears," the dowager spoke up, "I had planned a quiet night at home anyway. You should take the opportunity to go and enjoy yourselves. I am sure Lady Sarah would not mind the addition of Edward and Tom who will be happy to escort you, will you not?"

"Yes, of course," answered Edward quickly. He turned to Rebecca. "If you are going to insist on going, and I realise the futility of arguing the matter with you, then I want to be there to see what she is up to."

"So we're going?" Her eyes shone with excitement and Edward wondered how in the world anyone was supposed to refuse her anything. He doubted they ever had. And he was certain that he would never be able to.

"If you want to go, then we'll go."

Rebecca turned to Caroline with a questioning look.

Caroline sighed and finally relented.

"Fine. We shall go but I warn you, Rebecca, you are to behave."

"I will! Oh I am so excited. I shall write our acceptance immediately."

She jumped from her chair and ran from the room.

"Do not forget to tell her about the duke and Mr. Crawdon's attendance too," Caroline called after her.

Since Rebecca continued to tear up the stairs, Caroline could not be sure whether she'd heard or not.

****

Rebecca had heard and now, hours later, she fairly bounced around the drawing room waiting for Lady Sarah's carriage to arrive. Edward and Tom would meet them there. Rebecca imagined the hidden walks, the benches under overhanging branches, all of the discreet places she and Edward could steal some moments alone.

At eight o'clock on the dot Lady Sarah's carriage arrived. The girls bid the dowager a swift goodbye and quickly made their way outside. Even Caroline was caught up in the excitement though she urged Rebecca again to be wary of Lady Sarah.

"I shall be as civil to her as she is to me," Rebecca had stated firmly. "I am sure we shan't even speak to each other, there will be so much to do!"

Her excitement had been infectious and Caroline had soon allowed herself to relax and look forward to the evening's festivities.

The sisters entered Lady Sarah's carriage a little

hesitantly for they were not sure about the reception they would receive.

But the lady was all that was polite and cordial.

"Lady Rebecca, Lady Caroline. I am so pleased that you could join me tonight," she exclaimed as the girls climbed into the luxurious carriage.

Lady Sarah looked as flamboyant as ever. She wore a headband with such huge feathers Rebecca was half expecting it to take flight. Her dress was an eye-watering pink, the colour picked solely to draw attention, good or bad.

The neckline was scandalous even by the most liberal of standards, and Lady Sarah's ample curves were fighting what looked to be a losing battle to stay inside it.

Caroline smiled warmly in greeting but Rebecca held back. Lady Sarah certainly had made no outward changes so there was no reason to suppose she'd made any inside either.

"What wonderful news you had for me, Lady Rebecca, when you told me Eddie and Tom would join us. Such charming creatures, and so devilishly handsome!"

Rebecca merely smiled in response though her teeth felt sewn together.

"Of course," the lady continued, either oblivious to or uncaring of the disinterest from the other side of the carriage, "they were not always so stuffy and staid as they are now. La! The stories I could tell."

She smiled sweetly, probably anticipating questions from the younger ladies. But neither one was inclined to ask questions they would rather not hear the answers to.

Caroline, wisely, bit her tongue and said nothing. Rebecca, stupidly, let her mouth run away with her. Again.

"I hardly think they are stuffy and staid. Why, Mr. Crawdon's businesses must require a great deal of attention and as for Ed – I mean, the duke, well I think we're all aware of just what a big undertaking the Hartridge estates are."

"How sweet of you to jump to his defence, my dear,"

Lady Sarah grinned triumphantly, but Rebecca would not be baited.

"I believe I spoke of both gentlemen, my lady," her smile felt brittle and pasted on, "to whom are you referring?"

Lady Sarah laughed that ridiculous laugh again and Rebecca clenched her fists.

"Oh you are a coy one," she said at last, "but we will speak of it no more! Now, tell me, are you very excited about your first visit to the gardens?"

Rebecca was excited but decided that before they went any further in this charade they might as well be honest with each other about where they stood.

"Oh, we are beside ourselves with excitement, my lady," she answered, "though somewhat surprised at your invitation. I think it is safe to say that neither of us set out to be friends."

Caroline winced at Rebecca's bluntness but Rebecca really felt it was better to find out exactly what the lady was up to.

Lady Sarah's eyes narrowed slightly and she seemed to be thinking over Rebecca's words carefully. Finally, she let out and sigh and answered.

"I should not be surprised at your bluntness, Lady Rebecca. You seem to have quite the reputation of being — er — unusual. But I have no hidden agenda. I realise that I was rude to you in the park that day and I wanted to make amends."

Rebecca started to relax a little. That sounded reasonable and even nice. But Lady Sarah wasn't finished.

"Besides, we have a great deal in common, you and me. I thought it would help you to have a friend in the same situation."

"I do not know what you mean," Rebecca said carefully.

"I shall be frank, if I may, since our only companion is your dear sister," Lady Sarah spared a quick smile for Caroline but it did not reach her eyes. "I have seen the way Eddie is with you. And the way you are with him."

Rebecca was tempted to deny it but was more interested in what Lady Sarah had to say. She had a sinking feeling that it would not be good.

"I think it is obvious to everyone that there is an attachment forming. I just hope that you are keeping your wits about you. Edward was quite the rake in his day and though he has had to mature a lot, I cannot believe he has changed all that much in essentials. He is attracted to you. Any man would be, I suppose. Though Tom seems more taken with your sister."

At this, Caroline gasped and Rebecca spared her a quick, surprised glance, before turning back to Lady Sarah.

"He is not a bad man, he just cannot resist a pretty face," she continued flippantly, "I simply think you should take more care of your reputation."

Here, she dropped the smile and leaned forward, her face all seriousness.

"Edward will not marry you, Lady Rebecca. He is a duke and will only marry an appropriate girl. One of his family's choosing, I warrant. You are not dim-witted, so I am sure you are already aware of that."

Rebecca's heart sank and she could hardly breathe. Yes, she was aware of it. But she was going to improve. She had already decided to try harder. To change.

Lady Sarah had not finished though. The woman was relentless.

"Oh your lineage cannot be questioned. Nor your wealth. But, really, I think we all know that you would not be exactly in keeping with the idea of a duchess. I only urge you tread carefully. Men, especially men of the duke's stature will always come out of these things with barely a blemish on their reputations. But women! Well, I think we all know that once you are ruined your life is essentially over."

"That is enough," Caroline barked, finally having heard

enough of Lady Sarah's bitter ranting.

Rebecca had paled dramatically and Caroline was afraid she would swoon.

"It is alright, Caroline," Rebecca assured her.

She turned to Lady Sarah.

"I thank you for your obviously sincere concern," Rebecca bit out sarcastically, "but I assure you, no warning is necessary. The duke has not made any unwelcome advances toward me."

"I did not say they were unwelcome," Lady Sarah interjected.

Rebecca bit her tongue, literally, to stop from lashing out at the lady.

She did not, *would* not believe that Edward was the type of man who would use a woman so ill. And certainly not her. She believed him when he said he cared for her. She did.

"Regardless of what you think, there is no cause for concern about the duke and I, and I would prefer if you did not allow your imagination to run wild."

Lady Sarah laughed bitterly.

"My imagination? If only that were the source of my warning. It is not my imagination, my dear but bitter experience."

Rebecca felt as if someone had slapped her.

"What?" she whispered.

"You would not know, having been tucked away in the Irish countryside. Your precious duke and I were lovers and he broke my heart when he toyed with me then tossed me away deciding I was unsuited to the life of a duchess. And I see history repeating itself before my very eyes."

The carriage had come to a stop but none of the ladies made a move to alight.

"What happened in the past is no concern of mine," answered Rebecca a little shakily.

"The past?" laughed Lady Sarah, "It was right before he

went to stay with your family, my dear."

The door opened and a footman had lowered the steps and still Rebecca's eyes stayed fixated on Lady Sarah.

"Now, my dear," Lady Sarah continued, "let us put all of this from our heads and enjoy ourselves tonight. I am glad that I have warned you, I wish someone could have done the same for me."

She turned and exited the carriage.

Caroline grabbed Rebecca's hand.

"Oh, my darling," she cried, "please do not listen to that poisonous woman's lies. It cannot be true. I've seen how Edward looks at you, it is with the purest of love I am sure of it!"

Rebecca listened to Caroline's words but did not really take them in. Her mind was whirling. Had he said the same things to Lady Sarah as he had to her? Would he use her then drop her? Would he ruin her reputation to save his own?

She thought back on their conversations, their meetings. He'd been so studiously careful not to allow anyone to see them together. He had spoken words of admiration but not love.

Oh God, it could not be true. Surely he would have told her about a relationship with Lady Sarah. He would not have risked her finding out this way, would he? She needed to speak with him at once.

"Do not worry, Caroline. I am well. Let us join the duke and Mr. Crawdon. I believe I have some questions for our esteemed protector."

Chapter Twenty-Five

Edward checked his watch again and bit back a sigh of frustration. They were late.

"You can keep staring, cousin, it will not make them arrive any quicker." Tom slapped Edward on the back and grinned ruefully at his downfall. "You really have fallen desperately hard, have you not?"

Edward thought about arguing but what was the point? He meant to make his feelings known to Rebecca tonight and ask for her hand in marriage.

He knew that he should speak to her father first but he thought perhaps she would like for them to travel together to Ireland and inform her parents then. He could not imagine that they would object.

A niggle of worry gnawed at him at the thoughts of Lady Sarah and Rebecca being together. But he swiftly pushed it aside. Sarah was eccentric but not dangerous. She might fill Rebecca's ears with tales of his past escapades but they were not too bad.

He wondered if he should have told Rebecca about Lady Sarah and his past with her but a kiss or two during Sarah's debut Season was hardly worth mentioning, was it?

Finally, he spotted them through the crowd and had to stop himself from running to her. She looked breath taking as ever. He would never, ever be able to believe his luck if she were to consent to be his wife.

He loved her so much he thought it must be stamped on his head. And he did not care a jot! He smiled as he thought of how much he had changed, in so short a time.

Sensible and practical he may have been, but a sensible duke would not be considering grabbing a lady in front of the entire crowd and shouting his love for her from the rooftops!

The gardens were heaving with people tonight as usual. It was a unique place where classes mixed more than any other and working class folk gained entrance just as easily as the peerage.

Lady Sarah, Rebecca had informed them, had secured them a box right by the Promenade where they could easily see the dancing and musicians playing. Edward hoped that while the others danced and mingled, he could slip away alone with Rebecca and tell her his hopes and plans.

The ladies eventually made their way to Edward's and Tom's sides. Tom was quick to bow gallantly over their hands and use the most flowery of terms to describe their beauty. Edward stayed still and watched Rebecca. Something was wrong. She looked pale and drawn and would not meet his eyes.

He stepped forward to take her hand but she stepped immediately back and shied away from his touch. *What the devil?*

He looked at the other ladies present and noticed that while Sarah looked as flamboyant and happy as ever, Lady Caroline also looked pale and shot worried looks at her younger sister.

What the hell had Sarah done?

"Rebecca," he made to reach for her again but she

jumped away and spoke brightly to the group.

"Shall we find our booth? I am so very anxious to see what the gardens have to offer. I believe they have a quite potent punch that one simply must try?"

Tom laughed and answered cheerfully, "They do indeed, my lady. Though I would caution you against more than a mere taste. It is not for the faint hearted."

"Ah but I am far from faint hearted, my dear Mr. Crawdon. It takes more than a mere drink or a pretty word to touch my heart."

Tom wondered a little at the cryptic remark but the meaning was clear to Edward. A pretty word? She meant, clearly, the things he had told her last night.

His temper began to rise. She did not know how difficult it had been to open his heart to her, to be even slightly vulnerable. So long had he remained emotionless and cut off from those around him, the worries and responsibilities of his title leaving no room for the softer things in life. He had begun to think that Rebecca was the one person he *could* be soft and loving with, someone with whom he could be himself and not have to worry about appearances.

Someone he could laugh with and enjoy life with. Someone he could even climb statues with, he thought with a smile.

But her behaviour now? It was so very different to yesterday's that he was sure something had happened. This morning they had not been able to talk alone but she had seemed as happy to see him as he was her.

They had at this point reached their booth and Edward was momentarily distracted from his dark thoughts by the expression of wonder on Rebecca's face. She looked mesmerised by the sights and sounds around her.

The Vauxhall Gardens were certainly a sight to behold for the first time; he remembered witnessing the spectacle himself, albeit in a bit of a drunken haze.

She and her sister clasped hands as they scanned the crowds walking by, watched the dancers and musicians mere feet from where they stood.

He wanted to speak to her. To straighten this matter out. He had envisioned taking her on a stroll through one of the secluded pathways, stopping to watch the fireworks, which he knew she would love.

Suddenly, he could not wait a moment longer. He strode over to her and grasped her arm, turning her to face him.

"Rebecca."

"Your grace?" she answered coldly.

They were back to your grace? For God's sake what the hell had happened with Sarah?

"We need to talk."

"We are talking," she bit back.

Edward clenched his jaw as his temper rose. He should stay calm and reasonable, be gentle and polite.

"What the hell is wrong with you?"

Or not.

"Me? Not a thing, your grace. I am merely trying to enjoy the festivities. Be a dear and get some of this famous punch, would you? I believe I would like to dance."

She turned to Tom and gave him her biggest and most endearing smile.

He looked completely dazzled. *The traitor.*

"You will dance with me, will you not Mr. Crawdon?" she purred.

When had she learned to purr?

Tom coughed a couple of times, glancing nervously at Edward then back to Rebecca.

"I would be delighted to, my dear."

They left the box with an apologetic shrug from Tom to Edward. Rebecca ignored him and swept by with her nose in the air.

Edward ground his teeth.

"Well," started Lady Sarah, "there seems to—"

"Lady Caroline," Edward spoke over whatever quip Lady Sarah had been about to make, "will you do me the honour of dancing with me?"

Caroline looked a little taken aback at his harsh tone but conceded and took his arm.

"Do not mind me," called Lady Sarah sarcastically, "I shall be fine left unattended."

Caroline threw a nervous glance at Edward's stony profile.

"We really should not leave Lady Sarah alone, your grace."

Edward turned to address her.

"Since I can only imagine that she is responsible for the change in your sister, I cannot bring myself to behave very gentlemanlike towards her at present."

Caroline chewed her lip as if unsure whether to answer or not. Funny that she did the same thing as her sister. Of course, when her sister did it Edward felt as if his heart were being squeezed.

"The lady regaled us with stories of your past, your grace," she finally muttered.

"That does not sound so bad," said Edward carefully. He was no saint but he had never done anything too horrid.

Caroline looked up and he was surprised to see a blue fire dance in her eyes. Usually they were icy and calm, cold almost. Yet now they were spitting. So like her sister's in a lot of ways.

"Does it not, your grace?" She packed quite a punch into one little sentence. He felt like a naughty child being reprimanded.

"Er — no?" He said it like a question as he was unsure of where this was leading.

"I had thought that you knew Rebecca quite well, your grace."

"I do," he argued.

Caroline sighed and said, "I know my sister acts like nothing bothers her. I know she seems strong as iron. But she is a romantic at heart and she does not and cannot hide her feelings, though she thinks she does. Rebecca hurts deeply, your grace. Especially when let down by those she cares most about."

Edward frowned in confusion. He felt an icy dread begin to form in the pit of his stomach.

"Lady Caroline, what exactly did Lady Sarah tell your sister?"

Caroline blushed and glanced away before facing him again.

"It would not be proper for me to repeat it, least of all to you. Besides, it is for Rebecca to tell you, not I."

"Fine," was all the answer she got before Edward turned and dragged her over to where Rebecca and Tom were dancing. Without a word, he deposited Caroline in front of Tom and took Rebecca away, marching her straight off the floor and down the steps toward the makeshift forest past the booths.

Caroline and Tom both stared in amazement at their retreating forms.

Finally, Tom turned to Caroline with a grin and bowed.

"Shall we, my lady?" he asked and though he sounded as jovial as ever, there was a tightness to his voice.

Caroline stared at his outstretched hand for a moment until, finally, she placed her smaller one in his.

She looked up into his clear blue eyes and smiled.

"I'd be delighted."

****

Rebecca did not take kindly to being manhandled.

"Just what do you think you are doing?" she muttered

angrily as Edward frogmarched her down the path and away from the crowds.

Once they'd reached the relative privacy of the overhanging trees he stopped and turned her to face him.

"Alright. Tell me what has happened," he demanded.

"I am sure I have no idea what you are talking about," came the stiff reply.

"The devil you don't," his voice was very close to shouting. He did his best to moderate it.

"Last night, we seemed to have been on the verge of—well of moving forward." He could not bring himself to say what he desperately wanted to. Not while she was so hostile. "And now, now you are acting like a perfect stranger."

Rebecca knew there was truth in his words but she could not allow herself to act any differently. The only thing keeping her from sobbing was pretending that she was as uncaring and unfeeling possible.

She stared at him for a moment, willing herself not to soften until he told her the truth.

"Let me ask you something," Rebecca spoke sedately now, calmly. It made him even more worried.

"When you first met me," she continued in the same flat tone, "did you think I would make a good duchess?"

The question caught him off guard. He knew the answer would hurt her feelings but he would not lie to her. He would never lie to her.

"Rebecca" he spoke gently, wanting to touch her but knowing it would be the wrong thing to do. "When I first met you you'd fallen into a lake because you were chasing a kite," he said by way of explanation.

He hadn't directly answered her question but his answer was enough.

She nodded her head quickly, as though in a hurry to get through the conversation.

"What about when you first kissed me?" she asked

boldly. "Did you think I would make a good duchess then?"

He did not like where this was going.

"No," he answered honestly, though it killed him, "but I kissed you because I–"

"And all those other times," she continued speaking over him, "what about then?"

Well, this was easier.

"Last night I—"

"Before last night."

He swallowed hard.

"No," he answered miserably.

"I have only one more question," her voice was bleaker than he'd ever heard it and it hurt to know he'd made it that way.

"Did you have a relationship with Lady Sarah?"

He stared at Rebecca and could see from her expression that she wanted him to say no. And he hadn't, not really. But suddenly the few stolen kisses he and Sarah had shared as youths seemed a much bigger deal than they had mere minutes before.

"No," he answered though honesty compelled him to admit, "we kissed. A few times but it meant nothing. It was not even worth mentioning to you."

Rebecca closed her eyes and lowered her head but not before he saw the flash of pain.

"So you tossed her aside because she was not good enough for your precious title, is that it?"

"What? No! Of course not. Rebecca she meant nothing to me. Nothing. You are—"

"What?" Rebecca demanded, "I am what? I am not duchess material, you have admitted so yourself. And yet, you have kissed me. You kissed me when you *knew* that you would not want to pursue me. So it is true then. This is what you do? You— you seduce women, destroy their reputations and then move on to somebody more worthy?"

What the hell was she talking about?

"No, of course not. Why would you even think such a thing?"

"Lady Sarah told me about your sordid little past with her. She told me that you would not think me good enough, and she was right. You do not. And to think I wanted to change. To change everything about myself to just be more worthy of you. Worthy of your damned title." There were tears streaming down her face now but she did not care.

"Rebecca, Sarah is lying to you if she told you that we had anything more than a mere kiss or two. What I feel for you is—"

"Nothing," she yelled, "what you feel for me is nothing but lust. We both know I cannot be what you need in a wife. What you want. Yet you paid court to me in front of the whole of London and now, when you find someone you truly want, I shall be a laughing stock."

"Rebecca, calm down." He reached for her but she stumbled away.

"Do not touch me and do not tell me to be calm."

She took a deep breath and spoke again, this time with her voice devoid of all emotion.

"I am glad," she said, to his surprise. "I am glad to have found this out. What fools we both were, acting as if people would not talk. Would not notice how we preferred each other's company. Well, better to distance ourselves now. I am not what you want in a wife. And you are certainly not what I want in a husband."

Edward winced as her words struck him like a blow to the temple.

"You do not mean that."

"Of course I do. What would I bring to you but embarrassment and scandal? And what would you give me? A cage? A list of rules so restrictive that I would not even be myself? I fantasied that it would work Edward, but truly it never would. There has to be love for opposites to have a successful marriage. And there is no love between us. You do not love me. And I—I do not love you."

Her words felt like stab wounds as he stood and listened to her so casually deny that there was anything between them, to list all the reasons why they should not be together.

He felt so miserable he could weep and so angry he wanted to punch something.

"Do you mean that?" he finally asked.

She kept her eyes downcast and nodded mutely.

"No, Rebecca. If you will dismiss us, dismiss me so easily, you will look at me while you do it. Do you mean that?"

Her head remained bowed for some moments and in those moments Edward prayed that she would take it back. Finally, she raised her head and looked into his eyes with a cold, emotionless stare.

"Yes, I mean it."

Edward turned and left without another word, striding from the walkway and from the Vauxhall Gardens altogether.

Had he turned around, he would have seen Rebecca finally lose the last shreds of her control and drop to her knees as heartbroken sobs wracked her body.

Chapter Twenty-Six

Lady Sarah, having completed the second of her tasks while she had been alone in their booth, found Rebecca in a miserable heap on the ground.

Obviously she had done her job well.

"Oh my dear," Sarah cried rushing over to Rebecca with false concern. "Whatever can have happened to you?"

Rebecca was too distraught to do anything except let Lady Sarah guide her gently to her feet and lead her back toward their box.

"Come now, it cannot be that bad. Let us get you something to drink and you will feel better."

She poured a dark liquid into a goblet and pressed it into Rebecca's shaking hands.

"Drink, dear. You will feel as good as new."

Rebecca drank deeply. She tasted wine but something else too, a cloying sweetness that was at odds with the deep flavour of the wine.

She grimaced as it burned a trail down her throat.

"What is that?" Rebecca asked.

"Why, tis the punch you were so excited about tasting."

"I am not sure that I like it. It tastes — strange," Rebecca choked out as the fire built in her throat. "It is burning. May I please have some water?"

"Of course, but drink up first. Otherwise you will not feel the effects."

Rebecca's head began to swim. What was wrong with her? She felt sluggish and incredibly sleepy.

Lady Sarah tilted the rest of the contents of the cup into her mouth and she swallowed instinctively.

Something was wrong. The booth began to swim and the colours were too bright. Everything sounded so far away and even Lady Sarah's voice was becoming distorted.

"Pl-please get my sister."

"I sent your sister off to dance with Mr. Crawdon, my dear. She will be quite a while I would imagine. I convinced her that you were perfectly safe with the duke."

Rebecca felt nauseated. She felt violently ill and scared and she wanted Edward more than anything. But Edward had left because she had pushed him away.

She felt like crying again but her thoughts were so muddled she could not remember why.

"Do not worry, my dear," Lady Sarah's voice sounded close to her but she could not distinguish where. "The effects will not last long. Just long enough for you to be taken down a peg or two."

My God, the woman was insane. Had she poisoned her?

"I want Edward," were Rebecca's last words before she began to slip into darkness.

The last thing she remembered was Lady Sarah's voice again, sounding bitter and cold.

"Don't we all?"

****

As Rebecca slumped forward, Lady Sarah lifted her head

and gave a discreet signal. Within moments George Simons had climbed into their booth and covered Rebecca's unconscious form with a dark cloak.

"We need to walk her out of here," he whispered to Lady Sarah. But he hadn't taken his eyes from Rebecca's face.

Sarah began to feel uncomfortable. And a little scared.

"Mr. Simons," she started hesitantly. She did not like the look in his eyes — an almost insane joy while he watched Rebecca's helpless body. "Remember the plan. You are to leave her alone somewhere. Her reputation is to be ruined." She raised her voice now as the man did not seem to be paying any attention to what Sarah was saying. "Mr. Simons she is not to be touched."

Finally, the man turned to look at her and Sarah felt her skin crawl. She did not like what she saw.

"Y-you will stick to the plan?"

George merely smirked but did not answer. He lifted Rebecca and draped one of her arms around his shoulder.

"Help me," was all he muttered and Lady Sarah rushed forward to do his bidding.

She was beginning to regret her part in this wicked scheme. She had wanted to see the girl knocked from her perch. Everywhere she went it was 'Lady Rebecca said this' and 'Lady Rebecca wore that' and 'did you see the duke dance with Lady Rebecca?'

Sarah remembered a time when she'd had society at her feet. Her first Season had been ruined by an indiscreet affair with a married earl and she'd had to marry Robert Whitting, Earl of Salisbury to keep herself from utter ruin. And she'd lost Edward forever...

But suddenly it seemed ridiculous to have done all this to an innocent girl just because they'd shared a few cross words in the park.

"I said help me," George Simons' voice cut through her musings.

"I—I am not sure this is a very good idea after all," she whispered looking around frantically lest they be seen. "Perhaps I should just take the lady home."

"Did you get rid of the duke?" was his only response.

"What? Yes. Yes of course. They argued about something or other, I do not know what. Anyway I saw him leave in a towering rage. He will not be back."

"Right, well her sister will be back soon so we need to move her now."

"But I said—"

"I know what you said," Mr. Simons interrupted her, and now his expression was so fierce she was terrified. "And for your own sake, I am ignoring it. You will help me see this through or things will get very nasty for you."

Lady Sarah quivered in fear as she took in his countenance. How had she not seen how utterly deranged the man was?

She moved forward to help him and together they moved slowly through the pressing crowd dragging Rebecca's slumped form between them.

There were a few knowing looks and guffaws from the crowd at Rebecca's seemingly inebriated state. Thankfully though they saw nobody of consequence and so were able to move undetected by people who would recognise Sarah.

Finally, after what seemed like an endless trek, they reached the exit. Mr. Simons had a carriage waiting; it looked disgusting and disused. They walked towards it then he picked Rebecca up and dumped her none too gently into the back.

He turned to face Lady Sarah who, at this point, was so distraught that she was visibly shaking.

"Now, you get back in there and you make sure the snooty one don't come looking for her sister."

Sarah nodded mutely too afraid to do anything more.

But as he climbed into the driver's seat her conscience got

the better of her.

"Mr. Simons," she called. "You will still leave her in the hunting lodge won't you? The one you told me of?"

"You just do as you've been told," was her only answer then he sped off into the night.

What have I done? thought Lady Sarah in despair. But she would keep the secret. She could not tell of her part in it or it would destroy her and if Mr. Simons found out that she had told…

She squared her shoulders and went back inside to see this awful scheme through, wishing to God she'd never started it…

****

Caroline returned to the booth flushed with happiness having enjoyed herself more in these past hours than she had for the entirety of the Season thus far. It was easier somehow to let herself relax here. It felt as if the strict rules by which she lived did not matter as much inside these enchanted gates.

She smiled happily at her companion, Mr. Crawford, as he handed her a goblet of wine.

"I do hope this is not the punch you spoke to Rebecca of, sir." She smiled shyly up at him

"No, my dear," her answer came from Lady Sarah, "'tis merely a jug of wine I have procured just this moment."

Caroline glanced around then turned back to Lady Sarah with a slight frown marring her brow.

"Where is my sister?" she asked.

"Still off somewhere with Eddie, no doubt," Lady Sarah's voice was brittle as her smile. Her jealously was showing.

Caroline's frown deepened.

"I should go and find her," she said, "She has been alone with him for far too long."

"You do not think you should leave them if they are to

become engaged?" asked Tom.

Caroline stared at him.

"Engaged?"

"Of course," replied Tom, "I should have thought it would be obvious that those were Edward's intentions. The man's been driven half mad with wanting to do it since first light this morning."

"Oh my goodness, this is such wonderful news! Rebecca will be so happy." Caroline's eyes shone and Tom had to take a gulp of his wine to wet his suddenly parched throat.

"I hope that she is. I know Edward is worried about her reaction."

"How could he be? Surely tis obvious to anyone with eyes what her feelings are. And to know that he loves her? Why, it is the stuff of fairy tales."

"Careful, my lady." Tom smiled indulgently. "Your romantic side is showing."

A rosy blush tinged Caroline's cheeks at his words.

"Oh, I cannot wait any longer. Surely he has had time enough to ask. I must find her." She rushed from the box and Tom quickly followed grinning at her excitement.

Lady Sarah swallowed nervously. She knew they would not find either Rebecca or Edward.

They returned not long after, both of them now frowning.

"There seems to be no sign of them at all," said Tom. "And Hadley's just told us he saw Edward leave some time ago."

"How strange," Lady Sarah responded weakly. "Perhaps they have returned home."

"I am sure she would not go without telling me," said Caroline. "I know it seems foolish but I cannot help thinking something has happened."

"Come now, what would happen to her with the duke? I think we can all agree that she is in the safest of hands. Let us enjoy our night. There will no doubt be an explanation when we return." Lady Sarah pressed a drink into Caroline's hand and one into Tom's.

Caroline was still unsure but she knew Lady Sarah was right. Nobody would take better care of Rebecca than Edward. And the fact that they were most likely now betrothed made it a little more respectable for them to be gone as long as they were.

Besides, she was thoroughly enjoying herself as no doubt Rebecca was.

Lord Hadley came by their booth at that moment enquiring after Rebecca. He soon got over his disappointment at her absence when he caught sight of Lady Sarah's flirtatious glance.

"Will you do me the honour of dancing with me, Lady Sarah?" he asked as his eyes raked over her.

Lady Sarah smiled coyly and agreed and they both disappeared into the throng.

"Lady Caroline, it looks as if you are stuck with me once again," Tom spoke softly holding out his hand.

"I do not mind, sir," she answered shyly.

"No," he said as he placed her hand into the crook of his arm, "nor do I."

****

Rebecca awoke to a merciless pain in her head. She had no idea where she was and for a moment, blind panic set in. Surrounding her was complete darkness and the rocking motion she was experiencing was doing nothing to help her stomach, which was roiling alarmingly.

What had happened?

Why did her head hurt so?

And where the hell was she?

Blinking a couple of times to try to clear her vision and her head, she realised with some surprise that she must be in a carriage. A very old and unclean one judging by the smell.

Oh God, she really would cast up her accounts if it did not stop.

She could barely think coherent thoughts. Her head hurt and her mind felt fuzzy and strange. She sat up slowly but felt no better for it, and in fact the movement had caused her stomach to lurch.

She thought about calling out or banging on the roof or doing something to gain someone's attention. But some instinct told her to remain quiet. How she wished that her mind would clear so she could think logically but it seemed that the more she tried to focus the harder it became.

The pain in her head was becoming unbearable. She slowly lay back down on the smelly seat cushion and closed her eyes, trying not to inhale the stench surrounding her.

She could not think, feeling far too ill. She would rest a few minutes more then try again. Before sleep once again claimed her, her mind threw up one clear image— Edward walking away from her in anger. Though the circumstances were unclear, the thought made her heart ache. She slipped back into unconsciousness with a single tear trailing down her face.

****

Caroline was late down to breakfast the next morning having danced herself into exhaustion the night before.

Last night had been one of the happiest of her life. She did not want to dwell overmuch on the reasons why, just enjoy the memories and discuss the events with Rebecca.

She had been surprised to return to the booth last night to Lady Sarah's news that Edward had sent a message to their box to say that Rebecca was feeling tired and he was taking her home. But then, had he not escorted her home from the opera just the other night? Perhaps it was an excuse to spend some time alone.

Caroline had smiled at the thought of Rebecca and Edward being so much in love and had relaxed. Lord Hadley had joined their party so she felt a little better about how often Mr. Crawdon had claimed her to dance, though she had to turn away from Lord Hadley's and Lady Sarah's rather vulgar display.

She had come home much later than anticipated and was unsurprised to find that Rebecca and the dowager had already retired.

Now she rushed downstairs to find out Rebecca's wonderful news.

Upon entering the dining room she was surprised to find the dowager dining alone.

"Good morning, your grace," she greeted the older lady politely.

"Ah, there you are my dear," came her answer. "I had quite given you and your sister up this morning."

"My apologies, we stayed out much later than anticipated," said Caroline. "Though I am surprised that Rebecca is not up yet. Perhaps she really is unwell."

"Whatever do you mean?" asked the dowager.

"His grace returned her home quite early last night, your grace. It cannot have been after midnight. She was feeling unwell…" Caroline trailed off at the dowager's confused look.

"My dear, I did not retire until past midnight last night, in fact I was writing your mother. Lady Rebecca did not return home."

Caroline lowered the plate she'd been filling.

"She—she did not come home?"

She felt sure that the duke would not have been so stupid as to take Rebecca to his house. Rebecca would be completely ruined.

Without another word, Caroline ran up the stairs and burst into Rebecca's room. There she found Maura, cup of chocolate in hand looking as alarmed as Caroline felt.

"Maura," Caroline barked, "what time did Lady Rebecca return last night?"

"I—I do not know, my lady," Maura stammered, "she told me not to wait up, that she would be very late. But, her gown is not here and her night rail is still laid out. And her—her bed. It has not been slept in."

A panic gripped Caroline's heart and she looked frantically around the room as if searching for a clue as to what was going on here.

The dowager appeared in the doorway.

"Rebecca has not come home, your grace," Caroline said numbly. She could see by the older lady's expression that they were both thinking the same thing — she was in Edward's house.

Dear God did neither of them care about the scandal?

"I cannot think that Edward would do this," the dowager said though doubt tinged her voice, "he has never put so much as a foot wrong in Society since he gained his title. He would not do something like this."

"I think we should pay him a visit immediately," was Caroline's only answer.

The dowager nodded and left to send for the carriage. And Caroline wondered which of them she would strangle first.

Chapter Twenty-Seven

Edward was awakened by a pounding on his door and in his head.

"Go away," he bellowed as he turned over.

Bailey ignored his command and entered the room anyway. Edward was not surprised.

"Bailey," he croaked, "I am going to need one of your concoctions to rid myself of this blasted headache. And before you begin the sermon, do not. I have made a royal hash of my life and drinking an entire bottle of brandy is only the half of it. Not that it made me feel any better. I still could not stop thinking about the damned girl. She—"

"Your grace," Bailey, surprisingly, interrupted Edward and, not only that he sounded graver than Edward had ever heard him.

Edward lifted his pounding head to look at his valet. The older man's face was drawn.

"Good God man, what is the matter?" Edward asked jumping out of bed and throwing on breeches and a shirt. It was a testament to Bailey's state of mind that he did not even wince as Edward pulled clothes randomly from his closet and threw them on haphazardly.

"Is it my mother?" Edward demanded as fear seized him.

"No, your grace, the dowager is quite well," Bailey answered to Edward's relief.

But his relief was short lived as a fear unlike any he'd ever known gripped him at his shaken valet's next words.

"It is Lady Rebecca, your grace. She is missing."

Edward did not wait for Bailey to finish. He sprinted from the room and tore downstairs. He did not even know where he was going but the sound of voices drew him to the drawing room.

He entered and stopped dead in his tracks.

His mother was wringing her hands by the fireplace and Lady Caroline was sobbing quietly into a handkerchief on the chaise.

"What the hell is going on?" he demanded, fear making his voice louder and harsher than he intended.

"Oh Edward, it is Rebecca. She is gone. She is gone." Here his mother started to cry too and Edward could not get his head around the words.

"What do you mean, gone? Gone where?"

"We do not know, your grace," Lady Caroline lifted her head and her eyes shone with tears that spilled down her face. "We thought she was here."

"Here? Why would she be here?"

Caroline looked at him in exasperation before answering, "Because you brought her home last night when she was unwell. Only, her bed has not been slept in so we thought perhaps you had taken her here. But clearly you haven't and now I do not know what to think."

An icy feeling of dread settled into the pit of Edward's stomach.

"Lady Caroline." He walked further into the room and dragged his hands through his hair in agitation. "I have no idea what you are talking about. I did not bring your sister home. She — we, we argued and I left. Oh God, I left her there alone. I was so angry. The things she said! I—"

"You did not bring her home?" the dowager repeated, cutting into Edward's panicked confession.

"No I did not," said Edward then turned back to Lady Caroline, "Who told you that I did?"

"Lady Sarah."

Edward clenched his jaw then turned to his butler. "Get my horse. And hurry," he said as he swept from the room back to his bedchamber to ready himself.

"Your grace, I have taken it upon myself to send for Mr. Crawdon, he will be here directly," Bailey informed him as he helped Edward into his jacket.

"Thank you, Bailey."

"If I may be so bold, your grace, I think it would be wise to wait and hear what exactly happened last night before you go tearing off to Lady Sarah's."

"Wait?" Edward whirled round and snarled at Bailey, "wait while she is God knows where? That woman knows something and I intend to find out what it is." He took a deep breath and looked at his old friend and confidante. "Bailey, she has to be safe. She has to be."

His face crumpled in despair and he bowed his head as the weight of his panic bore down on him.

Bailey reached out and gripped the younger man's shoulder. He'd never seen his master lose his composure and he wasn't about to let him do it now.

"Your grace," he spoke gently but firmly, "I believe that the lady is safe and will be found. And I believe that you will try harder than anyone to bring her home. But you must keep your wits about you. You will not help her if you lose your mind now when you need it most."

Edward looked up into the wise eyes of his valet and smiled a little.

"You are right, Bailey. Thank you."

Bailey merely nodded and left the room.

Edward would get her back if it killed him.

****

By the time Edward's horse was ready, Tom had arrived and was in the drawing room with the ladies. He looked more serious than Edward had ever seen him.

"Tell me what happened," was Edward's only greeting to him.

Between them, Caroline and Tom told of last night's events, of how Lady Sarah had apparently received a message from Edward himself that he was taking Rebecca home. It only stood to reason then that she was behind everything going on here.

"I think it is past time I paid a visit to our friend, Lady Sarah," said Edward grimly.

"I am coming too," said Tom rising.

Edward did not argue.

He turned to his mother and Lady Caroline. "Will you remain here or return home?" he asked as he made his way to the door.

"We shall stay here, I think," the dowager answered. "I do not want to be at home with the servants speculating about what has happened. Yours do not know us well enough to pry."

Edward merely nodded his agreement before sweeping from the room.

Tom looked over at Caroline, curled up on the chair as if trying to protect herself from the horror of the situation.

He walked over and hunched in front of her, forcing her to look up into his face.

"We will find her, Caroline, I swear it," he whispered fiercely. Caroline nodded once and then, with a swift kiss to her head, he left to follow Edward.

Caroline watched them leave. *Dear God, I hope so,* she thought desperately.

****

Rebecca came to again and was relieved to find that although her head still hurt and her stomach still heaved, her vision had cleared and she seemed to have her wits about her a little more than last time.

The first thing she noticed was that it was bright out. Daylight was seeping through the flimsy curtains covering the windows. That must mean that they'd travelled through the night, 'they' being Rebecca herself and whomever had taken her.

The second thing she noticed, with surprise, was that she was no longer in a carriage. She appeared to be lying on a bed in a room that was surprisingly luxurious compared to the carriage that had brought her here.

Her confusion and instinctive fear mounted.

A fierce stabbing pain in her wrists and ankles that she had not noticed at first due to the overwhelming pain in her head drew her attention. When she looked down she saw, to her horror that she was tied up with tightly knotted rope.

Panic bubbled up inside her as she looked frantically around to try to ascertain where she was, but she did not recognise the place at all, sure she'd never been here.

She could feel her breathing becoming shallower as the panic threatened to overwhelm her and forced herself to remain calm. It would do no good trying to figure anything out in the middle of an attack of hysteria.

She slowed her breathing and forced her mind back to last night, dismayed to find she had no real memory of it. There had been the carriage ride with Lady Sarah and the horrible things the woman had said about Edward.

Edward... there it was again. That vision of him walking

away from her. They had argued. That was it! They had argued about the things Lady Sarah had said and Rebecca had told him — oh God, she'd told him that she did not love him.

He had left and that was really the only thing she could remember. So, where was she and who had brought her here?

Her breathing froze as the door to the bedroom slowly creaked open. And the panic that she had supressed mere moments before welled up in full force.

"Ah, you are awake." George Simons smiled widely. "I was beginning to think you'd sleep through the day as well as the night."

He spoke happily as if it were perfectly normal to have the daughter of his landlord tied up on a bed.

"Where am I?" Rebecca croaked hoarsely.

"We are in a hunting lodge a little ways outside of London. I won it from an idiot baron who had more money than talent for cards. Isn't it just like you lot, throwing money away, never having to work a day in your lives for it? Well, this is mine now." He paused and looked back at Rebecca. "And so are you."

Rebecca swallowed back the panic she felt. She had never heard him talk so much and his speech was rapid and rambling. There was an insane gleam in his eye. Rebecca feared he was quite mad.

"Mr. Simons."

"My name is George."

"I do not think it appropriate to call you that," she said carefully, wondering at his mood.

He threw back his head and laughed.

"Trust me, Rebecca," he deliberately used her name and stalked toward the bed. Rebecca's whole body stiffened in fright. "We will not have any cause for formality when I am done with you."

Rebecca bit back a sob of horror, not wanting to imagine what he meant but she was no fool. She wished with all her heart that Edward were here to keep her safe. To help her.

But even if he knew where she was, and how could he, who was to say that he would care? Rebecca had said awful things to him. And all because of what that horrible Lady Sarah said. Well, what if the lady had lied?

Stop it, Rebecca, she chided herself. This was hardly the time to wonder about the duke and Lady Sarah. She was tied up with a mad man for goodness sake.

"H-how did I get here? I do not remember."

"Oh, that was easy enough. Course I had to get around your precious duke first, did I not? Always hanging around. Always watching you. I did not like the way he looked at you, Rebecca. He looked at you like you were his. But you are mine. You know that, don't you?" he crooned.

He sat on the bed and stroked her face. Rebecca could smell the stench of old sweat and whiskey from him but did her best not to recoil from him. She had a feeling that any sort of negative action would tip him over the edge.

"George," Rebecca whispered, trying to keep her voice level, "you know that you cannot treat people this way. You cannot tie people up. You cannot kidnap them." She tried to sound as reasonable as possible.

"Oh I haven't kidnapped you, we're eloping," he said matter of fact.

Rebecca took a calming breath and tried again. She must attempt to reason with him, to keep from angering him, until she figured out what to do and how to get out of here.

"But what happened G-George? I do not remember much of anything save arriving at Vauxhall Gardens."

"Rebecca, you have to understand. You belong to me, don't you? You are mine. I knew it from the second I saw you. But you were so rude to me"— here he began to look angry and Rebecca was terrified— "so snooty, always looking down at me, letting people like that bastard the duke make you think you are too good for me. Well I showed him did I not? I expect he will try to find you, but by then he will be too late. You will be mine and he will not want you when someone else has had you first."

Rebecca began to feel angry, in spite of her fear, how dare he speak so casually of — of that?

"What the hell happened?" she yelled now, forgetting her panic, forgetting the pain.

"Ah there is the temper I've seen so much. I was hoping you'd have a little fight left in you, it will make the whole thing so much more *interesting*."

Rebecca bit back a retort. With disgust she realised that her fear and anger were exciting him.

She tried a different tact.

"I assume that Lady Sarah was somehow involved," Rebecca said now, "she was, after all, the only other person I was with last night."

His smile sickened her. "Clever girl. Yes she was involved, though the idea was mine," he stated quickly, as if she would somehow be impressed by his devious plan. "She slipped a little something into your drink and then helped me get you into the carriage."

Rebecca could not believe that the other lady would stoop so low. She must be as mad as Simons himself.

"But, why? Why are you doing this?" she almost sobbed.

The question seemed to anger him and he leapt from the bed and began pacing up and down in front of her.

"Why? WHY?" he shouted. "Why the hell do you think? Do you think your father would have let us be together? Or your precious duke? They all think they are better than me. Every one of them. Well nobody is better than George Simons. Not the fool who handed over this house, not your father and not *you*," he spat.

"And they'll know won't they? When we're married. They'll know I am just as good as any of you." He was breathing heavily now and his eyes were wild.

"I will not marry you," Rebecca argued. "I will not. How can you think I would after all of this? You cannot treat people this way."

Her words seemed to drive him forward and he loomed over her and placed a calloused hand around her throat. He leaned close so that she could see the bloodshot whites of his eyes. His breath stank and Rebecca feared she would gag.

"You will not have a choice, Princess. Not when I've taken you so that no other man will have you."

His other hand ran down her body and Rebecca did her best not to scream. The bastard would enjoy hearing her fear and she would not give him the satisfaction.

She closed her eyes and prayed that he would stop and mercifully, he did.

He moved away from her and went to a tray that she had failed to notice before.

"Sit up and eat," he demanded, then added with a leer that caused her skin to crawl, "You will need to keep your strength up."

He set the tray on the bed beside her and Rebecca saw her chance.

"George," she called softly as he made to leave the room, "I cannot eat with my hands tied."

He narrowed his eyes suspiciously.

"Please," she fought to keep her voice calm, "just untie me for a few moments, you can come back and retie the ropes when I am done."

He seemed to consider it for a moment then moved slowly back to her and pulled out a hunting knife.

Rebecca swallowed as it glinted in the dim sunlight.

"If you try to leave," he said quietly as he sawed at the ropes tying her hands together, "I will kill you."

Rebecca nodded her understanding and rubbed her wrists that tingled painfully with the blood rushing back into them.

Without another word, he turned and left the room slamming the door behind him.

Rebecca immediately began to pull at the ropes on her legs. She did not have the benefit of a knife and after ten minutes of trying, was sweating and exhausted. The pain in her head was worsened by dehydration but she dare not drink anything lest it was drugged.

She almost gave way to the fear threatening to overwhelm her but told herself not to give up. Rebecca fully believed him when he said he would kill her if he caught her trying to escape but really, what awaited her if she did not try? A fate worse than death.

Finally, when it seemed impossible that she would be able to release her ankles, she managed to half-slip one of her feet out. Pulling and tugging with all her might until the foot was free, she almost cried out in pain as the blood rushed back to the area, and the loosening of the tie on the left foot had tightened the rope almost unbearably on the right. Already her foot was beginning to swell and become discoloured.

But it did not matter. She could use her feet now. Stepping silently off the bed Rebecca stood up. Her head swam alarmingly and she gripped the poster for support until the sensation passed.

She looked round the room for something to use as a weapon should she need one. Her eyes fell on a sturdy looking candlestick and she crept over to the sideboard to retrieve it. Now, all that was left was to try to get out of the house undetected by the mad man and try to find her way back to London with no money, no help and absolutely no idea where she actually was…

****

Edward hammered at the front door of Lady Sarah's townhouse. It took what seemed like hours but in reality was only a few moments for a footman to open the door. Edward barged past the man without uttering a single word. When the footman made to step after him, Tom reached out and grabbed the servant by the arm.

"If you have a preference for your limbs to be attached to your body," he said cordially, "I suggest you do nothing save call for the mistress of the house. Tell her the Duke of Hartridge is here to see her. And he is not happy."

The footman's eyes widened in fear, whether of the threat or of the stature of the man who'd come through the door as if the hounds of hell were after him, Tom did not know. Nor did he care.

The sooner they could speak to Sarah, the sooner they would find Rebecca. He looked to his cousin's tense back as he roared for Sarah to come down at once. He was hanging on to his sanity by a mere thread, thought Tom. If anything happened to Rebecca it would destroy him. They had to get her back.

The butler had made an appearance at this stage and was doing his best to calm Edward down but Edward was in no mood to be told anything and was seconds from punching the man just to shut him up.

The noise level rose with Edward still bellowing for Sarah, the butler still begging Edward to quiet down and Tom shouting suggestions of threats for Edward to deliver to the butler.

Lady Sarah's appearance at the top of the stairs brought a sudden halt to the cacophony of sounds.

"Good heavens Edward, you will wake the dead with that racket," Sarah exclaimed as she moved slowly down the stairs. She was not yet dressed for the day and merely wore a robe over her nightrail. The robe was tied loosely and did nothing to cover the body underneath.

Ever the exhibitionist, thought Edward cynically.

"Where is she?" Edward asked without preamble.

"Good morning to you too," Sarah quipped flippantly.

"Damnation Sarah I am not in the mood. Tell me where she is or I will ruin you." His words were made all the more powerful by the cold stone-like expression on his face and the glacial tone he used. Had he shouted and raved, she would have believed him less.

"Where who is?" she asked innocently.

"Where IS she?" This time his shout was loud enough to shake the chandelier hanging from the vaulted ceiling of the hallway in which they stood.

Lady Sarah took an involuntary step backwards and Edward noticed for the first time some subtle changes about the lady.

For one, her face was paler than ever he'd seen it before. For another, her voice, far from the husky confident tone it usually had was brittle and shaky.

"You told Tom and Caroline that I had sent a message to you and told you I was taking her home. You and I both know that is a complete lie. So I suggest you start talking and talking quickly."

Edward was surprised when Sarah, usually so confident and arrogant, crumpled into a mess before his very eyes.

"I am sorry," she managed to say through the tears, "I am so very sorry Edward. It was only supposed to be a little trick. Something to put a spot on her reputation. T-to hurt her popularity in the *ton*. But he — I believe he is quite mad and I do not know what he has planned, I swear it. He threatened me. Told me that I must help him. That I must not tell anyone. Oh God, would that I had never listened to his insane plan. But I swear, on my life, Edward he was only supposed to leave her somewhere so that she would spend the night alone. But I think — I think he must have something more sinister in mind. I am sorry."

At this point her sobbing became so hysterical that she could not utter another word. The butler and a maid who had appeared from upstairs rushed to her side to lead her away.

"Stop," demanded Edward hoarsely. "Unhand her at once, I am not done."

"Please, your grace. She is overcome."

"Let her go or I will put a bullet in your head," he answered coldly.

The butler let go of Lady Sarah and instructed the frightened maid to do the same.

"You will calm down and tell me exactly what happened, Sarah," said Edward fighting his anxiety. He sent the butler to retrieve the earl's brandy before turning back to Sarah.

"Now," he said in as reasoned a tone as he could muster. He dreaded asking the next question because he knew the answer. He had failed to protect her from the one person of whom he should have been more wary. "Who is he? The man who took her?"

"I had not met him before the day she and I argued in the park." Sarah's words were coming between gut wrenching sobs.

"His name, Sarah," Edward did not relent.

"George Simons," she gasped.

Edward knew it. And his fear increased ten-fold.

The butler returned with a snifter of brandy and Edward shoved it into Sarah's hand.

"Tell me everything, Sarah. And make it quick."

Chapter Twenty-Eight

Rebecca's heart pounded furiously as she slowly opened the door to the bedroom in which George had deposited her. Praying to the heavens that the door would not creak she opened it just wide enough to slip outside.

She found herself at the end of a long corridor with a staircase halfway down. Rebecca felt a moment's indecision as she wondered what the best course of action would be. She had looked out the window before exiting the room to see if perhaps there was a tree outside or anything that could be used to climb down. But there was nothing but a sheer drop to the ground. Nor could she see any path or trail. Just fields for miles.

Now she wondered if she should check the rooms toward the front of the house or risk moving downstairs. Having no idea where Simons was there was only a second to decide. Finally, she judged it best to just make her way downstairs and try to get out the door. Then she would run flat out and hope to God there would be something or someone to help her.

She slipped down the stairs as slowly as she could,

listening intently for any sound or sign of Simons. But so far, she heard and saw nothing.

Her tension had reached fever pitch by the time she made it to the foot of the stairs. She could not quite believe she had gotten so far without incident. The candlestick was slippery in her sweaty palm but she gripped it with all her strength.

Her right foot was throbbing along with her head and she felt altogether more ill than ever before in her life. But she would not give up.

The front door came into view down a long, darkened hallway. There had been a change in the light and Rebecca could only guess that there was a heavy rain coming, if it was not already upon them.

Gradually, she made her way down the hallway to the door. Every room was closed making it nearly impossible to see but at least giving her a small chance of remaining undetected.

She made it to the door and took a deep breath. This was it. His attention was sure to be drawn the second the door opened. She would have to make a run for it.

Simons had removed her shoes at some point during the night or the morning and Rebecca had not stopped to try to find them. Sending up a quick prayer and keeping Edward's face firmly in her head, she wrenched the door open and ran outside.

She had no clue which way she should go but ran as fast as her legs could carry her. Not too far from the front of the house there seemed to be a wood of some sort and she headed for that, hoping that the trees would provide at least some shelter for her.

Her guess about the darkening sky had been right. There were dark heavy rainclouds racing about her and before she had even cleared the small front garden of the lodge they opened up and emptied onto the ground below.

Within seconds Rebecca was soaked. The material of her

dress became incredibly heavy and the gravel of the pathway tore her silk stockings to shreds. And still she ran.

She did not dare to look behind as she sprinted for the trees. She had just made it through the first of them when her heart sank as a shot rang out followed by her name. He had discovered her escape and he was shooting at her.

****

Edward and Tom left Sarah crying miserably and headed as fast as their mounts could carry them to a set of rooms in a seedy part of town that George Simons had taken on his arrival to London. It was not sheer luck that they knew of this place. Sarah told them, with some pride, that she had him followed after their first meeting. She liked to know whom exactly she was dealing with at all times.

Sarah's information had been scant but there was enough to know that a clue was awaiting them at Simons' lodgings. He had told Sarah he would take Rebecca to a hunting lodge on the outskirts of Town and that he would leave her there to find her own way back.

"By the time Rebecca returned," Sarah explained miserably, "everyone would know she was gone and she would be ruined."

"And did you not wonder why such a man would merely dump her in the middle of nowhere and then leave her untouched?" Edward demanded, a hot fury burning inside of him.

"No, I did not," wailed Sarah and he could tell that it was the truth. Sarah was malicious of that there was no doubt, but she would not sink to the depths of depravity that her partner in crime did.

"Why, Sarah? Why would you do such a thing?"

Sarah's eyes had filled with tears again.

"I do not know. Jealousy, I suppose. The girl had the

whole of London at her feet. Men adored her, women wanted to befriend her. She had the life I so desperately wanted. The life I should have had. And you. She had you, Edward."

Edward had been shocked at this confession. He and Sarah had never shared any sort of attachment. Yes there'd been a kiss or two some years ago but that had been it and then the scandal of her very public affair had blown up and she'd scarpered back to the country, only returning as a married countess.

"Sarah, there was never anything between you and I," Edward now said harshly. "Though I suspect you told Rebecca something different. That is why she was so upset last night, was it not? Why she thought that my feelings for her were insincere?"

His only answer was another tearful apology. But Edward had heard enough.

He moved to the door to leave but stopped just before exiting and turned back to the lady crying into her hands.

"I cannot think what to do with you until I have her back safe and well, but I will deal with you then. And, Sarah, I swear if he touches a hair on her head I will use everything in my power to make sure your life is completely destroyed."

Sarah knew that he meant it, too and she prayed to God that he would find Lady Rebecca safe. For all their sakes.

Now the men had arrived outside the filthy tenement in the East End where George Simons had his rooms. It did not take more than a guinea to gain admittance to his room by the wizened and toothless landlord that led them up the narrow staircase.

The man had no key for the door but Edward soon had it opened using brute force.

The room was filthy, covered in empty whiskey bottles and ash and it smelled as if something had died in it. But the thing that froze the blood in Edward's veins was discovered by Tom who was rifling through the lone desk in the room.

"Edward, I think you need to see this," Tom's voice called Edward from his task of searching under the bed.

Edward made his way over to the desk and stared in horror at what Tom held up to show him. There were pictures of Rebecca. Hundreds it seemed to be. Of her face, her walking by her father's house, one, sickeningly, in the window of what Edward could only guess was her bedchamber at home at Ranford. It seemed that Simons had committed his watching to memory and had drawn it all. There were pictures everywhere, some had spilled onto the floor and as Edward bent to retrieve them, he noticed a small leather-bound diary.

He opened it on a random page and scanned the poor writing, so poor that some parts were illegible. Perhaps Simons was self-taught in the art of writing for the words were badly written and grossly misspelled. But their meaning was clear and it put the fear of God into Edward.

It was about her, all about her. Notes of when he'd clearly been following her. Rebecca had been right to be concerned about him. Edward flipped hurriedly to the front and saw that the first entry was on the first day he'd ever seen her. And every single entry since had been about her. He had no time to study it intently but one thing was clear — the more it went on, the darker and more twisted the writing became. His unhealthy obsession fairly jumped off the page.

Edward flipped back to the last entry to see if they could garner any clues. He read for a short while before a feeling of nausea mixed with murderous rage had him dropping to the rickety wooden chair that sat at the desk.

"My God," he choked.

Tom reached over and plucked the diary from Edward's hand, scanning the contents quickly.

He swore and glanced in disgust at Edward.

"Edward I—"

"Do not," Edward interrupted him. "Just help me find her."

He did not want to talk about what he'd read. He wanted to forget it but it was burned into his mind and he knew he would have nightmares about it for years to come. A detailed account of the sick man's fantasies, his plans for what he meant to do when he had Rebecca alone. Edward felt the bile rise in his throat but shoved the thought ruthlessly from his mind. He would find her.

"Edward," Tom's shout broke through Edward's disturbed thoughts. "I know where he is."

Edward whipped around and saw Tom holding what appeared to be property deeds in his hand.

"The hunting lodge," said Tom with a grim sort of satisfaction, "these must be the deeds he won."

Edward snatched the parchment from Tom's hands and scanned it, his heart leaping when he saw the name of the property. Without another word the two gentlemen rushed from the room and to their waiting horses outside.

The sky was beginning to darken with black rainclouds and Edward knew there was a storm on its way.

He hoped it was not an omen.

"Please," he begged, "please let me reach her in time."

****

Rebecca crouched behind the trunk of a towering tree and stifled the sobs threatening to wrack her body. Never had she been so afraid.

The shots had stopped now and she knew that Simons was in close pursuit.

A paralyzing fear gripped her that made her afraid to move but afraid to stay where she was.

Think, Rebecca, think! Her mind whirled frantically. If she stayed where she was he would find her eventually. Her only chance was to keep running and hope she could find help from somewhere before he caught up to her. Or shoot her. She stood on shaking legs, her whole body soaking wet and shivering, and prepared to start running again.

Her feet were in agony and were bleeding and bruised beyond recognition but she must run. She must!

Before she could take a step, however, her stomach lurched as she heard Simons' voice ring out through the woods.

"Rebecca," he called, the wind taking the call and throwing it to the skies, "where are you?"

He laughed now and Rebecca tried desperately to figure out where he was, what direction he was coming from.

"Did you think you could escape? Where will you go, my Rebecca? You know you will not get far."

He sounded as if he were coming closer but Rebecca did not know if that was just her mind playing tricks on her.

"I told you," the shouting continued, "that I would kill you if you tried to escape. And I meant it."

Rebecca closed her eyes and tried to take steadying breaths. She could not stay here; she had to try. Give herself a fighting chance.

Mustering the vestiges of her courage she shot out from behind the tree and started to run once more.

Rebecca knew the second he had spotted her.

He yelled in triumph before starting his pursuit.

"Rebecca," he roared, "Stop."

But she did not stop. The trees thinned out ahead and Rebecca knew that she was coming once more to the edge of the woods, albeit further away from the lodge. Surely there would be a road there and if there was even a small chance that someone would be travelling on it, she would be saved.

Once again, Rebecca ran with all her might. He was gaining on her; she could hear the pounding of his feet on the wet forest floor. She was so close to the edge of the trees now. There was a small dirt track that ran alongside it and, in the distance, what appeared to be a farmhouse.

She would never make it to the house. But if she could make it to a surrounding field maybe a farmer or perhaps a layman would be working and could offer assistance.

Her legs felt perilously close to failing her but on she pushed. She had just cleared the trees when she felt Simons weight crush her and they landed with a *thump* as he tackled her to the ground.

Rebecca hit her head on what felt like a rock or perhaps a protruding tree root. Either way it hurt like the devil and completely dazed her for a moment.

When her wits returned she realised that George Simons was looming above her and he looked terrifying. In that moment Rebecca's control completely snapped and the full force of her panic pressed down on her. She screamed. As loudly as her lung would allow.

To her horror, Simons merely threw back his head and laughed. He had pinned her arms above her head and his knee was pressed painfully into her abdomen.

"You think someone will hear you out here? We're quite alone. And I think it about time I taught you a lesson."

Rebecca struggled with all her might. She felt a warm, sticky liquid run down her face from her head and realised with a fright that her head was bleeding from the fall. The world began to spin alarmingly but she could not lose consciousness now. She had to fight.

The candlestick had fallen in the scuffle and Rebecca twisted her head back to try and see it. It was mere inches ahead of her. She twisted and turned until she slipped out from under his knee then kicked out with the last of her strength and was satisfied to hear his grunt of pain as her foot connected with some part of him, though she knew not which.

He momentarily loosened his grip and Rebecca dived toward the candlestick. Simons had quickly recovered and dragged her back toward him. She hit out with the candlestick with all her might and miraculously made contact with the side of his head.

He immediately dropped his hands and stumbled backwards from the impact and the resulting dizziness.

Rebecca stumbled to her feet and staggered forward. Her vision was blurry and the world still spun sickeningly but she did not let it stop her progress.

The candlestick had only gained her seconds to make her escape. And she knew with a hopeless despondency that it would not be enough. And there was nothing left in her to fight with.

Looking up, Rebecca thought she saw something or someone rushing toward her but the darkness was claiming her again. As she felt George Simons' hands close around her and drag her to the ground once more Rebecca knew that she was lost.

She almost welcomed the darkness now; it would help her hide from the horror that was about to befall her.

Perhaps the darkness had already come, she thought in wonder seconds later as she heard a riot of sounds above her before a vision of Edward swam in front of her eyes.

"Rebecca, my love, can you hear me? There is so much blood, Tom. I do not know what to do. Rebecca, Rebecca please. Please hold on. Please do not leave me. I love you." His words ended on a broken sob and Rebecca vaguely wondered why her mind had conjured up such a pained image of her love before she finally lapsed into complete silence.

****

Edward rode until he thought his horse would collapse from the strain. He rode through the pouring rain as if his very life depended on it. And it did. If he were to lose her now, his life would be over. If she died, his heart would die right along with her.

He needed to save her for both of them. For he was

nothing without her.

And he had not told her. Not held her and told her how completely perfect she was. Last night, when she was saying all of those hurtful things, he should have told her then. Told her that the only duchess he wanted was her. That she did not need to change a damned thing. That she was all he ever wanted.

He could not be too late.

They rode for what felt like days until finally Tom gave a shout and pointed ahead and to the right. The lodge! They had arrived.

Edward was just turning to tell Tom to go round the back while he, Edward went through the front when the noise of a gunshot rent the air. They both pulled their horses up to listen. An icy fear gripping Edward's heart.

They strained to listen for any other noises and Edward thought he heard a shout. Then another.

"Tom," he said desperately, "that sounds like a man's voice does it not?"

Tom nodded his agreement and Edward signalled that they go forward more cautiously.

They had begun a slow trot when the distinctive sound of a woman's scream filled the air.

Rebecca!

Edward broke into a gallop and flew toward the noise.

They rode past the house, for the sound had seemed to come from the small woods on the opposite side of the track they were on.

They kept their eyes trained on the trees up ahead and suddenly Edward spotted a figure stumbling out. The figure of a lady. My God, it was Rebecca!

He was about to call out when the figure staggered to a stop and swayed alarmingly. Just then, another figure reached out and dragged the lady back toward the trees.

A fury such as he'd never known burst through Edward

setting his very blood on fire.

He would kill him. He would kill him with his bare hands.

Both Edward and Tom came to a stop at the same time, before the worst scene Edward could have imagined.

Rebecca's eyes were opened but worryingly glazed, her hair matted to her face with blood, and George Simons was leaning over her and tearing at her dress.

With a roar of rage Edward grabbed him and flung him bodily away from Rebecca. Before the man could even sit up, Edward was on him, pummelling him with a savagery he'd never felt before in his life.

He could feel Tom's arms around his chest, straining to pull him off the bastard but Edward would not be moved.

"Edward. Stop," commanded Tom but to no avail.

"I will kill him," Edward vowed ferociously, "I swear, I will kill him."

"Edward, please," Tom shouted, still pulling with all his might, "Rebecca. She needs you. She needs you Edward."

It was the only thing he could have said that would cut through the red haze surrounding Edward. He turned immediately and flew to her side, dropping to his knees by her head.

Her eyes were open but he could tell that she was fast losing consciousness.

"Rebecca, my love, can you hear me?" He tried to move the hair from her face but it was completely matted and the blood was still flowing. Tom hurried over and knelt on the other side of her weakened body. "There is so much blood, Tom. I do not know what to do." His voice was hoarse from fear, from the hot tears choking him, threatening to burst through.

He was losing her. He could see her eyes, her beautiful dark eyes, drifting closed. "Rebecca, Rebecca please. Please hold on. Please do not leave me. I love you."

And then the proud Duke of Hartridge who had not shed a single tear since he was ten years old bowed his head and cried.

Chapter Twenty-Nine

Rebecca awoke to unfamiliar sounds and smells, though the smells were delicious.

Her skull once again felt like it had been split in two and her mouth was dry as the Indian desert.

She was afraid to open her eyes, as she knew instinctively that the light pressing on her lids would hurt like the devil.

But finally her curiosity got the better of her and she lifted her lids cautiously, wincing as her thoughts were confirmed and the sunlight nearly blinded her. She blinked a couple of times trying to become accustomed to the light.

The source of the light was an open window to her right, the curtains billowing as a pleasant spring air floated into the room.

Looking around the room Rebecca knew that she did not recognise it. However, the fear of the last time she'd woken in a strange room was not present. The walls were white and clean. Simple, rustic and sparsely decorated. It seemed to be a farmhouse or cottage, she thought, as there were similarities between this and Martin's family cottage back home.

Rebecca looked down at the coverlet covering her, a

patchwork of bright colours and frowned. Where was she?

Her throat was painfully dry and she moved her head to the left in search of a jug of water.

Her throat closed altogether at the sight which awaited her.

Edward's giant form was curled into a small wooden chair. His legs were stretched out in front of him and his head had dropped to his chest, his arms folded against his abdomen.

What is he doing sleeping by my bedside? she wondered, though the sight of him brought a happy smile to her face.

Her mind felt strangely muddled and she furrowed her brow as she tried to remember what had happened.

Gradually the pieces began to fall into place and her mind swam with images of the nightmare she had recently lived through. The drugging, the bedroom in the lodge, the terrifying chase through the woods. She remembered it all; remembered George Simons pinning her to the ground. The sickening *thud* as her head had met the rock. She lifted her hand now, gently to her forehead and was dismayed to feel a large bandage covering a large portion of her forehead and hair.

I must look a fright, she thought, and then giggled silently at her foolish vanity.

Finally, she remembered, though unsure if it were a dream or not, Edward's wonderful face looking down at her, begging her to be well and saying that he loved her.

Surely a dream. But a beautiful one.

Had she not hoped with all her heart that he would come for her? That he would somehow find a way to rescue her? And he had. But how?

Rebecca was desperate for some answers, but first she was desperate for a drink.

Thankfully there was a pitcher and cup on a small table by the bed. As quietly as possible she sat up and was grateful to find that the room stayed in one spot, though the pain increased dramatically.

Closing her eyes and willing the pain to ease a little, she slowly reached for the pitcher of what was presumably water. On lifting it, Rebecca was caught off guard by how heavy it was and how weak she felt. She made a valiant effort to hold onto it but it was no use.

As if time slowed down, she watched as it slipped from her grasp and fell with a *thump*. The contents splashed out — and landed squarely on Edward's lap.

He yelled in surprise and leapt from the chair in one short movement.

The water spilled down his breeches and Rebecca could only stare in horror as he gasped and spluttered and tried to recover from the shock of being woken from a sleep with a jug of water to his—

"What the devil?" he shouted making a futile attempt to brush the liquid from his clothing.

"I am so very sorry," Rebecca croaked, surprised at how coarse her voice sounded. She really could have done with that water. "It was an accident."

"Isn't it always?" grumbled Edward, "How did you manage to—"

He stopped suddenly and his eyes snapped up from his clothing to her face. He stared at her for a moment before dropping to the bed beside her. He reached out a shaking hand and gently caressed her cheek.

"Sweetheart," he whispered reverently, "you are awake." Then he crushed her body to his and buried his face in her neck.

Rebecca thought she felt dampness against her shoulder as he pulled her tighter still.

"My darling, my darling," he whispered brokenly, "you are awake at last."

Much as she was pleased with the embrace, Rebecca was

starting to feel a little lightheaded from the lack of oxygen.

"Edward," she croaked, "when are you going to let me go?"

"Never," came the fierce reply.

Which was lovely in theory but in practice, quiet worrisome for her lungs.

"How nice," was her weak answer. "Only you are cutting off my circulation and it is a little difficult to breathe."

Edward released her immediately and settled her back against the pillows gently, as if she were a doll made of finest porcelain.

"How are you feeling?" he asked, his hand once again gloriously caressing her cheek.

"Ecstatic," she answered with a sigh.

Edward chuckled softly.

"Are you in pain?"

"My head, a little," she answered, "and my throat is terribly dry."

"Well I would offer you a drink," he quipped, "but I seem to be wearing it."

Rebecca smiled a little weakly at his joke.

"Do not move," he instructed as he picked up the pitcher and left the room.

He returned in moments with a fresh pitcher of water and an entourage.

Caroline, the dowager and Tom all rushed into the room after Edward.

Caroline and the dowager rushed to her side, both of them wearing huge smiles and tears on their faces.

"Becca, dearest," sniffled Caroline, "I am so glad you are awake." She grasped Rebecca's hand and wrist in a tight grip and Rebecca was surprised at the stab of pain. She yelped and Edward, who had reclaimed his chair while the ladies greeted Rebecca, leapt up and was by her side in a split second.

"What is it? What is wrong?" he asked, worry etched on

his features.

Rebecca smiled at his obvious concern. *I could get used to this.*

"It is nothing," she assured him, "a small pain in my wrist." She looked down and was shocked to see a ring of purplish bruises around not only that wrist but the other too.

"From the rope," he told her gently.

She swallowed over a sudden lump in her throat. It was as if seeing the bruises brought the whole episode back in one swoop and she began to shake violently.

"Rebecca," the dowager leaned over her in concern.

"I am well," Rebecca assured her as much as she could, but there were tears building at the back of her throat and to her embarrassment they began to stream down her face.

"I am sorry," she blubbered, "this is so silly."

"Oh no, no it is not. After everything you have been through. Everything he did," wailed Caroline and suddenly her quiet tears turned to noisy sobs.

Edward and Tom shared a startled look and turned to the dowager to calm the girls down. But the lady had pulled both of the girls into an awkward embrace and was wailing loudest of them all.

"My poor, brave girl," she crooned over and over.

"Good God, they'll flood the place," said Tom in alarm, "do something."

"Me? I do not know what to do. You are better with crying women. You do something," retorted Edward.

They both looked back to the snivelling females as if hoping that the tears would have miraculously stopped. But on they went.

Eventually Edward tired of having to wait to speak to Rebecca about all of the things he wanted to say so he gently prised his mother away from her and pushed her toward the door.

"Tom," he said pointedly, "be so kind as to ask the lady

of the house to prepare some sweet tea for Mother. I believe she is in shock."

Tom nodded and held the door open for the weeping woman.

Now, Edward thought grimly, *the sister.*

"Caroline I—"

"That is quite alright, Edward," Caroline gulped. They'd reached a point over the last couple of days where titles and formal names seemed ridiculous. "I am sure you want some time alone with Rebecca." She turned to Rebecca now who thankfully seemed to have stopped crying. "I will come and sit with you soon, dearest, if you are not too tired."

Rebecca smiled and squeezed Caroline's hand before the older girl swept from the room followed by a somewhat scared looking Tom. *What is it about men and their fear of crying women?* she thought distractedly.

"Are you well?" Edward approached her cautiously as if afraid she would become a crying mess again.

"Yes, I am quite well now, thank you," she responded. "I do not know what came over me."

"Delayed reaction, I would imagine," he answered gently.

He filled the cup with water and held it to her lips. She drank gratefully and thought she had never tasted anything so delicious.

He put the cup down then sat on the bed and grasped her hand, staring at her in concern.

Eventually she laughed. "Edward I am well, you do not need to watch me so closely."

He smiled a little self-consciously and Rebecca's heart melted at the sight. Her arrogant, proud duke looking embarrassed by his concern.

"Where are we?" she asked, wanting to know everything that had happened since that last awful moment in the woods when— she froze. *Oh God. Had George Simons — had he?* She could not even think it.

Edward watched in alarm as Rebecca visibly paled.

He reached out and cupped her face in both hands.

"Sweetheart, what is it? What is wrong?"

Rebecca could barely bring herself to speak the words but she had to know.

"In the woods. Mr. Simons said — he said he was g-going to—?"

"No," Edward answered understanding at once what she meant. It tore at his heart to see the fear in her eyes. "He did not touch you, Rebecca. Not, not in that way."

Rebecca felt almost faint with relief. It had been her biggest fear. What had he said? Nobody would want her if he had her first. Thank God he hadn't.

"As to where we are," Edward continued, "we are in a farmhouse not far from the lodge."

Rebecca vaguely remembered seeing a farmhouse from the woods and wondered if it was the same one.

"The people here have been incredibly helpful and kind. As soon as we found you we brought you here. The lady of the house, a formidable farmer's wife by the name of Mrs. Brown took care of you while her son fetched the doctor and her husband, the local magistrate. I am ashamed to say that I was not much help. To you or anyone."

Rebecca reached out and grabbed his hand.

"You saved my life," she said simply.

He smiled but it faded almost as soon as it appeared.

"I thought I was too late," he said softly and his voice was raw with emotion, "I have never known fear until that morning when they told me you were gone. And when I finally found you. When I saw him and what he was trying to do. The blood on your face" —his own face turned white with fury and his eyes gleamed with remembered hatred— "I could have killed him there and then. I should have," he spat.

"No you should not," answered Rebecca firmly. "You are

not that type of man and I would not want you to be. W-what happened to him?"

"The magistrate came and took him away. We will never see him again, that I can promise you."

"He put up quite a fight, I warrant," she said.

He looked, to her surprise, a little embarrassed.

"Well no. Not really," he answered. "He was unconscious. And tied up."

Rebecca eyed him speculatively.

"And how did he end up in that state?"

"I punched him. A lot. And then we had to tie him up in case he awoke before the magistrate arrived."

"I did not think you a violent man," she teased.

"When it comes to someone trying to harm you," he answered all seriousness, "I will be the most violent man on the planet."

Rebecca gulped at his tone and expression. She could well believe it. He was a force to be reckoned with to be sure.

He suddenly smiled again.

"Besides, you are one not so innocent yourself, my lady. You made quite an impact with that candlestick of yours." He looked so impressed that she flushed a little with pride.

"I was not going to go down without a fight," she answered.

He gave a bark of laughter. "Nor would I expect you to my love."

"How came my sister to be here so soon?" she asked now, a question that had not occurred to her until now.

"We wrote as soon as we had you settled, darling. My mother and Caroline were beside themselves with worry."

Rebecca frowned in confusion. Even if Edward had written straight away, it made no sense that they would have gotten here so quickly. Unless —

"How long have I been unconscious for?"

He took her hand and planted a soft kiss on her palm

before answering. "This is the third day."

"The third?" she asked in shock trying to sit up. "But, but how? What happened?"

"You lost consciousness in the woods and we brought you straight here, as you know. Your head" —he closed his eyes as if the memory pained him— "it was bleeding quite a lot. You remember hitting it on a rock?"

She nodded and he continued with his tale.

"The doctor. He — he did not know when you would wake, or even if," his voice shook and Rebecca's heart ached for him.

He looked intently into her eyes now. "I have never been so afraid in all my life. I have died a thousand deaths waiting for you to awaken. I have not left your bedside."

"In three days?" she asked.

He shrugged.

"Edward that is insane. You must be exhausted."

"Do you think I could have left you? What if you had awoken and wanted me?"

There was an awkward little pause then Edward spoke again.

"The doctor has been sent for. He wanted to know the second you awoke."

"Will I be allowed to go home?"

Edward smiled.

"Try to be patient, my love."

There was that word again. *Love.* He had called her his love several times now and every time he said it her heart stuttered a little.

She remembered him, kneeling by her body, saying that he loved her. Was that memory or dream? Dare she ask?

"There are those wheels turning again," Edward joked. "Will you not tell me what you are thinking of?"

Rebecca thought back to her plan to confess her love for him. Was she brave enough to do it now? Thinking of how close she had come to death and how it felt knowing that she would never see him again, Rebecca knew that she was brave enough. Life was too short to live with the regret of things unsaid.

"Edward." She started licking her lips nervously. His eyes darkened as they took in the action. *Interesting.*

"The night in the gardens, the night we argued, I should not have said the things I said. Lady Sarah said—"

"I know exactly what Lady Sarah said," Edward interrupted furiously, "and what she did. Trust me, she will not harm you again."

"What did you do?" Rebecca asked momentarily distracted. She had forgotten all about that lady, so unimportant was she.

"I suggested she leave Town and hide herself away on her husband's Scottish estate. Her husband's very remote, very isolated Scottish estate," he said wickedly. "And I told her if she ever returns I will ruin her, completely and utterly."

Rebecca swallowed, once again awed by how intimidating he could be.

"Rebecca" —he leaned forward now and clasped both her hands in his— "I swear to you that she lied. There was never anything between us and not because I toss women aside, but because I never felt anything for her."

Rebecca smiled, knowing that there was truth in his words. Should have known from the very start.

"And as for me thinking whether or not you are duchess material" —Rebecca tensed a little here. There was no denying that she was certainly *not* duchess material. And when this story got out amongst the *ton*... well, she would be deemed even more scandalous.

"I think you will make a wonderful duchess." Rebecca stared at him in disbelief.

"Edward," she said with a pained little laugh, "we both know that is not true."

"Of course it is true," he argued.

"No," said Rebecca sadly, suddenly feeling miserable because he was trying to make her feel better but really, what had changed? "It is not. I am scandalous! I am clumsy, accident-prone, I never say or do the right thing and when people hear of this..." she trailed off disconsolately.

"You are not scandalous," Edward replied smiling gently, "a little unorthodox and very entertaining, but not truly scandalous. Yes you are clumsy and accident-prone but those are some of your most endearing qualities. You say things that make an entire room laugh, when you are not charming the occupants with your warmth or astonishing them with your intelligence."

Rebecca was blushing at the compliments he was firing at her. And he seemed sincere in them all.

"People love you, my darling. You have only been in Town a few short weeks and the place is eating out of your hands. You have brought life and fun and joy to my life. Laughter to my mother's home. You are the only person I've ever known who can brighten a room just by being in it. You say the most outrageous things and forever keep me guessing and I love that about you. You bring a welcome chaos to my far too organised existence."

"And when people hear of this," he continued, his eyes softening and his face looking so tender it made her want to cry again, "they will know what an incredibly brave and strong woman you are, who fought with every breath in your body to save yourself from the most unimaginable horror. And they will know how I did all that I could, and would do so very much more, to save the woman I love."

All the breath left Rebecca's body in one giant whoosh. Did he just say—?

"Did you just say 'the woman you love'?" she asked.

"Well of course," he answered a little confused.

Rebecca laughed at his confusion. She laughed as the

purest of joy burst into her chest.

"What do you mean 'of course'?" she demanded breathlessly.

"I mean of course I love you. I have loved you, probably from the first second I saw you chasing that silly kite," he said with a smile.

"Oh Edward," Rebecca managed to sniff before promptly bursting into a fresh set of tears.

Edward looked at her in panic.

"Rebecca, do not cry, I beg you. I did not mean to upset you. If you do not love me it is all right, I promise. You do not have to. I love you enough for the both of us. All I ask is that you give me a chance. A chance to make you happy. I swear I will spend every day trying to make you happy. And I will not even be sensible," he finished desperately.

Rebecca laughed through her tears.

"Yes, you will," she sniffed. "You will be sensible and practical and charming and witty and arrogant and wonderful," she said with a smile. "You will be all of those things I love you for."

It was Edward's turn to look amazed.

"You love me?" he asked. Well, demanded more like. "You love me?"

"Well of course," she answered mischievously.

His smile was one of pure, unadulterated joy and he gathered her in his arms and kissed her until she was panting.

"Marry me," he said pressing tiny kisses down her jaw, around her ear, careful to avoid the bandages. "Marry me quickly before I expire from wanting you."

Rebecca's newfound joy faded at his question and she pulled herself out of his arms.

Edward frowned at her.

"What is it sweetheart?" he asked worriedly.

"I cannot marry you," Rebecca whispered miserably.

Edward's heart sank.

"Why the hell not?"

"Mr. Simons, he said that when he'd — well, after he'd f-finished with me that no other man would have me. That I would be ruined. If people do not believe that you arrived on time, if they think he—"

"Rebecca," Edward cut in, "I do not care what people think. I do not care what they might suspect. I would not even care if I had been too late, though it would kill me to know it for the rest of my life. It already kills me to know what you suffered," he said bleakly, "and I shall never forgive myself for leaving you alone that night. Never."

Rebecca made to answer but he shook his head slightly and continued.

"Even if I had been too late, do you really think me so fickle, such a monster that I would blame you for any fate that befell you? That it would make a jot of difference to how I feel about you? Nothing, *nothing* will ever change the way I feel for you and how much I completely and absolutely adore you. Please say you will be my wife."

"Edward, I love you so very much and nothing would make me happier than to be your wife but I cannot be a duchess, truly I cannot. I do not even want to be one!" Rebecca answered miserably.

Edward stayed silent a moment.

"Alright," he said at last.

Rebecca told herself to grow up and not be disappointed that he agreed with what she wanted without even putting up a fight.

But Edward was not finished.

"I shall make you a deal," he said, moving to sit against the head of the bed and pulling her to rest against his chest.

"Marry me and try your hand at being a duchess for, say a year. If you do not like it, and if people do not worship you as I do, then I will hand over the title to Tom and be done with it."

Rebecca stared at him open mouthed.

"You cannot be serious."

"I am serious."

"But, but that is madness. Edward, you cannot give up the dukedom. It is your life."

"Wrong," he answered gently. "You are my life. And much as I enjoy my duties as duke I am not willing to sacrifice my only chance of happiness for it. I will live anywhere you want and do anything you want, my darling girl. I will walk to the very ends of the earth. I just want to marry you."

Rebecca smiled a luminous smile, her eyes shining with the purest of love for this wonderful man who was willing to give up so much for her.

"Maybe," she whispered as she leaned up to plant a shy kiss on his lips, "maybe being a duchess would not be a terrible thing."

"Let us find out shall we?" asked Edward lowering his head to hers.

"Yes," agreed Rebecca against his lips. "Let's."

And then neither of them spoke for quite some time.

Epilogue

The dowager's household was a flurry of activity as everyone prepared for the end of Season ball. This year's was, of course, extra special since it was now to be the engagement ball to celebrate the union of Edward, Duke of Hartridge and Rebecca, daughter of the Earl of Ranford.

The invitations had become even more sought after since the announcement of the betrothal.

Rebecca had been reluctant at first to allow the dowager to throw such a lavish party for them since she had not seen or spoken to her own parents. When they returned to London, she had written to them with the news of course and they had been, as expected, beside themselves with happiness.

The countess had assured her that her father would be fit as a fiddle by the time the wedding arrived and that they should, of course, celebrate the engagement in their absence. She promised to throw something similar when Rebecca and Edward returned to Ireland after the Season.

They would get married on her family's estate with only a few close friends and family in attendance.

"All the more reason," coaxed the dowager, "to have a

lavish engagement party for your friends here."

Once Rebecca felt certain that her parents would not mind, she consented.

She had regained all of her former strength and vivacity since the accident and, thankfully, was not scarred from her brush with the rock.

When they had all returned to Mayfair, London had been buzzing with gossip about the kidnapping and Lady Sarah's swift departure straight after it. Rebecca's fears, however, had been unfounded. Nobody thought of her as anything more than a poor victim and Edward was delighted to have been painted as some sort of knight on a white horse.

He'd smugly referenced it every day since they'd returned.

Rebecca sat at the dressing table while Maura put the finishing touches to the most intricate hairstyle she'd ever done. It was beautiful. She had managed to tame Rebecca's unruly curls so that some of them fell in a river over one of Rebecca's shoulders. The majority of the hair had been pinned up in a riot of curls giving Rebecca the look of a Grecian princess.

Her dress had only arrived moments ago and Rebecca had smiled when she read the card from Madame.

"The greatest works of beauty take time to come together. Enjoy."

Rebecca thought of the journey she'd come on with Edward to get them to where they were now and decided that Madame spoke a lot of sense.

Maura finally finished with her hair and Rebecca moved excitedly to the box. She took a deep breath and reverently opened the lid. Her gasp matched that of Maura's behind her.

The dress was a deep bronze, more vibrant than Rebecca, as a debutante had ever worn before. Her mind threw up images of the scandal she would create wearing such a bold colour. Then she thought of Edward's face and his reaction should she wear something so daring and knew that she would.

Maura quickly helped her into the gown, making light work of the laces at the back.

"My lady," Maura breathed seemingly stuck for words. She merely nodded her head then gestured for Rebecca to look in the mirror.

Rebecca turned slowly and her mouth dropped open at her reflection.

The dress was a masterpiece; there really was no other word for it.

The sleeves fell just off the shoulders exposing a greater expanse of skin than Rebecca was used to. The neckline fell in a deep V and was trimmed with the most delicate of lace. The short sleeves were made entirely of the same lace so although her shoulders were covered there was the hint of them on show.

The satin material shone in the candlelight and the overlay of lace was dotted with tiny diamonds, which sparkled and made the dress seem somehow enchanted. Not content with that amount of drama, Madame had added a train of satin and lace that swept behind Rebecca as she walked.

I will certainly make an impact, she thought with a smile of feminine pleasure lighting up her face. The clock chimed telling Rebecca it was time to go and greet their guests. The dowager wanted Edward and Rebecca in the receiving line since it was their first official event as a betrothed couple.

Rebecca turned and gave one last smile to Maura then went downstairs to greet her fiancé.

Edward waited impatiently at the bottom of the stairs. Incredible how mere months ago he had not even known Rebecca existed and now he missed her when he did not spend every waking moment with her. Their wedding could not come soon enough. He could not wait to make her his.

He had been very sedate in his affections since the incident with Mr. Simons. No other reason than the fact that she would soon be his wife seemed to have snapped the last of his self-control and it took every ounce of willpower he possessed to keep his distance from her. He worried that even one passionate kiss would lead them past the point of no return and he wanted to wait. For Rebecca.

A noise on the stairs drew his attention and he looked up to see his fiancé appear.

His jaw dropped open.

Hang waiting, he suddenly thought ferociously, *it is the most overrated thing in the world.*

Rebecca came to a stop in front of him and waited for him to speak. But he could not. She had quite literally rendered him speechless.

"Edward, are you well?" Rebecca asked smiling coyly.

She knew, the minx. Knew the effect she had on him.

"I — you—" he stuttered before coming to a stop once again.

But Rebecca did not need the words. The look in his eyes told her everything she needed to know.

Caroline appeared next and both Edward's jaw and Rebecca's dropped a little this time. Though the gleam in Edward's eyes was missing when he looked at Caroline, and that was enough for her. The gleam belonged to Rebecca alone.

He also recovered quickly enough to pay Caroline a compliment on how well she looked.

Caroline's dress was as dramatic and beautiful as Rebecca's. Caroline's was a chiffon creation of sea green which did incredible things for Caroline's ice blue eyes.

She looked like a Scandinavian goddess, Rebecca thought, coolly and intimidatingly beautiful.

Rebecca would watch Mr. Crawdon's reaction with interest.

"Caroline, you look really quite beautiful," Edward bowed over her hand and Caroline favoured him with a grateful smile before moving into the ballroom to oversee the setting up of the orchestra.

"Hmm," said Rebecca playfully.

"What is it darling?" asked Edward, running a finger along her collarbone and making her shiver with excitement.

"You call my sister beautiful yet cannot spare a word for me," she teased.

Edward grinned wickedly.

"The words I have for you my love are not appropriate for the receiving line of a ball, I assure you. They are for the privacy of the bedchamber and nowhere else." This he whispered in her ear and chuckled softly at her whimper.

"Patience, my beauty," he said softly.

Rebecca turned to look him square in the eye.

"Have you ever known me to be patient?" she asked.

He grinned. "No."

"And why start now?" she asked with a wink.

They would later argue about whose fault it was but either way, they missed the receiving line, were late to their own party and arrived looking so flushed and dishevelled that they were the talk of the Town once again.

Caroline stood watching the dancers glide gracefully through the steps of the waltz. She was unaware of the attention coming her way looking as beautiful as she did in Madame's creation. Her eyes scanned the room and her breath hitched when they made contact with the deep blue of Mr. Crawdon's. He was staring at her as if she were a meal to a starving man. Caroline knew she should look away, that it was most improper for him to look at her so but she felt trapped in his gaze. He walked slowly towards her and Caroline's heart rate sped up. He stopped just inches from her and Caroline had to tilt her head to look up to his too handsome face.

"What you do to a man with your beauty, Lady

Caroline," he drawled.

Caroline did not know quite what to say in response to such a forward remark so she stayed mute. Like a dolt.

"Shall we dance?" he asked and she remembered their wonderful evening in Vauxhall Gardens, though she should not think of it. But what was one dance? It would be unusual not to dance with him at the engagement party of her sister and his cousin.

He held out his hand to her and she placed hers in it. She tried not to react to the feel of his hand through her glove.

It was a dance, she told herself as he led her to the floor. Just a dance.

****

Rebecca waltzed in Edward's arms and felt like she never wanted to stop.

"Do you think it would cause a terrible scandal if I were to kiss you now in front of all our guests?" asked Edward.

"Yes I do," she answered firmly, "and your mother would not be impressed."

"Nor yours, I imagine."

Rebecca smiled a little sadly. "But she would not be here to see it."

"Darling, do you remember when you asked me to teach you to fence and I refused."

"You did not refuse to my memory," she grinned.

"You are mistaken. I *did* refuse at first. And then you looked at me with those damned eyes and I gave in almost immediately."

Rebecca smiled unrepentantly.

"Do you remember what I said?" he continued.

"Something about giving me anything to make me happy as long as it was in your power to do so."

"Yes well, I think you will find my powers stretch to

retrieving missing relatives," he said with a smile.

"What?"

He turned her gently and pointed across the ballroom. There, standing with the dowager were her brother Charles, her mother and her dear papa looking a little pale but mostly as well as ever.

Rebecca gasped then flew across the room and straight into the arms of her family, hugging each of them fiercely. Edward followed at a more sedate pace, happy to see the glow of delight on her face.

He came up behind her and placed a hand on the small of her back. And then, Rebecca caused a terrible scandal in front of all their guests by kissing her fiancé soundly on the mouth.

About the Author

Nadine Millard is a writer hailing from Dublin, Ireland. Although she'll write anything that pops into her head, her heart belongs to Regency Romance.

When she's not immersing herself in the 1800s, she's spending time with her husband, her three children, and her very spoiled Samoyed. She can usually be found either writing or reading and drinking way too much coffee.

BLUE TULIP
PUBLISHING

Printed in Great Britain
by Amazon.co.uk, Ltd.,
Marston Gate.